BRIDES
OF
BLOOD

ALSO BY JOSEPH KOENIG

❖

Floater

Little Odessa

Smugglers Notch

Joseph Koenig

BRIDES OF BLOOD

GROVE PRESS
New York

Published by Grove Press
A division of Grove Press, Inc.
841 Broadway
New York, NY 10003-4793

Published in Canada by General Publishing Company, Ltd.

LIBRARY OF CONGRESS CATALOGING-IN-PUBLICATION DATA

Koenig, Joseph.
    Brides of blood / Joseph Koenig. — 1st ed.
        p.   cm.
    ISBN 0-8021-1536-5 (acid-free paper)
    I. Title.
PS3561.03345B75   1993
813'.54—dc20   92-14155
                                                CIP

Manufactured in the United States of America

Printed on acid-free paper

Designed by Kathryn Parise

First Edition 1993

1   3   5   7   9   10   8   6   4   2

For Knox and Kitty

But now in blood and battles was my youth,
And full of blood and battles is my age,
And I shall never end this life of blood.

MATTHEW ARNOLD
SOHRAB AND RUSTUM

If you think of what you must do to save your country,
Annihilate the liars.

DARIUS I

BRIDES
OF
BLOOD

---❖---

F rench prostitutes had been flown in to celebrate the acquittal. The favorite was Marie-Christine, a blonde-haired girl said by the Paris bureau to be a thirteen-year-old virgin. Braless, wearing underwear with Minnie Mouse on the elastic, she looked to be about ten—a real prize. Nicole, Sylvie, Ghislaine were there for the judges, SAVAK generals who had labored over the evidence for a year before bringing the case to trial. The fifth girl, a pale beauty from Lyons, was intended for the prosecutor, but he had turned down the invitation to stay at home with his wife. Rather than let her go to waste, Farmayan, the defendant in the notorious case, had taken her to bed with Marie-Christine, which had pleased the younger girl in ways he had not anticipated.

In truth Marie Christine was nearly fifteen, and well used, her virginity restored by Swiss doctors who had stitched fetal lamb tissue across the entrance to her vagina. The orgy in the penthouse suite of the Royal Teheran Hilton had gone on until dawn, when the girls were returned to the airport by military car. In eight hours they had earned ten thousand U.S. dollars for their pimps, and been lavished with fine Persian miniature paintings, souvenirs of their brief visit to Iran, which they would trade for drugs at the first opportunity.

At 9:00, the tribunal at SAVAK headquarters was called to order for the start of testimony in support of the verdict arrived at in advance. The young prosecutor who had spent the night in his own bed looked wearier than anyone else. In a parched tone that betrayed his discomfort he detailed the charges. Colonel Farmayan was accused of the rape-slayings of two leaders of the Democratic Association of Iranian Women during interrogation at Evin Prison, the latest in a string of similar outrages.

Farmayan, thirty-nine, dozed through the opening statement. Not until the prosecutor revealed that, acting as his own chief investigator, he had located two eyewitnesses did the defendant sit erect in his chair.

"In light of the overwhelming evidence of his guilt," the young lawyer told the court, "and the likelihood that he will commit the same offense again, I am asking for the accused to be put to death. Would natural law be so accommodating, I'd request two consecutive sentences."

All three judges glared at him. At 11:30, before the eyewitnesses could be called, they ruled that there was no case and Farmayan had been found innocent. The prosecutor raised his voice in objection, and was silenced by the threat of contempt if he persisted. Appeal would not be considered.

For a week the prosecutor brooded. The verdict had never been in serious doubt. When he was assigned to the murders he had been made to understand what was expected of him. An acquittal would not be a black mark on his record, but regarded as the opposite, a strong foundation for advancing his career. He had protested that he wanted no part of it. A plan to guarantee a just sentence was already taking shape in his head.

On the eighth day after the trial the prosecutor left early from work, complaining of nausea. It was a short drive to his apartment, where he changed from his uniform into a suit purchased from an old clothes peddler. A soiled cap pulled low over his forehead completed the transformation. He drove back to headquarters in his wife's car, a yellow Thunderbird dripping new-car smell, and idled the engine at the curb.

When Farmayan came outside, he was with two agents on leave from Paris. They went to a black Mercedes-Benz at the corner, and Farmayan unlocked the passenger's door. The prosecutor took shallow breaths. If the men got into the car together, his plan would have to be scrapped. After talking for five minutes Farmayan clapped the others on the back, and they walked away laughing. The prosecutor was not far behind as Farmayan went around to the driver's side and sped off by himself.

The Mercedes-Benz left the city headed southeast into the desert. The Thunderbird dropped back several car lengths to allow a bus between them. At the Varamin turnoff the bus exited the highway, leaving the black sedan the only other vehicle in either direction. Bandits patrolled the road at night. It occurred to the prosecutor that he had put his life in jeopardy in two different ways, two ways at least, something he had not given adequate consideration to before.

The full moon was over his shoulder as he stamped on the gas and ran alongside the German car. Farmayan stared so intently that for a moment the prosecutor was convinced he'd been recognized. He pointed to the Mercedes's rear tire, and then sped ahead, watching the mirror. Farmayan continued half a kilometer before pulling into a narrow turnout.

The Thunderbird veered onto the shoulder, raced back in a hail of gravel. Farmayan was crouched beside a wheel with his thumb pressed against the rubber. "Friend," Farmayan said, "whatever you think you saw, nothing's gone soft except for your—"

Abruptly, he stopped. His hand inside his jacket was too late by seconds. The driver of the Thunderbird had a revolver out, and now he pushed the cap back from his brow.

Farmayan did not seem alarmed. He stood up slowly, hands at his sides.

"If there's something you need to discuss with me, there are easier ways of getting my ear," he said.

Salt grit stung the prosecutor's eyes as a tractor-trailer barreled down the far lane. He pulled the gun close against his body. Tears blurred his vision; he fought the urge to blink.

"Well, what is this about?" Farmayan snapped at him.

"It's about justice."

"Justice for me? It has the bad smell of something else."

"And for the women you murdered. I was unable to present my best evidence at the trial."

"You did well enough, under the circumstances."

"Please spare me any compliments. My part was to lend legitimacy to proceedings that were a hoax from the start."

"A professional courtesy any of us would have been glad to extend to you," Farmayan said. "It is impossible to function effectively as guardians of the state with the threat of harsh punishment hanging over our heads for every small conflict with the law."

"I'm not here to debate the merits of SAVAK's charter. The trial will continue from where it was interrupted."

"Don't be absurd." Farmayan started to turn away. The prosecutor steadied the gun at his heart, holding him there.

"One thing puzzles me," Farmayan said. "Who were your eyewitnesses? There were no witnesses I was aware of."

"I had none. It was to convince myself of the utter corruption of the court that I said they existed."

"It's too bad you've suffered this late attack of conscience. With brass balls like yours, your future in SAVAK would be boundless."

The prosecutor recoiled as if the most slanderous allegation had been leveled against him. "My resignation is on General Nassiri's desk. I was naive—"

"You still are. Those women were anti-shah filth not deserving even of the scraps we fed them in Evin. No crimes were committed against them."

"They were human beings."

"Subversives," Farmayan said disgustedly. "A lesser form of life."

The colonel's lack of remorse was duly noted by the prosecutor. "Have you anything to say in your defense?"

"It's pointless to continue this foolishness."

"Then you had better pray."

"Pray for what? Forgiveness? Forgiveness from you? *My* conscience is clear."

"The little French girl I've heard so much about—you had better pray she will be your footstool in the other world. Do it now."

Because he had not expected Farmayan to plead for his life the prosecutor was not disappointed by his silence. Farmayan dropped to his knees. He cupped his hands against his chest, touched his forehead to the ground. The prosecutor stood over him with an unlit cigarette in his lips. Dust from another big truck forced his eyes shut. When he opened them again, Farmayan was reaching inside his jacket. A silver automatic snagged on a lapel as the prosecutor put two bullets in his head.

The prosecutor went back to his car and took out a gallon can from the trunk. To the driver of a passing van he was a Good Samaritan in aid of a disabled vehicle. He emptied the can on the black sedan and the corpse. Pausing to examine his work, he lighted the cigarette and dropped the match without extinguishing it.

Farmayan burned with a hard flame sending out yellow streamers to the German car. Its heat bathed the prosecutor in sweat that soaked through his shabby suit. The Thunderbird was on the pavement again when a fireball erupted over the turnout. A secondary explosion launched dull skyrockets overhead. The prosecutor put his foot close to the floor, rolled up his window against a sudden chill.

· 1 ·

"*Jews and their foreign backers are those who seek to snare the very foundations of Islam and pave the way for Jewish domination through-out the world. Since they are a crafty and active lot my fear is that, may Allah forbid it, they will one day achieve their goal. In collusion with the cross worshipers they plan first to humiliate and then eliminate Islam in Iran. May Allah never let us see such a day.*"

The old man's fury roiled the heavy air. Mud-brick walls reflected his protest, batted it along crooked streets, and cloned a mob's curses, his message blurred by feedback as it multiplied again, now the battle cry of an army.

A white Paycon with loudspeakers mounted on the corners of the roof carried the word from the southern slums. The small car jerked, stumbled, and lurched back over its trail, washed the pavement in the yellow spray from its headlamps. The driver, vigilant against the enemies of the faith, kept one foot always on the brake. A skewed beam beside the passenger's window plied the sidewalks. Deterred by the rough walls it sought out arcades and shaded alleys, heroic monuments to the recent war dead. Tumbling haze displaced the light along empty avenues as the Paycon climbed into the heights of the city and drifted on its green edge.

The beam wavered there despite the motion of the car, which stopped suddenly alongside a row of benches. Brightness congealed around a woman whose head lolled back over the top slat. At that odd angle she appeared no

7

more than twenty, and not beautiful, her best features the double sin of a swarm of loose hair and scarlet lips that were weakly parted.

"Whore," someone said inside the car.

"Drunk in the bargain." The driver cut the engine, damping the head-lamps, but not the taped sermon that blared overhead.

Four women squeezed out of the car, sisters in black habits, invisible against the night but for eyes, and shiny noses, cheekbones, olive raccoon masks, and of the leader—the most devout—not that much bared, a corner of cloth gritted in her teeth and only one glaring eye unhidden. The women were Pasdars, guardians of morality, their jurisdiction immodesty and licentiousness in its myriad guises. They marched beyond the range of light and surrounded the stuporous figure on the bench.

"Cover yourself!" The lone eye took in bare wrists and ankles protruding from a black garment identical to her own, colored lips and nails—a catalogue of felonies. "This is the Republic of God."

She tilted a jar of clear fluid at a stained rag, and swabbed the criminal's face until the red was gone. The girl seemed not to care, or even notice, putting up no resistance as a second measure of acetone removed the offending color from her fingers.

Another of the quartet pulled a loose veil over the wild hair, but could not cage it all. "Slut, hide your nakedness." She threatened worse than acetone. "Where is your shame?"

The girl's chin snapped against her breast as she was prodded from slumber. The Pasdars took her under the shoulders and hauled her up on marionette legs. She showed no interest in supporting her weight; soon, neither did the women. When they tried to sit her down, she dropped like a stone. Not troubling to put out her hands, she broke her fall with her nose. A Pasdar produced an unsoiled handkerchief from the folds of her black chador, but there was no blood to speak of to mop up. Nudging the girl onto her side, she looked into her senseless face. Tangles of brown hair poured off one shoulder, exposing a scorched circular wound behind her ear. The Pasdar listened for breathing, she felt for a pulse, pressed close to fill the empty heart from the violent pounding in her own chest.

The loudspeakers quieted as the tape ran out. A blast of static announced their immediate return to life.

"Remind the peoples of the danger posed by Israel and its agents. Recall and explain the catastrophes inflicted upon Islam by the Jews. We see today that the Jews, may Allah damn them, have meddled with the text of the holy Qur'an . . ."

———

Approaching Niavaran Palace the djoubs ran almost clear. Plane trees nourished by the snowmelt they brought down from the mountains lined the boulevards. An American car, an aged Thunderbird, tracked the greenery north through suburban Shemiran, a motorist preferring dead reckoning to the directions he had copied in his notepad. The dry wind was infused with the flavor of summer gardens and the odd pocket of cold spilling down from the Elburz Range. Like the djoubs, the motorist's thoughts were clearer here, too, a novelty that soon wore thin. He opened the glove compartment for a flask that he kept buried under the *Administrative Regulations Governing the Revolutionary Courts and Public Prosecutor's Office*. He drank with little pleasure, businesslike, alcohol as basic to the task at hand as the guns he wore under his shoulder and in the small of his back. "Punishment for drinking liquor is eighty lashes whether it is a man or a woman," he recited as he reinterred the empty under the law book. "Article 131, the law of Houdoud and Qesas."

Turning into the teeth of holy rage, he homed in on an apartment complex on Saltanatabad Avenue below the former royal estate, two modern pale brick high rises that mirrored each other across a tiled courtyard set back from the sidewalk. Double-parked beside a white Paycon pumping out the Imam's wrath from crackling speakers was a Range Rover of the Komiteh, the Committee for the Revolution. The Thunderbird pulled in several car lengths behind. As the motorist swung his legs out, he breathed against his palm and sniffed his breath. "A man is to be whipped while standing with his body naked except for a cover on his private parts. But a woman is to be whipped while sitting with her dress tied to her body." He went back to the glove compartment for a stick of gum. "Article 132."

Bleary-eyed families, the wives and daughters wrapped dutifully in long head scarves, looked down into the court from gray windows. The faint light of the nearest streetlamps extracted from the tiles a bluish luminescence, so that the squad of Pasdars might have been standing on the surface of a shallow pool. With them were a couple of bearded men who made sharp, nervous gestures with Uzi automatic rifles. A girl stretched out on her side in the center of their small circle seemed to have washed up against the benches. The driver of the Thunderbird went to the white car and pulled the cassette from the tape player, silencing the old man's ranting. Some of the apartment windows immediately went dark. As he turned toward the court, he thought an Uzi was pointed his way. But nothing was very clear anymore, and he couldn't be sure.

"Police only!" The way was barred by a Komitehman staring past him at the Thunderbird. "You will have to go around."

He opened his wallet. The Komitehman looked doubtfully from his face to the color snapshot with his ID.

"Your name, please?"

"Bakhtiar." His stomach gurgled loud enough to hear. Sour gas bubbled in his throat. He corked it with his epiglottis.

"And your rank, if I may ask?"

Not quite a slap in the face, the question served a similar purpose. The Komiteh's duty was to protect the borders and the Revolution, his to chase after counterfeiters, rapists, thieves, and killers, miscreants whose threats were aimed only indirectly at the glory of God. As it would be on the road to paradise, the simplest of the men with the Uzis, even an illiterate like this one, took precedence over officers of the National Police where their responsibilities overlapped.

Darius Bakhtiar relaxed his throat, let out a vodka belch. "Lieutenant colonel."

The black curtain parted around the girl, and he dropped to his knees beside her. The smell of acetone stung the linings of his nose.

"Who touched this woman?"

The Pasdars kept silent. A Komitehman in a fatigue jacket zipped to his chin despite the August warmth bounced a light into Darius's eyes.

"What does it matter?" he said. "It was done."

Darius cupped the flash against his palm. "Who are you?"

"Bijan." The name, signifying nothing in itself, was followed by a pause, and then the kicker: "From the Bon Yad Monkerat."

Darius swallowed another burp. In consultation with the ayatollahs in the highest ranks of government, the Committee for the Revolution was charged with enforcing the prevailing moral tone. While lesser Komitehs held sway in tiny fiefdoms throughout the city, some claiming barely ten or twelve blocks for their turf, the Bon Yad Monkerat oversaw all of Teheran from a posh villa seized for the Revolution from an exiled merchant family. Bijan was the number two man.

Darius pushed the number two man's light at the body. With his thumb and forefinger he separated the charred fringes of skin around the wound behind the girl's ear. A metal nub glinted dully in yellow bone like a poisoned pearl. "The angle of the bullet, where the gun was fired, that's lost for good."

"Whatever." Bijan shrugged. "The case is unimportant. She was a prostitute. When the Pasdars found her, her nails and face were painted. She was half naked. You know these people better than I, the sordid nature of their squabbles. It is only thanks to God they haven't all destroyed themselves yet."

Darius rolled the girl onto her back. Scratches from her hairline to her swollen eyes had crusted into a brown grid.

"This woman was beaten on several occasions before tonight," he said.

"It was God's will." Bijan leaned his Uzi against his leg. He carved a block of halvah with a penknife, and gave the other Komitehman the larger piece. "Violence is a way of life for them, existing as they do. A beating was something she asked for, the natural preliminary to such a death."

"Since you know so much, why did you send for me?"

"Do I have to spell out everything, Lieutenant Colonel?" Bijan chewed with his mouth open. "The National Police must attend at all such tragedies, no matter how wearisome. It is the law."

Darius looked into the mountains. Teheran was built on a plateau that angled sharply into the Elburz. It wasn't hard to imagine that a giant hand had curled back the north end and was poised to spill everything—cars, sidewalks, acres of new skyscrapers—into the endless desert to the south. It occurred to him that, if he could find a place to stand, it would be a sight to see.

He scratched his smooth chin. Where trimmed beards, like yellow Thunderbirds, were considered unbecomingly decadent, to be clean-shaven was to skirt the borders of criminality. Bijan had a point. What was the use of knocking himself out? With a few strokes of lipstick the girl knowingly had signed away her future. Under the dress code of the Komiteh the use of makeup carried a penalty of seventy-four lashes. The girl, if she were a believer, already was at the gates of heaven. If not, at least she had escaped from hell. In Darius's hand, the light traced bold parabolas around the benches, then returned to the body. "Tell me," he asked, "where is all the blood?"

Bijan examined his Uzi, wary of a trick question.

"She's been shot," Darius said impatiently, "but there's hardly any blood."

"The Pasdars cleaned it."

Bijan turned to the women for confirmation. The leader's eye blinked like a slamming door. "Only the face." She held the veil an inch from her mouth. "The nails, her hair—we touched nothing else."

"In that case, it's simple," Bijan said. "She was killed someplace else and brought here."

"In that case," Darius said, "nothing is simple."

Evidence was deteriorating, the investigation—not begun yet—in a mire from which there was slight likelihood he would be able to extricate it. Even so, he had several hard facts to work with. The victim was not a married woman caught in flagrante delicto with another man. Had that been the case there would have been no need to dispose of the body here, since an aggrieved husband had the right, under the law, to kill his errant spouse without being prosecuted for murder.

Darius shooed the Pasdars away. He straddled the body and pressed his lips to the girl's neck. His eye was so close to the partially exposed bullet that he was tempted to pop it out.

"What do you want from her?" asked Bijan.

"She's started to cool. It's hours since she was killed."

"You are taking her temperature?"

"In a manner, yes."

"Orally, I assume."

Bijan's mouth was distorted by the halvah, but Darius couldn't fit a smile anywhere on it.

". . . Then we can go now."

"Not yet," Darius said. "I want you to secure the scene till officers arrive. Also, you haven't told me what things looked like when you got here."

Bijan was shepherding the Pasdar women to the street. "You don't need our help. Before Islamic justice replaced the old system, the criminal police were ten times as busy as today. Still, they performed their duties."

"I wouldn't know," Darius said.

"A plague of murder afflicted the people. Killers understood they would not be dealt with severely, so they kept the city in terror. Under the new law it has been made clear what punishment awaits them, and everyone can walk the streets in peace."

Darius glanced back at the corpse. "Tell her."

"You are wasting your time," Bijan said. "If you should bring this probe to a successful conclusion, no one will care. The girl is not worth the effort; to find her killer is no accomplishment. He has done the nation a service. If you don't recognize what has happened, let me paint you a picture. It was a lovers' quarrel—if love is the word for what transpires among their kind. They had battled before, you said so yourself. Tonight it got out of hand.

Perhaps she even liked it that way. The boyfriend shot the girl, executed her, judging by the location of the wound, and left her where she would not be traced to his place."

"You've found witnesses?" Darius said. "Spoken to people who saw the body being dumped?"

Bijan cut another piece of halvah without finishing what he had in his mouth.

"Did you try? How many hours did you let go by doing nothing before you called?"

"Not long," Bijan said. "First we had to satisfy ourselves that the matter was of sufficient seriousness to bother the National Police."

"An idiot would know right off that this was murder."

"Good, good." Shouldering his rifle, Bijan went after the women. "I see you are already on your way."

The old man's ranting began again as the Paycon scurried from the curb. Unformulated questions suggested answers inside the tall buildings; but without the Komiteh on his side Darius was beating his head against the walls. The investigation, molded in official apathy, would bind him to sterile routine until an improbable resolution was delivered from above. Had the girl eluded her killer, and the crime been merely the flagrant use of makeup, resources would have been made available to prosecute her. With the assault on public order having climaxed in her death, however, only a cursory probe was demanded. The logic was unassailable—and the system grew fat on its perversity. For proof there was Bijan, the Komiteh's crown prince, who had chalked up another success by declaring the murder not worth solving. In no aspect of the case did Darius see profit for himself. While a good arrest might earn a few pats on the back, to accede to the failure desired of him eventually would cost him his job. He turned his face into the breeze. Cool air dispersed some of the fog in his brain, and heightened the sadness that never went away. Clear thought, he decided, was an acquired taste, a luxury well beyond his means and narrow prospects.

Again he crouched over the girl. Judging by her perfect teeth, she had been well off, rather than poor, likelier a city resident than her country cousin. In her pockets he found eighty thousand rials and a tortoiseshell compact; nothing else he might use to identify her. There was no label or laundry mark in the black garment.

He wandered away from the benches to call for assistance and to search perfunctorily for additional evidence. When he looked back, a boy of about fifteen was standing over the body. On a string around his neck Darius saw the Key to Paradise with which thousands of children had walked the Iraqi warfront as human minesweepers, secure in the knowledge that their entry to heaven was guaranteed by the talismans stamped in a Taiwan plastics factory. The boy poked at the corpse with an aluminum crutch and lifted the girl's hem above her thigh.

"Get lost," Darius said.

The boy hammered the ruined face. "Shit on your mother's grave." His shout Ping-Ponged between the buildings as he vaulted away on one leg.

Darius smoothed a bloodless gash under the girl's eye. Wounded again, she appeared younger—a vulnerable sixteen—her untanned skin blemished only by the old scabs and the assaults suffered after death. Dissolved in acetone was an expression to attach personality to her bland remains.

Police cars rolled up where the Pasdars had been parked, and men in baggy uniforms got out and rubbed the tightness from their thighs. The rumpled procession could not be blamed on the hour. Under the new order, neckties, too, indicated a pronounced lack of piety; but the fashion of the National Police had not been restyled to accommodate the revealed truth. Buttons were left undone, and undershirts and tufts of hair sprouted from open collars. A black Paycon was edged out by a Nissan for the last spot at the curb. The Paycon slunk away, then roared back head on and bounced up onto the sidewalk and over the tiles.

The plainclothes investigator behind the wheel caught Darius in his lights. "If I made no sense on the phone," he called out, "it's because I was having a bad dream, and you woke me. What have we here?"

"Another nightmare," Darius said.

Mansur Ghaffari dropped his high beams as he steered toward the benches. A slender, almost gaunt blond man, he was half a foot taller than any of his colleagues. Ghaffari was third-generation National Police, his mother's father having been one of a handful of Swedish army advisers imported in the early 1920s to establish a constabulary under Reza Shah. "Do I remember your saying she was shot behind the ear?"

"Don't take my word."

Ghaffari kept his distance from the body. "The photographer is done with her?"

"You have my permission."

Ghaffari's nostrils twitched as he took the dead girl in an awkward embrace. "A nightmare for us," he said, and whisked away a fleck of red from the mouth. "Damn witches, they did everything but steam-clean her. It's incredible they had the presence of mind to call."

"The Komiteh did," Darius told him. "She's *their* gift."

Ghaffari tilted the girl into the light. A uniformed officer leaned over his shoulder, watching them cuddle. Darius asked, "What are you waiting for?"

"I was just . . ." He was not much older than the dead girl, a recruit patrolman returned to duty after three months at the National Police Academy. Though the young man had been sent for schooling in criminal investigation, Darius suspected a field of study along the more practical lines of issuing traffic citations. The role of the police gradually had been usurped by the Komiteh, until its police duties consisted primarily of writing tickets. Because salaries had been cut commensurately, most officers moonlighted as security guards. "We just want to know if there is anything special you need."

"Second sight."

"Sir?"

"Never mind. Cordon a wide area around the body; this court soon will be as busy as the bazaar. Videotape the entire scene. Include the buildings and sidewalks, then hunt for clues. Go along both sides of the street and note the license plates of every car parked within four blocks."

The patrolmen had wheeled a gas-fired generator onto the court. Roaring like a motorcycle, it was hooked up to arc lights, which were positioned around the benches. Ghaffari looked behind the girl's ear. "A contact wound."

"But not the cause of death," Darius said. "There's no blood on the tile—"

"The Pasdar is fanatical also about cleanliness."

"Or on her chador, not in the amount you'd expect. Someone wasted a bullet on a perfectly dead girl."

Ghaffari patted down the black garment. "No papers."

"No nothing."

"I can take her fingerprints on the spot. If the Bon Yad Monkerat is involved, this is top priority."

"They want to make an example of her," Darius said.

"What example? She's been murdered."

"The kind that's buried in an unmarked grave."

The uniformed officers strung a rope between the benches and a triangle of iridescent traffic cones, and then clustered around like fighters hungry to enter the ring. The twenty-four-year-old criminalist who doubled as police artist, seeing Ghaffari move the body, put away his sketch pad to hunt for the mother lode of clues. Eighteen months out of the academy, in over his head in a job spurned by veteran investigators because it allowed no opportunity for graft, he kept a criminology text inside his evidence kit at all times. The tiles were as clean as a dinner plate. For want of anything to do he scraped some of the dust between them into a clear envelope.

Darius stepped over the rope and started across the court with Ghaffari hurrying after him.

"The girl was roughed up over a period of time," Ghaffari said. "Last night was simply the coup de grace. When we get her to the morgue, I'll bet we find she's been tortured."

"No bet."

"Why are we looking for witnesses, when there won't be any? You know whose work this is."

"I do?"

"It has all the earmarks of one of *theirs*."

"What do *theirs* look like? Has anybody seen one in years? Aren't *theirs* planted at night near the Fountain of Blood at Behesht-e-Zahra? . . . No," Darius said, "the Komiteh has its reasons for wanting us to go easy on this, but not because they're responsible."

"Such as?"

"They say the girl is a whore. It could even be they're right."

They entered the sweltering lobby of the building closest to the benches without waking a doorman nodding beside the intercom phone.

"Apparently security at this complex is not a problem," Ghaffari said.

"What doesn't exist rarely is a problem."

The elevators were out of service. Full electric power was limited to daylight and evening hours in most areas of the city. Water was available part of the day on the days it was available at all. The air was sticky from bathtubs kept filled all the time.

The investigators sprinted up several flights of stairs and came out in a corridor reeking of the spicy sauce called khoresh. Ghaffari pounded on a door on the side of the building overlooking the death scene. "Police!" both men said.

Light footfalls faded inside the apartment. "Open up," Ghaffari demanded.

Darius conjured a family frozen in mid-step, holding its collective breath until the angel of death had passed by. "Try somewhere else."

Two apartments away a door was edging shut. Darius wedged a foot in the space and straightened his leg. The panel gave slowly, then flew back, and he staggered into the arms of a man wearing striped pajamas.

"Thank you for inviting us in." Darius flashed ID.

"You can't— This is a religious household. My wife and daughter are not dressed." The three-day growth on his cheeks Darius attributed to lazy grooming or a recent conversion. "If you would return later, when they are properly clothed—"

"It will be too late."

A head popped out behind a corner, and a girl of about fourteen in a VIRGINIA IS FOR LOVERS T-shirt dashed barefoot across the doorway. Darius pushed into the living room. Flat woven carpets were piled three deep beneath a floral print oilcloth, a sofray, used as a tablecloth for eating on the floor. On a convertible sofa a handsome woman in her mid-forties inhaling through a cigarette holder made the same sucking sound as someone lighting a pipe. Her frosted hair was in curlers, and blue tears were frozen under her eyes. The woman clutched a robe around her throat but didn't hide her face or run away. A violin concerto floated through the smoke she kept moving with the back of her hand.

"Bastards," she said, "what crime is this?"

Music corrupts the minds of our youth, the Imam had said. There is no difference between music and opium. Music leads to fun, and Allah did not create man to have fun. The aim of creation was for mankind to be tested through hardship and prayer.

All this Darius knew by rote. If an existence devoid of pleasure was at the heart of the divine plan, then he had moved closer to God than ever had been his intention. With nothing in life but his work, it was the difference between opium and homicide that had become obscure for him. For the doggedness with which he broke the great majority of cases he was in debt to the mullahs who ruled the land and were the generals in God's war against fun.

The woman slid a portable tape player from between the cushions. Training it like a death ray at his heart, she turned up the volume full blast. Her husband made a grab for the machine, and she twisted away and shielded it behind her back.

"Bring me to Evin Prison," she sobbed. "See if I care."

Darius held out his palm. Sobbing, the woman surrendered the cassette. Darius drew the curtains from glass doors and stepped out onto a terrace that looked down on a kidney-shaped rock garden.

"Where are we in relation to the courtyard?" he asked.

"Just around the corner. The apartment has a northern exposure," the man boasted.

Darius leaned over the railing to study the rare flora below. How many weeks since he had been this close to grass and a handful of shrubs? There were few parks in Teheran, and most of them were sodded in concrete. In the courtyard the gas generator coughed.

"I apologize for the music," the man was saying. "My wife is very tense. There was some disturbance outside, and she couldn't sleep. The classics help soothe her nerves. Please, do not mention it to the Komiteh."

"Have you or your family heard anything out of the ordinary tonight?"

"The Imam's sermon on the Jews, if that is not ordinary."

"Nothing else?"

"The sirens of the police."

"You shouldn't play music so loud." Darius returned the tape.

"I understand." The man smiled knowingly.

Darius didn't smile back. "You'll wake the neighbors."

"What was that racket about?" Ghaffari asked in the corridor.

"Mozart." Darius pounded on another door. "Those people couldn't have seen anything. Let's try here."

An old man opened, hiding his face behind a liver-spotted hand. He was completely bald but for a few silver threads in the pink flesh below the crown of his head. "Excuse me," he said, and then he yawned. "You woke me." He took off wire frame bifocals and buffed each lens on a sleeve of his housecoat. "You are—"

"Police." Ghaffari was already inside. "We need a few questions answered."

The old man pressed the glasses to his puffy eyes and curled the temple pieces over his ears. Darius noticed he had more hair in his ears than on his head.

"Please come in," the old man said to their backs. "I will make some tea."

Darius whirled on him. The Komiteh were forbidden to accept food or drink in the homes they visited, because of the strong chance of being poisoned, and he had applied the rule to his squad. "*National* Police." He walked through the kitchen into an unlighted room. "We'll be a minute, and you can go back to sleep. We want to look out your window."

The old man hesitated. "There is a viewing fee . . ." He laughed, unamused, and followed them onto a logjam of rolled carpets. Since inflation had destroyed the value of the rial, Persian rugs had become legal tender among those members of the upper middle class that had not been ruined. The penalty for taking carpets illegally out of the country was death.

"May I ask what this is about?" The old man yawned again—forced it, Darius thought. When his hand came away from his mouth, it was shaking.

Darius stared down into the street as a morgue wagon moved between the massed police cars and parked close to his Ford. An attendant in a stained lab coat opened the double doors in back. A blackthorn cane rooted in the asphalt, and then the coroner, Dr. Baghai, stepped out, smiling and shaking hands with everyone like a playwright on center aisle on opening night.

Darius turned away from the window. The old man was still yawning. His hand hadn't quit shaking.

"Thank you, sir," Darius said. "For you, this is about nothing."

Ghaffari peeled back a corner of an antique Lavar Kerman carpet. "We're passing up a good arrest. He's smuggling, you know."

"We're here to investigate murder."

The stairwell reverberated to the sound of a brigade marching out of step over a bridge, and then Hamid, the young criminalist, dashed into the corridor alone. "I've been up to the top floor and down again, trying to find you. The dead girl—" He puffed out his rib cage to take a deep breath. "We have her identified."

"Good work," Ghaffari said.

"How?" Darius asked.

The criminalist had Darius by the sleeve. "Her mother is waiting downstairs."

"I'll talk to her alone," Darius said. "I want you to canvass both buildings with Lieutenant Ghaffari. I'll expect written reports."

In the street, uniformed officers pressed around a woman who sat rocking on her hips beside the body. Ululating, she tore at her hair as she smothered the girl's forehead with kisses. When Darius put his leg over the rope, she made a fist and pounded her breast.

"Mother—" he began. The woman peered at him through her tears, then resumed wailing.

"Mother, my heart goes out to you." Darius locked into her gaze. Without changing tone, he said, "Someone shut off the damn generator. She can't hear me."

Silence brought with it a watery twilight that calmed the woman the way darkness stills a caged bird. The trilling ceased, and her sobs were spaced further apart. From inside the folds of her chador Darius heard the clacking of worry beads. "Is this your daughter?"

"Tahera." The woman caressed the scratched cheek. "She is just sixteen."

"And her last name?"

"Taleqani."

"Mother Taleqani, tell me when was the last time you saw Tahera."

"When?" Time was an alien concept. "Two years? Three? Yes, three," she said. "For three years she was gone."

"Mother Taleqani—" Of all the distasteful aspects of police work, what he had no stomach for was grilling the survivors of murder. In little real sense could many be said to have survived. Endurers, he would have called them. Existers—the momentum of their broken lives rapidly winding down. The woman beside the body, judging by the whistling in her lungs each time she let out a sob, soon would be at a dead stop. "I'm sorry," he said, "but there are more questions about your daughter I must have answers for."

The woman grieved quietly, braced for the next assault.

"Three years is a long time. Were you in contact with Tahera before tonight?"

"Yes."

"I see." He betrayed all the involvement of a doctor discovering a spot on a lung. "Do you know where she was?"

"Yes."

"Where?" he asked.

"She was in purgatory," the woman cried. "But now she is in paradise."

The moment of calm was slipping away. "Who did this to her?"

The woman beat her chest with such force that Darius felt the shock of the blows. "You did!" An arthritic finger, shiny as bone, pointed where the punches echoed in his heart. "You murdered her." She took her case to the crowd outside the rope. "Stone him," she pleaded. "Crush his skull to powder. He murdered my child."

"Mother Taleqani—"

The woman screeched her misery to the heavens. She threw herself on the corpse, watered it in tears.

A hard object jabbed into Darius's shoulder, and he looked back at the crowd as Dr. Baghai reached him a second time with the tip of his cane. "I can give her an injection, if you like." In hopes that he might lose a patient to a sudden resurrection the coroner went nowhere without a full doctor's satchel. "Otherwise it may take several days before she is lucid."

"Will she stand up under interrogation?"

Baghai gestured indecisively with his stick. "A drink would be better."

"For everyone concerned," Darius said.

The rope thrummed in his fingers as a teenager in a light summer chador slipped inside the cordon. She put an arm around Mrs. Taleqani's heaving shoulders and murmured in her ear. Mrs. Taleqani shook her head. She kissed the corpse, cajoled it forgivingly to come home while the teenager tried to bundle her away.

Darius jerked the rope. The traffic cones danced like bobbers on a struck line. "Mrs. Taleqani can't leave. She's a witness in a murder case."

"My mother knows nothing about murder," the girl said.

"Tahera was your sister?"

"That's right."

"And your name?"

"Farah Taleqani. But I don't see—"

"I'm Lieutenant Colonel Bakhtiar, the investigator in charge. Information about your sister is badly needed. Your mother is overwrought and not responding. It's essential that you answer for her."

Farah Taleqani raised the rope above her head.

"Without your cooperation," Darius said gently, "it will be that much harder to find the killer."

"I can't help."

"Tell us about the last time you saw Tahera. Start there."

"Very well." The young woman paused to calculate her words. "It was three years ago next month. Tahera was at school, and she told her girlfriends that she had dreamed she saw the Imam without clothes. It was a joke. That night, the Komiteh came to our house and took her away. For questioning, they said. We never saw her afterward."

"Where was she?"

"Tahera was tortured to death. Word reached us from the prison."

"Impossible. She died tonight."

Farah Taleqani stared at him with her mother's vacant eyes. "This girl is not Tahera."

"But Mrs. Taleqani—"

"My mother has spent three years searching the city for her daughter. Each day she goes into the streets to look, always to look. It is not the first time she has found someone else's Tahera."

The crowd parted as she prodded the sobbing woman under the rope.

Darius did not turn away until they disappeared across the street. "About that drink . . ."

Baghai stepped on Darius's toes in his hurry to get at the corpse. His thick fingers probed in the area of the head and neck while the attendant recorded his observations on a clipboard. "You started without me," he said.

"The body was compromised by the Pasdars when I arrived."

"You should always finish what you start. When we have her on a slab, I'll sit back and let you." Baghai lifted the head. "You've seen the wound in the mastoid bone behind the right ear? A small-caliber weapon, almost touching the skin, was fired from above and slightly to the left of the girl. The slug entered her skull from what I would estimate to be an angle of greater than forty-five degrees. Do I have to tell you it didn't kill her?"

"What did?"

Baghai opened his arms wide.

"The time of death?"

"The body has chilled noticeably, but rigor mortis has not begun. A rough guess on a night like this would be about eight hours earlier, about—" Baghai brushed his cuff back from his watch. "Nine P.M., more recently if she was brought from a room without air-conditioning."

The coroner pressed one hand over the other, and leaned on the handle of his cane. "We are ready to remove her to the morgue. The autopsy will be the first order of business. Will you attend for the police?"

"For the girl, too."

He stayed with the body while the attendants brought Baghai to the wagon. Glancing up at the windows he spotted a blond head in an eleventh-story apartment, Ghaffari insulated by double panes from the virulence of murder. The rising sun was in his eyes when he walked back to his car. It glinted off the flask of vodka as he wrung out the last drops.

❖ 2 ❖

With a week's stubble Darius was a Chicago gangster. More than that—Rasputin, the black tundra of his beard melded into the blacker tangle that cascaded over his ears, while his coal eyes burned with a hard, feverish gleam.

He dabbed a brush at a bar of brownish soap, and worked the thin lather into his skin. Photographs edged the cracked mirror on the wall. Those showing him unshaven had been taken twenty years ago, when like others of his generation he had flirted with the Imam's brand of Shi'a Islam. In another, which was a few years newer, he braced with boyish pride in the uniform of a United States Air Force Reserve officer trainee. It was this photo that he returned to as he wielded his razor like a portraitist's brush, defining subtleties only hinted at by the camera.

Ghaffari sat on the lid of the toilet, smoking a Turkish cigarette. "I never saw these pictures before. Frankly, I like you better with a beard."

"So do I," Darius said.

"And with a woman." He flicked his thumbnail at a faded Polaroid of Darius in his ROTC blues. His arm was around a pretty girl with brown, windblown curls. A flowery kerchief was tied over the back of her head, and she had on a montoe, a shapeless, ankle-length coat. Barely visible in the background was the west portico of the United States Capitol. "I didn't recognize you at first. You're smiling."

"Shit." A red splotch marred the portrait. "I assure you it won't happen again." Darius tore off a sheet of toilet paper, and crumpled it against the nick. "What did you find after I left?"

"What we expected. No one heard a shot or scream, and because of the brownout no lights were on at the court." Ghaffari returned the photo to the mirror. "I visited thirty apartments, and at all of them I was told the same thing, that at night it's impossible to see to the benches."

"And during the day?"

"Many of the units are like the first one we visited—without a view of the court; although from the upper floors it's easy to see into the private homes across the street."

Darius angled the razor under his nose, scraping away at the underlying pallor to get at a few stubborn hairs. He used an Iranian blade, an aptly named Shark; when he glanced in the mirror again, his upper lip was awash in blood.

"You're the only man I know who keeps pictures of himself on his mirror," Ghaffari said.

"To remember me by."

Searching for a match Ghaffari went into Darius's office, a waiting-room ambience of gray walls and gray carpeting. A threadbare sheet had been tossed over a couch upholstered in torn vinyl, and a bolster pillow was squashed against the armrest. In a large outer office burly men in various stages of uniform dress breakfasted on melon juice and coffee cake while civilian clerks beat on manual typewriters. He returned to the bathroom without the match. "Why don't you sleep in your own bed for once?"

Darius screwed the cap off a green bottle, and held it to his nose. "It's not worth fighting the traffic, when I have to be at the morgue by ten."

"You never go home. There are corpses who spend less time at the morgue than you."

"They don't know what they're missing. Look, Mansur, it would be nice if you could stop poking your nose into every little thing I do."

"What other friends do you have to tell you that your behavior is cause for concern? You see so little of your wife, it's a mystery why you bother to stay married. Considering all the time you spend here, it would be more practical to move into one of the cells downstairs, and Farib can come stay with you during visiting hours."

"Now, I think you may have something," Darius said.

Ghaffari hung his head in surrender until he saw the beginnings of a reluctant smile. Taking the bottle from Darius, he milked it of a drop, and transferred a whisper of scent to the underside of his jaw. With liquor outlawed, alcoholics had bid the price of aftershave and cologne to the equal of French perfume. "You should lay off this stuff."

"Why?" Darius snatched back the aftershave, sloshed it on his face and neck.

"You waste it like water."

Darius poured more onto his tie. "A pretty girl is waiting."

The coroner's office was housed in a building the color of mud brick several blocks from police headquarters. Darius went in through the viewing room where Teheran's bereaved gathered each morning to claim the bodies that sprouted like malevolent toadstools on the streets. Corpses waiting to be identified were stored in the basement morgue, and brought up for inspection on a glassed carousel. The building resounded with an iron clangor like the housing of a huge engine. Descending into a chemical bouquet of formalin and urine, of cold sweat mixed with the foulness of death, Darius had the sensation that he had skipped the intermediate stations of dying and burial to arrive intact in the bowels of hell.

A room the size of a downtown block was a benign necropolis under the rule of men in surgical gowns and masks, the nether side of the living city three stories above. A dozen slabs were inhabited by corpses in various stages of destruction. To each was assigned a young doctor as squeamish as a schoolboy investigating a frog. Flitting from table to table was the stooped figure of Baghai.

A body without a face lay under fluorescent strips. In the most devout neighborhoods a splash of sulfuric acid was vigilante justice for women found wearing makeup. Blindness or disfigurement was the usual sentence, but too often it was administered with an excess of zeal. Baghai claimed from the chest cavity a gelatinous heart, and placed it in a shiny pan— Baghai, who hadn't the decency to fill the air with cigar smoke, to pretend to be offended by premature death.

He stood behind a pathologist tracing a Y-shaped cut on a cadaver whose lower torso had been crushed to the thickness of a book. Steadying the tremulous scalpel, Baghai forced it through the brittle flesh on both sides of the sternum, and slid it to the sexless pubis. When the incision was complete, he curled his fingers inside the slit. The body opened with the sound of shredding cloth.

"Only suicides leave hesitation marks," he admonished the doctor.

Darius loosened his tie and inhaled the scent stored there. The racket was deafening. The refrigerator motors whirred in harmony like a robot section of an orchestra. Warm air rushed in through the loading dock as another gurney was brought inside. Darius recognized the attendant from Shemiran as Baghai waved him to the only vacant slab and said, "This one goes to the head of the class."

Baghai tore away the sheet with the flair of a magician whipping a tablecloth from under a setting for twelve. All color was drained from the girl's face, leaving the bland residue of pain. Her limbs had begun to stiffen; the attendant had to force her arms against her sides to remove the chador. Underneath, a scoop-neck dress clung to her like silk snakeskin.

"Islam's critics," Baghai said, "would have us condemned as practitioners of pagan cruelties. Before you, though, is evidence of how far we lead in equality of the sexes. In Europe and the Americas women dress provocatively to win the admiring eye of a man. But the chador prevents women from being regarded as mere sex objects. As a result, they are free to wear what pleases them close to their heart."

"For her," Darius said, "the chador was a disguise, not a political statement."

Baghai fumbled with the zipper. "The dress is fetching, but the girl is not. She must have expected that its glamour would wear off on her."

A lace bustier prodded the girl's small breasts into thin sensuality. Patterned stockings completed the transformation.

"Make an extra set of pictures," Darius said. "The Komiteh will have a good laugh."

"Conclude nothing from what you see. You would be amazed at how many modest women dress like her under the chador. Some sew their own frilly garments."

"I doubt she's Iranian. Not from Teheran, anyway."

"Teheranis have the same fantasies as women everywhere."

"But a different expression," Darius said. "She seems too compliant, too accepting of death. Like an Arab."

"It could be she is a foreigner. Saudis in particular are obsessed with seductive lingerie. Not having had to live under the tyranny of a Westernized shah, they've never known a time they were not liberated by the veil." His dry cackle trailed off into coughing. "I speak from professional experience only."

Baghai searched the lace for a zipper. "Cut her out," he told the attendant.

Darius blocked the scissors. He snapped open a panel at the crotch, and the attendant eased the girl out of the bustier.

"I see you've had experience of a hands-on nature," Baghai said.

Darius inspected the label, then folded the garment as though the girl would be slipping into it again when she was done on the slab.

"We will start now," Baghai said.

"First let me have the bullet. Try not to scratch it."

Baghai's arthritic fingers moved deftly as he trimmed the ragged skin around the mastoid bone. "We should be done in an hour. Get some fresh air. I'll send for you when we have compiled the preliminary report. Only a word of warning: don't eat before you return."

He tweezed the slug, let it fall into Darius's palm. "Small caliber. A twenty-five, at most."

Darius sealed the bullet in an evidence envelope. "I've had my fill of fresh air."

"Very well, then, we will begin with the external examination. If it agrees with you, stay for the cutting."

Baghai lowered the light. "Deceased is an unidentified female," he began in his dry voice, "approximately eighteen to twenty-five years of age. The body is generally well developed and well nourished. Weight . . ."

"Fifty kilograms," the attendant said.

"Height . . ." Baghai referred to a ruler etched into the slab. "One point six meters.

"Body found on 3400 block of Saltanatabad Avenue, Shemiran, approximately five A.M., August twenty-first. Time of death, from eight to twelve hours. Gunshot wound of the right mastoid bone. The bone shattered but not swollen. A black hole, eight millimeters in diameter, rimmed by abraded skin with powder tattoos in a radius of seven centimeters. Body was found by the Pasdars and cleansed with acetone prior to examination. Body pale in color. Rigor mortis apparent in the limbs, and . . ." Baghai manipulated the head, a chiropractic adjustment. "Neck muscles.

"Deceased's hair is black and straight. Eyelashes black and mascaraed. Pupils round; irises dark brown. There is a purplish swelling around the left eye, and scabs approximately nine centimeters long and one half centimeter wide across the left cheek to the edge of the upper lip. Slight swelling on the left side of the jaw."

Darius noticed that outside the lace corset the breasts were flaccid, the colorless nipples inverted. Baghai dictated similar observations to the attendant.

". . . No surgical scars." Baghai placed his hand on the flat, fishy stomach. "Pubis clean-shaven. Subdural hematoma approximately three centimeters in diameter on the upper right thigh, and . . ." He spread the legs indecently, and readjusted the light. "My God, this girl has been infibulated." With a speculum he opened her. "In a lifetime I thought I had seen everything, but this—"

The voice was not Baghai's. Baghai had no feelings. When a cluster bomb had crashed into a Rey kindergarten during the war with Iraq, Baghai by himself had autopsied the mangled remains of thirty-seven children, and then gone out to a fine Firdowsi Avenue restaurant to explain his findings to military intelligence.

"This woman may well have been Arab," the imposter said. "I pray she is not Iranian, that we haven't come to this."

Darius stared at the coroner.

"You're the expert on Arab women. Do I have to explain?"

"An amateur expert," Darius said. "They're a hobby. Once were."

"This is not for amateurs." Again the voice of dispassion. "Among our co-religionists on the Arabian peninsula, it is not unknown for the external genitalia of female children to be surgically removed. The rationale is that a woman will have no interest in engaging in illicit sex when she is incapable of taking pleasure from it. In West Africa, there are tribes that perform female circumcision because they believe the clitoris is a dangerous organ that makes men insane. This much, at least—" Baghai smiled half-heartedly, "is accurate."

"That's what was done to her?"

"And more. During infibulation, after the exterior genitals are removed, the legs are bound together for several weeks to prevent the scar tissue from being torn apart. The vulva is sealed, and a splinter of wood placed in the wound to allow for elimination. The vulva remains closed until it is cut again, or forced open. Infibulation permits virginity to be proven before the brideprice is paid. Our Arab cousins are obsessed with all this."

"At her age the scar is still intact?"

"There was no scar," Baghai said. "The operation was performed no more than two weeks ago, and the stitches ripped out before the wound healed. For a child, a baby, it would be torture. In a woman the agony must be indescribable. Why she would submit is beyond my understanding."

"There was a gun at her head last night. Probably it wasn't the first time."

Baghai put down his instruments. He attached a flash to an old Japanese box camera, and tunneled between the girl's knees.

"The coroner's office maintains a black museum," he said. "The record of

this case will have a special place. If you would like prints for your friends at
the Komiteh and Pasdar—"

Darius was blinded by the flash. "Don't give them ideas."

He was in the viewing room, watching the frozen parade on the carousel,
when the attendant reached him with the preliminary report. He scanned it
while hurrying downstairs. "You haven't listed any cause of death," he said
to Baghai.

"I could no more find a cause than a reason. I've removed the internal
organs for laboratory analysis. It's possible she died of sepsis. Infibulation
generally is performed by a barber using the same filthy razor with which he
shaves his male customers. Coarse horse hair is used for the sutures. Infec-
tion is the rule. Medical science can't explain why someone would shoot a
girl who is already dead, or why she had to suffer mutilation."

"When will the lab results be ready?"

"In several days. Until identification is made, I'll keep the body. I may
want to look at her again."

"You've seen torture before," Darius said. "Could she be one of *theirs?*"

"When the Komiteh learn of a new cruelty, they don't hesitate to employ
it. Lately, we are finding Coca-Cola in the lungs of people who have died of
painful means. By shaking the bottle into a nostril they make the most
laconic prisoner talk. But they can't take credit for her. Let me show you
why."

Darius averted his eyes as the coroner lifted the sheet.

"You can look."

Baghai had exposed the girl's feet and was stroking her arches. "Unmarked," he said. "She hasn't been subjected to the bastinado. Nor are there
scars. The Komiteh may come up with the odd new trick, but they never
forget the old."

Ghaffari was gone from headquarters, no one knew where. Darius went to
the Avenue of the Islamic Republic, formerly Shah Avenue, to see the
Revolutionary Prosecutor.

Fayegh Zakir was a painfully thin man with an oversize head and blunt,
swollen features that gave the impression he was feeding on himself. His
office was next door to the men's room, the air saccharine with disinfectant.

It was a windowless cubicle furnished plainly with an old desk and chairs left by previous administrations. The trappings of modesty, Darius knew, fell away at the property line of his home in the posh north Teheran neighborhood of Africa, which he had purchased for cash equal to forty-seven years' salary.

Darius touched his perfumed tie to his nose, and went in with the preliminary autopsy findings. Zakir gestured to a seat in the cloying draft from the men's room. "What is this?"

The Revolutionary Prosecutor regulated the activities of the Komiteh, issuing the warrants under which they entered houses, seized property, and made arrests in questions of security and intelligence. Under the law, the Revolutionary Guards had little power without his authorization, and could be dismissed or jailed at his order. In point of fact, Zakir lived in fear of the Komiteh, whose grumblings about insufficient vigor had hounded the last four of his predecessors from office.

"A fresh homicide." Darius didn't sit. "A girl was discovered by the Pasdar murdered at the new apartment complex on Saltanatabad Avenue below Niavaran. We don't know who she is, or how she died. Baghai dug a bullet out of her head, but it was put there after death. There was evidence of sexual mutilation."

Although he was alerted to major crimes by the Komiteh, Zakir demanded a separate briefing from the police. The feeling of both agencies was that they were working at cross purposes, which often they were.

"Fourteen rapists, plus eight killers were stoned to death last week at the Sports Stadium in Bushehr." Zakir slid a Daily *Kayhan* from under the report, and tapped his finger against the front page. "You'd think that would put the fear of God into anyone contemplating murder. The crazy bastards don't read the papers, though. What leads do you have?"

"None."

"Is Ghaffari working with you?"

"He inspected the apartment houses for witnesses."

"He is a capable officer. The investigation can be left in his hands without worry. There is a more pressing case I want you to take over."

"What's more urgent than murder?"

Zakir leaned across the desk, lowered his voice. "Last night, four armed men broke into a house on Bobby Sands Street." Bobby Sands Street, at the rear of the British embassy, had been Royal Street prior to the Revolution, when it was renamed after the Irish Republican Army gunman who had starved himself to death in an English jail. "They roughed up the occupants, bound them with adhesive tape, and made away with carpets and furnishings valued at many millions of rials.

"How many killed?"

"None, praise to Allah, but the family received a terrible fright. They are the son and daughter-in-law and grandchildren of a big turban man from Isfahan, Ayatollah Golabi. We must find the people who did this, and put them quickly in the ground with those bastards at Bushehr."

"This is more important than murder?"

"If people like the Golabis lose their key, and are locked outside the house, *that* is of greater concern than the death of such a girl."

"Give me the report," Darius said. "I'll find someone to look into it."

"You will handle it personally."

"When I have time—"

"First the robbery. You are not in the U.S. now. This is how we do things here."

He did not need to be told. A jumble of priorities ensured that every job in Iran was infinitely more complicated than it appeared on the surface. The diligent worker was the one who took on more than he could accomplish, promising that sometime in the future, with God's help, surely he would fulfill his task. Held to that standard of endeavor, Darius's performance as a criminal investigator was found to be wanting. Having closed virtually every case to cross his desk, he was faulted for a lack of initiative. What more could he do? he had asked Ghaffari. Go on a murder spree himself? Arrange for mountains of unsolved cases secure in the knowledge that he could put a killer behind bars for each one? It was either that, Ghaffari had advised, or forget that he'd ever lived in the United States, or else go back there to stay. And because the three strategies were equally attractive, and one was as improbable as the next, Darius had settled on another way out of his bind and shut his ears to all criticism except the flood that came from himself.

"Ayatollah Golabi is extremely powerful," Zakir said. "He will make our lives miserable until we find who did this. After he has his carpets back there is nothing he won't do for us. What can the girl do?"

The question was not meant for Darius, who got up to leave.

"You are not working for the shah anymore. You're in no position to dictate. If it weren't for the turban men, you'd wish you had been sent to Bushehr."

Darius sniffed his tie as he went to the door. "She can give us peace of mind," he said.

The young criminalist, Hamid, was pacing the corridor when Darius returned to headquarters. "We have learned something of major signifi-cance," Hamid said. "The superintendent of the apartment complex says the electric ran well into the evening yesterday; it was not until midnight that power was cut, and the lights went off in the court. Obviously, the body was brought sometime after that, and before four-thirty, when the Pasdars arrived."

"Why?" Darius asked.

"Because . . ." Hamid reviewed the case in his mind before committing himself. ". . . those are the hours when it was dark."

"Where is the rule that a body cannot be gotten rid of in broad daylight without being noticed?"

Hamid held himself stiffly. He gave Darius a sheet from a yellow legal pad. "Here are the license plates that you wanted noted. All but two are registered to residents of the neighborhood. Of the others, one is from Azerbaijan Province, and another reported stolen from Rey last week. We have taken over an apartment on the top floor, and are keeping our eyes on the vehicles. Tomorrow morning, we'll set up roadblocks to ask motorists if they saw anything."

Darius entered his office to find Ghaffari at his desk, making a paper plane of yellow paper like Hamid's.

"Doesn't miss a beat, that boy," he said. "I'm one hundred percent convinced he'll find whoever stole the car from Rey." He refolded the paper, streamlined the wings. "This is a list of all convicted sex offenders in the city over the last fifteen years. The computer is not working. Records compiled it by hand."

"Why go back so far?"

Ghaffari test-flew his plane without letting go. "When the penalty is death, recidivism is discouraged. I suggest we look for someone who left prison prior to seventy-nine."

"Sex fiends don't wait that long before going after their next victim. Not any longer than you.

"I've been good, a faithful husband. I—" He protested too vehemently. "You briefed Zakir?"

"Yes— And I almost forgot. Congratulations. The Revolutionary Prosecutor has put you in charge of the case."

"What about you?"

"As of now, I'm looking into a *big* one, a break-in at the relatives of a turban man near the British embassy."

"That's nuts. Who is he protecting?"

"Don't be insulted, Mansur. Soon as you show progress, he'll replace you with Hamid. And after him, one of the recruits. And then he'll order an arrest, somebody the Komiteh wants out of the way."

The yellow plane made a belly landing next to the trash basket. "Farib called."

"Where is she?"

"She had the same question about you."

"Did you explain?"

Ghaffari put his feet up on the desk. "Go home, Bakhtiar. That's an order from the new homicide chief. Tell her about this girl yourself."

Darius wove through the noonday crush, taking whichever streets the traffic offered. Policemen stood out of the way as drivers ignored signals, rode on the sidewalk to avoid bottlenecks, and converged on gridlocked intersections where honor was stained by yielding the right of way. Although an official car was at his disposal, he preferred the old Thunderbird with its German radio that pulled in snatches of popular music from U.S. Armed Forces Radio in the Persian Gulf. He drove past the Muslim Theological School at Baharestan Square, and parked in the underground garage of a twelve-story apartment house. Orange letters were spray-painted on the whitewashed wall behind his spot:

THE ROAD TO SALVATION:
FAITH, HOLY WAR, AND MARTYRDOM

The floorboards groaned beneath the carpeting. He stepped over dusty suitcases in the foyer, and tossed his jacket on the couch. The three-room apartment had been considered luxurious when the building went up during the early 1970s oil boom. But the thin walls were no match for the stench of dombeh, frying lamb fat, and the gulping toilet next door. On the television was a photo of him at the former Shahyad Tower on the western approach to the city with a curly-haired girl who was wearing a green head scarf and had stolen his smile. Colorless images flittered across the screen. Darius stared absentmindedly at a mullah sermonizing on the evils of idolatry and sexual deviation.

In the bedroom a sleeping woman held herself tightly on a sliver of the double mattress. He sat next to her, and studied the aquiline nose that plastic surgeons had whittled a step beyond perfection. Gold droplet earrings were lost in her thick curls. "When did you come back?" he asked.

Her lips parted, and the red tip of her tongue tasted them. Her eyes darted around the room. Not happy with what she saw, she closed them again. Propped on an elbow she rubbed the lids with her knuckles like a child. "Where were you?"

"A woman was murdered. I had to work all night."

A knife edge of sun sliced across her cheek. Held to the scrutiny of natural light her complexion was flawless, which she attributed to having given up makeup and alcohol.

"Tell me about Qom."

"Uncle misses you," she said.

"He's well?"

"It was 118 degrees yesterday, and the pollution does his asthma no good. But he will never leave."

"You spent time with him every day?"

"When I was not at the mosque." Farib scratched her forehead. Just below the hairline was a thin callus from the stone that she pressed her head against while crouched in prayer. The Qur'an forbade touching any man-made object during discourse with God. "You might visit sometime."

"You know my feelings," he said. "It would be hypocritical—"

"It's your duty as a Muslim to go to the holy city and pray to the Almighty."

"Your uncle is a turban man, and he doesn't object."

"If uncle forgives you for not attending to your religious obligations, it's because he is a saint. As a woman, such forgiveness is beyond me. You can make an appearance at the mosque, even if it means nothing to you. For what he did for you he is still criticized everywhere."

"It was more than ten years ago. How long will I be repaying my debt?"

"For eternity," Farib said. "You owe him your life."

Darius kissed her, and she yawned. Reaching under her chador, she removed sturdy cotton panties of Syrian manufacture. The chador surrounded her like a tent as she rolled onto her stomach.

Darius touched her shoulder, and she hiked the chador above her hips. Farib's bottom was as creamy as her face. Once, he had asked her if this was also because she abstained from alcohol, and she had stopped talking to him for a month.

On her knees she said, "What are you waiting for? It's your right."

"We aren't from a village still in the dark ages. We can make love like human beings."

Dutifully, she took off the chador, turning over onto her back. Her body was pink and fresh, as if she had stepped out of her skin. Darius nuzzled between her breasts, marched his lips along her slender throat. He pinched a hair from a corner of her mouth, and kissed her again. Farib's arms remained at her sides. She was as responsive as the pillow.

A woman, it was written, was possessed of greater desire than a man—nine times more—and was not to withhold herself when her husband wanted her. The nature of a man was to utilize this desire at his pleasure, to respond to what already was there in her. Farib, for all her professions of orthodoxy, adhered to stubborn heresies in the interpretation of her wifely responsibilities. Darius pulled away.

"If I don't please you anymore, take another wife. "It's your right," she said. "Or a temporary wife, for when I'm not here."

She sat up. "Or divorce me. I won't fight it. Just pronounce a talaq, and it will be done. Surely, that's not too hard for you to do. Unless you're afraid my uncle may forget he once had reason to save your life."

Darius went back into the living room. On the ring with his apartment keys was a brass key, which—when there was someone to share the joke with—he called his Key to Paradise. He unlocked a cabinet in the wall unit. Removing a bottle of Russian vodka, he poured some into a collins glass.

He switched channels. A mullah in a black turban, which indicated he was a direct descendant of the Prophet, took the place of the other on the screen.

"We recognize no absolute values besides total submission to the will of the Almighty. Our teachers say, 'Don't lie!' But the principle is not the same when we serve God. He gave man the precious gift of lies so that we can protect ourselves at times of danger, and puzzle our enemies. Should we adhere to the truth at the cost of defeat and jeopardy to the faith? We believe not. Our teachers say, 'Don't kill!' But the Almighty himself instructed us how to kill . . ."

Farib had slipped into a University of Maryland sweatshirt and blue jeans.

She stood at the mirror brushing her hair, a fleeting image of the woman he had married. Their eyes made contact in the glass. "Have you finished poisoning yourself?" she asked.

Darius put down the vodka in a swallow. "Got to go," he said. "It's a big case. I just wanted to say hello, see how you were—"

"I was well, thank you." Farib dropped the brush on the bare cosmetics table. "You look tired," she said. "There's time for you to nap. I'll be out of your way. I have shopping to do."

Darius took her place at the mirror. Knotting his tie, he watched the chador fall over Farib's shoulders and swallow her whole.

"A *very* big case."

· 3 ·

Workmen had dug up Hafez Avenue and gone away leaving it a watery trench, a catchbasin for the djoub. Darius parked in the shallows close to the former British embassy whose brick walls were blackboards of revolutionary rhetoric.

THE SPIRIT OF ALLAH HAS COMMANDED: ANY COMPROMISE IS TREASON
TO SLAY AND BE SLAIN FOR ALLAH: THAT IS THE EDICT OF RUHOLLAH

The sidewalks were empty, the flooded gutter devoid of traffic. Darius walked slowly, playing the rare midtown quiet against his nerves. At Bobby Sands Street he took a running start across the gorge. His shoes squished as he let himself inside a walled garden on the corner.

A cement blockhouse set in a jungle of azalea and jasmine was guarded by a Komitehman with an Uzi. Darius said, "Police," and waited to be asked to produce identification. The Komitehman lowered his gun. He went to a lawn chair under a tattered Cinzano umbrella, and turned up a sermon on a portable radio.

The mist from a revolving lawn sprinkler broke the sunlight into pocket rainbows. Above a plastic wading pool a swing creaked in the breeze. The door was opened by a boy of no more than eight wearing a felt cap that budded in fuzzy mouse ears.

"Is your father at home?" Darius asked him.

The boy nibbled a white strip around a green apple with big mouse teeth, and ran inside the house. Darius entered and looked around a large room paneled in walnut. Embroidered drapes kept the sun off fine elephant's feet Bokhara carpets that lay three deep on the hardwood floors. The walls were lined with religious texts dating back to the seventeenth-century Sufi mystics. Darius heard an adult voice, and followed it into a room filled with baby furniture, where the boy squatted in front of a television.

The cap fell off as the boy turned around. Darius saw a bulbous head and narrow eyes, the patrimony of the religious elite. For generations the women most desired as brides in Iran had been the daughters of their future husband's father's brothers. Children like this one were a common result.

The boy giggled, and looked back at the screen. Darius poked through the rooms, but saw nothing around which to construct an investigation. In twenty minutes he was ready to leave. The Komitehman had returned to the door, but now faced inside, as though having let him too easily into the house he would rectify the mistake by keeping him prisoner.

Darius said, "This *is* the Golabi home that was burglarized?"

The guard said nothing, thought about it, nodded.

"The child's parents will be back soon?"

"I don't know."

Darius gave him his card. "Have them contact me at my office."

The guard stepped aside, and Darius went out to the car furious with himself for wasting time that should have been spent hunting a killer. The only crime he had found was perpetuated in the genes of the misshapen child. He had gone far enough with Zakir's charade. Sooner than probe the burglary he would accompany Farib on a pilgrimage to Qom.

Dredged from his subconscious the murder case came back to him with several hard theories attached. In no manner were Iranians involved; for the girl to have been ruined as she was pointed unmistakably to Arab hands. As far back as elementary school he had been taught that the Arabs were a cowardly lot of Sunni heretics who prided themselves on their lust for innocent blood. Torture was not unknown in the long history of his country. But the Persians were a compassionate people, and the judicial application of pain traditionally was limited to the bastinado, the melancholy flogging of the soles of the feet.

He spent the remainder of the afternoon at the train stations and airport, searching for witnesses to the girl's arrival in the city. The photo he showed, a black-and-white Polaroid snapped at the crime scene, made no impression on anyone, perhaps—as the baggage clerk at Iran Airlines told him—because the young woman he was looking for appeared to be sleeping. When he returned to headquarters there was a note on his desk that Baghai had called. He reached the coroner at the morgue as he was going home.

"What news?"

"In all the hubbub of finding the mutilations," Baghai said, "I didn't examine the body as carefully as I should have. In the crook of the left arm was a crusting sore, extremely deep. My assumption was that it was a severe rash, like several others I saw, but when I looked closely I noticed a cluster of tiny punctures in the skin."

"She'd injected herself regularly?"

"There aren't enough marks to indicate she had taken narcotics over a long period of time. She may have become an addict recently, or previously smoked the drugs before graduating to the use of needles."

"Could she have died of an overdose?"

"Of an overdose, of bad dope, of intentional poisoning. Of anything else," Baghai said. "In any event, it's no longer our case. This is about drugs, and drugs are the Komiteh's jurisdiction."

"No," Darius said. "It's about torture. And murder."

Darius thanked him and hung up. Heroin addicts were a rarity in a country where the illicit drug of choice was opium. He rubbed his smarting eyes, and the room pinched in at the walls. As it rebounded, he felt compressed in turn. A blurry figure in a blue suit came into the office and stood at the door. "Yes?"

A bearded face with high, sloping cheeks and black hair the texture of iron filings assumed character as Nader Mehta stepped close to the desk.

"The girl's fingerprints are not on record."

Mehta once had been chief of investigations for the homicide squad, the brightest of the rising stars in the National Police. A Zoroastrian by birth, he was officially a "believer," like Jews and Christians of "the people of the book," to be treated with deference, although not as equal to Muslims. When the Revolution dead-ended his career, he had retreated into the records department and the mysticism of fire-worshiping ancestors who had ruled Persia before the Muslim conquest. Though such interests officially were frowned upon, Darius—like many Iranians—was fascinated by his country's pre-Islamic past, and every spring on Red Wednesday, during the Now Ruz new year's celebration, he joined Mehta in a leap over three bonfires of desert thorn, chanting, "My troubles and my pallor I cast into your flames. Your warmth and rosy cheeks for me."

Darius said, "Send her card to Khuzestan Province. She may be an Arab. If not from another country, then one of ours."

Mehta made no move to go. "What do you call Jewish babies that are not circumcised?"

"Huh? I'm no good at riddles. You tell me."

"Girls," Mehta said, but didn't laugh. "With them it's girls."

"You'll send the card?"

"The files in Khuzestan are in worse shape than here." Mehta looked at him sadly, the curator of a museum with no capital for acquisitions. "The only decent records are the Komiteh's. You might ask . . . No, you might come to them on your knees, and beg for a peek."

"They've told me to mind my own business."

"Then why are we chasing all over to identify her?"

"What would you do instead?"

"Seek solace from God."

"God won't find her killer."

"And from this." Mehta lifted the flap on his jacket pocket, and Darius saw the neck of a pint flask. "Let the sin be on me."

Darius took the bottle and unscrewed the cap, brought the vodka to his lips, then paused to say, "There's plenty to go around."

After the evening shift had come on duty, and he was on his own time, Darius drove south from the administrative district of Ark. Near the central bazaar traffic thickened, and the sidewalks were sluggish with pedestrians. Down stone steps he entered the bazaar through the gold sellers' quarter, and stood there while his ears grew accustomed to the din. Under a faienced arcade six thousand shops and stalls undulated for ten kilometers through the heart of the city. He pushed into the crowd, which swept him to the copper beaters, and beyond to the rug merchants and traders in textiles, gem cutters and tile makers and leather crafters whose booths gave off an oily, animal smell neutralized by the sweetness of bakeries and the charcoal smoke of cello kebab, square chunks of lamb served on a bed of rice. Between the wool dyers and lumber traders, at a narrow stall no deeper than a closet, he stopped to watch a man bent over a bench cluttered with tin cans.

The man pounded the cans with a rubber mallet that did not mar the labels stamped with a picture of a tree burdened with sun-ripened peaches. When they were reshaped to his satisfaction, he wove them into a mat of Pepsi-Cola cans. These he fashioned into a suitcase, which he finished off with a leather handle. Looking up to admire his handicraft, he saw Darius, and turned away.

"Farhad, don't you say hello to an old friend?"

"You're no friend of mine," the suitcase maker answered.

"That depends on your point of view. I'd say I'm the best friend you have in this world, and maybe the next."

Farhad placed another can on the bench. A glancing blow scraped the green crown from the peach tree, and he threw it away. "I can't work with you jabbering at my back."

"Then look at me."

Reluctantly, Farhad faced him. His skin was loose beneath hollow black eyes. Thin on top, he was going gray at the temples. Farhad was twenty-four. "You don't have any business with me," he complained. "I've been clean."

Darius smiled unpleasantly. "It's a new service of the National Police. We look after the health of all our old friends."

Farhad didn't see the humor in it. "Ask the Komiteh," he said. "They'd know if I was using."

"But I'm already here." Darius grabbed the suitcase maker's wrist, and rolled his sleeve above the elbow. Farhad's bicep was a shriveled knot of scars, but there were no fresh abscesses or punctures.

"Why don't you make yourself useful, instead of bothering me, and hire out as a bodyguard for a mullah?" Farhad said.

He buttoned his sleeve, hammered another can. Darius watched over his shoulder, then kicked him behind the knee. Farhad went down, grazing his jaw on the bench and recoiled onto his back. Darius was all over him. He tore off the suitcase maker's shoes and flung them into a pyramid of spoiled cans. Farhad's feet were two sizes too large for his shrunken body, the skin yellow as parchment. Along the instep the veins were swollen red, and drained into suppurating wounds between his toes.

"I *should* call the Komiteh," Darius said. "You'd learn who your friends are."

"Eat rooster shit."

Farhad's heels swept under Darius's chin. Darius poised a jab at the scarred soles, but pulled it when the suitcase maker screamed in anticipated pain. Disapproval became the verdict in the murmuring at his back. A crowd stretched to the rug merchants, all eyes on him. "Keep moving," he said coolly. "The show's over. Let's go."

Grumbling, the shoppers drifted in search of the next attraction. Darius pulled Farhad to his knees, and backed him over the bench.

"What do you want?"

Getting information from an addict was next to impossible, Darius knew, even when there were funds to pay for it. Properly softened up, however, Farhad would not be as quick to fall back on the lies that were his natural line of defense. Darius brought out the picture of the girl. There were few heroin users in Teheran that Farhad did not number among his friends, and enemies. "Ever see her before?"

The suitcase maker scarcely glanced at the snapshot. He shook his head as he picked up his mallet.

"Look again."

"I never—"

Darius stamped on his foot.

"Monday," Farhad moaned. "This time of day."

"Where?"

"In the Shah's Mosque, here at the bazaar. You crushed my—"

"Who is she?"

"I don't know."

Darius tapped his foot beside the suitcase maker's.

"I swear it."

"But you talked?"

Farhad made a gasping sound that Darius took for a yes.

"What about?"

"What do you think?"

Farhad's thin smile irked Darius, who ground his heel into the suitcase maker's toes. "How much did you sell her?"

"*She* was the one with the goods." Moisture was running from Farhad's eyes. "Her price couldn't be beat."

"Your lucky day."

"I told her to get lost."

"Why?"

"She wouldn't say where she'd got my name, or how she knew I was in the market for good stuff." Perched on one leg Farhad caressed his wounded toes.

"Everyone knows your name."

"She was moving kilos." Farhad looked sadly around the tiny stall. "Grams are my speed now."

"Who did you send her to?"

"That kind of weight, I don't know anybody who could handle it."

Darius lifted his heel.

". . . It's the truth."

"Any idea why she was desperate for quick cash?"

"What does anyone want with serious money these days? It's not cheap to find a place in Beverly Hills."

From the top shelf Darius brought down a grip fabricated from small cans that formerly had contained baby French green peas. "How much?"

"Seventy thousand rials," Farhad said. "Planning a trip, too?"

Darius moistened his thumb as he counted out the bills. "Wouldn't that be nice?"

Darius drove back to his place on Baharestan Square. Exhausted, he was nevertheless too keyed up for sleep, and continued into the suburbs. The electric was off at the apartment complex in Shemiran, the black surface of the courtyard like a subterranean sea. He sat on the bench where the body was found, looking up at the buildings. Why had the girl been left here? Why not in a park, or vacant lot, or any of a thousand bombed-out ruins downtown where she would have remained undiscovered for weeks? Had she been killed upstairs, he asked himself, and her body gotten rid of at the first opportunity? Or was it more than convenience that linked the mutilated Arab girl to Saltanatabad Avenue's déclassé elite.

He slunk down until the back of his head rested against the top slat, and he was looking into a window covered by a yellow curtain. Shoe leather scraped the tiles with the hiss a blade makes on a barber's strop. A flash of khaki and then the barrel of an Uzi caught his eye. He reached for ID, but quickly showed his empty hand. The assumption being formulated by the man with the rifle was not necessarily that he was going for his wallet.

Red-rimmed eyes and drawn cheeks insinuated themselves as a mirror image of his own. Bijan's day had been longer even than his.

"Trying it on for size?"

"What?" Darius asked him.

"I saw you sitting here like the dead girl. For a moment I thought you might be dead, too."

"Who would harm me? I have no enemies."

"Neither did she."

"Is that a fact?"

"A theory of mine," the Komitehman said. "Another is that it would be better for you to concentrate on the burglary at the relatives of Ayatollah Golabi."

"There was no burglary."

"You have the soul of a prophet. Your calling is to reveal the truth." Bijan sat next to him with the Uzi between his knees. "But in Islam all truths were revealed long ago. Muhammad was the last prophet, and he is dead more than a thousand years."

"New questions come up every day," Darius said. "The prophets didn't anticipate the modern age."

"Nothing is new," Bijan answered with conviction, "merely things that are not as they appear to be at first glance. For instance, dig deep at the Golabis' and, if God wills it, you will uncover a robbery like countless others."

"And if I dig here, what will I find?"

Bijan gazed at the apartment houses. It seemed to Darius that he focused on the bricks rather than glimpse inside the windows. "The girl was an Arab, a narcotics addict. It is not the responsibility of the National Police of the Islamic Republic to sort through the world's garbage."

"How do you know she used drugs?"

"On reflection it is plain."

"Nothing is plain," Darius said. "Dr. Baghai almost missed it."

"We have our sources."

"Your people killed her. That's your source."

"Slander against the Committee for the Revolution is a crime for which the penalty is years at hard labor," Bijan said. "If you persist in such remarks, be prepared to back them up with fact."

"She *was* yours."

"I don't understand what you mean by yours. The Pasdars found her body. We alerted the police, who took her away. So it follows that now she is *yours*, am I right? I came to tell you that pursuing more relevant investigations will enhance your worth to the Revolution. If you would rather waste time on a prostitute, it is up to you, of course, but—" Bijan slid his hand along the oiled barrel of the Uzi, fondled it—teased it, Darius thought. "But not useful to anyone."

"How did you know—"

"That the girl used drugs? I told you—" Bijan stroked the muzzle, and wiped his hand on his pants. "The Komiteh has its sources, even in the morgue."

"I don't mean that," Darius said.

"What?"

"How did you know I was here?"

Farib lay on her small piece of the mattress with her elbows like barbed wire around her body. Vaguely, Darius remembered when she sprawled across the bed and could not sleep unless he was pressed tight beside her. Over the years she had gravitated to one side from which he was excluded except upon invitation. He noticed a leg almost off the mattress. If he did not repair his marriage, soon she would be sleeping on the floor, or else he on the couch. In the morning he would offer to go shopping with her, look for nice things to put in her new valise.

Stepping out of his clothes, he raised the blanket. Without benefit of surgery Farib's body was nearly as perfect as her nose. It was Darius's complaint, never expressed, that he slept each night with the Venus de Milo, and worried about leaving smudges. Perversely, he anticipated her rages, when bloodless lips or the clumsy gesture that proved her to be human inspired new love—and more frustration. His eyes full of her cool beauty, he climbed under the covers trying not to brush against her.

He was awakened by the phone. Too tired to move, he lay on his chin and listened to it ring. When it stopped, he opened his eyes. He was alone in bed, the room flooded with late-morning sun. The ringing began again. He hurried into the kitchen, and picked up on the extension.

A whisper he couldn't put a name to asked to speak to the lieutenant colonel. With the receiver against his shoulder he brought the teapot under the faucet. Running water washed away the cobwebs, and he recognized Farhad on the line.

"I've been thinking about the girl," he was saying. "Possibly, there are other things I remember about her."

"What things?"

Farhad had his own agenda. "Before I tell you, there's a small favor you can do—"

"Keep out of trouble," Darius said, "and you won't need favors."

"It's not for me—for a friend, a girl very much like the one we talked about."

"What kind of trouble is she in?"

"Evin Prison," Farhad said. "That kind."

A sound meant to be ironic laughter came out of Darius a grunt. "No one has influence there. Not even the Komiteh can get people out of their jails."

"If they know someone is interested in her case, they'll go easier on her."

"I have some doubt about this sudden improvement in your memory," Darius said.

"I've always given you good stuff."

"You have the same credibility as any other informant, which is to say not much."

"She'll be *just* like that girl, if you don't help."

Darius put a light under the teapot. "Give me a taste of what you have, and I'll tell you what it's worth."

"Nothing for nothing."

"Bye, Farhad. I'm not going up against the Komiteh, and then find out you've been building castles in air." He heard other voices, one inquiring about the price of a valise.

Farhad said something he didn't catch, and then, in a whisper: "The girl told me she had twenty, maybe as much as thirty kilograms of Afghani white heroin, very high-grade, almost pure. And she knew specifically who she wanted to move them to—a mutual acquaintance in Dharvazeh Ghor, who she could not locate. I told her where to look."

"And then?"

"The buyer—do what you can for my friend, and I'll give him up to you."

"You appall me, Farhad. Where's your criminals' code of honor?"

"What does *he* know about honor? He's a fucking thief who's beating me out of a ten percent finder's fee."

"Tell me more."

"This is all you get for free. Will you help?"

Darius forced hesitation into his voice. "I'll be at the bazaar in a couple of hours."

"No, I've already been seen too much with you. How well do you know Dharvazeh Ghor?"

"I can find my way around."

"On Martyr Rafizadeh Street there is a school that was bombed during the War of Cities, and never torn down. If you want to know about the girl, about both girls, be there at seven."

"I can't give you any guarantees about your friend."

"If you won't try—*then* it's guaranteed what will happen to her."

Dharvazeh Ghor, at the retreating edge of the desert, was home to the poorest of Teheran's poor, day laborers and sweepers in small factories, who lived in iron-roofed shanties for which a single squat toilet over an open sewage pit served dozens of families. The Martyr Rafizadeh Street School had been a pet social project of the new regime. It was less than a year old when an Iraqi missile crashed into the lunch room, killing and maiming nearly two hundred children. No funds were available to rebuild the structure, which stood now as a memorial to the slaughtered youngsters. Though the roof was gone, the walls remained intact but for empty windows and door frames. Dharvazeh Ghor in its entirety appeared to Darius as a monument to shattered hope. New construction had been limited to wedding bowers for the war dead, waist-high shrines decked with colored pennants, and tin amulets in the form of St. Abbas's consoling hand.

Darius had assumed that Farhad would be waiting outside. For fifteen minutes he paced the sidewalk before clambering through the wreckage into a classroom. The cinder block walls were papered over with revolutionary posters showing Muslim warriors being raised to heaven on the backs of white horses. Rows of splintered desks faced a blackboard that was a Rosetta stone of juvenile script. A rat half as long as its hairless tail paddled away from a yelping dog that followed it around the edge of a water-filled crater. The walls, the floors, the sliding door of the coat closet were black with ancient blood.

Spasms of light glinted off rubble piled in a doorway like tailings from a vein of base metal. Darius stood on the broken brick eye to eye with a picture of the Imam that stared down on a mahogany desk set among file cabinets and empty bookcases. Farhad was slumped behind the desk in an oversize leather chair with his head against his shoulder. He was wearing a knit skullcap and a long-sleeve shirt rolled up above one elbow. A shoelace was knotted around his scarred bicep; the vein bulged purple in sallow skin. A burning candle was glued to the desktop beside a spoon that was bent back against its rusted handle.

"Hey," Darius said. "Hey, you, wake up. The party's over."

Farhad's shoulder was a spindly lever that propelled him toward the floor when it was disturbed. Darius grabbed him under the arms and let him down slowly on his back. He pressed an ear to Farhad's chest, but heard only his own blood pulsing through his head. Like an errant dart in the suitcase maker's pants cuff was a hypodermic needle attached to a reddish eyedropper.

Ghaffari arrived behind the morgue attendants, who stood out of the way while he photographed the body. With each flash the dead man's image was fixed as indelibly in Darius's brain as on film. Ghaffari swept a light into the corners, got down on his knees to follow a trail of white powder under the desk to a crushed bit of chalk. He took a second set of pictures to be safe, then went outside to wait with Darius while the body was strapped onto a gurney.

"It's a successful man who dies doing what he likes best, so it's fair to say he led a fulfilling life." Ghaffari loaded a fresh roll of film into his camera.

"Besides, with an addict what else can you expect? I know what you're thinking, but have you ever heard of one dying of old age?"

"The timing is too convenient," Darius said. "If he'd kicked off tomorrow, or the day after, then I might be persuaded it was accidental."

"That's all it was. No one needed him silenced, because he had nothing of importance to say. He was toying with you. He didn't know any more than we do."

"Possibly." Darius was distracted by the corpse being carried out through a window. "Still, for my only witness to die just as we were about to talk—"

"Is pure coincidence," Ghaffari said. "Where do we go from here?"

"You go with him to the morgue. Stay till Baghai tells you exactly how he died." They walked across the street, and Darius poked his head through the beaded curtain of a wedding bower. Edged in candle stubs on a bed of withered roses was a framed portrait of a teenage boy who had died on the Basra front. Droplets of red wax clung to the cheeks like tears of blood. "I'm going back to Shemiran."

"Why?" Ghaffari snapped two pictures of the school building. "We've squeezed that lemon dry."

"What else is there?"

The lights were on at the apartment complex, but OUT OF SERVICE signs were taped to the elevator doors. Darius climbed to the top floor, and worked his way downstairs through tenants who insisted they were asleep, or not at home when the body was placed in the court. The tenth-story landing resonated with Beatles music, which he traced to an apartment in the line whose fourth-floor resident was the old man with the rugs. He knocked. A noisy argument started up in another unit, and he let his eyes drift past the elevator and back along the other wall through the garbage strewn around the incinerator. When he turned to the door again, a pinpoint of light was focused between his eyes.

"Who is it?"

The voice was a husky contralto in counterpoint with the music. The fifth Beatle, he thought, like the Twelfth Imam—the Lord of the Age, who had disappeared in the ninth century—was fated to walk the earth unrecognized into eternity. He pulled out his ID and dangled it up to the peephole like a small fish he'd caught. "Police," he said.

"What do you want?"

"Open up, please."

"I'm not that interested."

"Immediately."

Two dead bolts turned, and he was looking at a green-eyed girl whose straight blonde hair danced on her slight shoulders. The pale glow of her cheeks he credited to an insufficient diet and golden down that was faintly visible in harsh lamplight. More startling than her beauty was her boldness in not hiding it. She was wearing a sleeveless, above-the-knee dress of thin summer fabric, the neckline a gentle V between lightly freckled breasts.

The first question was automatic: "Is your husband at home?"

"I have no husband."

Single women were discouraged from living alone. Women like her did not remain single for long. His experience had been that few homicide investigations didn't pose more questions than they answered. Contradiction was the skeleton on which the best cases were fleshed.

He stepped inside without being invited. He had seen the same shabby broadloom rug and convertible couch, the bruised table and chairs in other apartments that he had come to recognize as furnished units. The music blared from a tape player on the bathroom sink beside several articles of soapy underwear. He shut off the water, which the young woman had seemed to believe masked the sound.

"I'd like to ask you about the body found in the courtyard."

She fixed him in a venemous stare. "I didn't kill her. Does that answer the question?"

"In part." Though he believed himself to be incapable of blushing, Darius's face felt hot. "Were you awake at that hour? Did you notice anything?"

Her expression didn't change, but the effort in holding it started her lower lip to quiver. "I heard sirens, but was too sleepy to get out of bed. In the morning the neighbors told me what had happened. Everything I know is second-hand at best."

"Your name, please?"

"Maryam Lajevardi."

Darius jotted it in his notepad. "And what did the neighbors say?"

"That a girl had been shot, and her body left downstairs to be discovered. And the police had been here for most of the morning."

"To be discovered? What do you mean by that?"

"Those are their words," she said. "You'll have to ask them."

"And, you say, you slept through it all?"

"Like the dead." Maryam Lajevardi palmed the cassette, as though she were concealing vital evidence.

"I assure you," Darius said, "this concerns only murder. I don't care about music."

"One mustn't close one's mind to anything. You may find you enjoy the Beatles."

"It's forbidden."

"*There's* the crime." She dropped another tape in the machine, turned up the volume on a heavy metal group.

Her lip was fluttering wildly. She clamped it under her front teeth as Darius went into the living room. The apartment looked down on the courtyard, affording an unobstructed view of the benches where a tired-looking old man sat smoking a cigarette. Yellow draperies wafted from the window in a light breeze.

"Are you a student, Miss Lajevardi? Do you work?"

"I'm employed at the D. Azadi currency exchange on Firdowsi Street." Darius rubbed the yellow cloth between his fingers.

"You haven't written it in your little book." Her lip was out of control. "Selling traveler's checks," she said to quiet it.

Obscured by an accent Darius couldn't quite place, her voice had softened to a throaty whisper. "Miss Lajevardi," he asked, "what are you doing living here alone?"

"Is it against the law to have my own apartment?"

"Answer the question, please."

Her lip was still. She bit it anyway as she sniffed back tears. "You won't make me go back?"

"Back where?"

"Bandar-e-Shah."

"That's where you're from?"

She nodded. "My father is the manager of the state caviar factory there."

"What brings you to Teheran?"

"What has this to do with the girl—"

"Will be for me to decide," Darius said.

Without exhaling, she took a deep breath. "Last month I turned twenty-two. In the eyes of my father I officially became an old maid. It was arranged for me to marry the foreman of the factory. He's forty-seven, coarse, crude, uneducated—a religious fanatic as well. I took what money I had saved and came to Teheran. I've been living here for six weeks."

"And?"

"And? And?" Maryam Lajevardi blew her nose in a man's colored hand-kerchief. "Isn't that enough? Are you asking what comes next for me? How can I tell you, when I don't know myself?"

Darius touched his pen to his notebook, and the young woman stopped sniffling. "You won't report that you found me?"

"No," he said. "That's not my job."

"Because if I'm forced to go back, it will be the murder of two girls you'll be investigating."

"One more question. How do you live in Shemiran on what you bring home from the currency exchange?"

Maryam Lajevardi went into the kitchen, and tore open the cabinets above the sink. Waxy white paper lined the bare shelves. "I starve."

A blue service taxi had run an Iran Peyma bus into a streetlight, and emergency vehicles blocked all lanes of Saltanatabad Avenue. Darius drove onto the sidewalk around the accident, and then continued downtown. Of nearly three dozen witnesses he had spoken to, Maryam Lajevardi alone merited a follow-up interview. How much of that could he credit to her short dress and the warm promise of her silken skin? How much to the melodrama of her escape from a brokered engagement? Even if her story had been delivered to wring the last drop of sympathy from him, in its endless complications he'd heard it too many times before to discount it out of hand. Minus the tears supplied on cue, the lip willed into a spastic bout of vulnerability, he had little cause to view it with skepticism.

At a red light Darius shut his eyes and conjured the image of the young woman. His mind's eye could be counted on to circumvent the cleverest guise while going to the heart of uncooperative witnesses and suspects. What came to him most vividly about Maryam Lajevardi was her breathy voice, the defiance of authority that she was at loose ends to contain. Hearing it again in his head he decided the tone was too excitable for a native of the Caspian; he had supplied her brash words with the wrong accent—or *she* had. Her speech, as well as her coloring, seemed in part foreign, which might explain why he had gotten nowhere with the bullying tactics that as a rule produced quick results with men and women made docile through generations of submission to Islamic decree. Intrigued now, he played over the voice until he had located the faint accent in central Europe, or the shores of the Mediterranean, or else, he thought briefly, in a corner of his brain that would invent a lonely, beautiful woman who was also an outsider in her own land. Already he was looking forward to their second talk. When no good reason came to mind for putting it off, he angled toward the curb, prepared to wheel into a U-turn.

He never heard the car that ran up his tail and slammed the Thunderbird into the intersection. Returning to consciousness, he was vaguely aware that if he hadn't had his foot off the brake, the whiplash would have snapped his neck. He doubted he'd been out for more than twenty seconds. His nose was running. He wiped it on the back of his hand, and blood spilled between his knuckles. Two teeth had been driven through his lower lip. In the mirror was a caricature from a new school of realism of a helpless Dracula with bloody fangs. Touching his tongue to a jagged incisor, he went out to inspect the damage to his car.

The bumper was dangling, the trunk lid jack-knifed over the spare tire. He was sick on the blood and the smell of gasoline. The other vehicle appeared to be unscathed. It was an American limousine, an old Chrysler with a grille like the jaws of a road-grading machine. As it disentangled from the Thunderbird, the loose bumper came away with it.

"Stop right there!" His words were thick, shaped by a swollen tongue as clumsy as a big toe against the roof of his mouth.

Silvered glass offered little of two figures in the other car's front seat. The Chrysler shifted into drive, the torn bumper throwing off sparks like a lit fuse. Darius stuck out his palm, but the heavy limousine kept coming. It was ten feet away, and gaining speed, when he flung himself onto the Thunderbird's trunk. The impact put him on the asphalt on his back.

The Chrysler stopped, and two men in shiny jackets stepped out and watched him struggle to his knees. They were heavily bearded, and wore aviator's lenses of the same mirrored glass as the Chrysler's windows. The shorter one, from the driver's side, steadied him against a lamppost. A tire iron came out of his companion's sleeve like a snake shedding satin skin. Darius shied away, and a muffled gong hummed against his back. He tried to run, but his legs weren't up to it. The driver held him there with one hand.

The taller man rubbed his wrist, took a practice swing with an overhand motion. Darius slithered behind the lamppost. The tall man shortened his arc, and the blunt end of the iron found Darius's heart.

Darius toppled sideways into the street. He looked up into reflective sunglasses that pictured a tortured beetle on its back. His finger was through the trigger guard of his shoulder gun when the short man took it away. Tears distorted his vision as the tire iron came down against his ribs.

Too slowly he was losing consciousness; he cursed his high threshold of pain. He bicycled his legs, and a shoe flew off, and his foot collided with something soft, the sensation like kicking a pillow. One of the men said, "Unnhhh," and there was the sound of puking, and then the smell.

Darius closed his eyes. Numb, he might have been dreaming it was someone else being worked over but for the feeling in his chest that he was suffocating, which grew worse with each blow. The metal bar clattered in the gutter, and he was hauled to his feet and then pushed toward the Chrysler. He planted his feet, but had little strength to resist.

"Move, damn you!"

The squawk of a car horn startled him, and he gagged on a mouthful of blood. The return of his senses came with a fresh rush of pain, and the realization that kidnapping would precede his murder. He fought back with energy drawn from a closed account.

The driver shouted, "Let's go, he's done anyway," and Darius felt himself falling into the street.

The man he had kicked grunted in assent. He snatched up the tire iron, and pounded it in his open palm. Darius buried his head under an umbrella of his arms. The bar sizzled in air, then crashed against his bare sole. All the pain in the world traveled the length of his spine and exploded in his skull. A blessing, it sent him reeling into blackness.

· 4 ·

It was night, and he was moving. Of that much he was certain.

The road was a washboard beneath the wheels of the vehicle, a panel truck of some kind. Through greasy windows in the back doors he made out hardscrabble farms in sandy fields. These were obscured by swirling dust storms, the gerd bad, or round winds, which meant he was being brought south into the desert. When he raised his head to see more, pain put him flat on his back. The top of his skull was jouncing like a loose lid. His brain issued the command to press down on it, but his hands didn't respond. Adrenaline washed a heavy weight over his heart.

In the light from an overtaking car he glimpsed a leather strap across his chest that pinioned his arms to his sides. A woman sat beside him, and slightly behind. Blackness sloughed off her chador, and spread over the desolate country. The torn road jarred him to alertness in which he questioned why the men from the Chrysler hadn't killed him when they had the chance. Thinking made his head hurt that much more, and he craned for a landmark instead. A cool hand on his cheek forced him back against the pillow.

"You're awake?"

Let them find out for themselves. If it was his secrets they were after, not even torture would unseal his lips.

"Darius?" The intimate tone invaded his spirit. What had he blabbed while he was out? "How are you feeling?"

He laughed—and the cool hand pulled away. The voice was a hallucination. So why not the pain?

The woman's head grazed the roof as the truck hit a huge pothole. She bent over him, and the veil came away from her face. Farib's smile lasted several seconds before disintegrating under its own weight. "Lie still," she said, "you have a fractured skull."

Her fingers traced a gauze dressing around his forehead. Did the doctors, he wondered, use black gauze for the fractured skulls of descendants of the Prophet?

"Where are we? Why am I tied?"

A blatting sound escaped him as the truck shuddered on a patch of gravel. They were over pavement again when Farib unbuckled the strap. He brought up his right hand sheathed in a gauze mitt. Farib snipped the tape, and the mitt fell apart. The hand felt dead against his cheek.

"You wouldn't stop clawing at the bandages," she said. "We had to wrap your hand."

Darius made a clammy fist around the railing of his stretcher. "I don't remember."

"At Pars Hospital," she said. "The doctors didn't know at first if you would surv— You're not a good patient, Darius."

"What day is this?"

"Monday. You were in the hospital four days."

"Where are you taking me?"

"To Qom."

"Tell the driver to turn around."

"You need quiet," Farib said. "Three ribs are broken, and you've suffered internal injuries. Your kidneys are bruised."

"I'll recuperate as quickly at home. Faster . . ."

Farib filled a paper cup with water from a pitcher. At the next stretch of smooth road she brought it to his lips. Darius hiked himself up on her arm. The lukewarm water felt as good on his face as down his throat.

"It's better for you to be away from Teheran," she said. "The men who did this to you, Mansur says they may try again to kill you."

He had an answer for that. He had a good answer for every argument she could raise. But being right didn't seem so important now as getting some rest. He shut his eyes, but just for the moment, till he had strength to explain why it was pointless to hide. Next time he looked, the moon had dimmed as the sun edged into its territory, and then a rough equilibrium was achieved in which the stars were extinguished and pink streaks opened the sky from east to west. He sat up, answers at his command, but it was Farib's turn to sleep.

The desert gave way to hillside vineyards, and then to a city the color of the reddish brown sand. The ambulance stopped at a house listing into a small garden as though an earthquake had yanked it from the foundation and only the windblown dirt propped it up. Farib squeezed his hand as the doors opened, and two men carried his stretcher outside. Darius guessed the temperature was well over one hundred. The superheated air was thick with dust and the stench of open sewers. Blue flies dived at his head, but he was too weak to fight back. The stretcher levitated, put down wheels like a plane, and he landed in the shade of a pomegranate tree beside a goldfish pond. Green finches nesting among the red-and-white flowers had bleached the ground around the roots. Farib took the veil from her teeth, and motioned in the direction of the tilted house. "In there, please."

The pink sky ran up against the whitewashed ceiling of a corridor that opened onto a room with two sealed windows. No air moved through the wind towers, ventilation chimneys built into desert homes to catch the meager breeze. Darius was parched. He called for water, but Farib didn't come. The men wheeled him into a corner, and left him there like a stick of broken furniture.

A shadow was moving over his body, and he followed it with his head like a sunflower in thrall to the sun. A turban and a silver beard running to white were too close to focus on. Having seen all he cared to, he lay still to wait for more sleep, which didn't come. When he looked again, the turban and beard were arranged around Uncle Hormoz's worried face.

Darius smiled, thought he did. The men from the ambulance brought him to a bed that creaked like a boat in high seas when he was set down on it. Someone told him he needed sleep; and easily persuaded now, he complied.

It was the hottest part of the day when he woke. A cot had been placed near the bed, and Farib was sprawled across the mattress under a thin sheet. On a yellow sofray between them was a water pitcher and a salad plate topped with chunks of goat cheese. When he reached for the food his arm refused to cooperate, and he knew he had been strapped down again.

The buckle was positioned so that he could free himself without help. Like a diver rising from great depths, he sat up slowly, and dangled his legs. The heat had spoiled the cheese, but he wolfed it down before the taste could register. Tonight he would dream of kebabs and vodka.

He drank four cups of water, bitter Qom water filtered through the salt flats on which the city was erected, and then he walked around the bed without taking his hand from the mattress. Farib's new suitcase lay open on the floor. Beneath patterned chadors were his tan slacks and some rayon shirts. He dressed himself, but hadn't the dexterity to fasten the buttons. Tasseled loafers were cached in knit shoe bags; but in a traditional home it would be a grave insult to his host to wear them inside, and so he padded about the room in stocking feet. A faint breeze seared his wounds through the bandages. Farib moaned in a sexual dream, and kicked off the sheet.

He was an encyclopedia of pain. Although he had few pretensions of vanity, his facial injuries troubled him most. He gazed into the window, which returned little of himself in the filthy glass. Farib disdained mirrors, but he thought there might be one in the bathroom. On butter legs he stumbled down the corridor until he was too weak to go further or turn back. His knees sagged then, and pawing at the wall he surrendered to powerful hands that gathered him around the middle, and held him upright.

"It's not the first time you've had to bear the consequences of my impulsiveness."

"God willing, let it be the last. You weigh a ton." Hormoz swept him toward unpainted double doors. "Are you looking for someone?"

Darius's fingertip followed the unfamiliar outline of his lips. "In a manner of speaking . . ."

Hormoz was Farib's favorite uncle. As her father's eldest brother, and a highly respected cleric, he might have been expected to provide a bridegroom for her from the most brilliant of Qom's religious students. At the start of their three-year engagement, when Darius had found out that Farib was the pampered niece of a professor at the Faiziyeh Theological Seminary, he had despaired of the family allowing the match. But Hormoz had turned to Islam late in life, after amassing a fortune trading tobacco in Europe, and had encouraged his own sons to emigrate to infidel Paris, where he was rumored to support two younger, illegitimate children. He had raised little objection to Farib receiving a Western education, or for choosing as her future husband a young lawyer in Washington on a government scholarship to study the American legal system for reforms applicable to Iranian courts.

In Qom Hormoz was venerated as a marja, a mullah whose behavior was an ideal to be emulated by other clerics. The old man was seventy-one, the only relative Darius had regular contact with.

Hormoz's windowless room was little larger than the back of the ambulance, hotter even than the inferno where Darius slept next to Farib. A candle sent its flame straight up into dead air suffused with the flavor of mint leaves and tobacco. A man whose suit jacket hung loosely from round shoulders waited for Hormoz beside a satin pillow. Desert dust seeded clouds of his stale sweat.

"Excuse me for a minute, please." Hormoz left Darius slouched against the doorpost. "A good friend is here to see me."

Hormoz took his place on the pillow. His visitor came forward, and Hormoz allowed him to kiss his knuckles. Hormoz took back his hand with a few crumpled bills pressed into the palm. He squared the edges between his fingers, and transferred the currency to his other hand, then slipped it back to the man, who bowed graciously and shuffled out of the room.

"Nuri is unusually devout." Hormoz motioned Darius to a green pillow beside the wind tower. "As a bureaucrat in the Ministry of Endowments he's greatly inconvenienced by the Shi'a strictures against accepting government employment until the Twelfth Imam comes back as the Lord of the Age. Since he cannot in good conscience take his salary, he gives it to me, and I return it to him as a present. It's his now to do with as he sees fit."

Hormoz produced a dull mirror the size of a postcard. Darius buffed the glass on his pants leg, and leaned toward the candle.

"What do you see?"

"They say that inside every fat person there's a trim beauty struggling to break free. It's not so different for the rest of us. Allow me to introduce the inner Lieutenant Colonel Bakhtiar of the National Police."

"He's no beauty," Hormoz said.

"A homicide investigator makes his living off the carnage of predators more remorseless than himself. His is a buzzard's face—an occupational hazard."

"A fool's. You weren't spared from execution to die piece by piece."

Darius tilted the mirror, watching as his cheeks blanched. "For what great purpose, then?"

"Don't be impertinent. Farib has her hands full with you. You drink too much, and too openly."

"Vodka eases my nerves."

"You have the steadiest nerves a living body could want," Hormoz said. "You drink because it is forbidden. You've sabotaged your career by going out of your way to antagonize everyone in a position to hurt your interests."

"The fact that I'm breathing antagonizes those people."

"All the more reason to watch your step."

"It antagonizes Farib, too."

"She doesn't see the harm in adopting a civil line, rather than cornering your adversaries and applying pressure until they feel they have no choice but to strike back."

"The bastards who cracked my head did not lack breathing space."

"Must I play devil's advocate for the shah's former magistrate?" Hormoz used a chain of stone prayer beads to count silent repetitions of Allahu Akhbar, God Is Great, while Darius studied his injuries from every angle. "Very well—over ten years ago, you disposed of the SAVAK murderer Colonel Farmayan, whose pleasure was to broadcast the taped screams of those he tortured so that he might destroy the will of new victims. Unlike the killings he prided himself upon, Farmayan's death was clean and painless. Good men and women are alive today thanks only to you. And what was your reward? To be thrown into SAVAK's most infamous prison. For what you did, you should have been given a medal."

Darius did not feel deserving of a medal. A better prize was never to be reminded of his crime and the Evin condemned cell from which his resurrection was still not complete. Crushing despair lingered in his system, a microbe that flared up when his resistance was weakened by memory or bad dreams.

"The Revolution reprieved my life. It's enough."

"The ayatollahs got off cheaply. Farmayan was the embodiment of the sickness of the reign of the Pahlavis. Shooting him was a gift to the nation."

"You're forgetting something." Darius clutched his ribs as he shifted his weight. "He was my boss. Evin Prison was my workplace as well."

"Darius, do you know who the Malamati Sufis are?"

Anticipating real pain, Darius groaned. "With all due respect, your sermons accomplish more when you save them for Friday prayer services."

"The hypocrite is corrupt in his heart," Hormoz intoned, "but makes a show of being good. The Malamati, the self-reproacher, is good inside, but pretends to be evil so that people will hesitate to invest their trust in him. I think you may have some Malamati Sufi in you."

"It would have been news to my father. He raised me as a Twelver Shi'ite, the same as you."

Hormoz snorted at the interruption. "The point is that it is forbidden to be Malamati. A man's self-respect goes beyond his own concern. A believer is forbidden to engage in any action that will damage his honor or his prestige in the community. Islam forbids us to pretend to be what we are not, and pretending to be evil is no different than assuming the guise of a man of virtue."

"If I were pretending," Darius said, "would your intercession have been required to save me from death?"

"Crimes worse than yours have been forgiven. That you and Farmayan were members of the same agency is irrelevant. He was a torturer—you hunted foreign spies. Compromise was a way of life in those days, too." Hormoz clacked his beads loudly, and started another count of thirty-three repetitions. "The years before the Revolution made for few heroes. God knows you were one. Allow the ayatollahs to use you, to sing your praises as one of the former elite, who, having seen the error of his ways, eliminated an enemy of the believers, and made himself valuable to the Islamic Republic."

"Now is not an auspicious moment to announce my candidacy for sainthood." Darius tilted the mirror for Hormoz to see swelling behind his ear.

"The understanding by which you were reprieved hasn't strengthened with time," Hormoz said. "There will be nothing I can do to repair the damage if you weaken it further of your own accord. Many of the friends who assisted us before are dead now or in hiding for their own lives."

"My attackers had fresh complaints. A woman was murdered, and I've been warned off the investigation."

"Warned by whom?"

"By everyone it touches. The Revolutionary Prosecutor, the Bon Yad Monkerat, even the victim seems determined that her killer not be found."

"How does a criminal homicide involve the Komiteh?"

"Are you acquainted with a Bijan, who is a big shot with the Bon Yad? I've heard he was once a student at Faiziyeh."

"Bijan is a common name."

"He's a common type." The weak movement of hot air through the wind tower raised shivers across Darius's back. "I thought he might have earned special distinction at the madreseh."

"Once there was a student of mine too slow-witted to aspire even to becoming a mullah. He was such a poor reader that he acquired the Qur'an in the old manner, by rote, and never inquired into the meaning of the words he parroted. He left the religious life to go into the family trade, but was no better suited for copper beating than driving the devil out of souls. Subsequently, he drifted into the army. Though he was given every opportunity, he was too inept to die bravely in battle. Praise to God, he found his niche in the Committee for the Revolution. I believe *his* name was Bijan—Bijan Farmayan."

"A close relative of the colonel's?"

Hormoz shrugged. "It could be they're simply from the same clan."

"If you would please find out," Darius said. "It's not only the investigation he wants to put a stop to."

"Why, what else?"

"It's me."

Farib sat well back on the other bed, unable to contain her mild revulsion. When Darius stirred, she slid into bed with him without dirtying her feet on the floor. She was wearing leopard skin panties that he had bought for her at a Washington sex boutique, and seen her in once before, when she had modeled them for him at his dingy student boarding house where female guests weren't allowed upstairs after 10:00. A year's romance conducted mainly in museums and repertory movie houses, but not at all in the Georgetown dorm room that she shared with three religious girls, had won her a modest engagement ring, and for Darius the opportunity to make love to her with record haste. Put under notice not to expect a next time until their wedding night, he had presented her with the panties as his shy way of telling her that the relationship could not regress and go forward simultaneously. Rather than endure another semester with the hopeless roommates, she had acceded to his demands, excelling at the game of sneaking up his fire escape to spend every night together; the excitement of the break-in a reward in itself, to be savored above the desultory screwing it prompted.

She hooked her thumbs in the elastic, and wriggled out of the leopard skin with a measure of lewdness that struck him as something she had rehearsed in a mirror. Then she tugged at the drawstring of his pajamas. As he raised his hips the room cartwheeled, and he fell back against the mattress. Farib snuggled beside him, careful of his ribs. Someone's heart was palpitating like a frightened animal trapped between them, and the odd thing was to discover that it wasn't his. Digging under Farib's shoulders, he scooped her onto his body.

"You don't have the strength," she said.

Darius put her hand inside his pajamas. Farib giggled artificially, and her tongue swiped at his ear. "That's not what I mean. The doctors said you mustn't strain yourself."

"It wouldn't be any strain, if you'd—"

She eased him inside, devoured him, her customary dryness overcome although he'd hardly touched her. Floating on elbows and knees, anchored by pink nipples burning into his chest, she rode him as passionately as his damaged body permitted.

What, he wondered, was going on with her? Did every man need his head cracked open in order to arouse his wife?

"And this . . ." she whispered into the ear she'd licked, "is just a hint."

Conversation could wait—had waited forever; but, feeling her start to hold back, he said, "Of what?"

"Of how things will be in paradise."

The sweat ran cold under his back.

"In paradise everything will be as wonderful as the Qur'an promises," she said breathlessly. "We could be together in paradise, Darius, if you'd live cleanly, and attend to your religious obligations."

"We'd make love into eternity?"

"In paradise you'll be a king."

"And on earth—"

"I'll be your houri," she went on faster. "One of many. Everything you wish can be yours."

Sadly, he thought, he could not be bribed, incorruptibility one more of his faults. Had he wanted other women, he would take a second wife, a sacrament in the eyes of Farib and, possibly, God. But he desired only the wife he had, who, in her confused embrace of Islam, viewed a husband who would treat her deferentially as a threat to heavenly bliss.

He felt himself slipping away from her. He rolled his hips, and was gone.

"Darius? Did you hear?"

It took every ounce of strength to shove her off him. "Paradise is giving me a headache," he said.

Darius was awakened by the summons of the muezzin calling the faithful to prayer. In the darkness he sensed that Farib's cot was empty. Sitting up too fast, he had to steady himself against the wall. Possibly she had been right, and he *was* still too weak to make love to her. But he preferred to find out without agreeing to terms that had less to do with an orgiastic eternity in heaven than with her own brand of hell on earth.

She came into the room in her white prayer chador. The callus at her hairline was livid under a gray smudge from her prayer stone of pure Mecca clay.

"How are you this morning?" she asked.

Pressed against the wall, he tried to look at ease. "Much stronger. Anytime you're ready, we can leave for home."

"Not yet. I've been to Fatemeh's shrine every day to pray for your recovery. Now that you're feeling well, you can give thanks yourself."

Stronger didn't mean he had the endurance to argue with her. He laid out a change of clothes on the bed. "Give me a few minutes to get dressed."

"How can you even think of going there without bathing first." Farib kept his shoes and socks locked up in her suitcase. "You know that sexual sweat is forbidden."

Along with blood, urine, feces, and the touch of an unbeliever, the perspiration produced by sexual excitement was one of about a dozen substances considered ritually unclean.

"If I was sweating last night," Darius said, "it was because of the damn heat."

But he wouldn't mind a shower. On previous visits to Qom he had felt clean only during the scattering of religious festivals when he accompanied Hormoz to the ritual bath. Now he let Farib herd him into the tile bathroom that had been installed in the ancient house since the last time he was here. The salty water made for thin lather; but in fresh clothes, his hair damp against his ears, he felt as though he had shed layers of skin. Ten minutes after joining Farib outside in the predawn blast furnace, he needed another shower.

They walked alongside the muddy bed of the Qom River close to the Faiziyeh Seminary. The streets were clogged with the maimed, the blind, and insane seeking cures at the shrine of Fatemeh, sister of the great-great-great grandson of Hussein, the seventh-century leader of the Shi'ites. Vying for the pilgrims' trade were miracle workers who tugged at Darius's sleeve barking their qualifications to heal his head. Religious music blared from the minaret loudspeakers that had blasted him from sleep.

A legion of unattached women wound through the gateway in the high wall. All ages, sizes, and dialects were represented among them, and in common only the veil, and abject despair.

"Hookers," Darius said disgustedly in English.

"They do nothing immoral. The holiest of men employ seegahs from time to time."

Darius was sorry he'd opened his mouth. In matters of religion Farib was the last true defender of the faith.

"The Prophet gave them his blessing," she said.

Seegahs were temporary wives, who, in exchange for a small sum of money, contracted themselves to a man for a predetermined period. The religious laws, even those proscribing capital crimes such as adultery, came equipped each with its own legal loophole, and it was the seegah to whom the Shi'a traveler turned for companionship in a strange city. A contract might run from an hour to ninety-nine years, but the temporary wife received none of the benefits of her permanent counterparts; any children she bore had no legal right of inheritance. The sole requirement for becoming a seegah was that the woman not be "addicted to fornication."

In their own quarter of the courtyard were the mohalels, the seegahs' male equivalent. A woman divorced three times by her husband was forbidden to return directly to him. Mohalels were available for a sexless one-night stand culminating in a quickie divorce that left yesterday's bride free again to remarry her original husband.

The courtyard was paved with old gravestones arranged around the main building of the shrine. At a shallow pool in the center of the court the pilgrims made their ritual ablutions. Farib tunneled through the mob to plunge her arms in the filthy water, and to splash some on her forehead and nose. As Darius wet his fingers, a few drops landed on his cheek. More than ever he wanted another shower.

"I'll see you later at uncle's," Farib said, and started for the women's entrance. Darius watched her pass barefoot through an anteroom of the shrine's golden dome. Mirrors in the ceiling of precious metals dissected her into cameos edged in silver and gold. She kissed the right doorpost of the tomb chamber, and lit a candle from another pilgrim's stub. Swept up in the procession around the sandalwood sarcophagus, she joined her wails to the mourners' din in the ecstasy that had eluded her the night before.

Darius stood at the men's entrance under the arched portal. Spotting Hormoz in his capelike abayah at the head of a group of students, he followed into a side room where Hormoz recited a prayer with the copious tears that were the mark of a famous marja. Measured against Farib's sobs the old man was found wanting in his fervor. Darius knew Hormoz as an intellectual who tested his faith daily against the reason of a world he never had turned his back on. Farib, better educated, and Westernized, had blinded herself to the contradictions of dogma frozen in obscure, seventh-century political rancor. But her weeping was not for the sister of the eighth imam exclusively, but to be shared with the martyr from the District of Columbia, who, caught up in events she couldn't control, had taken sanctuary in the veil.

Hormoz clacked his stone beads while he chanted "Forgiveness" three hundred times. Snatches of prayer recalled from religious grade school came together on the back of Darius's tongue. They dissolved there like a crumbling pill as he left the shrine, rubbing the sore spot in his chest.

Hormoz's house was an open hearth under the rays of the morning sun. Darius played the brackish water of the new shower against his depleted muscles. He needed a shave, but Farib hadn't packed his razor. Using cuticle scissors, he trimmed a week's growth to several days' stubble, and then he cut away the dressing from his head. The wound was too sensitive to go near with his fingers. He rubbed color into the wan stripe high on his forehead, and combed wet hair over the bald patch surrounding his stitches.

A draft of hot air blistered the skin across his shoulders. He squinted at Hormoz stenciled in the doorway against the low sun.

"I saw you at Fatemeh's shrine," Hormoz said. He came down the corridor diffidently. When his wife was still alive, this part of the house had been the anderoun, the inside, or women's area, which he seldom visited. His room was the biroun, the outside, or master's apartment. "In your bandages you looked like a holy man."

"The National Police are masters of disguise."

Hormoz patted Darius's rough cheek. "What disguise is this?"

"A well man." Darius splashed cold water against his face, and then he toweled off. "I'm returning to Teheran."

"Farib, too?"

"That's up to her. But I've been away from work too long."

"She'll be disappointed. Ayatollah Ardebili, the former chief justice, will be at Faiziyeh this afternoon to talk about proposed changes in the laws of Houdoud and Qesas. She asked that you be allowed to sit in."

"What else has she planned for the period of my recovery?"

"There are seminars every day during the month of Muharram," Hormoz said. "And she thought you might visit Mobarakabad and other famous mosques."

"It's futile to attempt to make me devout—even in my weakened condition."

"She knows. But it's become clear to her that the marriage has no future so long as your lives continue in opposing directions. As it is, you've grown apart. The need for you to remain my nephew is not a sufficient foundation for an enduring relationship."

"Since one of us must change, let it be her. I've tried—"

"Farib already has changed."

"She can change back."

"Do you believe that is still possible?"

Darius borrowed more hair from his temple to conceal the white patch. "No," he said, "not really."

"Grant her the divorce she wants, and the freedom to find her way." Hormoz's stone beads came out, and silently he began counting Allahu Akhbars. "If you feel in jeopardy not being under the protection of my name, then you must flee as so many others have. You've lived outside the country before. Farib agrees that was the happiest part of your life. You speak excellent English, you have an American university degree. You came back from Washington more American than Iranian in attitude."

Darius wanted to interrupt, but deferred to the older man.

"You don't see yourself as others do," Hormoz went on adamantly. "To believe anything is possible if you set your will to it, to place confidence in your judgment above all others, these are not Muslim traits."

"I didn't need America to teach me to be the way I am." Darius could not contain himself. "From childhood I thought I would fit in comfortably there. But as an Iranian, as myself, not as a forced convert to a secular religion with a different set of uncompromising demands."

"Certainly you don't fit here. It will be easier for you in the United States, or Britain, or anywhere in Europe for that matter. I've asked myself often why you haven't emigrated up to now, and concluded it was for the sake of your marriage. That will be of no consideration any longer."

"You're too quick to credit me with selflessness," Darius said. "When you were enumerating the baggage that always travels with me, there's one item you left out."

"What is that?"

"Which land would open her doors to a murderer convicted and sentenced to death under the laws when Iran was not regarded as a pariah nation? Everything that was said about me at the trial was true. I *am* a ruthless killer with few qualms about destroying my perceived enemies. Why else would the ayatollahs have spared me? Who better than they can sympathize with that philosophy? There's not a country on earth that will offer me a safe haven, no country wiser than this one."

"All the more reason to use the Revolution to preserve your life," Hormoz said. "I'm an old man; you can't take cover behind my reputation forever. I may die at any moment."

Darius filled a cup from the salty tap, and toasted Hormoz with a sip. "A long life to you, dear uncle," he said. "A very long life."

❖ 5 ❖

Thirteen stripes of red and white were painted on the doorstep of a cinder block house off Shush Avenue, the border of the southern slums. White stars of David alternated with the hammer and sickle in a square corner of blue. Someone in waffle-sole shoes had stamped all over the stripes while the paint was wet; foot traffic had worn away most of the blue. "Walking on the enemy" was casual warfare in the patriotic quarters of South Teheran.

Rocking on his heel, Darius vaulted over the flag. His momentum carried him into a hallway in which a trail of burned flashbulbs tapered into blackness along a bare floor. From where he stood he saw Ghaffari huddled in a closet with Hamid, the young criminalist, and listened to them cursing in the dark.

"Shut the damn door," Ghaffari shouted. "You're spoiling the film."

"I didn't know," Darius said.

"What? It's you?" Ghaffari backed out of the closet holding a camera that was strapped around Hamid's neck. Shading his eyes, he sized up Darius. "You don't look the worse for wear."

"I'm fine." Darius stared past him into the dim rear of the house, where uniformed officers had given up any attempt at looking busy. "Fine," he said again, cutting short Ghaffari's diagnosis. "Where are they?"

"This way," Hamid said, and squeezed past the patrolmen. Outside the

69

bedroom Ghaffari said, "Watch it," and Darius turned his toe from a puddle of vomit just beyond the door.

A Japanese lantern softened the light from a frosted bulb over a double bed on which a man and woman lay in one another's arms. The couple were in their early to mid thirties, Darius estimated, and were nude above a sheet that clung damply to their hips. A black crater in the woman's forehead might have been made with a rock, or a bit of lead. Rivulets of gore crusting against her face and neck were shiny between globular breasts. A hole in the man's armpit scarcely had leaked color. More had hemorrhaged through his nose.

The bedding was soaked with the woman's blood; the vaguely metallic smell was everywhere in the room. Darius lifted the venetian blinds, but no light entered. The windows had been blackened with flat paint, and were nailed shut. A scrape in the glass several centimeters above the sill allowed a sliver of a dirt alley pocked with footprints.

"The neighbor boy brought Najafi, that's the male, unsweetened tea, coffee cake, and a Daily *Jomhuri-e-Islami* every morning at nine," Ghaffari said. "The boy showed up at the usual time today, and when no one let him in he knew something was wrong. He went into the alley, but couldn't see inside. The house was unlocked. He looked in all the rooms before he came in here. That's when he lost his own breakfast."

"This Najafi—" Searching for an exit wound, Darius found a crisscross of raised stripes between the man's shoulders. "Do we know him?"

"Just the name, and what little the kid gave out," Ghaffari said. "He'd been here six months, and rarely left the house."

"He lived with the woman?"

"No, but he didn't lack for company. People came and went at all hours."

"How the bullet caught him under the arm," Hamid said. "Someone must have stood over them with the gun, and automatically his hand went up in defense. It wouldn't shock me to find out the lady had a husband."

Darius grunted noncommittally, and drew back the sheet. The girl was in panties, the man nude except for black socks with DEATH TO ISRAEL in stylized script over the ankles. "Who is she?"

Ghaffari shrugged. "You want to talk to the kid?"

Darius's head shook slightly. By bending the woman at the waist, he was able to free Najafi's arm. A red crescent was tattooed at the base of the thumb. The other four fingers ended in smooth nubs at the knuckles. Darius peeled off the DEATH TO ISRAEL socks. The left foot had been severed cleanly across the instep, and a prosthesis was attached to the stump.

"Let Mehta know we're interested in a Mr. Najafi with a record showing convictions for theft." He noticed raw welts tangled around the elbow. "And possibly drugs."

The woman's arms were waxy smooth, unblemished, and still flickered with heat in the armpit closest to her heart. Black-and-blue marks on her chest did not appear to be fresh. Darius hiked the bloody sheet over both victims. "Print them right now," he said to Hamid.

Ghaffari came in with a boy about fourteen. The boy was short for his age, and had oily skin erupting into blackheads between his eyebrows and in the shallow creases around his nose. His eyes darted from Darius to Ghaffari without acknowledging the bed.

"This is Eskander," Ghaffari said.

"You found them?" asked Darius.

"Yes," the boy said proudly.

"Where do you live?"

Eskander pointed out the blackened window. "Next door."

"Did you hear shots?"

"It's very noisy on this block, always lots of loud cars. Even at night. I heard nothing."

The way Eskander's stomach was grumbling as he edged away from the bed, Darius was afraid he was going to lose the rest of his breakfast. "Can you tell us Mr. Najafi's first name?"

"He told me to call him Jamshid."

"Did he mention where he lived before he came here?"

"I'm sorry, sir, but this is all I know. I told the other policeman—"

"You've been very helpful," Darius said. "You can go now."

Ghaffari, watching the boy run from the room, said, "He has to have more than that. Why didn't you get a little tough with him?"

"He's too scared as it is. Soon he'll be answering in yeses and nos, whichever he thinks we want to hear. Give him a day for the colors to fade, to see this in black-and-white, and you won't be able to shut him up."

Somewhere in a far corner Hamid was shouting, "Come here, come quick."

The foyer was deserted, except for two of the officers with nothing to do. Darius ran inside a black living room, the kitchen, and through the backyard to an outhouse where Hamid lay on his belly, shirtless, one arm in a squat toilet consisting of an oval hole in the floor edged by two chipped slabs of porcelain. The water hose that is used instead of toilet paper in traditional

Iranian homes was tangled between his feet. His face was screwed into an expression of disgust the more grotesque for a losing struggle to hold his breath. A brick of white powder in clear plastic lay against his leg.

Hamid gagged as he ducked his head into the pit. His fingernails made clawing sounds against the underside of the floor. He wriggled down until the porcelain was a life preserver around his chest. Then his free hand waved weakly in triumph, and Ghaffari pulled him out by the ankles clutching another white brick.

"I knew if there was dope anywhere," Hamid said, sucking air, "it would be in here."

Darius opened the smaller bag, sniffed the contents, put some on his tongue, swallowed.

"My God," Ghaffari said, "you took enough to kill four men. And you still insist the beating didn't damage your brain?"

"It's quinine."

Ghaffari tasted the other brick. "This one is milk sugar. He was hiding enough white powder to cut several kilos."

"All that's missing," Darius said, "is the heroin."

"There's nothing else in there," said Hamid, who couldn't stop dry-washing his hands. "Just shit—"

"You did well," Darius said to the unhappy criminalist. "I hate to think where we would be without you."

To reach Records in the sub-basement of police headquarters Darius had to pass through Supplies, which was mostly bare walls, and Evidence, where the steel shelves were bowed under bricks of Afghani hashish and un-processed Turkish opium poppies, crates of untagged handguns and counterfeit Seiko watches. A little girl's chador crusted with blood was wrapped around the serrated blade of an electric carving knife. African elephant tusks seized from a trader in illicit wildlife formed an ivory gibbet for the carcass of a baby mountain gorilla that some comedian had strung up by a silk noose. A dark wall stacked floor to ceiling with green quart bottles reminded Darius of a hotel wine cellar, when such things were allowed.

In a bare metal cage Mehta was slumped over a table with his head in his arms. Darius rattled the gate, but the records chief didn't stir. The humid air was overloaded with alcohol spiced with a chemical tang that Darius couldn't identify, although the taste had found a familiar place on the back of his tongue.

"Hey," he shouted into the cage, "Hey Nader, hey you, open up."

Mehta raised his head. His elbow collided with a tumbler that emptied its contents across the tabletop before shattering against the floor. Mehta's chin dropped into his arms, then he picked himself up and stretched. He was wearing a sweat-soaked T-shirt, boxer shorts, and solid red socks in scuffed wingtips. Glass crunched underfoot as he stumbled to the gate.

Darius trod inside cautiously. He bent for a large sliver, and his sinuses cleared when he held it to his nose. "What's this?"

"Poison," Mehta said.

"One hundred proof, unless I miss my guess."

"Don't know, I wasn't there when they ran it through the still." Mehta's words were indistinct, his breath as powerful as the chemical smell on the glass. "We nabbed another gang of bootleggers while you were away. Six thousand quarts of scotch whiskey were poured into the djoub. The rest were brought here to be held for evidence at the trial."

"How much was that?" asked Darius.

"Fifty bottles."

"I must have seen two hundred on the shelves."

"Then there's plenty more to get rid of," Mehta slurred. "What the hell, trial's not till winter."

"It's good to see you're keeping busy."

"Stuff'll kill you, you let it." Mehta twisted the cap off a fresh bottle, and offered Darius the second swallow. "But it's slow death. You could make it last into next year, and still have plenty left over to put away the bootleggers for life."

A tumbler half full of flat water stood on the table beside an empty pitcher. There was no sink or fountain in the sub-basement, and water was not to be wasted. Mehta followed the example of the Imam, who had learned the value of water in his seminary days at Qom, when the drinking supply was obtained in part from catch basins. Legend was that the Imam would fill a glass, and save what he didn't use until he was thirsty again, whether eight hours later, or the next day. Darius tightened the cap on the bottle. "What did you find out about Jamshid Najafi?"

Mehta's chin jutted at a bank of file cabinets. Darius removed a manila folder from the wire basket on top. "This file is for a Khalil Pakravan," he said.

"Jamshid Najafi, Khalil Pakravan, it's the same guy. Anyway, his prints were on Najafi's hand."

Khalil Pakravan, according to the record, was a native of Ramsar in the

Mazanderan region on the Caspian Sea. Upon leaving school at thirteen, he had found work helping his father as bathhouse attendant at the hot springs near the beachfront Grand Hotel. Caught going through the luggage of the West German minister of tourism, he was paroled to his family in lieu of jail time, at the cost of his job and his father's. From Ramsar he had drifted to Teheran, where he was arrested at nineteen for burglarizing the Vitana Mother Biscuit factory on the Old Karaj Road. At his trial in Branch 139 of the Penal Court, he was found guilty of hadd, or theft for the first time, and sentenced under Article 138 of the Law of Houdoud and Qesas to the loss of four fingers of the right hand. Ten months later, he was picked up in the parking lot of the former Royal Teheran Hilton in the Mercedes-Benz 560 SL of the Saudi oil minister. The sentence for a second-time thief was "the dismembering of the left foot from the lower part of the protrusion so that half the foot and part of the place of anointing remain." Since his last conviction, Pakravan had kept out of trouble, although a note placed in the folder by a south Teheran patrolman indicated that he had been questioned without charges being pressed in connection with the street sale of a large amount of shireh, a popular narcotic that was the liquid residue of opium. Pakravan's father and mother were deceased, and the whereabouts of a sister were unknown. A half-brother owned a small restaurant on Hejab Street in downtown Teheran.

Clipped to the record was a photo of a good-looking boy with a freshly shaven skull. A disembodied hand at the back of his head was forcing his face toward the camera. Darius flipped the picture over. The mug shot was dated less than five years earlier, before Pakravan had made the career change from theft to heroin that had left him a spent cripple at twenty-seven.

"What have you got on the woman?" Darius flung his jacket over the back of a chair, opened his shirt.

Mehta's reply was a snore. His head burrowed deeper into his arms.

"*Nader?*"

"Nothing. She's clean—never been printed."

There was another file that merited the trip to this sweatbox. Letting himself out of the cage, Darius went into a locked storeroom that was the archive of criminal investigations cleared prior to the Revolution. For forty-five minutes he combed the steel cabinets fruitlessly, until under the Ls, where it had no reason to be, he found a folder with his name on the tab. Nothing had ever given him greater satisfaction than to read the reports of the criminalists stymied by the execution-slaying of the mass murderer Farmayan, the most feared inquisitor in all of SAVAK. No fewer than twenty detectives had been assigned to the case, and this in the days when the homicide bureau was a top-flight investigative body. The folder had been thick as his fist when he borrowed it surreptitiously during his first months with the National Police, and must have been pulled and misfiled since the last time he had taken it home. Now it contained only the record of his final questioning before charges were drawn up, and a few yellowing documents from the appeal.

Because Ibrahim Farmayan's body had been found in a desolate highway wayside known to be frequented by bandits, the case had fallen under jurisdiction of the National Police as a suspected robbery-homicide. Not until the remains were identified as those of a SAVAK colonel was the investigation taken over by Farmayan's subordinates in the shah's secret police. Carbons of subsequent entries to the record routinely were sent to the agency that had handled the initial probe. These, however, had been edited by the military censor, so that the National Police glimpsed only the bare bones of the case against Darius. The huge gaps in the file would be in possession of the Komiteh, which had taken over SAVAK's functions under the new regime.

Reviewing the notes of his interrogation by the assistant to the Deputy Prime Minister for National Security Affairs—General Nassiri, the director of SAVAK—it seemed to Darius that the lies he had answered with were so clumsy that he must have wanted to be convicted. Abandoned to the mercies of the military magistrate serving directly over him, he had declined to beg for compassion, instead unburdening himself of a sanctimonious admission to having eliminated a vile monster. There was a snapshot of a very young man in this folder, too, a faded Polaroid documenting the collar-length hair and flared sideburns that even then were nearly ten years out of fashion, except as they were etched in his memory of Washington in the early 1970s.

The smell of bootleg was assaulting his olfactory nerve. He poured an inch in Mehta's reserve tumbler, and put it down in a gulp. Surviving this trial by fire, he measured out two fingers more to get him through the transcript of the unsuccessful appeal of his death sentence. Large blocks of text had been blacked out with a marking pen, making piecemeal the thrust of the prosecutor's statement against him. Left untouched by the censor was the testimony of secret witnesses in opposition to the appeal. Of the four Farmayans who had spoken that day, the victim's nineteen-year-old nephew, Bijan, then a student at Faiziyeh Seminary in Qom, had argued most persuasively for death.

Ghaffari drove. Darius, relegated to navigator's duty by the destruction of his car and residual dizziness from his cracked skull, directed him through a morass of streets renamed to accommodate the new religious-political line.

"Is this good Hejab Street we're looking for," Ghaffari joked, "or bad Hejab?"

Hejab meant the proper style of Islamic dress and personal grooming. Every Friday, during prayer services at the major mosques, crowds of the faithful would shout, *Down with bad hejab.* Hejab Street, prior to the Revolution, had been Los Angeles Boulevard.

A motorcycle accident had stopped traffic in both lanes. As Ghaffari gunned his overheating engine, Darius found himself staring at a woman on the sidewalk whose head scarf was fastened under her chin with a silver brooch. What he had taken, at first, for the evidence of a sleepless night on her face was almost definitely a touch of mascara. He looked back over his shoulder, eyeing the woman, who smiled flirtatiously and immediately turned away.

Incredible. Had he been present when the Imam returned from exile in France he would not have witnessed a revolutionary more dangerous than the frightened woman. But the Imam was dead for a few years now, and tomorrow perhaps another woman would find courage to push back her veil to reveal a wisp of hair. After that, who could say? A touch of rouge? Some lipstick? And then an exposed wrist, and arm, and—Praise Allah—a bare ankle? From that point it was a short step for the nation to embrace nudity and fornication, all varieties of copulation with beasts as proscribed in the holy texts. It was truly incredible what you saw on the streets these days.

Pakravan's Fried Chicken was surrounded by a declining residential neighborhood that had not fared well in the War of Cities. A gas station on the opposite corner had taken a hit from an Iraqi bomb, and the explosion of the underground tanks had transformed several blocks of apartment houses into black ghosts. Pakravan's was a single-story building with large, inward-slanting windows above a sealed takeout counter, and walls of red-and-white brick trimmed in aluminum. Looking down from the roof was a plexiglass replica of what might have been a Kentucky colonel, but for yellowish paint that had smeared a wispy goatee all over the cheeks, and an open collar sketched crudely on top of a string tie.

When the homicide detectives entered there were no customers at the lunch counter that was the restaurant's Formica spine. Above one of six cramped booths was a poster showing a woman's bare head circled in red with a broad stripe slashing through shoulder-length hair. Superimposed over the illustration of bad hejab was a long scarf wrapped around the hair to conceal every offending strand.

SISTER, the illustration was captioned, PLEASE BE MODEST.

Under the poster three women sat at a table sipping tea through sugar cubes clenched in their teeth. The woman facing the oversize windows had opened her chador and was nursing a newborn from her exposed breast.

A man with a fry cook's smoky pallor looked up at Darius and Ghaffari from a chopping block on which he was positioning a watermelon as though it were a baby about to be sacrificed. "Today's luncheon special," he said, "is honey-fried—"

Darius intercepted soiled menus. "Are you Mr. Pakravan?"

Admitting to nothing, the fry cook pulled out worry beads, and passed them through his fingers. Darius suspected that he was performing a divination to find out whether his visitors could be trusted before inquiring who they were. It was hard not to snatch the beads from his hand. He wished, momentarily, that he was back in America, where the superstitious were ridiculed to their face.

But he could no more interfere than walk away from the restaurant without answers to his questions. Something in his own character that also rejected pure reason had weighed in his decision to leave the United States; as a homicide investigator in a poor country he had come to rely on intuition over costly technology. Yet, if he had abandoned the West to escape the tyranny of reason, he had gotten more than he bargained for when he returned to Iran. In the clash between science and religion he remained an observer, holding his allegiance for the more civilized system, whichever that turned out to be.

The fry clerk put away the beads and did not look at Darius again. He tested his blade against a callused thumb, and then hacked through the melon's thick rind.

"What kind of trouble is Khalil in now?" he asked Ghaffari.

"His troubles are over," Ghaffari said. "He was shot dead yesterday in a house off Shush Avenue."

Pakravan was preoccupied with replacing the menus against a napkin holder. Darius read his bland reaction as a shield against grief. The blade divided the melon into quarters, and eighths, and Darius made a mental note to inquire into bad blood between the Pakravans, and to mark the fry cook as a suspect if any were found to exist.

Ghaffari, waiting for tears, and then information, said, "This is your brother we're talking about. Do you understand what I told you?"

"Too well. If you're here to see me shocked, you'll go away disappointed."

"Some sorrow would be sufficient," Darius said.

"Khalil exhausted my capacity for sorrow years ago. The Komiteh used to come by regularly to let me know of each new scrape he'd gotten into, and warn me he had better change his ways. After the last time, I told them what I'm telling you now, that he wasn't my brother anymore, I'd cut him out of my life as permanently as they had cut off his foot."

"Even so," Darius said, "we need to learn what he was doing at the house."

"Selling heroin? Fencing stolen goods?" Pakravan avoided looking at Darius's ID. He hunched his shoulders to say, Why ask me? "Those were the only occupations that suited him."

The melon slices were arranged like pink flower petals on a cracked plate. A counterman brought them to the nursing woman.

"Khalil was the light in my father's eye. He had been accepted as a student at the Madreseh of the Shah's Mother in Isfahan. I had big plans for him. As the older brother, I would support him with my restaurant until he completed his education and became a famous mullah. But with puberty, Khalil changed. He was interested only in earthly pleasures. It wasn't long after that he lost his hand, and was deprived even of the satisfaction of touch. So much for the life of a sybarite."

"Who were his friends in Teheran?" Darius asked.

"Not mine."

"His enemies, then?" Darius spread the photos of the Shush Avenue victims on the counter. "This is Khalil?"

Pakravan nodded.

"Who's the woman?" Darius asked.

"I never saw her before."

Darius added a morgue shot of the girl found murdered in Shemiran. "What about her?"

Pakravan blotted his fingers on his shirt, and snatched up the photo. "That's Leila. She was my sister's friend when they were growing up."

"You're certain? Look again."

"Well, she's lots more mature than the last time I saw her, and here she looks— But, yes, the timid mouth, it's definitely her."

"What's her last name?"

"Darwish. What happened to her?"

"Like your brother," Ghaffari said. "Tell us everything about her."

Pakravan's shoulders heaved, and he took a short breath. "She was just a little kid who lived several streets away, and went to school with my sister. She was always hanging around our house, but I can't say I ever talked to her. I heard she went away to college . . . but who remembers?"

At last Ghaffari had his tears. "Does her family still live there?"

"I see her mother sometimes when I'm back in the Mazanderan. She's a fine woman. Her husband is Arab, but Shi'ite. Originally from Iraq."

"What else?"

"What else can there be? In my head Leila is always eight, my sister's playmate, dressing up their dolls for formal tea parties. I didn't make a study of her. I didn't know she would end up like this, and the police would be interested in every little thing."

"Where's your sister?" asked Darius. "We want to talk to her, too."

"Like Khalil she went her own way." Pakravan wiped away his tears—more than Ghaffari could use. "A second time my parents' hearts were broken. I cut her out of my life, too."

The caller, a Captain Eshragi, had a reedy voice that long-distance transmitted to Teheran in pulses of barks and hisses.

"I apologize for taking so long, but the Darwishes live on a plantation outside Lahijan. Phone service is undependable at best, and no one was at the house the two times men were sent out. It's only because a patrolman ran into the mother at the post office that we have anything to report."

"You're acquainted with the family?" Darius held the receiver away from his ear. He spoke loudly, as if to a deaf man.

"We've had certain dealings with them."

"Concerning the daughter?"

"The daughter, *and* the father." Through the clutter Darius made out a Caspian accent that was the basis for Maryam Lajevardi's artless imitation.

"Leila Darwish should be twenty-four now. Six years ago, she was one of a few students allowed to attend the University of Moscow on a scholarship made available by the Soviet-Iranian Friendship Society. Despite her father,

Leila was nonideological. She had no links to communist organizations, else she would not have been let out of the country."

"The Komiteh in Guilan Province permit the National Police to examine their subversives' files?"

"To compile them." Brittleness crept into Eshragi's voice, making his accent nearly impossible to decode. "I myself was the officer designated to assess her political reliability."

"Please, go on," Darius said.

"Leila Darwish rightly viewed the scholarship as her only opportunity for advanced education. When she came home after her second year, she was interviewed again and was determined to be unsympathetic to the socialist system. She didn't enjoy her stay in the Soviet Union, and spoke of little other than starting a teaching career here. Over the next couple of years she wrote often to her family of those plans. Shortly before she was to take her degree, the letters stopped coming. Her parents contacted Moscow but received no cooperation from the authorities. This was at the height of the campaign against the Red Satan, when there were few lines of communication between the two countries. The girl was reported missing to us, and we put out a nationwide alert in case she surfaced in Iran. Since that time the family has been in the dark. Now you announce that she's been found murdered on a bench in Teheran. It's hard for the mother to accept."

"Why is that?"

"Mrs. Darwish had consoled herself with the fantasy that her daughter had fallen victim to political intrigue, and would return as some sort of post-revolutionary heroine. She is grieving as much over the manner in which Leila died as for the fact of her death."

A conversation between two women was bleeding onto the line. Darius screwed the phone against his ear. "And the father?"

"He's a hardheaded old bird, still an ardent Bolshie. We keep an eye on him, but there's never anything to report. It's doubtful he has illusions about Leila. His fantasies are too precious to waste on a daughter."

From the derelict used-car lot of the motor pool Darius selected a green Pay-con, and test-drove it north toward the old Shemiran Road. Several blocks from headquarters traffic detoured around police barricades. He continued onto the sidewalk, and inched through the pedestrians massed on the curb. A patrolman stormed toward him, snorting through a whistle in his teeth.

"You can't get through." The officer pointed to a sign on the barrier: ALL

BELIEVERS ARE SUMMONED TO TAKE PART IN THE FLAGELLATIONS IN OBSER-
VANCE OF IMAM HUSSEIN. "It's the celebration of Ashura," he explained.

Darius threw the Paycon into reverse, but was pinned there by the swelling
crowd. Children moved through the traffic jam on foot, offering sweets,
newspapers, and American cigarettes for sale to a captive clientele. Yesterday,
the Ninth of Muharram, legions of the devout had marched along the
boulevards wailing, "Yah, Hussein," in memory of the third imam slain at
the seventh-century massacre of Kerbala. On Ashura the men returned to
flay their bodies with leather thongs and chains. The Pahlavis had banned the
religious parades on the grounds that too often the celebrants mutilated
themselves in their passion. Under the ayatollahs they were not only permitted, but encouraged.

Darius heard ritual chanting as broad columns of men dressed all in black
appeared whipping themselves over one shoulder and then the other with
chains attached to a short pole. They were followed by a man clanging brass
cymbals to set the beat for their flagellations, and by more marchers, who
pounded their hearts with the flat of their hands, and wore red headbands
proclaiming, IRAN HAS BECOME PALESTINE. HOW CAN MUSLIMS NOT SPEAK
UP? and ISLAM IS AN ETERNAL TREE. IT NEEDS THE BLOOD OF MARTYRS TO
BLOSSOM. A man in the last row split open his skull with a chain, and
collapsed into the djoub as the throng rounded the corner and moved on.

Ashura had drawn even Shemiran's taghoutis, or unbelievers, and bad
hejabis to the parade downtown. The desk at the apartment complex on
Saltanatabad was unmanned, guarded by a doorman's cap. Outside Maryam
Lajevardi's apartment, expecting more of the Beatles, Darius was treated to a
chorus of furniture skating across the floors. Perhaps, he thought, there was
more truth to her story than he had admitted. But if Maryam were moving
out as she'd said, she wouldn't be taking the rental stuff with her. He
knocked, and the racket stopped. No one answered, though; not even when
the doorbell triggered somber chimes, and the unlocked door yielded to his
shoulder.

A bookcase had been emptied onto the foyer floor. He went into the living
room over leather-clad Persian poets, and back issues of *Today's Woman*, the
monthly magazine of the Iranian Women's Association, offering tips to the
middle-class mothers of large families on how to raise a dowry for their
youngest daughters. "Miss Lajevardi," he called out. "Miss—"

Imported underwear and dark hosiery were strewn inside a bedroom
whose walls were a gallery of psychedelic art and British airline posters
showing miniskirted girls in bouffant hair, a tardy summons to Swinging

Sixties London. A man in a Harris tweed jacket with leather elbow patches stood with his back to the window, shoulders rocking from side to side as though he were trying to slice himself through the venetian blinds. The gray skin had slipped from his cheeks, and collected in folds under his jaw. Only his eyes and the haggard skin around them were three-dimensional behind lenses in steel frames. A sparse beard was set off by a luxuriant mustache. Darius had the impression that the effort to raise facial hair was so draining that he had been able to pull off the trick only on his narrow upper lip.

"Who are you?" asked Darius.

The man came forward around an unmade bed. After a false start the thin lip went to work behind the mustache. "I might ask the same thing."

He spoke too rapidly for Darius to place his slight accent. When Darius flashed ID, he took it from him and studied it for twenty seconds. "A friend of Maryam's," he said finally.

"Her friend's name?"

"Zaid Rahgozar."

"Where is Miss Lajevardi?"

"Maryam was called home."

"I was told her family didn't know where to find her."

"It was on very short notice," Rahgozar said. "Her relationship with her parents has improved a great deal recently."

"Is that why you've taken it upon yourself to ransack her apartment?"

A smile retracted Rahgozar's lip under the glossy mustache. "Maryam has found a more affordable place to live, and she asked my help in bringing some things there. I'm going to drive them over, so they will be waiting when she returns."

Darius booted a yellow dress onto the bed. "Where is her new place?"

"I . . . I have the address written on a piece of paper."

"Let me see it, if you don't mind."

Rahgozar's left hand frisked the right side of his body, then the procedure was repeated right on left. Darius unbuttoned his own jacket, and reached into the sweat circle under his arm.

"It's here somewhere," Rahgozar said, and sprang before Darius had the gun out.

Darius sidestepped the flying body. He dipped a shoulder, prepared to slam Rahgozar onto the mattress, and opened himself to a sharp elbow to the forehead. The blow had no immediate effect. He was a couple of steps behind the fleeing man, and gaining, when his legs quit suddenly and he stood paralyzed as Rahgozar ran out of the apartment.

Darius staggered to the wall intercom, waited through ten rings for the hat on the security desk to answer. A tingling sensation in his limbs was moving into his torso. The room began to revolve like an amusement park whip. As it picked up speed, it spun him onto the bed. Stretched out on his back with the gun on his chest, he listened for Rahgozar's return, chewing the inside of his cheeks so he wouldn't black out.

He had no idea how long he lay there. There was a triptych mirror on the dressing table, but he decided he didn't want to know how he looked. When his vertigo passed, he went to the refrigerator for ice, which he held to his forehead in a dish towel compress. A search of the apartment turned up nothing that interested him more than would the intimate possessions of any beautiful woman. Either Rahgozar had taken what he came for, or it was an item of little obvious significance.

Finnish vodka hidden in a scuffed armoire saved the morning from utter disaster. The cap had never been unscrewed. Expensive, black market vodka was not a practical source of calories for a woman with nothing to eat. So the bottle was the gift of an admirer, who wanted alcohol on hand when he visited. Some lamb and fresh vegetables would have been faster to warm Maryam Lajevardi's heart.

One last time he went through the rooms, and then called Ghaffari at the office.

"Put out an alert for a Zaid Rahgozar, about forty," he said. "One hundred and eighty centimeters, seventy kilos, blue eyes, graying hair, and eyeglasses in metal frames, dressed in a brown tweed sport jacket, black pants. Broadcast it citywide and to the Mazanderan. He's wanted for questioning in connection with the murder of Leila Darwish."

"You've found a new lead?"

"Lost it," Darius said.

"Are you okay? You sound groggy."

Darius wrung water from the dish towel. "I bumped my head."

"Better get yourself together. The Komiteh's been calling all morning."

"What do they want—a progress report on the robbery at the Golabis' that never happened?"

"They want you," Ghaffari said. "At two. At Bon Yad headquarters."

A block from the old American embassy, officially renamed the U.S. Den of Espionage, Darius spotted a parking space on Takht-e-Jamshid Avenue. Angling toward the curb, he was extra careful not to drop a wheel in the deep

djoub. The djoub was dry, the Teheran water department having decided to
flush clean the Ashura parade route by diverting water through the system of
underground tunnels that was as old as the city. Takht-e-Jamshid was now
Taleqani Avenue, but not even the Komiteh called it that.

The Bon Yad Monkerat mansion was a three-story dwelling of Mediterranean design with stucco walls and a tile roof. Through the side gate
Darius glimpsed a patio of broken bricks edged in lank grass, the only green
in what had been a large desert garden. A gummy puddle that was dark
red at the property line ran to pink over the sidewalk and into the djoub. It
was not unheard of, Darius knew, for a sheep to be slaughtered outside the
Bon Yad's door by the family of a prisoner putting up a substitute for the
blood of their relative. Darius felt suction against his heel. He glanced back
at scarlet tracks that followed him like a guilty conscience inside the gray
wall.

Leaded-glass windows projected a mosaic of colored light onto the floor of
a corridor crowded with Komitehmen. A teenager swaggering under the
weight of his Uzi and the two sets of handcuffs on his belt loop brought
Darius upstairs, knocked on double doors, and pushed them open without
waiting for a summons inside.

Darius stood in the threshold of an airy office that had been the master
bedroom when the merchant family still lived here. Two desks were positioned too close to the walls to take advantage of a pool of strong natural
light. The eastern exposure afforded a view of the old embassy used now as a
school for Revolutionary Guards. In shadow to his left a man in gray-black
camouflage pored through files like those Mehta kept. There was one folder
on the other desk, where Bijan sat picking his teeth with the corner of a
matchbook.

"It's good to see you back and feeling yourself." Bijan was wearing tailored
fatigues with razor-sharp pleats that reminded Darius of Fidel Castro in his
custom military uniforms thirty years after the institutionalization of the
Cuban Revolution. Bijan looked inside the folder. Underneath was a bowl of
red pistachio nuts, which he nudged toward Darius. "A moment, and I'll be
with you. Have a seat."

Gilt scrollwork showed through the whitewash under the high ceilings.
Darius looked outside into a kidney-shaped swimming pool clogged with
brown leaves. Behind the graffiti-scarred wall of the embassy compound
young men in khaki were walking from the large brick building that had
been the chancery. Three empty pools and two netless tennis courts, the

smokeless stacks of a small power plant, gave the vast complex the look of a country club gone to seed. In a cathedral of tall pines was the marble mansion where the ambassador had lived.

"A beautiful home with a glorious view." Bijan stared at him over the top of the folder. "Too bad the family who lived here had to leave the country."

"Maybe they'll return someday."

"In their fondest dreams," Bijan said. "I doubt they will come closer than that. The family were supporters of the Pahlavi dynasty, as loyal as the people who lived in that other fine house with the marble walls."

"Maybe they'll come back, too—"

A full-throated scream, not manly, but unmistakably from a man, rose from the lower floors. The harsh acoustics of the bare office reassembled it into a shriek of terror that froze Darius in his chair.

Bijan put down the folder. "Yes?" he asked. "You're all right?"

"What did you want to see me about?"

"In its own time. We were talking about the family whose home this was. I met them once myself; they were not bad people. In 1953, when that bastard Mossadegh was prime minister and wanted to hand over the government to the Tudeh, Ayatollah Kashani lectured the faithful on their duty to support the shah against him. The family acted in the best interests of the nation. They were very patriotic . . . ."

"Yet they've been forced to flee."

"Politics!" Bijan pronounced the word with a sneer of contempt rather than the polite sarcasm that had been his tone up till now. "As I remember, the first director of SAVAK was a General Bakhtiar, Teymour Bakhtiar. Was he any relation?"

The question was a bludgeon; the denial it begged would put Darius on the defensive. He dodged it with silence.

"No?" Bijan answered for him. "It was just a hunch I had. Still, you must be proud of a clansman achieving a position of such authority under the monarchy."

"Did you send for me to trace my family tree?"

"Genealogy is a hobby of mine. Until I told him, the boy who brought you here did not know that his great grandfather was Ayatollah Bafqi, who Reza Shah dragged by the beard into the yard of Fatemeh's shrine because he opposed the 1928 statutes forbidding the wearing of turbans. Bafqi was a saint, and it shows in the boy's blood. There are other families whose lineage is not as noble."

Darius had nothing to say to that either. Bijan said, "Narcy?" and the man in the gray-black fatigues went out of the office.

"I have news about your murder case," Bijan said in a voice devoid of enthusiasm. "Through our network of informants we've been able to determine the identity of the girl found slain in Shemiran. Her name is Leila Darwish, from Lahijan. Her father was an Iraqi, who relocated to Khuzestan in the early 1940s. According to our information, the girl had been living in Teheran as a prostitute."

"By which I take to mean she was a bad hejabi."

"Try to refrain from speaking as a lawyer. Time is too precious to waste quibbling over semantics. The girl had given herself to dissolution. Whether she sold her body, or yielded it for her own corrupt pleasure is of minor concern."

Darius cracked open a pistachio between his teeth. The meat inside was rotten. "When can I see your informant?"

"That is impossible. Our people in the street operate under guarantees of confidentiality, the same as yours."

"I need to know where he obtained his facts."

"There is little I can't tell you myself. The informant made Leila Darwish's acquaintance in north Teheran, and briefly they were sexually involved. When she took her things from his apartment, she didn't tell him where she was going. He learned of her death by seeing her picture in the newspapers. You've been trying to connect the killing to the murders of a couple of drug peddlers near the railway station; but all that the victims have in common is they were taghoutis not deserving the honor of a homicide investigation."

"Where did her dollars go? Where is the heroin?" Having evaded Bijan's bludgeon, Darius tossed back darts.

"The Committee for the Revolution is duty-bound to share its information with the criminal police, and to make its resources available wherever they may be of use. The informant must remain anonymous, though. He has nothing to add concerning money or drugs."

Bijan slid the folder toward Darius, who looked inside at photocopies of the autopsy report on Leila Darwish, her death certificate, fingerprint card, and typed notes on her personal history that read as if they had been transcribed from his conversation with Captain Eshragi. Not one fact extra. The Komiteh routinely tapped the phones of the National Police, but Darius ran the homicide bureau under the assumption that the Revolutionary

Guards were alternately too lazy and arrogant to monitor the bugs. It was a tribute to the progress he'd made that they had seen fit to appraise what had been gleaned. Unless it was to give him a hard pat on the back, however, he didn't see why Bijan had wanted him here.

"I need more than this."

Bijan tunneled through the nuts before finding one he liked. "Talk to the girl's family. Although I am not trained as a detective, they seem the obvious source of clues."

"Phone service to Guilan Province is spotty at best. Order the informant . . . to meet with me." The informant who doesn't exist, he'd nearly said, but for a look from Bijan that the talk might suddenly end. "His identity will not be compromised."

Bijan snatched another nut off the top of the pile. "You are not trying hard, if you let bad phones interfere with your investigation. Lahijan is less than three hours by car."

"Outside Teheran the National Police have none of the prestige of the Komiteh to compel witnesses to talk."

"Authority can be extended to you," Bijan said. "But, as the suggestion is mine, I should advise you not to take it. The Caspian is far from the capital, and politically unstable. The Komiteh can't ensure your safety in a region still inflamed by the brutalities perpetrated by your former colleagues."

So this was what he had been summoned to hear: the choice between graceless surrender and being goaded into a trip far from Teheran, where he might be removed from the case by harsher means. He accepted it as further praise, a tacit understanding that he was closing in on something important.

"I don't see the risk."

"Hassan Darwish was long active in leftist radical circles. He may not appreciate that you've taken it on yourself to intrude in the affairs of his family."

"Knowing I've come about his daughter—"

"His daughter is dead. Your investigation is no favor to her—or to him," Bijan said. "After reviewing the record on Darwish that was inherited from SAVAK, we don't regard the possibility of an arranged attack on your life as farfetched. The man is an accomplished provocateur. The communists recruited Darwish as a teenager in Iraq in 1941, and sent him to Khuzestan to build up Arabic-speaking cadres in the Tudeh Party. In 1944, he received the attention of the nation when he organized mass strike meetings at a factory in the holy city of Qom. The mullahs responded by dispatching a gang of seminarians to fight the atheist claque. But Darwish and the Tudeh beat back the students, and the strike went on for some time."

Bijan showed him a photo of a pockmarked man with thick black hair and a flowing mustache clad in a military-style shirt and a flat cap with a star above the cloth bill.

"Stalin?" Darius said.

"Hassan Darwish. In those days every member of Tudeh, every man who could raise them, had mustaches like those."

Bijan gave Darius the picture to keep. "For six, maybe seven years, Hassan Darwish's activities are a mystery to us. In 1953, when Mossadegh was under attack from all sides, we know that Darwish was with his wife in south Teheran, organizing in the big locomotive factory near the railway station. The Darwishes, like the rest of the Tudeh, believed their moment had come. But Mossadegh was not the stooge they took him for. With the Soviets breathing down his neck, he sought help from the Americans. What he got was more than he bargained for. He got the CIA."

"I'm familiar with Iranian history."

"Thousands of Tudeh were rounded up and slain," Bijan went on. "Hassan Darwish was more fortunate than many other communists, such as his wife, who did not survive her stay in the shah's prisons. After ten years he was paroled to Lahijan, where he found work in the tea farms. Today he is remarried, and the assistant to the manager of one of the largest plantations in Guilan Province—"

Another shriek echoed in the hollow room. It choked, and then it died, releasing Darius toward the door.

"In the Caspian he is like a pasha," Bijan said after him. "If I were you, I would trust no one."

· 6 ·

Over the Elburz's icy saddle the dry Iranian plateau drops through cypress forest and jungle to the Caspian shore. Darius skirted the high snowfields via the winding Chalus River Road, arriving at a drab riviera of shuttered dance halls and cheap family hotels, beaches segregated by sex where women bathers floated on the languid water like black jellyfish in the billowing folds of their chadors. Dunes edged the coastal road that brought him gradually into slopes stitched with emerald tea plants. Women protected from the sun in white head scarves were stooped over the bushes like pale, flightless moths. No men worked the rolling fields. Only a woman's hands were gentle enough to pluck the fragile plants.

Outside Lahijan Darius spotted the tile roof of the mausoleum of a forgotten saint, and followed rutted switchbacks to a plantation in the hills. A Bedford truck swung around him into the lot, spraying gravel against the wall of a barracks-like building. The driver performed a few deep knee bends, mounted the porch, and dropped coins in a machine that dispensed four brands of orange soda. Darius, disdaining calisthenics, went stiff-legged after him. "Where do I find Mr. Darwish?" he asked.

The trucker pressed the frosted bottle against his forehead, then held it at arm's length as though the soda had been spoiled by the heat. He tilted the neck toward a man staring out a screen door at the fields. The man's stern features were expressionless; to Darius it seemed he couldn't make up his mind what sort of lousy mood to be in. "That's him there," the trucker said.

Darius entered a breezeless cubicle behind the door. "You're Hassan Darwish?"

Anger accumulated in the orbits of the man's eyes, and spilled over his face. "Which sons of bitches sent you? I was told only that someone would be here to waste my time."

Darwish turned his empty gaze back to the fields. Viewing him in profile, Darius decided that the revolutionary of forty years ago had learned to make himself elusive by surrendering only his smallest fragment to public scrutiny. Though he appeared younger, Darius estimated him to be in his late sixties. His flowing mustaches were silver-gray, as was the hair that was still so thick it seemed to be all of one piece. But there was a peculiar absence of luster from his dark eyes and skin. The Red Army–style cap and cossack tunic of a Tudeh agitator had been exchanged for a pinstriped shirt with a starched collar, a gray suit, and red-and-blue striped tie that called more attention to itself than anything in Darius's closets.

Darius flashed his identification too quickly to focus on. "National Police," he said. "I'm here about your daughter, Leila."

Darwish's face went slack, and hung on his cheekbones like an identity that had outgrown him. "If Leila's brought you this distance, you must know more than I."

There were vacant chairs in the office, but no invitation to sit. Darius pushed a seat close to the desk. "When was the last time you spoke with her?"

"I haven't heard from Leila in more than two years. But—" Darwish's laugh sounded like impolite coughing. "I don't have to tell you. A report is filed every time I wipe my ass. Probably on the original paper."

Taking into account his weathered look, Darius judged Darwish's health to be sound enough to tolerate the details of his daughter's death. He spread four photos over a *Teheran Times* on the desk.

"Do you know these people?"

Turning slightly from the window, Darwish stabbed a finger at the girl found dead in Shemiran. "That's Leila."

There was no change in expression, but the lusterless eyes had acquired a thin gloss. Impassivity was a trait that Darius often found had been refined to the greatest degree in an Evin Prison torture cell.

"What about the others?"

Darwish separated Farhad and the Shush Avenue victims from his daughter. As he studied them through half lenses, his eyes gradually lost their sparkle. "I don't recognize them."

Darius retrieved three of the photos. Darwish folded his glasses inside his vest, alone again with Leila. "When did she die? The police here are kept deliberately in the dark about everything."

"Two weeks ago. Her body was found in north Teheran."

"Why was she killed?"

"There are few leads. It's why I've come to talk to you."

"Do you expect me to believe you traveled from Teheran without knowing in advance the answers you want to hear? I won't lend my name to an attempt to frame any comrades."

"I have no expectations," Darius said. "There was a bullet in her head, but it may not have been the cause of death. And she was— It's all I can give you, but my condolences."

"Save them. Leila and I fought bitterly, and had stopped communicating some time before she disappeared. The estrangement was more deep-seated than postadolescent rebellion. It would be condescending to her memory to say I thought we would ever be reconciled."

"You heard from her last when she was still at the university in Moscow. With your friends in high position there, someone would have responded to an appeal for information."

"My friends are either dead, or in disgrace," Darwish said. "The Gorbachevites removed them from power, those they didn't make my enemies."

Darwish adopted an expression like Hamid's when he was about to poke his head in Najafi's toilet. He looked up from the picture so Darius would have its full benefit.

"Hasn't Mrs. Darwish got any contacts in Moscow?"

"Leila's mother is not political. She knows no one in what was once the Soviet Union, or even Teheran. I met her in Lahijan at a time I was forbidden to leave Guilan Province. The arrangement suits her to this day. It was her decision to report our daughter missing to the authorities. I wouldn't have given them the satisfaction."

"You cared so little for her?"

"Leila was a self-sufficient girl, who always had a clear idea of what she wanted, and what she had to do to obtain it. Considering our differences, I didn't find it worrisome that she had distanced herself from her parents."

"Such disregard for a daughter," Darius said, "is outside the bounds of human decency."

"From your crude interrogatory manner, I gather you're an expert on what goes on beyond those bounds. I spent some years in a jail of yours where it was the mode—"

"I'm not here to discuss *my* background. You didn't inquire into your daughter's whereabouts because you didn't want to know where she was. Why not?"

"That's untrue. Leila was a disappointment even as a child. We were never close."

"Stop, please," Darius said. "You communists, despite your contempt for the customs of the bourgeoisie, are not well known for the latitude you allow your children to run their lives. You would have followed her every move."

"From which textbook did you make a study about us?" Darwish glared haughtily, but then sucked back a sigh as he stared at the picture.

Darius realized that the old radical remained the prisoner of his discipline, helpless to ask about the facts of his daughter's murder out of fear that he would give up more information than he received.

"You really don't know, do you?"

"I refuse to answer any questions of yours. Your story about my daughter's death is a fabrication. If not, you probably share complicity. Under neither circumstance will I dirty myself talking to you."

Darius had had his fill of the aging tyrant, whose sensibilities he no longer felt compelled to protect. "There were facts I neglected to mention, because I thought you should be spared the unpleasantness," he said. "I was mistaken; you're entitled to know everything. Before she was shot, your daughter was sexually mutilated."

"In what manner?" Darwish asked formally.

"The coroner found that she had been infibulated."

"I'm unfamiliar with the term."

"It means—" Darius's anger failed, and he softened his voice. "Suffice to say she was hurt gravely."

"I have the right to know," Darwish demanded. "Explain what you mean by infibulated."

"Her clitoris was surgically removed, and her vagina sewn shut."

"It has the ring of something a former agent of SAVAK would invent in his spare time."

"He might, if he were Arab—" Darius slammed the bottle on the newspaper. "Are you too pure to cooperate in finding who maimed and murdered her?"

Darwish's chair came closer, but his head scarcely moved. Slouching, he maintained his distance from Darius. "Leila was proud of her heritage. Although she was raised in a progressive, internationalist household, she considered herself foremost a Pan-Arabist. Nothing came ahead of her people's fight against the imperialists and the Zionist entity. As this was a struggle we shared, I was supportive of her decision to play an active part."

The trucker came back through the office. Darwish paused until the screen door swung shut behind him. "Her mother has never been told, but after Leila's last year in Moscow she was recruited for training in a guerrilla unit that would be sent to southern Lebanon to infiltrate Israel's upper Galilee."

Darius said, "The mutilations were not performed by Israelis."

"Nor by Palestinian Marxists," Darwish snapped at him. "The quality of the volunteers the guerrilla camps attract is not high. The ignorant dregs of Iran and the Shi'ite villages of the Bekaa that are monuments to backwardness find playing soldier to their liking."

"You dismay me, Darwish. I thought communists transcended concepts of national pride, and all men were brothers."

"Which communists are we talking about? These bumblers are no more communist than my daughter. Leila was an Arab chauvinist—as a child she was a Nasserite. This was the basis of the bitterness between us. Leila rejected my communism the way . . . the way bourgeois teenagers look down their nose at the values of their parents. She was a religious fanatic who voluntarily took up the veil and was allowed to attend school in the Soviet Union because her beliefs were well known to the Komitehmen who watch me all the time. The camp she was assigned to wasn't run by Tudeh Fedayeen fighters, but by more damn fanatics—the Revolutionary Guards."

"How, then, if she was with her unit, could she have turned up slain in north Teheran?"

"I don't know."

"Where was the camp?"

"Far from the Caspian. More than that she couldn't say. The girls were brought there for religious indoctrination and instruction in basic military skills."

"You heard from her? When?"

"She called several months ago," Darwish said, "to inform me that she would be completing her training soon, and was to be given a special mission outside the country. 'At the cutting edge of the holy war against the infidels' was how she described it, which I took to mean she'd been ordered inside Israel, or Afghanistan, possibly even the Sudan—someplace where the forces of repression murder each other for the glory of God. She boasted of the importance of her role, that she would accomplish more for her people in twenty-three years than I had in a lifetime. Conditions in the camp were excellent, she said, and her comrades very enlightened. She was lying. Her years at home had not been spent with eyes closed. Leila recognized reaction and superstition for what they were, even as she immersed herself in them. I ordered her to leave the camp while there was still the opportunity. Her answer was that the cause she was fighting for was greater than her comfort. I called her an idiot. She laughed at me. Not an idiot, she said, but a Bride of Blood—whatever that ghoulish title designates. I lost my temper. I told her to go to Israel to be killed with the rest of the fanatics, if that was what she wanted. It was the last we talked."

"She must have let something slip about the camp where she was stationed."

Darwish started to shake his head automatically.

"Think!" Darius said.

"You'll never find out what happened to her. She was dead when she put on the chador. It was only a matter of time before her physical body ceased to exist."

Darius got up to leave. As he reached for the morgue shot, Darwish pulled it away. "I want this."

"There are better pictures to remember her by."

The photo started to tear. Darius let go, and Darwish smoothed the glossy paper around his daughter's head. "I burned those a long time ago," he said. "Like Lear, I expected too much from my child."

Darius made nothing of it. His schooling under the reign of the shah did not permit the study of Shakespeare, who wrote too well of the bloody end of vain kings.

He went out to the car still feeling the pain of the lonely old man wrestling him over the mangled snapshot of his slain daughter. From the flask in the glove compartment he refilled a soda bottle with good Swedish vodka seized just yesterday from an SAS pilot who had brought six cases into Mehrabad Airport looking to turn them over quickly for rare Agra Allower carpets. The bottle was cool against his crotch as he coasted along the switchbacks to the lake shore. Replaying the interview in his mind, he was sorry he hadn't demanded to speak with Darwish's wife. What corner of Leila's personality had been passed down through the Iranian side of the family? Her father's legacy was a propensity for bad politics and standing fast to their tragic conclusion. The capacity for enduring needless suffering, he suspected, had been inherited from her mother.

Hamid arrived empty-handed; Ghaffari, minutes later, with two bottles of Mehta's best evidence. When Farib opened the door, Ghaffari's lanky body swayed in the light breeze off the balcony, and he said, "You look beautiful today. Beautiful as a bride."

Hamid had never been to the Bakhtiars' before. Made uncomfortable by the occasion he stood on the balcony and looked down at Baharestan Square, at women carrying old bolt-action rifles as they marched eight abreast in front of the Muslim Theological School shouting, "Death to Israel, Death to America, Death to World Zionism." Darius shut the sliding glass doors, and Hamid walked into a corner of the living room with his hands stuffed inside his pockets to study the Impressionist prints on the walls, and then stare awkwardly at Darius.

"Yes, Hamid, is there something you wanted to say?"

"I— It concerns the Darwish case. This is a bad time. It can wait."

"Why? What's better than murder to take our minds off our small problems?"

"Dr. Baghai called when you were in the Mazanderan," the criminalist began uncertainly. "The same .25-caliber gun with which Leila Darwish was shot also fired the bullets into the drug addict and his girlfriend in south Teheran."

"Does that surprise you?"

Hamid shook his head, his lips pressed tight. "The findings of the lab on Leila Darwish's death were not so obvious. In addition to the opiates a poison was introduced into her system."

"What kind of poison?"

"Dr. Baghai didn't know."

"How was it administered?"

"That was not determined. The lab report came back negative. Samples of her blood were sent to the serology unit at Mehregan Hospital in Isfahan. They didn't turn up anything either."

"It would seem the one thing we know is she *wasn't* poisoned," Darius said.

"Dr. Baghai says it's a poison we've never encountered before."

"A convenient theory."

"But all we have," Hamid said. "And, speaking for myself, an unknown poison is preferable to having to hunt for a means of death entirely new to forensic science."

Farib had prepared a lunch of tass kebabs and rice. No one had any appetite, no one but she. Ghaffari put a bottle on the table, and screwed off the cap. As he touched the neck to Darius's glass, Farib came out of the kitchen, where she was eating alone. "He can't," she said, and covered the glass with her palm. "Under the law he mustn't be intoxicated, or in a rage, when he pronounces the talaq."

"But, dear Farib," Ghaffari said, "how can you expect a sober man to do such a crazy thing? It's why I brought whiskey."

Farib was clearing the table when Darius said, "You'll have time later," and assembled everyone on the sliver of a balcony. Below, the parade was over; yellow leaflets fluttered like confetti in the traffic flooding into the square. Hamid and Ghaffari stood against the railing with Darius between them, forming a semicircle around Farib, to whom Darius said casually, as if the idea had just occurred to him, "I make my wife free, upon remittance of her dowry."

Farib tugged her veil higher under her eyes.

The divorce would not become final until Farib had completed three menstrual cycles. By pronouncing only a single talaq, Darius had left open the possibility that they might reunite. A more common form of divorce would have had him say the talaq three times, requiring Farib to remarry before they could be wed again. Darius had offered a three-talaq divorce, but she had declined.

"I won't ask for the unused portion of my dowry," Farib said. "It's yours to do with as you see fit. So you should not expect any part of your milk fee to be returned." A milk fee was an amount of money paid to the mother of a bride as reimbursement for the cost of bringing her up. "Nor do you have to pay for my maintenance. My father has agreed to support me until I take another husband." She backed into the apartment. "One other thing . . . Don't forget to inform the authorities we're no longer married."

Watching her walk to the bedroom and shut herself inside, Darius became aware that the holster in the small of his back was funneling sweat into his pants. His face felt hot.

"Well, that's done with." Ghaffari brought out the other bottle, and placed it in Darius's hands. "What are you looking angry about?"

"There's nothing left of her dowry," Darius said. "Farib and I were agreed that the dowry was a medieval custom, and since we were a modern couple I couldn't accept any goods from her father for myself. We sold everything, and I opened a checking account in her name from the proceeds. All of it was gone on clothes before we left Washington."

The old Shemiran Road was littered with cars butchered for parts by shade tree mechanics and left on the sidewalks to rust. Into the Elburz foothills the cross streets turned plush, and then semirural, mimicking a country village but for prices straight from European capitals. Darius bore east beyond the shah's summer palace. Slim poplars lined the way to Manzarieh Park on the green flank of Mount Towchal.

The International Boy Scout Jamboree had been held at Manzarieh the year Darius was fourteen. Somewhere there was a photo of him swaddled in merit badges beside the statue of Lord Baden-Powell that had stood at the entrance to the park. During the war with Iraq an ayatollah had claimed Manzarieh's nine hundred square kilometers as a recuperation center for Revolutionary Guards. Two hundred youngsters from Muslim and third world countries were installed in a dormitory on the grounds; but none had seen action at the front. They had come to "The Institute" to learn Islam and guerrilla warfare under the tutelage of Hezbollah, the Party of God.

Darius was struck by the sheer beauty of Manzarieh, which disqualified it as the camp where Leila Darwish had been sent for training. Towchal's lush slopes were too bucolic to inculcate sufficient ferocity in pampered young women who aspired to the sobriquet Brides of Blood. The mountain re-mained popular with hikers for its spectacular vistas of the Elburz and the city. For those who forgot the two-kilometer exclusionary zone behind the barbed wire perimeter of the institute, the outer fence was electrified.

Darius peered inside the main gate at a dozen men kneeling on prayer rugs beside a pond. When their devotions were concluded, they rolled up the rugs and exchanged them for Kalashnikov rifles, which they broke open under the rigorous eye of a Japanese or Korean in an army jacket with red stars on the lapels. A basij, a volunteer from the Foundation of the Oppressed on Earth, came out of the gate house carrying a Kalashnikov at port arms. The banana clip was conspicuously in place. "Go back," he commanded. "You can't come in."

Darius dangled his ID out the window. The volunteer waved him away without looking at it. This was no embarrassed illiterate, but a disciplined soldier under orders to prevent unauthorized persons from entering. Darius swung into a U-turn. A Mercedes limousine pulled up to the gate house, and the guard went back inside and raised a red-and-white semaphore. Darius continued around into a full circle, cutting ahead of the limo through the open gate.

Hunched over the wheel, he raced onto the grounds. With outsiders barred from Hezbollah installations, no mechanism existed for reaching the leadership of the camp. His objective was not the school buildings directly ahead, but to create a disturbance that would end in his surrender and interrogation by party stalwarts, who might answer *his* questions. The Mercedes sped after him, and he swerved aside and fit the Paycon in its square shadow, kept the German car's thick steel between the Kalashnikovs and himself. Three mullahs in camel's hair abayahs stared anxiously from the rear seat, making him feel like a bandit heading off a stagecoach. When their chauffeur angled a small revolver at his head, he gave up the chase and stood with his ID in his hands high above his shoulders.

Guardsmen in black ski masks shoved him toward a building that had been the administration hub of Empress Farah University when the late school for girls had taken Manzarieh for its campus. His wallet and guns were brought inside an office while he was made to wait in the corridor for forty minutes, and then he was bundled into a jeep and driven across the site of the old Boy Scout encampment to a bare field scattershot with craters.

Deeply tanned men were crouched around a mullah who was rooting in the earth for a metallic device from which half a dozen spines protruded on top. The mullah reburied the object under a thin layer of sand, then dug it up again while the tanned men jotted notes in looseleaf binders. After several repetitions the mullah said a few words in Arabic, and the class cleared out to the edge of the field. The mullah drew a revolver with pearl grips from his abayah and fired at the object in the dirt. Darius covered his eyes as a thunderous explosion lifted a sandstorm that the wind carried into the mountains. All of the men clapped and whistled. Some scratched feverishly in their books.

The driver of the jeep turned over Darius's wallet to the mullah. The cleric looked quizzically at Darius as he matched clean-shaven features to the photo in the ID and to the handguns that had been presented to him like a small offering. He dismissed the class, and came over to the jeep. "Manzarieh is off-limits," he said. "The National Police have no jurisdiction here."

"I need to find out about a young woman who was a volunteer at a camp for Revolutionary Guards."

"You could have been killed, crashing in—should have—had the basij at the gate been doing his job." He flipped the wallet shut and returned it to Darius. "Proper channels exist for obtaining information. Contact the Komiteh in your district, and apply through them. All reasonable requests are responded to in good time."

"There is no time."

"Then the request is unreasonable."

"You haven't heard me out."

"It's enough you weren't shot. Leave now."

The driver floored the jeep, which spun its cleated tires and then lunged forward as Darius leaped out. The driver let go of the wheel to pull his gun. He looked toward the mullah, who shook his head slightly, an economy of motion that Darius was aware could have been horizontal with no more effort than up and down.

"The young woman was murdered. Manzarieh is only a couple of kilometers from the site in Shemiran where her body was found. Someone here must know about her."

"You have just attended a class on the concealment and safe removal of antipersonnel ordnance in rural areas. This is not women's work. Do you see women in this camp?" the mullah said. "I would have been notified of anything like that occurring close by."

"Her name was Leila Darwish. Tell me how to find which camp was hers."

"There is nothing I can do," the mullah said, and began walking away.

"An innocent woman was tortured and slain." One quick step was all that Darius took after him; the driver hadn't holstered his gun. "She deserves a full inquiry into her death."

"Perhaps. Or perhaps the kinder deed is to let the matter rest." The mullah stopped, but didn't look back. "You had better go before too much is made of your being here. Tonight the basij will talk of nothing but your brazen act. It's not good . . . not good for you. I would lock you up, but for—" He turned to Darius. "Do you know me, Bakhtiar."

"No."

"I am Sheik Javad Salehi. Years ago, I was a student of your wife's uncle at Faiziyeh, in the disciplines of logic and Persian history. Hormoz was a brilliant teacher, compassionate, a father to his pupils—my good friend to this day. He spoke warmly of his niece's new husband in America—so much so that sometime later, without meeting you, I voted to reprieve your life after the murder of Ibrahim Farmayan."

Salehi waited, and Darius heard the click of worry beads.

"Not even a thank-you . . . ?"

A volley of rifle fire delivered its mournful report through the camp, and after that a single shot.

"You owe me something," Salehi continued. "Hormoz used to read to us from your letters from the United States. You were one of the few who adapted readily, yet you chose to return to Iran. Why?"

"The government invested a good deal of money in my schooling so I could better serve the people. I couldn't renege."

"Others did," Salehi said. "The government changed."

"But not the people—not much."

"That was not Hormoz's interpretation. During your typical infatuation with the United States, your wife wrote that you had been offered several jobs with prestigious firms. Her uncle remained unshaken in his faith that you would come back."

"Why bring this up now?"

"Among the most highly regarded faculty members at Manzarieh are our 'moral preceptors,' who have spent time in the West, and returned with firsthand knowledge of the crisis afflicting the so-called democracies. The youth must be made to see that the West is strangling on its degeneracy and that, God willing, Islam will triumph in the hearts of men. We would be honored to make a place for you as a moral preceptor that will not interfere with your regular duties with the National Police."

Why, Darius wondered, in a ruined economy with raging unemployment was he everyone's first choice for a job? The Revolutionary Prosecutor, the Bon Yad Monkerat, couldn't find enough for him to do. Now a place on the staff at "The Institute" was his for the taking. As if Salehi had known he would turn up—as if the Revolutionary Guards wanted him occupied with anything other than the hunt for Leila Darwish's killer.

"Is the enemy so seductive," Darius asked, "that the volunteers have to be taught to hate it?"

"Our youth grow up enamored of the West from television and movies. They are captivated by its hedonism, including—sad to say—many who wish to bring it down."

"My friends also viewed the West with disdain," Darius said. "Who among us hadn't had it crammed into his brain that when Islam led the world in science and philosophy Europeans were still living in caves? We came flaunting our spiritual superiority—and were overwhelmed by America's richness. When we returned home, our guilt boiled over into hatred of the West for opening our eyes to how backward we were. Few of my friends could remain in Iran . . ."

"Were they so greedy for material comforts?"

"Everything they'd been taught to believe appeared as lies," Darius said. "How could Islam be the final revealed truth of God when life was far better in the infidel West? Those who returned to stay became more Muslim than Muslim to show they rejected the things they secretly craved."

"But not you."

"In the U.S. I was more American than American. I was only fooling myself—and then not even me. That's when I came home."

"Your objectivity alone qualifies you to be a moral preceptor. The basij will respect your honesty."

"There's nothing I can tell the volunteers, nothing they want to hear. All I can do for them is find who murdered their comrade."

"Without my assistance," Salehi said. "For security purposes one camp very often is unaware of what the next is doing, or even where it is."

Under Salehi's thin beard Darius noticed a scar that reached around his chin to both cheeks. "What about the camp of the Brides of Blood?" he asked. "Is its location secret, too?"

"It would be impossible, strictly speaking, for any of the Brides of Blood to turn up near Manzarieh." Salehi's friendly tone had become neutral. "They are headquartered far from here, and have no business in the capital."

"Where?"

"Outside the country. If you have to ask— How much do you know about them?"

"Next to nothing," Darius confessed.

"The Brides of Blood are the most esteemed young women volunteer fighters for Islam. Each one is a virgin, who has dedicated herself to avenging Imam Hussein by doing battles with the enemies of the faith."

"What kind of missions do they take on?"

"To kill, and to die for the faith. The girls who drove trucks filled with dynamite into the Zionist positions in southern Lebanon, they were Brides of Blood. Their reward was a martyr's death, and instant admission to paradise, where Ayatollah Aqda'i has said that Hussein will select husbands for them from the most devout and physically beautiful of young men."

"But where—"

"Lebanon," Salehi said.

"Be specific. I need details, every fact you have."

The jeep cut between them, and the driver flung open the passenger's door. Again Salehi shook his head, and put a foot up on the bumper.

"In southwestern Beirut," he said, "in the harbor district known as Ouzai, is an elite encampment whose volunteers are mainly Shi'ite girls from Lebanon, plus a few Iranians. They are divided into a number of fighting units. The one that has brought the most glory on itself is the Sayyidah Zaynab Brigade, which has embraced a martyr's fate to drive the Israelis out of the land. Theirs is the forward base of the Brides of Blood."

"You'd be doing an immeasurable service by writing a letter of introduction into the camp."

"A service? For whom—for you? For Leila Darwish? Not the girls."

"Please, you've given me this much. A little more and, I think, I can wrap up the case."

"You're deluding yourself, Bakhtiar. If there was a chance you might succeed, I wouldn't have told you anything."

"What? I don't understand."

"Seven weeks ago, commandos from Acre, in the belly of the Zionist beast, landed four rubber dinghies just south of Beirut. From the beaches they proceeded unmolested to Ouzai and massacred the innocent girls. After taking what they wanted, they planted explosives in all the camp structures. For eight hours fire raged in the rubble. There were no survivors. The coffins returned to the families for martyrs' funerals contained only blackened bones. That is why I don't want to talk about it: each girl's memory is too precious to be defamed by such a death. And that is why the girl found slain in Shemiran cannot have been a Bride of Blood—because the Brides of Blood no longer exist."

Salehi climbed into the jeep, and tossed out Darius's guns. "Do you want to know more? Ask the Jews. They have the duty roster, the order of battle, the names of informants and spies, all the records. They can tell you *everything* about the Brides of Blood."

Two volunteers escorted Darius back to his car. The semaphore went up when he was fifty meters from the perimeter, and the guard came out and waggled the Kalashnikov good-bye. His evidence pad was in the glove compartment, but not the flask that he had filled from two cases of premium bootleg that he had moved into his new apartment ahead of his clothes. He saw himself as a moral preceptor lecturing thirsty fanatics on where in

Teheran to find the best vodka. Who was to say it wouldn't be his most valuable service in the cause of the Islamic Republic?

His subconscious already had begun to process the new information. He scribbled furiously, taking notes on his talk with Salehi before the facts were tainted by sober opinion. Whether Leila Darwish had known about the destruction of the camp, or had tired of life there, was beyond the range of his inquiry. Safe to say that she had been on a foreign mission at the time Ouzai was overrun and, instead of returning to Lebanon, likely had spent her final weeks dodging the Komiteh in Teheran while she tried to dispose of several kilograms of heroin. Slow to discover what poor material she was for a Shi'ite martyr, she would seem to have compounded the error by attempting to finance a new life out of proceeds expropriated from the old.

He stopped writing. Safe to say that nothing was safe to say, or to commit to paper. Thinking was safe; but, without alcohol as a lubricant, too often created painful friction and heat. He had allowed Bijan to steer him down one blind alley after the next in the belief that it was *he* who was doing the manipulating, which he saw now for the same arrogant delusion that had brought Leila Darwish to Teheran to deal heroin under the nose of the Komiteh.

Bijan's agenda was the mystery within the mystery. Having failed to persuade Darius to drop the investigation, he had joined it as a partner generous with information detectives had gathered on their own. Darius put no faith in the notion that he wanted simply to be kept abreast of progress he could not prevent from being made. Nothing at Homicide remained hidden for long from the Komiteh. Bijan's interest in the case was in controlling its direction, now urging Darius to delve deep into Leila's past. It was as if a secret had been forgotten by the last person on earth to know it, and Darius was needed to bring it to immediate light, to whisper it in Bijan's ear. Had Leila been that person? Had Farhad? Darius did not anticipate a future brighter than theirs if the Komitehman wasn't given what he wanted. And if Darius didn't fail? Bijan did not need excuses to get rid of anyone. Hatred for the murderer of his uncle burned bright as ever in his eyes.

The sun descending through a pall of soot colored the city in liquid orange. Below Niavaran a steamroller ground layers of steaming asphalt into the road. Traffic was detoured through steep avenues of grand villas erected in the last years before the Revolution. As he was admiring what was meant to be a Tudor-style estate in an English garden, a white Chevrolet hurtled across two lanes of traffic and cut him off. He slammed the brakes. The Chevrolet slowed with him, and he was forced to wheel around the corner to avoid a crash.

The near miss was accomplished reflexively with little anger directed toward the driver of the other car. Who better than a policeman understood the Iranian penchant for reckless driving? Traffic signals were meant to be ignored. The rules of the road were as theoretical as the Imam's outline for the working of the Islamic state. Under the law it was legal to run down jaywalkers.

He had been shunted onto a street of smaller houses, which he followed downhill assuming that it would rejoin the old Shemiran Road. At a cross street called Qods the way narrowed to a single lane that was blocked by an ambulance. Two paramedics sat on a litter in the middle of the street smoking cigarettes beside a body under a gray blanket. On an average day six Teheranis lost their lives in traffic accidents, most of them at night when women in black chadors virtually were invisible, and there were days when it seemed he witnessed every one. More than moral preceptors, he thought, what were needed in the camps were instructors in defensive driving.

One of the paramedics, a huge man with a stethoscope like calipers around his bull neck, came over to the Paycon. "We are sorry, sir," he said, "but he cannot be moved until the police arrive."

Darius shifted into reverse, but the white Chevrolet was on his bumper now. "I'm a police officer," he said dispiritedly, "let me have a look."

From the compact form outlined under the blanket, the body already had been disturbed. There was no blood, or broken glass, or skid marks in the street, nor vehicles other than the ambulance.

"Were there witnesses? Did anyone see the car that ran him down?"

The medic on the stretcher blew smoke through thin, cracked lips. "No."

As Darius peeled away the blanket, a jab to his kidneys doubled him over in pain. "Don't move, don't say anything," the big man ordered.

The corpse flung its gray shroud over Darius's head. Darius's shoulder gun was taken away while other hands probed for his reserve pistol. Another kidney punch started him toward the ambulance. When he felt the bumper against his leg, he locked his knees and wouldn't go further.

"Get in!"

Two quick, hard blows came down on the top of his head. Someone said, "Don't, you almost killed him last time." Lighter punches raining on his shoulders wearied him and put an end to his resistance. Holding himself still, he listened for Farib's husky voice to tell him that she was bringing him someplace quiet and safe, then shut his ears to his labored breathing and the click of handcuffs behind his back, the shriek of tires as the ambulance hurtled down from the mountain carrying him into the steaming city.

❖ 7 ❖

In blackness Darius concentrated on tracking the movement of the ambulance, which immediately had turned onto a level street and veered left again without slowing. A long, straight decline gave the sensation of increasing momentum. The next turn, a sharp right, spilled him across the floor. To imprint the route in his memory he began a silent litany of "Left-downhill left-right—" then "Left-downhill left-right gentle left—" knowing that the imprecise directions could be plotted as easily over the map of any large, hilly city. Nevertheless, he didn't quit until the ambulance raced around a small park, or square, spinning him in circles on his back. After that, he occupied himself with staying wedged against a wheel well, where he best could keep from becoming goods damaged in transit.

The wheels ran over a bump, bloodying his nose against his knee. The ambulance was still rocking on its springs when he was dragged outside with the blanket bunched around his head and brought along a gravel path. A cat in a bag, he thought, would know the feeling. The voice he had heard before said, "You're coming to steps now." Raising his foot for them, he would have pitched headlong down the flight had someone not pulled him back by the shoulders.

He descended into a haze of camphor and turpentine. A door opened on dry hinges, and he was thrown onto a bare mattress and chained to a pipe against the wall. Left alone on his knees, he wore himself out trying to pull down the building. By tossing his head like a horse he was able to shake off the blanket. The room was in darkness; he'd gained nothing but a twinge in his neck and a view of a strip of dim light beneath the door. His eyes stung with foul, anxious sweat. Voices penetrating the low ceiling were lost to him when a refrigerator chugged loudly into its cooling cycle.

Lacking alcohol, he wanted sleep—any means of blanking his fear. Measured breaths stilled the hammering in his chest, but not the wild thoughts that made a kidnapper of everyone he knew. His enemies were too numerous to sort out, delineated unclearly from those few of his acquaintances he believed to be friends. He shut his eyes to slow the rush of ideas. When he opened them seconds later, it was like waking from a long nap.

A man was paused several steps inside the room. He was about twenty-five, wearing a broad-billed infantryman's cap and leather sandals. Loose-fitting corduroy trousers were hitched around his pinched waist with a web belt. The automatic rifle in his hands was loaded with the straight clip of an American M-16. He tugged a cord overhead, and Darius bowed his head in the glare of an unshaded bulb.

"Do you recognize me?" he asked, positioning himself directly under the light.

"No."

"That's because you're not looking closely." The muzzle of the M-16 levered Darius's chin into the glare. "Take a good look."

Darius squinted at gray eyes in grayer shadow under the soiled cap, smooth features that would not be improved by the character beginning to shape them.

"I am Saeed Djalilian, the son of Daoud Djalilian. Do you see his face in mine?"

What Darius saw was the kind of anger he associated with the relatives of criminals he had been responsible for putting away, so volatile he equated it with possession of a dangerous weapon.

"You knew him as Dave Djalilian. The same Dave Djalilian whose memory you profaned by working for the Komiteh."

The name might have been taken from another man's past. The threat of the M-16 alone was personal.

Two men came quietly inside. One of them, still wearing his paramedic's jacket, wrapped a heavy arm around Djalilian, who sank under its weight. The other, ten years older, thirty-five kilos lighter, was a wiry man of about fifty whose cheeks were cloaked in a yellow beard. Djalilian stared at him with angry eyes, which were turned away by his soft gaze. Soft, Darius thought, but sure, and infinitely unyielding. He recognized those eyes, and now the face behind the flowing beard, but took no comfort from familiarity. As a young lawyer in Sazeman Atelaat Va Amniat Keshvar, the State Organization for Security and Intelligence, SAVAK, he had been assigned to the Special Intelligence Bureau under the directorship of Colonel Massoud Ashfar, who for the slightest lapse in judgment, and sometimes for none at all, had turned that penetrating gaze on him. Ashfar had fled as power dwindled from the shah, and was rumored to have sold state secrets to finance his getaway. Incredibly, here he was, having aged little over the years, except that his beard, which in the old days was already long and gray, was now the ragged mask of a sage.

"Saeed," Ashfar said, "this is not the way we treat a guest. Would you be so kind as to bring food and something to drink? Lieutenant Colonel Bakhtiar must be hungry after all he has been through today."

Djalilian didn't move. The man in the paramedic's jacket released him with a shove that sent him stumbling through the door.

"Be patient with Saeed," Ashfar said to Darius. "He is impulsive, and allows emotion too often to interfere with doing his job."

Darius scraped his chain against the pipe. "I have no patience."

"What better opportunity to acquire some?" Ashfar put out his hand toward the heavyset man. "You remember Baraheni."

Darius had said, "No," when the name came to him. Khosrow Baraheni had been a ranking interrogator in SAVAK's Anti-Sabotage Committee headquartered on Farrokhi Alley, which was chartered to launch investigations into the activities of anyone it desired without seeking the approval of the courts. Baraheni was a SAVAK legend, a Galileo among torturers, who had turned his particular world upside down when he discovered that by applying a samovar to the small of the back and heating the water inside to the boiling point, he could reduce the most taciturn of men to a babbling font of information.

"You would be advised to be cautious in Saeed's company," Baraheni said suddenly. Trained as a listener, Baraheni rarely had anything to say in the past. "He doesn't like you."

"Because of his father?" Darius addressed the question to Ashfar. Someone else always had answered for Baraheni, who in the intervening years at least had acquired the use of language and no longer seemed to go around drenched in the blood of his victims. "I never heard of him."

"He was an obscure cipher clerk on the Iraq desk, who may have brushed past you once or twice in the halls," Ashfar said. "The new regime was still looking for the keys to the toilets on Farrokhi when he was bringing the fanatics his codebooks. They put him in Evin, and hanged him during the first wave of executions in seventy-nine. The kid has built him into a great hero; and you, for having the temerity to survive, as a devil. We told him to be gentle with you that time in Shemiran, but he isn't with us to be gentle. It's going to take a while for you to get to know and like each other."

"What do you want?" Darius asked.

Ashfar furrowed his brow to suggest that he was considering every nuance of a deceptively complex question. "We want you, Darius. We want you."

Darius shook his head.

"You haven't heard us out," Ashfar said.

"There's nothing to talk about."

"He's living too well." Baraheni's voice was the rumble of a slow freight. "He's a big shot in the National Police, in bed with the Komiteh on the side. Why give up everything that goes with that just to help the people?"

"You're judging him too harshly. Darius Bakhtiar is a man of high moral conviction who would never place his selfish interests ahead of those of the nation." Ashfar put up a boot on the mattress. Darius smelled dog excrement on the heel. ". . . Or his former comrades."

"Aren't you curious about us?" he asked Darius. "What has it been—it must be close to fifteen years since we've spoken."

"We made it out of Teheran just in time," Baraheni cut in. "Another twelve hours, and the fanatics would have had us swinging from the gallows with Saeed's old man. For months we lived like animals, till we expropriated the funds to get started in Europe. Since then we've stayed in London, twice in Germany, all over Switzerland and Belgium. Last year we came to France."

"We're settled in a little suburb of Paris," Ashfar said. "Wonderful place. Great wine cheap as water, terrific food, more blondes than you could have in a lifetime."

"Too bad you didn't leave Iran, too," Baraheni said.

"He was in prison. You remember—that sorry business about Farmayan."

A muscle twitched in Baraheni's cheek, drawing a sneer on that side of his face.

"But what is best about Paris," Ashfar went on, "is the community of loyal countrymen that has settled there around the royal family. Quality people—

the senior commanders of the Army Aviation Service Group, two thirds of the air force generals from the Soviet and Turkish borders. It would warm your heart to see how many of our compatriots have established themselves comfortably in Europe. And every last one of them doing whatever is in his power to restore Crown Prince Reza to the throne as head of a modern, incorruptible constitutional monarchy. That's why we've come back, to lay the groundwork for his return."

Where in years gone by Ashfar had the relief of pain as a prime selling point, reduced circumstances, thought Darius, had forced him to support his positions with argument before announcing his terms. But even without the authority of government backing he remained imposing, exuding the threat of bodily harm as other men gave off a bad odor.

"You'll let me know when the baby shah is ready to leave France," Darius said. "After looting the treasury, I doubt the Pahlavis have any great desire to see Iran again."

Ashfar laughed. Baraheni joined in, covering his mouth with a massive hand, the slow freight rumbling through a tunnel.

"Did I say something funny?" asked Darius.

"It's quite sad, actually." Ashfar held on to a frozen, joyless smile. "They told us the masses were waiting to rise up against the fanatics and were hungry for leaders to organize them, that they would forget the past and welcome us with open arms. It hasn't been like that. Your friends in the Komiteh, they would be glad to have us. But they are the only ones."

Djalilian came in with bowls of the thin stew called abgusht and naan, oval pancake-shaped bread, and set the tray down at the edge of the mattress. Ashfar unscrewed the lid from a plain glass jar, and poured an inch of clear liquid into each of four tumblers. Darius pulled his head away when Ashfar brought a glass to his lips.

"Did you snatch the right man? The Darius Bakhtiar I used to know never refused a drink."

"Maybe bootleg isn't good enough for him," Baraheni said.

"I think it's our company he finds distasteful. I think he would rather be someplace else." Ashfar emptied Darius's glass into his own. "Well, no one is forcing him to stay against his will."

Baraheni inserted a key into the handcuffs. Darius's numb hands swung around his hips, and he looked at them as if he had never seen them before. His eyes shifted toward the open door, and back to Ashfar, whose gaze could have burned through the steel shackles. He estimated the chances at close to even that he could be up the stairs before the others were on their feet or drew guns—even though that was what they were expecting him to do. The refrigerator went off. He heard footsteps on the upper floor, and he sat down and tasted the stew.

"Saeed," Ashfar said, "apologize to Lieutenant Colonel Bakhtiar for hurting him in Shemiran and treating him so shabbily today."

Djalilian's spoon went dead in the air. He stuffed his face with bread, and gestured that he couldn't talk with his mouth full.

"You have to."

Baraheni pinched Djalilian's cheek in mock affection, squeezing pasty saliva onto the mattress.

". . . Sorry," Djalilian mumbled, and rubbed color into a white streak alongside his lips after Baraheni let go.

"Saeed's a good boy," Ashfar said to Darius. "A hard worker. Almost as hard as you were at his age. But it's less than two years since he fled west; he still has rough edges. That's why we tolerate his excesses, why we've been willing to tolerate yours. We don't want much—just some help in getting back home."

"I don't work for the passport office. You can leave the way you came in."

"That's a fact," Ashfar said. "But, frankly, we arrived in Iran with limited funds, and those are all but gone. What fun will there be in returning to Paris to live in poverty?"

Darius was about to shake his head again, when Baraheni pressed his cheeks between meaty hands and tilted his face at Ashfar. Darius heard bones creak, felt his skull compress . . .

"In the six weeks we've been back," Ashfar said, "we've found out that Afghani heroin is being brought regularly into Iran."

"Where did you get your information?"

"Listen." Baraheni squashed Darius's mouth shut. "He's telling you."

Ashfar swilled vodka. "The fanatics have a low opinion of narcotics smuggling, and enjoy nothing so much as stringing up drug traders side by side in public places. They regard their part in this filthy business as doing the work of God, as they describe any criminal enterprise that serves their purposes. None of the drugs remain in Iran. They're destined for transshipment to North America, where they can be applied to subverting the will of the despicable Great Satan, while bringing in badly needed hard currency for the Islamic Republic. The most recent shipment, as you know, has been diverted. It is our patriotic duty to retrieve it, and spoil the plans of the fanatics."

". . . And save the Americans from the consequence of their illicit appetites," Baraheni said.

"Good point."

"How did you learn about the heroin?" Darius asked.

"You mean, how did we know you were working to find it?" Ashfar said. "Have you forgotten the old days, what good spies we were? You were one of the primary contacts we wanted to establish in Teheran. Before we made approaches, however, we had to learn your current thinking. So we started following you around. Every time the heroin changed hands, sooner or later you turned up. That morning on Saltanatabad Avenue when the girl was found slain, you were too busy with the corpse, or else you might have noticed Saeed and myself among the crowd of spectators. Or maybe not, as we had on chadors. When you connected the heroin so quickly to Najafi, Baraheni suggested you must be working with the smugglers. I had to remind him that you're a policeman trying to run down the drugs for legitimate ends, the same as we." Ashfar smiled; but not Djalilian, nor Baraheni, who shifted his grip to Darius's arms.

"Saeed and another friend were supposed to bring you here for a talk—not to beat you and leave you bleeding in the street because some people came by and frightened them off."

Knowing the answer, asking because it was expected of him and he was afraid to deviate from Ashfar's script, which so far as he could tell called for him to remain alive at least into the foreseeable future, Darius said, "What are you proposing?"

"Help us to put our hands on the drugs, and we'll bring you out of Iran with us."

"But who is going to prevent Baraheni from putting his hands on me?"

"You see, Saeed?" Baraheni said. "Even a murderer has compunctions."

"You will transport the heroin yourself," Ashfar said. "We trust you not to screw us out of it. Once you rejoin us in Paris, you'll be under the protection of French law. Until then, you are the law. Your well-being is not in such great jeopardy as you pretend. I would venture that you'd set other considerations aside if we could bestow a French visa on you, let alone asylum or citizenship."

A nerve rubbed raw transmitted the energy to break out of Baraheni's grasp. "Then we're agreed—what you're proposing is an impossibility," Darius said. "Be realistic, or let me go."

"Nothing is impossible." Ashfar snapped his fingers, then examined his empty hand like a conjurer who had made a ridiculously large object disappear in air. "We have access to excellent French ID; stolen and bought, not forged; driver's license, social insurance card, immigration papers, military discharge documents for a man of your age, general appearance, and background. Ever want to be in the French Foreign Legion when you were a kid? Here's your chance to be a bona fide Legion veteran entitled to all medical and legal benefits that go with twenty years' service. We can pull you out of this hellhole, and get you started on a new life in Europe with a tidy sum in the bank."

Darius pictured himself a retired Legionnaire crumpled in a Parisian alley with Baraheni's knife in his back, an expression of pained bewilderment combining his own cynic's distrust with Gallic resignation. "Up to now, you've been picking my brain," he said. "You haven't told me anything about the heroin."

"You're not in much of a position to make demands," Baraheni said.

"Bakhtiar never was one for jumping into the water without wetting a toe first, except, I suppose, when it came to Farmayan. What he's asking is not unreasonable." Ashfar refilled Baraheni's glass from the jar. "On approval," Ashfar said to Darius, "we will let you have the name of the girl shot to death with Najafi in south Teheran."

"You knew her?"

"Thanks to Saeed. We hadn't been in Teheran two days when we realized the people weren't ready to rise up against the fanatics. We were bored, disheartened, scared—I don't mind telling you; nursing our meager funds until something came along to make our mission worthwhile. Saeed alone was enjoying himself. He's from Isfahan, and this is his first time in the capital. He was out every day, taking in the sights, when he ran into a girl he had known at home. A drug dealer had captured her fancy, and quickly lost it, rather a repulsive fellow whose daily beatings were starting to wear on her. She asked Saeed if he wouldn't mind helping her to rob her boyfriend for fifty percent of the profits. Saeed didn't know what to make of it. Valuable time was lost before he passed on what she had said. A meeting was arranged for the Museum of Archaeology, where the girl told us Najafi was storing kilograms of Afghani heroin in his house—" A heavy object crashed to the floor upstairs. Djalilian would have snatched up the M-16 had Baraheni not beat him to it and put it out of reach. "This is not what we came to Iran for. It's the kind of thing we have been fighting all our lives. After much debate, we concluded the drugs were going to be sold in any event, and the greater evil would be to let the dealers have the proceeds. While we debated, others went into action. The night before the robbery was to take place Najafi and the girl were murdered, and the heroin apparently taken from its hiding place."

"You were inside the house?" Darius asked.

"Twice before the police. Once after."

"What did you find?"

"Not a thing." Ashfar took more vodka for himself. "Dope is a contemptible occupation. Already the smell of shit is on us. But if we don't turn up the heroin ourselves it is going to the U.S. and the money to the fanatics, and better we should stink from that than they. If you come over to our side, you will be treated as an equal partner. If not, if you get to the drugs ahead of us and return them to the Komiteh, it will be on *your* conscience. Are you listening?"

Ashfar waited to hear his answer. Darius waited with him.

"I'll take that for a yes," Ashfar said abruptly. "The girl's name is—was Sousan Hovanian, a Christian, originally from the Armenian quarter of Isfahan, where her parents are caretakers of the Vank Cathedral. She was twenty-three. Any more questions, save them; you know as much as we. More . . ."

Marched upstairs with the blanket over his head, Darius listened in vain for the voices he had heard through the ceiling. Djalilian went with him into the back of the ambulance, and to guard him against his guard so did Baraheni. As they retraced a twisting route into the heights, Baraheni regaled the younger man with stories of how he had disposed of the shah's enemies, the expedient murders of left-wingers pinned on Muslim zealots of the right, who then were tortured to death for refusing to confess to crimes about which they knew nothing. His intended audience was Darius, who discounted the message of each grisly account. It was illogical for Ashfar to attempt to recruit him to locate the heroin and then order him slain while the offer stood. As illogical as shooting Najafi and Sousan Hovanian before they could tell where the drugs were to be found.

"Farmayan was a good friend of ours. Everybody in the bureau was shocked that he took a bullet without a fight." The voice was still Baraheni's, but directed at Darius it lacked humor. "It threw a fright into some of the weak sisters when they heard. They thought the fanatics had sent us a message. We knew better, Ashfar and me. To get close to him the killer had to be someone he knew. The part that gave us trouble was that you would have that much guts."

The blanket was torn from Darius's head, and he was looking into the black bores of two guns.

"Nice equipment," Baraheni said. He patted the weapons with the rough affection of a doctor delivering twins into a sorry world, and stuffed the barrels inside Darius's waistband.

The air sweetened as the way grew steeper. Darius tossed the blanket around his shoulders, but could not warm himself against a chill that had eaten into his bones. Soon the ambulance stopped, and the door was opened by the tall man who had gotten in the first lick when Darius was worked over in Shemiran. Keys were pressed into his hand, and his gunbelts slung over his arms. "Three from the corner," the tall man said, and pointed him at the curb.

Walking away into the darkness, Darius experienced the sensation of a bull's-eye burning into his back. Halogen beams washed over him like radar locking on to a target. The roar of the engine starting up again sent him diving between parked cars. As he fumbled for his guns, the ambulance raced down the center of the street. His Paycon was parked where the tall man had said it was. The ambulance ran a red light and disappeared while he jabbed the wrong key at the door.

He locked himself inside, and swept out the glove compartment for the flask that wasn't there. His guns had been returned with the clips intact, the firing chambers empty. He drove home to his new apartment composing the report of his kidnapping, reciting the details out loud because there was no one he could entrust them to. While Ashfar and Baraheni decided whether they wanted him silenced, it was worth more than his life to keep them out of the Komiteh's hands. One word that he had been in contact with SAVAK expatriates, and the Revolutionary Prosecutor would declare him in enmity with God, and corrupt on earth, crimes for which the penalty was crucifixion.

Vodka from the freezer took some of the chill out of his bones. He asked the long-distance operator to connect him with the National Police in Isfahan. "Isfahan is half the world" had been common wisdom since the sixteenth century, when the city was the grandest in Persia. Tonight, with phone service cut off, the ancient capital might as well have been on another planet. The smart thing would be to have Bijan put the Komiteh in Isfahan to work confirming Sousan Hovanian's identity. But that was the smart thing. A better thing was the vodka. He fell asleep clutching its dregs to his chest.

He was up at 5:00. He showered, and because it was the sabbath, made a concession to the new reality by not shaving. In an hour he was at police headquarters. He teletyped a request to Isfahan for information about Sousan Hovanian, then went downstairs where Ghaffari was waiting to drive him to congregational prayers at the University of Teheran.

Basijis armed with German G-3 automatic rifles ushered them inside the walled campus. In a plaza the size of several soccer fields tens of thousands of men knelt on prayer rugs toward an unadorned stage. The delegation from the National Police were clustered in the shadow of a television camera platform. At the end of the row of the newest recruits Darius set down a white prayer stone that was his last birthday present from Farib. After attendance was taken he would leave early, as he always did, pleading the demands of a major investigation.

The stage was a breakwater in a khaki sea buffeted by a tide of white turbans. A crater in the concrete near the Foundation of the Oppressed and Deprived memorialized the worshipers killed when a Khalq Fedayeen guer-rilla had blown himself to bits with TNT several years before. An ayatollah from Shiraz, whom Darius had never heard of, was imploring the faithful to donate blood for Lebanese Shi'ites battling surrogates of the Zionists south of the Litani River. He was followed to the rostrum by Ayatollah Maraghehni, the head of the Supreme Judicial Council, who pledged to the crowd that the government had no intention of restoring relations with the United States.

"We have welcomed the severance of ties, and this is the word of the Imam, officials, parliament deputies, and people from various walks of life. Global arrogance led by the Great Satan lacks wisdom. In their unmanly propaganda the Americans have defamed us before world public opinion, and have introduced Iran and every other revolutionary country as suppor-ters of kidnapping and have thus deceived many a country into believing this."

Darius wondered what he had been deceived into believing about his murder case, the absurdities he had clung to because a false trail under his feet was less frightening than a free-fall through a void. The evidence alone didn't lie, but much of it had nothing to say, not to him. With dental records unobtainable for Sousan Hovanian, he would pay from his own pocket to bring a relative to Teheran for a look at the body, and to prolong the illusory comfort of gradual progress. The heat reflected off the plaza's bare walls gathered like dust in the prayer rugs. It boiled the alcoholic sweat from his body, which he was determined to replace at the first opportunity. Ayatollah Maraghehni finished his sermon on the Great Satan, and launched into another.

"We guarantee the people the administration of justice and equity in every aspect of social and economic life. The laws of the state look at wrongdoers and offenders with the same eye irrespective of their social position. It has been brought to our attention that miscreants in the army, the bureaucracy, and most notably the National Police have escaped punishment for long-standing misdeeds that demand retribution. Rest assured that the law will catch up to all transgressors, including those who believe that, because they are charged with enforcing it, they are outside its reach."

The entire line of recruits turned toward Darius. He faced them down with a stare borrowed from Ashfar until they bowed their heads in a prayer that was neither to him, nor for him, but a plea to God just to make him look away.

The ayatollah stopped for a drink of water, and resumed less stridently. "I want to laud the teachers of the nation on the occasion of National Teacher Week, and to pay tribute to the educator at so many madresehs and the University of Teheran, Ayatollah Motaharri, who was martyred in this city on May 2, 1980 . . ."

A martyr's death was the highest honor the regime could accord. A hypocrite's death was the greatest disgrace. In between, thought Darius, was the living death that was his. He clenched the prayer stone in his fist. The clay shattered into gritty dust that seeped through his fingers. Somewhere, he had heard that the summer temperature in Paris never went much above eighty degrees.

· 8 ·

Saturday morning, when Homicide normally was held down by a lone recruit, Darius was at his desk by 8:00. Within the hour Isfahan called, a Sergeant Kamoushi reporting that Sousan Hovanian was unknown to the National Police in that city.

"Did you send a man to the Christian quarter?"

"We never went to Jolfa when we were five hundred strong," Kamoushi said. "Now that we are fewer than forty officers, I can't waste one on the pork eaters. Let them kill themselves for all I care."

Jolfa, Darius remembered from three days in Isfahan with a SAVAK tribunal investigating a counterfeiting ring, was the old Armenian neighborhood where the Christians who had built much of the city were segregated from the believers across the Zayendah River. "Until they do," he said, "I must insist that the request for information on the girl be honored."

"I will ask for her birth certificate," Kamoushi said uncomfortably. "But it will be several weeks before you have it, if at all."

It took twenty minutes to establish another connection to Isfahan, half an hour before Darius was put through to Vank Cathedral and the caretaker called to the phone.

"Hello, what do you want with me?" Maria Hovanian asked in a voice as fragile as the wires that transmitted it.

117

"I'm calling about your daughter, Sousan . . ." Darius accepted the woman's silence as assent to continue, but gently. "We have reason to believe she may recently have been in Teheran."

"Sousan? My Sousan is a child. She never leaves my side." Maria Hovanian laughed uneasily. "What do the police in Teheran want with my little Sousan?"

The same sick feeling that seized his guts Darius sensed tightening its grip on the woman. "I'm sorry to have bothered you," he said. "I made a mistake."

"What about this Sousan?"

"Never mind. I'm glad to say it doesn't concern you."

"Please, I would like to know."

"Very well," Darius said. "A woman with the same name as your little girl was found murdered in Teheran. It's plainly a case of mistaken identity."

"How old was she?"

Static crackled on the line. "What?" Darius said. "I can't hear."

"How old was this Sousan Hovanian?"

"About thirty."

"Once, I had another Sousan. She was my eldest, a secretary in the National Committee for Health Planning." The poor connection didn't mask Maria Hovanian's struggle against tears. "When the Revolution came, she lost her job. They said to her there was no place for a Christian in the government of the Islamic Republic. Sousan sat doing nothing in the house, except for several hours every day when she went to the cathedral to help us clean, and to pray to the Blessed Mother. After two years, her prayers were answered. The Blessed Mother told Sousan to convert to Islam, things would be better. Sousan became Muslim and went to live on the other side of the river. Ten months later, my other Sousan was born. My Sousan is . . . would be her sister."

The woman paused to take a mouthful of air.

"Conversion wasn't enough for Sousan. She needed to show the people of her new faith that she was as observant as they, that she was more religious than God. She joined the Isfahan Pasdar, and went looking for bad hejabis. One day she went out with them as usual, and vanished. My late husband spoke to the Komiteh more times than I can remember. They didn't know where Sousan was, they told him, and it would be better if he stopped bothering them. He reported her missing to the police, but we never heard anything from them either."

"The National Police in Isfahan?"

"Yes," the woman said.

"They have no record for her."

To talk to a stranger was to dare trouble for an unbeliever. To talk openly to the authorities was to encourage it. Mrs. Hovanian shouted her defiance: "Why would I lie to you?"

Why hadn't she, thought Darius, when no one had been truthful with her, not even the mother of the prophet she worshiped as God.

"I have good reason to believe the woman found dead in Teheran is your daughter," he said. "Will you accept a bus ticket and come here to identify her?"

"No."

"Mrs. Hovanian—"

"I mourned long enough. I won't begin again."

"Can you send us her photograph? Even one old picture might be useful."

"Take them all," Maria Hovanian said. "I haven't looked at them since she went. It's more than I can bear to dream of her."

When he arrived at headquarters at noon the next day, a package wrapped in newspaper was sitting on his desk. Hamid followed him into the office accompanied by a clean-shaven man of about seventy, whose fine white hair curled over gnarled ears and flounced against his forehead.

"Mr. Garabedian is from Isfahan," Hamid said. "He won't let anyone open it but you. It might not be a bad idea to have it X-rayed."

"I come to Teheran each week to visit my son," the old man said. "Maria Hovanian told me to see the parcel personally into your hands. The mails—" He made a spitting sound. "They are worse than useless."

Darius sent him away with a thousand-rial note pressed into his palm. The newspaper was taped around three black-and-white photographs of a pleasant-looking girl with large, liquid eyes. The blurred background was an unrecognizable expanse of beach crowded with bathers in rubber caps. The girl, no more than fourteen or fifteen, was wearing a modest one-piece swimsuit that would have landed her in jail had she shown herself in it since the Revolution. On the back of each photo was written *Sousan Hovanian, summer 1975.* A magnifying glass brought out the girl's begrudging smile, but not Darius's conviction that he had seen her face before. The bland optimism of the pretty teenager was long gone from the woman found shot to death in the Shush Avenue dope den. Maria Hovanian could not have provided pictures more ill-suited for identifying a murder victim had she selected some of Sousan in a chador.

The phone rang. A fit of coughing answered Darius's quick hello. He pulled the receiver from his ear and listened from a distance to Dr. Baghai's raspy, "Bakhtiar?"

"I was about to call you," Darius said. "I've obtained pictures of the girl I believe was killed with Khalil Pakravan. They're not the best, but—" Darius thought it out of character for the coroner not to have interrupted to correct him about something. "This doesn't concern her?"

"No," Baghai said. "We've been able to determine conclusively the cause of death of the other woman, Leila Darwish."

"Poisoning, as you suspected?"

"It's not something that can be explained over the phone." The coughing began again, harsher. "I'm at my place in Jamshidabad, near the old race course at Elizabeth II Boulevard, or whatever it is they call it these days. Come over right away."

The road was a speedway for fire engines. Darius placed a blue flasher on the dashboard and pulled close behind a tank truck, drafted it to a communal bathhouse off Englehaab Avenue that was engulfed in a cyclone of flame. Screaming sirens bled into the hysteria of women crying their pain to whoever would listen. The women beat their breasts wandering dazed and blind, or crouched on the sidewalk, while those too badly burned or injured lay moaning among rows of corpses. Swarms of children shrieking for their mothers ran through the inconsolable mob. The block was ringed by Revolutionary Guards, Uzis leveled at a crowd of spectators.

As Darius got out of his car, a section of blackened tile crashed down on a young mother cradling a toddler in her lap. The woman toppled over dead, and the child fell on his head and went into convulsions under her body. Darius ran onto the sidewalk. A Guardsman rammed a rifle into his chest, and drove him off the curb. "Stay back," he commanded.

Darius pushed his ID at the Guardsman, who batted it away with his gunstock. Darius drew back a fist, and was grabbed from behind and wrestled into the gutter.

"Let go," he yelled. "The baby—"

"You can't do anything for him." A firefighter in a coal scuttle hardhat pinned Darius's arms behind his back. "The Komiteh has given orders to shoot anyone who tries to help."

"What? Are they out of their minds?"

"The women who were in the baths . . . many were naked; none are properly dressed. The Guardsmen say it is worse for them to be seen like that than to die in the fire."

Darius quit struggling. The sirens relented, and brownish smoke lifted anguished sobs through the bathhouse's torn skylight.

"The building is very old," the fireman went on, "at least one hundred and fifty years. Not twenty minutes ago, when the baths were filled with women and little children, the floor gave way. Many of the bathers fell through to the furnace used to make the hot water. Few were uninjured. There are scores of them still trapped in the basement. We pulled out eleven women and fourteen children before the Guardsmen forced us out . . ."

Darius stood out of the way as other firefighters trained hoses on the blaze. The weak flow from the tankers was overmatched by flames feeding on the wood framework of the structure. The bathhouse burned to the level of the street before disintegrating into the basement, where the fire was extinguished in huge cisterns and pools of water.

It was a numbness of the spirit that kept him there. Was there any nation but his that valued the modesty of its women above the sanctity of their lives? What men were so shamed by their obsessions that they had invented a God to quell the instincts that made them human? In the middle of an idea he switched his thoughts to English, distinguishing himself however little from the mob. Another fire engine pulled up, and he turned quickly away, fearful that the face he would see reflected in the polished brass was no different from the rest.

The women's screams followed him back to his car. Shutting the windows served only to trap the horror inside with him. He continued north spinning the knob on the dead radio, racing the engine to drown it out.

Baghai lived in an apartment house erected in the 1950s, before the new construction code had been drawn. It was of a common design put together around a flimsy skeleton of light steel I-beams, defying earthquakes and gravity on the integrity of the pasty mortar between the bricks. Darius had seen more than one building like it collapse without warning, perhaps nudged by the breeze, the floors sloughing off like pancakes on a tilted platter. Entering one filled him with the same apprehension he experienced each time he belted himself into a plane.

Yet the electricity rarely went out in Jamshidabad, which was several blocks north of the University of Teheran, and Baghai's elevator most always was in service. Out of habit he took the stairs to the third story, to a dark studio that reeked of the morgue. Darius was undecided whether Baghai brought the smell home in his clothes, or if he had captured it in the medicine bottles covering a table beside the convertible sofa on which he lay on his back like a frail, invalid bird.

"Are you trying to scare me?" Darius asked him. "Or do you really feel as bad as you look?"

"Pull up a chair, and be quiet."

"You're not up to this. Call me at the homicide bureau when you're better. We can talk more comfortably over the phone."

"But not so privately. My telephone is tapped, and eavesdroppers are everywhere. And there are things that should go no further than you and I." Baghai pushed himself into a sitting position. "Have you learned enough about Leila Darwish to tell if she had been anywhere near Indochina?"

"That's a peculiar question."

"Answer it anyway."

"The final months of her life were spent in a guerrilla camp in Lebanon with occasional excursions through the Middle East and possibly into Africa. I've heard nothing about Indochina. Why do you want to know?"

Baghai's body was racked with coughing. He pointed to the table, and Darius uncapped a bottle of red fluid that the coroner measured on his tongue and swallowed. Another spasm shook him, and then he lay back, exhausted.

"It was a hunch I had—" The stink of the morgue was on Baghai's breath. "I sent specimens from her body to the laboratory we usually use for that kind of work. The lab was not qualified to perform the necessary tests, and I had to send them to place after place until I found one that could do what I wanted. By the time the results came back, I was sick, and didn't learn until this morning that the cause of her death was mycotoxin poisoning."

Darius looked at him blankly.

"Mycotoxins are a rare strain of poison produced by certain fungi, in this case grass or wheat fungi, which prevent human body cells from manufacturing protein. In sufficient dosage death is the result."

"How much is sufficient?"

"A very, very, very small amount."

"How did the mycotoxins get into Leila Darwish's system?"

"I can't tell you."

"Well, who would have had enough to prepare a lethal dose?"

"Another mystery," Baghai said. "I know little about them, and most of that comes from a single article I recalled seeing in a scholarly journal several months ago. The article was written by a pharmacologist from the Poison Unit at the Imam Reza Medical Center at Mashad Medical Sciences University, in Mashad, whose previous fame had rested as coauthor of a study on the effects of mustard gas."

"He did the lab work for you?"

Baghai coughed into a tissue, and crumpled it under the pillow. ". . . Some other medical school. He refused to acknowledge my request."

"And there's no indication of how the poison was administered?"

"None at all," Baghai said. "That's why I asked if the girl had been in Southeast Asia. You see, in the early 1980s, the U.S. Defense Department charged that the Soviets had supplied mycotoxins to the communist forces in Laos, who used them as chemical weapons against the Hmong tribespeople allied with the Americans. People coming into contact with the substance developed headaches, nausea, skin sores, intestinal bleeding, and difficulty in breathing before ultimately dying. Whole villages were wiped out, their populations eradicated. But in the confusion of war, and the remoteness of the area, few reports of mass death reached the attention of the world press. The Hmong, those who survived, called the goo they found spattered on the devastated villages 'yellow rain.' Biologists in Canada and Malaysia scoffed at the U.S. claims, asserting the yellow was in reality the droppings of giant Asian honeybees, *Apis dorsata*, which swarm over the countryside on extremely hot nights in mass defecation flights."

"Mass what . . . ?"

"The bees' larvae are sensitive to temperatures above ninety-two degrees Fahrenheit. During these flights the bees shed about twenty percent of their body weight, and thus are able to cool themselves and their hives. The skeptics insisted that mycotoxins were next to useless as chemical weaponry because they are hard to work with, and not nearly so effective as, say, various nerve gasses—or mustard gas."

Baghai reached for a paper cup. Darius carried it into the kitchen alcove and brought it back with a pitcher of ice water.

"Those are skeptics," Baghai went on. "Among realists are U.S. scientists who obtained samples of yellow rain from leaves and rocks and in water collected near battle sites in Laos. Analysis determined them to be a chemical called T-2, a mycotoxin that is a product of a common mold which often contaminates cereal grains. Later, the Americans obtained a Soviet gas mask which contained a spot of T-2. The conclusion was that the Russians were employing mycotoxins in a test program of new chemical agents in conflict situations." Baghai's body shook again, and Darius guided the cup to his mouth. "In this part of the world there has been recent talk of Iraq rebuilding improved stores of chemical agents that were ruined in the war with the Americans. After the combat, you may remember, United Nations inspectors destroyed a gun barrel not quite a meter in diameter and forty meters long that would have enabled the Iraqis to hurl chemical shells as far as northern Israel and eastern Iran. If they are producing mycotoxins in large amounts, millions of people throughout the Middle East are in jeopardy of a hideous death at the whim of the madman Saddam."

Darius helped him to settle into a more comfortable position, and tossed a blanket over him. But for the feverish warmth of his body, and the constant movement of his hands, the coroner was indistinguishable from one of his clients.

"Based on what I've been able to find out, Leila Darwish was nowhere near Iraq," Darius said. "Still, I'd like more information about mycotoxins. The girl was of Iraqi descent."

"The name of the pharmacologist credited with the article I read is Dr. Manuchehr Karrubi. He may be more forthcoming with the police than he was with the coroner's office."

"What about the woman murdered near Shush Avenue?" Darius asked. "Did you have her body tested for the poison?"

"The findings were negative. The bullet in her face wasn't put there for effect."

Darius showed him the photos from Isfahan. "Are these suitable for positive identification of the victim? They're more than ten years old, closer to fifteen."

Baghai stood the pictures upright among the vials of pills. "I'll be back to the office before the end of the week. As it turns out I have bacterial pneumonia, which kills as quickly as mycotoxin poisoning, but usually is curable when treated in time. We'll see then."

"It can't wait," Darius said. "Tell your assistants to allow me access to the body."

"You're not competent to make a ruling."

"It's her. All I want is another look, to satisfy myself."

The phone was ringing. Baghai's elbow cleared the table of bottles as he grabbed for it. "He is," he said, and handed over the receiver. "Lieutenant Ghaffari has been looking all over for you."

"You have leads?" Darius said by way of hello.

"No, I— This is more important. Otherwise I wouldn't have bothered you."

"What, then? A new load of bootleg? This month's *Penthouse?*"

"I'm serious," Ghaffari said. "It's about life and death—mostly death."

"Whose?"

"Mine, unless you help. I have to see you."

"Meet me at the morgue in an hour."

"What better place . . . ?"

Baghai was standing medicine vials on end when Darius gave back the phone. "Tell the interns I'm coming by with the lieutenant. I'll call later to let you know what I've concluded."

As Baghai replaced the receiver, his arm swept the table clean again. "What makes you think I'm interested in the opinion of amateurs?"

Desert wind had wafted the smell of the fire all the way to Jamshidabad. Darius followed the spoor downtown to Englehaab Avenue. Mounds of debris had been bulldozed onto the sidewalk in front of the water-filled pit where the bathhouse had been, scorched towels, and sheets, and canvas wet wash carts, a jumble of women's clothing on a pyre of shattered tile and black timbers topped by a sodden, headless teddy bear. A lone fire truck stood guard over the sizzling rubble. Darius slowed to peer into the foundation at a molten tangle of lead plumbing.

Ghaffari's life-and-death problem could be written off in advance as girlfriend trouble. The road focused his thoughts again on Leila Darwish. Had the nascent Arab nationalist established ties with Baghdad? Was her service as a drug courier for the Revolutionary Guards a screen for activities as an Iraqi agent? A yes to both questions still did not explain how she had become exposed to mycotoxins, or whether the poisons were being developed for chemical warfare by Iran's enemies. Better for all concerned that she had been targeted by a swarm of giant bees. But, then, why was he the one who had ended up in shit?

The morgue was under siege by ambulances backed up around the block. Spotting Ghaffari parked across the street, he wheeled into a neat U-turn and pulled up alongside him.

"It's a madhouse." Darius was watching the loading platform, where an intern who needed to make up a week's lost sleep was directing the bodies of the fire victims inside. "I'll have to come back later."

Ghaffari slipped into the passenger's seat, and went immediately for the bottle in the glove compartment.

"Who is she?" Darius asked. "A foreign tourist? One of your old flames?"

Ghaffari looked at him so unhappily that Darius considered it a personality defect that he was unable to feel sympathy for a friend.

"It's Sharera." Sharera was Ghaffari's wife, whom he had met through an introduction arranged by Farib. "She's making all kinds of unreasonable demands."

"What does she want?"

"She wants me dead," Ghaffari said. "She's found out about my latest affair."

Darius groaned.

"You, too? Really, what's the big deal? The girl was just young stuff that I—" He appealed hopefully to Darius, whose expression hadn't changed except to calcify around the edges. "She was nothing. But Sharera is blowing it up into something huge, and is threatening to turn me in to the Komiteh." He unscrewed the cap from the bottle. "I don't deserve this."

Ghaffari's gaze shifted to the morgue, where the line of bodies had turned the corner. He pointed to an empty litter mixed in with the others. "There," he said, "that spot is reserved for me. I need a ticket out of this crazy country."

"What you need is a lock on your zipper." Darius took back the vodka. "Do you know what they're handing out these days for adultery? One hundred lashes. And that's if they're being lenient. Last month, the Zahedan Penal Court approved a death sentence for a nineteen-year-old girl who had slept one time with her husband's younger brother."

"Please, don't give me any more good news."

"Under the new law the penalty for a married man having sexual relations with a woman other than his wife—"

"You sound like a lawyer."

"I *am* a lawyer," Darius said. ". . . is death by stoning. 'The condemned shall be hooded and partially buried in the vertical position,'" he recited, "'men up to the waist, and women up to the chest. The executioners shall circle the condemned and throw stones at them. The stones should not be too large so that the person dies on being hit by one or two of them, and they should not be so small either that they could not be defined as stones . . .'"

"Are you trying to scare me out of fooling around? I'm already scared. See—" Ghaffari snatched the bottle, and brought it to his mouth. "My hand is shaking."

"Will the girl confess three times in court?" Darius asked.

"Huh? She's not a mental case."

"Does Sharera have four male eyewitnesses?"

". . . nor an exhibitionist."

"Does Sharera have eight female eyewitnesses?"

"Like I said—"

"Then the burden of proof remains with Sharera," Darius said. "The odds of such a sentence being returned against a male defendant are about a million to one. It's just something for you to think about."

"It's *all* I've been thinking about. If Sharera goes to the Komiteh, there's an excellent chance I'll lose my job. Worse, Nahid's family are from a powerful clan in Qashqa'i, and I'll have her brothers, her uncles, her cousins gunning for me. You don't know these Qashqa'is. They're primitive people. They shit behind their tent and scrape dirt over it like a dog. They'll hang my nuts from their camel saddles if word of this gets out."

"What do you want me to do?"

"Speak with Sharera. She respects you, she hangs on every word that passes your lips."

"That may have been, before the divorce. She probably hates my guts now."

"Not so much," Ghaffari said. "Someone has to talk sense to her. Have I ever asked you for anything?"

Darius looked across the street. The line of bodies was endless. The young doctor who had come outside to supervise the loading dock had broken down in tears. Darius took a long pull on the bottle, and locked it in the glove compartment, then sprinted away from the curb.

Ghaffari's small single-story house was set behind an ivy-covered wall in a neighborhood near the Azadi monument in the western part of the city that had not changed in twenty years. Its four rooms were furnished in the old style with cushions and pillows on the floors, which were layered with Hamadan carpets that had been in Ghaffari's mother's family for generations. A low table in the living room supported a twenty-seven-inch color television and a vase containing a single dog rose. The door was opened by a little girl in a floral-patterned indoor chador who ran into her father's arms and was covered with his kisses. Over Ghaffari's shoulder she eyed Darius as though he were a child molester. Shahla was nine years old, the legal mature age for a female, and thus obligated to wear the veil.

"Where's your mother?" Ghaffari asked her.

"In the garden," she said, suddenly bored. "Digging."

"Tell her I've brought home company, and then you can go out to play."

Shahla took off her chador and whipped it into a corner. Underneath she had on pink-and-yellow spandex shorts and a striped polo shirt. Soon a woman came into the house munching on a cucumber. When she saw Darius, she let her veil fall down around her neck. Darius took her right hand to kiss, but she pulled it away and whisked invisible dirt off her knuckles.

"It's been too long since we've had the pleasure of a visit from you," she said.

Sharera had been Farib's friend when they were growing up together in Pol-e-Rumi in north Teheran. Darius still thought of her as a robust, athletic teenager who spent summers on the tennis courts and her winters skiing on Mount Dizin. After the Revolution, tennis was forbidden to women because the skimpy outfits revealed too much of their arms and legs. The ski slopes were segregated by sex to prevent collisions between the sexes. Sharera seemed to have shrunk and put on weight at the same time. Gardening did not burn as many calories as active sports.

"Sharera," Ghaffari said, "bring us melon, some tea."

"Please don't bother," Darius said. "I can't stay long."

"He's asked you to be our marriage counselor, hasn't he, Darius? He said he would do it." Sharera had given up her feeble pretense that she was happy to see him. "There's nothing to discuss. I've warned him time and time again that I won't put up with his fooling around, and yet he insists on seeing other women. I don't want to press charges, but what alternative do I have?"

"Mansur has given me his promise that he will stop." Even to him it sounded inane. He might as well be telling the wife of an alcoholic that her husband had pledged never to take another drink. "Isn't that right, Mansur?"

Ghaffari nodded forlornly.

"I've heard those words one hundred times. A thousand," Sharera said. "They mean nothing."

"You know what the revolutionary courts will do to him?"

"Not nearly enough."

How had he been trapped in the middle of this domestic bloodletting when he could be enjoying an afternoon at the morgue? He would run from the house if it didn't mean possibly losing his only experienced investigator. "That's one way of looking at it," he said. "But do you have any idea of how it will affect you and Shahla? Do you understand the disgrace attached to being an adulterer's wife?"

"Understand?" She had begun to shout. She glanced out the window at the little girl playing in the yard, and immediately lowered her voice. "Who understands better than I? I've made a career of it—a life. No, Darius, I've thought it out and, painful as it will be, anything is better than constant humiliation. Last month, he gave me a disease. Did he tell you that, the great lover?"

Ghaffari went into the kitchen. He came back with a fifth of Chivas Regal, and poured it over the lip of a shot glass.

"Sixty-five thousand rials for that bottle," she said. "He has plenty of money for his pleasures. How much do you think he has for his wife and daughter?"

Darius felt himself becoming envious of Ghaffari. Rather than turn away from her husband, retire to the baths and the company of friends, Sharera would battle to keep her marriage. Unlike Farib, she remained a modern woman—in spite of the chador, a feminist.

"I can't allow you to do it," he said, "no matter that Mansur deserves it. I'll vouch for him. If he goes back on his promise, I'll make him suffer so, he'll wish the Komiteh had him."

"I don't know why you bothered to come, or why I'm listening." Sharera paused, and the room filled with the sound of her breathing. She looked toward the window again, and then stood with her back to it. "Okay, I won't do anything this time, but if I find out he's been with a woman again, you'll pay, Darius, just as though you'd slept with her yourself, and it was we who are married."

Ghaffari, watching her stalk out of the room, put a glass in Darius's hand, and filled it. "What a funny thing for her to say."

Darius savored the flavor of the premium scotch as Ghaffari stared at him with his head cocked.

"My God, Mansur, you're jealous."

Ghaffari tossed down the remainder of his drink.

"I'm not sleeping with Sharera," Darius said. "If I was, she'd want to turn me in, too."

Ghaffari put his arm around Darius's shoulder, and kissed his cheek. "What you did for me . . . in more ways than one, you saved my life."

"I don't know what for."

"Neither do I, not if I can't have Nahid." Ghaffari looked at Darius to see if it was all right to smile, and thought better of it. "Let's go back."

The Paycon's battery was dead. Ghaffari jump-started it from his old Plymouth, and they headed east.

"Baghai thinks Leila Darwish was poisoned by her killer," Darius said.

"Tortured, shot, filled with drugs, poisoned," Ghaffari said. "This case has everything."

"Except good clues." Darius showed him the photos from Isfahan.

"Who's the kid?"

"Sousan Hovanian, when she was maybe fourteen," Darius said. "I want another look at the body."

Ghaffari grunted and turned his attention to the traffic. As they came to Hafez Avenue, he glanced toward the facade of the dowdy Park Hotel, Teheran's oldest. "You can let me out here."

Darius touched the brake. "Why? Do you need to use the bathroom?"

"Don't ask questions. Just do it."

"What's gotten into you?"

"There you go again, damn it."

Darius drove up to the curb, and Ghaffari started out of the car. "I can never repay you for—"

"You have a date," Darius said.

"It's almost a week since I've been with Nahid. The Park is the only place where we . . . where she feels safe seeing me."

Darius angled away from the sidewalk. The door swung in against Ghaffari's knee.

"Ow, what are you doing?"

"Didn't you hear what I told Sharera? I gave her your word, *my* word, you'd quit."

"It's the last time, I swear," Ghaffari pleaded. "Just to tell Nahid good-bye. I can't leave her waiting in the lobby. She'll worry, she'll get into big trouble. The hotel will report her."

"They'll report her to *us*."

Darius sped into traffic, which pulled them away from the hotel. Sulking, Ghaffari opened the flapping door wide, and then slammed it shut. The bodies were gone from the streets around the morgue. Darius was reminded of a theater that had put on a late show to accommodate crowds for a surprise hit.

A new odor stood out from the chemical stew of the autopsy room, a smoky essence that was the flavor of the day. The intern Darius had seen weeping on the loading dock, a Dr. Kashfi, looked up at the detectives from a slab where a boy about four years old lay with his internal organs exposed to bright light like an intimate secret betrayed. Humming tunelessly, he unlocked a refrigerator unit, and wheeled out a steel gurney. "This is her," he said, and went back to the slab.

The photo of Sousan Hovanian fluttered to the tile floor as Darius lifted a green sheet. The body was shriveled and black. A point of bone protruded from a disintegrating chin where the girl's face had begun to slough off the skull. One of her breasts was as firm, as well shaped, as . . . inviting, he thought, as in life. The other was putrid flesh eaten around to the ribs by maggots.

"How was this allowed to happen?" he demanded.

Kashfi hunched lower over the child's body, and buried his head in the Y-shaped incision. "There have been power outages all summer," he said, and "there's no money for gas for the emergency generator. There's nothing we can do for the bodies we don't get to right away, but hope they don't spoil before the electricity comes back on. It's why I'm working late tonight."

"Let me see the laboratory report on Leila Darwish," Darius said, "and everything you have on this girl."

Kashfi wiped his hands on his gown. He went into the coroner's office, came back quickly with two folders.

The newest entry in the Darwish file was a letter from a pathologist at a clinical testing lab. Darius had a hard time penetrating the medicalese, which seemed to say that although the doctors could not state with one hundred percent certainty that Leila Darwish had succumbed to mycotoxin poisoning because they never had encountered a case before, the evidence indicated to their satisfaction that that was what had killed her. As Darius looked inside the other file, Ghaffari burped into his cupped hand.

"Get some air," Darius told him. "You're green."

"Blue," Ghaffari said. "What have you got there?"

"The autopsy report on Khalil Pakravan's girlfriend." Darius pulled out a color Polaroid. "When was this picture taken?" he asked Kashfi. "I've never seen it."

"I shot it myself," the young doctor said proudly. "I'm photographing every cadaver as they come in, until the power problem is rectified."

Darius put the photos from Isfahan on the slab beside the Polaroid. The Shush Avenue victim appeared years younger than in her picture, as though it were the parts of her face weakened by the process of aging that had been the first to decompose. From the contour of the head, the general configuration of features, a pronounced widow's peak on the low hairline, and the European roundness of shallow-set eyes, he was convinced the dead girl was Sousan Hovanian.

"What do you think?"

Ghaffari nodded grimly. "She's the missing piece in the puzzle, the link between Leila Darwish and her killer, and what became of the heroin."

Darius switched off the light over the body, and Kashfi returned it to the refrigerator unit.

"This is the break we needed," Ghaffari said. "It's just a matter of time until the pieces fall into place."

Darius shook his head.

"No?" Ghaffari said. "She's not?"

"Nothing falls into place unless we put it there. And I don't see our next move."

❖ 9 ❖

S leepers were available by reservation only on the night flier to Mashad. Darius purchased a second-class seat, and entered a stifling compartment occupied by a mullah in a black turban. To while away the fifteen-hour ride to Iran's second holiest city, nine hundred kilometers northeast of Teheran, he had brought along the back issue of the *Journal of the Iranian Research Organization for Science and Technology* featuring an article by Professor Manuchehr Karrubi on "New Developments in the Application of Mycotoxins for the Suppression of the Immune System in Human Organ Transplants." As the station began to sneak away from them, the mullah opened a greasy paper bag of nuts and raisins, and offered some to Darius.

"You are possibly European?" he asked.

Darius nudged the bag back toward its owner. "What makes you say that?"

"The way you are dressed, and your taste in literature." The mullah showed Darius his own reading, the *Epic of the Kings*, by the tenth-century Persian poet Firdowsi. "It is not unusual to see foreign tourists at this time of year. Unbelievers are not encouraged at Imam Reza's shrine in early summer, and what other reason can there be to make such a long, hot journey?"

While Darius read, the mullah dozed until the evening call to prayer, when he dropped to his knees facing the rear of the train and, at an oblique angle beyond that, Mecca. After prayers, dinner was announced. Darius waited till most of the passengers had returned to their compartments before going to the dining car. The menu was limited to cello khoresh, lamb on a bed of rice topped with a spicy vegetable-and-meat sauce flavored with walnuts. Though he was hungry, he kept walking to the lavatory at the end of the car. Inside his jacket was a rare bottle of Caviar brand vodka that he had found hidden among his old clothes when he moved. Caviar brand was a light Iranian vodka that had sold for about three dollars a fifth before the Revolution shuttered the distillery, and which had inflated in cost at a rate exceeded only by black market dollars. He drank standing over the toilet, which was stopped up with an empty pint bottle of bootleg not good enough to piss Caviar onto, although that was what he did.

At ten, two hours late, the train pulled into the station in the northeast corner of Mashad. Sharing his taxi downtown was the mullah from his compartment, who would not think of allowing him to his destination without a glimpse of the golden dome and turquoise blue cupola of the shrine of Imam Reza that was the focal point of the summer pilgrimages.

The mullah left the cab at the old bazaar and disappeared in a sea of weathered Mongol faces, of men in the baggy, pajamalike pants of central Asia and Afghanistan, and women wearing blue chadors. Darius instructed the driver to take him east from the city. The Imam Reza Medical Center was housed in a grimy brick building in the center of a grimy brick complex that had been a large factory. Darius left the cab along the access road, and proceeded on foot to a double chain link fence topped with concertina wire. In a corner of a flat expanse of land in which nothing grew a backhoe scooped out the pebbly soil and crafted it into low mounds. Darius watched as the bucket of the backhoe carried the remains of several lambs and young goats to an open trench perpendicular to the fence. None of the animals appeared healthy. Many were deformed, if not mutants, the fur discolored and the raw flesh blistered, in some cases eaten through to the bone. A pink umbrella shielded the operator of the backhoe from the sun. He was a totally bald man, without eyebrows, lashes, or hair anywhere on his pitted cheeks, and he wore a surgical mask over his mouth and nose. As he pulled away from the fence, he squinted at Darius with a lone, milky eye.

Darius cut back through a wooded area to the main entrance of the medical center, and showed his police identification to a guard. He was brought into the lobby and told to take a seat and wait. He waited—ten minutes in alert anticipation, and after that lost in thought, a wide-eyed sleep from which he was summoned when his name was called by a red-haired young man who brought him to the elevator. His escort was slim, in his late twenties or early thirties. He was wearing a lab coat speckled with scorch marks either from a caustic chemical, or the harsh TIR cigarettes that he smoked furiously, racing to consume as many as he could before they were outlawed as the health hazard they obviously were.

A black skull and crossbones was stenciled on the wall of the top-story corridor through which cool air was propelled by a series of hissing vents. Skylights angling upward from the dark ceiling allowed dusty light into an otherwise modern laboratory. The red-haired man flicked a fingernail against a beaker on a centrifuge, and then started the machine by whacking it. The noise it made, or his unhurried manner, made Darius's skull throb where the stitches had been. "I don't have all day," he said. "Tell Dr. Karrubi I'm here."

"I am Dr. Karrubi."

He turned up the flame under an alembic, then brought Darius into a windowless office cooled by floor fans in three corners, and leaned against the edge of his desk. On the walls, among framed degrees from German universities, was a photo of the Imam in his student days at Qom glowering at the camera. "What information have you come for all this way that could not be obtained from competent sources in Teheran?" he asked.

"It concerns the death of a woman named Leila Darwish."

Karrubi, apparently uninterested, was looking above Darius's head. Darius turned around and saw more diplomas, more pictures of the Imam, whose hooded eyes were fixed on the young pharmacologist.

"She was found in a northern suburb of the capital. The coroner's office sent specimens from her organs to the poison unit for a determination of the cause of death."

"The particular case eludes me," Karrubi said. "We are swamped with work from medical examiners all over the country."

"How many cases of mycotoxin poisoning do you see?"

"As I said, I don't recall—"

"Mycotoxins are your specialization. How can you not remember someone dying like that on the streets?"

"I am just a simple researcher," Karrubi said. "There is not that much that I know about the subject."

"Such modesty is an admirable trait, but somewhat out of character," Darius said. "I've seen your article in the *Journal of the Iranian Research Organization,* and just several months ago you were clamoring for recognition of the breakthroughs you've made. I doubt anyone in the world knows as much as you."

Karrubi took cigarettes from his lab coat and lay them on his desk. He lit a fresh one from a five-centimeter butt.

"I need to find out how Leila Darwish ingested the poison that killed her," Darius said. "From my understanding of the article, mycotoxins are rare in nature."

"I can't answer."

"You must have some hypothesis."

"I prefer not to make guesses."

"Not even educated ones? It would be negligent of you to have no theory to explain the death of this woman. If people are succumbing to mycotoxin poisoning in Teheran, the implications are grave."

"It's outside my purview. Our experimentation is limited to the possible uses of mycotoxins in overcoming autoimmune rejection of transplanted organs." A gray worm of ash dropped onto Karrubi's lap. He whisked it to the floor, and crushed its glowing tail under his heel. "Since you lack a theory, consider that she ate bad mushrooms. That is the most common manner of death from mycotoxins."

"The poison that killed Leila Darwish was from the same strain of wheat or grass fungus utilized by some countries in chemical weapons. Among the tissue specimens sent to you were sections of skin marred by severe burns and rashes. The woman did not receive those injuries rubbing up against a poisonous mushroom."

"May I say politely that I do not know what you are getting at. Or, to be more accurate, that you don't. We are in the business of medical research," Karrubi said, "of learning to save lives, not to study more horrible ways of taking them."

"Perhaps as a by-product of your experimentation such discoveries are being made."

"Definitely not. The singular application of the knowledge obtained here is a reduction of suffering."

"Mycotoxins killed that girl," Darius said.

"If you are interested in the murderous uses of chemical agents, I would advise you to focus your investigation on the criminal scientists of the Zionist regime of Baghdad. It is a well-known fact that they have been engaged in that kind of research for years."

"The girl was never to Iraq."

Karrubi took a step away from the desk. "The laboratory that performed the analysis for you will be pleased to provide additional information, I am sure," he said. "There is nothing left for us to discuss."

"Doctor Karrubi—" Darius was out of his seat, toe to toe with the pharmacologist. "You're not a suspect in this homicide, yet you've evaded my questions as if you were. Why is that?"

Karrubi patted his pockets, then reached down for his cigarettes. "I won't stand for being badgered. You have no jurisdiction in Mashad. Leave now, or I will call the guards to have you removed."

But the choice was not Darius's to make. Men in uniform burst into the office and dragged him through the lab in a brawny pas de deux in which his toes scarcely brushed the floor, one of the guards hustling him along the hissing corridor while the other went ahead opening fire doors. The freight elevator was waiting to catch him. The operator, a worn man in a vested suit with white broadcloth showing through the elbows, and alligator skin showing through that, brought him to the basement tilting his nose as though he were another load of garbage.

Somewhere he'd lost his sunglasses. He went outside squinting against the noonday glare. His stomach was grumbling about the meals he had missed since leaving Teheran. There was no place to eat around the campus, no place where *he* would eat. A city whose wealth was imported in the pocketbooks of religious pilgrims could not be recommended for its cuisine.

He went back toward the bazaar, and had lunch in the coffee shop of the Iran Hotel. Exhausted, and with nothing to do until the next train left that evening, he paid fifty thousand rials for a room in which to nap.

He woke around 5:00, craving vodka and his own bed, too groggy to try to catch his train, or to care. He shut his eyes again, and slept through the late-afternoon and evening call to prayer.

After a shower, he went downstairs. His reward for the frustrating trip would be supper in Mashad's former three-star hotel. The last traces of the dining room's old elegance were fossilized in the antique carpets on the walls, and the gilded, mismatched bone china. He ordered fesunjun, duck in pomegranate juice with ground walnuts, and maol shair, a nonalcoholic beer.

At the height of the dinner hour the dining room was a quarter full. Three tables away a young mullah was feeding chicken to a seegah twice his age. Beside them, four Orientals jabbered loudly in bad, status symbol English. Under a crystal chandelier marred by missing bulbs a lone diner was studying a menu at a round table for eight. Darius gazed at the thin, gray man, who pointed silently when the waiter came for his order. The man's plump mustaches, his diffidence, recalled Zaid Rahgozar so vividly that Darius preferred to believe he was hallucinating rather than attach credibility to such coincidence.

His salad was like paper in his chalky mouth. The man *was* Rahgozar, had to be, the amazing coincidence no coincidence at all, but a mutual interest in mycotoxins and the leading poison expert in Iran. When Rahgozar walked from the dining room, Darius trailed him as far as the elevators. He watched the indicator light turn red for the seventh floor, and then went to the desk.

"The man who just went upstairs," he said. "Mr. Rahgozar—"

The clerk looked up from the register. He was a short man with a nose of such prominence that Darius couldn't understand how his eyes worked in concert.

"Can you tell me what room he's in? We were supposed to meet in the lobby, and apparently I've just missed him."

"Seven twenty-seven," the clerk said. "I'll ring him for you."

Darius reached over the desk, and pressed the clerk's hand against the receiver. "That isn't necessary."

He slipped into a phone booth from which he could keep an eye on the elevators. The long-distance operator put him through to Ghaffari's without difficulty. Sharera picked up.

"Let me talk to Mansur," he said.

"He isn't home. I haven't seen him in two nights. Darius, you know where he stays with his slut. Tell me where, tell me, and I'll go there now and brain the two of them."

"I would," he said, "except I need him. If— When you hear from him, have him call me at the Hotel Iran in Mashad."

"Have you got a girl, too?"

"This is important, Sharera. Tell him what I said, and if he's out all night tomorrow, you'll know he's here with me."

When Darius stepped off the elevator on the seventh floor, three of the Orientals were loitering in the corridor, cursing in Japanese as their companion tried to force the key into their door. He waited until they were inside, and then knocked on 727.

"Who's there?"

A good question. In his excitement at discovering Rahgozar at the hotel he hadn't planned out how to get close to him.

". . . Room service."

"I haven't ordered anything."

"Six jujeh kebab dinners were requested for seven twenty-seven," Darius said. "I'll be happy to take the cart back to the kitchen, but *someone* will have to pay for them."

"One minute." The door was opened by the thin man with the glossy mustaches, who was wiping his face in a towel. He was in tassel loafers, pants from a black suit, and a tattered undershirt. Soapy water ran off his forearms into the carpeting. Darius waggled his gun, but the thin man was dabbing at his eyes and didn't see it, or chose not to. Darius shoved him inside.

"My money is in my wallet." He nodded toward a black jacket on the bed, "but hardly adequate compensation for the loss of a hand."

Remembering their last confrontation, Darius backed him all the way into the room, and chained the door. Rahgozar blotted his eyes some more, but still didn't seem to recognize him. "I left the water running," he said, and started for the bathroom.

"Stay where you are." Darius went first into the bathroom. A toilet kit lay on the edge of the basin. He folded a straight razor into its handle, pocketed it, and then turned off the water.

The thin man grabbed for his jacket. Darius ripped it away, and patted it down. There were no weapons. In the inside pocket was a passport with a red cover. Darius opened it to a photo taken at a time when the thin man was thirty pounds heavier, significant weight in a ferocious ridge of muscle above his eyes. The information under the picture was in Cyrillic. Darius made his way slowly through the Slavonic letters, spelling out Zaid Rahgozar, age forty-two, birthplace, Baku, Azerbaijan Soviet Socialist Republic. He flipped the passport to the cover, which was embossed in gold with the emblem of the new government in Moscow.

"This is a Russian diplomatic passport," he said.

"Very good, you get an A in East European languages. Now, if you don't mind, I would like to speak to my embassy." Rahgozar put out his hand, and Darius expected him to snap his fingers. "Give me the phone."

Darius waved his gun, freezing the thin man beside the bed. He poked the muzzle in his side, and Rahgozar sat.

"No calls."

"You know the law," Rahgozar said. "As the holder of a diplomatic passport, I'm immune from interrogation and arrest."

"Is that Russian law?"

"Quit pretending you're thick between the ears, Bakhtiar. There's not a nation on earth that doesn't respect the special rights of foreign envoys."

"We have no law like that in the Islamic Republic," Darius said flatly. He shredded the passport. Tossing the pieces in Rahgozar's lap, he asked himself which statutes he had violated, how much greater the potential penalty he was bringing down on his head than anything Rahgozar was liable for.

Rahgozar rubbed his hands against the prickling flesh of his upper arms, and pulled the jacket over his shoulders. "This provocation will not be overlooked by my government."

"Which government is that? Why, in these times, is a native Azerbaijani working for the oppressors of his people?"

"Unlike most Iranians," Rahgozar said, "I know who my real enemies are, and not all of them are to be found across foreign borders. I demand you call the Russian embassy."

"You're in no position to make demands on anyone."

Rahgozar was watching droplets of blood dribble onto the white bed-spread. He touched his chin, smearing crimson on his face. "Let me have the towel. I'm bleeding."

"It's something you may have to get used to," Darius said. "You have been attempting to deal in a large quantity of heroin. Possessing narcotics in this country calls for a sentence of death. If you have anything to say in your favor, you had better say it to me."

"What heroin? There's no heroin here. Search the room."

"Your *friend*, Maryam Lajevardi, is a principal figure in a case involving several brutal murders and the importation of opiates into the Islamic Republic. The drugs are from Afghanistan, where the Russians have been involved intimately for more than a decade. Both the woman and the drugs are missing. It doesn't require a great stretch of the imagination to see what you were doing at her apartment."

"Not with an imagination like yours," Rahgozar said. "You'd better call."

"The most recent shipment from Afghanistan was deflected from its destination by an acquaintance of Miss Lajevardi. You've been trying to find it. You came to the apartment looking for drugs, but the drugs weren't there."

Darius's spiel, the circuitous line of questioning, was the flourish of a magician's empty left hand as he readied an object to be materialized before a gaping audience. Now he opened his right hand to the spotlight.

"You've been observed at the Imam Reza Medical Center," he bluffed, "in the vicinity of the poison unit. Why is a foreigner interested in Iranian research into substances with the capability of being utilized as chemical warfare agents?"

Rahgozar moistened a finger on his tongue. He rubbed the red spot on his chin.

A lousy bluffer, Darius tried again. "We know about the mycotoxins."

"The what?"

"We know why you want them . . ."

"I'm just a simple dope dealer," Rahgozar said. "This is beyond me."

"Where they're going . . ."

"Then why are you wasting time on me?"

"And what they're intended for."

"Is that supposed to shock me into emptying my heart to you? You *should* know—you're working for the people who had them stolen."

Darius, wondering too long what Rahgozar meant, groping for a follow-up, saw his advantage slip away while the thin man stared at him disbelievingly.

"Fuck, you don't know," Rahgozar said, "you don't know a damn thing. They let you learn you were looking for drugs, for thirty kilos of heroin and a Russian who wanted them. But you did better than that, didn't you? Better than they had any right to expect. You found out about the mycotoxins, too. Except they never told you what they're for, and you still don't know, and it bothers you." He used a corner of the bedspread to wipe the blood off his face. "My God, an Iranian with the vestiges of a conscience. Drop the case while you can, Bakhtiar. You don't want to end up like Leila Darwish. It's not a comfortable death."

"And when I find the mycotoxins," Darius interrupted, "what do you suggest I do with them? Turn them over to the helpful agent of the peace-loving former Soviet Union?"

"It's too late. Burn them, or take them into the Gulf and sink them in deep water. You'll be doing yourself . . . doing the world a favor."

"Who are you?" Darius asked.

"A dead man."

"You've been exposed to the mycotoxins?"

"I wish I'd come that close. I'd have swallowed the damn stuff, gotten rid of it that way, if I had to. Do you know what Iranian medical researchers are doing with the small amounts of mycotoxins they've been able to obtain?" A veneer of perspiration put a keener edge on Rahgozar's sharp features.

"Dozens of Iraqi prisoners of war still listed as missing in action are housed at the poison unit for use as human guinea pigs. From time to time Dr. Karrubi locks one inside a sealed chamber, and then pumps mycotoxins into the air. Sometimes the guinea pig is given a gas mask to wear. No matter. When the poison comes in contact with his skin in sufficient concentration, he's done."

"What is the source of your information? Do you expect me to believe—"

"I don't care what you believe," Rahgozar said. "I'm dead anyway."

"How—"

"*You* killed me. The others were too stupid to see I'd have to come here, but they're smart enough to follow you."

What others? Darius was about to ask. But how did it matter? Whether it was the Komiteh that the thin man was afraid of, or Ashfar and Baraheni, or the Revolutionary Prosecutor, or his own men from the homicide bureau, the only difference it would make to Rahgozar was between a public execution and a private one.

"No one knows I'm in Mashad," he said.

Rahgozar laughed at him.

"We're a civilized race," Darius said in a voice so calm that its soothing effect was not lost on himself. "Don't be too quick to accept the things that have been drummed into your head about us. You're not going to be harmed. I'll do what I can for you, but first you have to tell me everything."

"You're a flea, Bakhtiar, a flea on the backside of a beast that's going to scratch you out of its hide when you become too much of a nuisance. What can you do for me?"

"I give you my word, my word as a man of conscience, to help."

"No good. Call the embassy. It's my only chance."

Darius shook his head. "First tell me the connection between the heroin and the mycotoxins."

"You get nothing till you make the call."

"The Darwish girl . . . How was she exposed to the mycotoxins?"

"Time is being wasted." Rahgozar fished a pack of cigarettes out of his jacket. "Let me have a li—"

Darius followed his gaze to the knob twisting in the door. He drew his shoulder gun as the panel was hammered open and four men rushed inside, a collage of khaki shirts and trousers, short hair and unkempt beards, the other constant the large military revolver clenched in each intruder's hand. Four weapons trained on him, and he dropped his gun on the floor. Rahgozar sat where he was, chewing fiercely on the unlit cigarette.

The intruders were badly disorganized. They prowled around the room looking in the closets and drawers, going over territory their companions had covered, individually examining the contents of Rahgozar's new suitcase, and peering out the windows and into the corridor while Darius anticipated the momentary arrival of reinforcements or enemies. None of them said anything until the youngest, a man of no more than thirty, gave up the search and came over to where Darius stood beside the bed.

"We are Revolutionary Guards," he said. "We heard what was happening and came in to save you."

"What was happening?" Darius asked. "Nothing was happening here."

"This man is a Russian agent. He was threatening your life and the security of the Islamic Republic. We have been following him since he arrived in our city."

"I've had him under watch for several hours," Darius said. "No one else was near him."

"They've been on your tail," Rahgozar said. "That's what he's trying to tell you."

A Guardsman wearing white socks inside buffalo skin sandals swung his gun across Rahgozar's mouth, mashing the cigarette against the thin man's cheek. Rahgozar brushed it away, and with the tip of his tongue flicked out bits of broken teeth as though they were tobacco crumbs.

"We will take over from you now," the young Guardsman said to Darius, "and continue the questioning." He transferred the heavy gun to the other hand, and pointed it at Rahgozar. "Put on your shoes," he commanded.

When Rahgozar made no move to obey, the man in the sandals swung his pistol again. Rahgozar leaned slightly out of the way and took him by the arm. A short, snapping motion of his wrist launched him across the room, where he crash-landed against the window, squirting blood from both nostrils onto the glass. Rahgozar laced his shoes. He removed a fresh shirt from the valise and fastened the sleeves with silver cuff links. He put his jacket on over it and stood with his arms hanging loosely at his sides.

"This man is my prisoner," Darius said.

"And you," the young Guardsman said, "if we see fit, are ours."

"So long, Bakhtiar." Rahgozar allowed the gunmen to push him around the bed. "Thanks for making that call."

As Rahgozar walked to the door, the Guardsman he had flung into the window fired his gun. The large-caliber bullet caught him high on the shoulder. Rahgozar's back twitched, and he broke stride, but kept moving. A second shot dropped him to his knees in a Christian attitude of prayer. It was the young Guardsman who fired the third slug that entered the back of Rahgozar's neck, and put a hole the size of a small coin in the wall.

"He should not have tried to escape," the young Guardsman said.

Darius drew his other gun, and swept it around the room. It felt light in his hand, a harmless affectation.

"You don't seem to appreciate that we saved your life," said one of the men who hadn't spoken before. "Possibly, you know better than we. I would suggest that you were in collusion with the Russian."

"What is a homicide investigator from Teheran doing in Mashad?" asked the Guardsman in the buffalo skin sandals.

"You had better go," the young one said to Darius, "while you have the chance."

Darius walked around the body. Rahgozar had fallen reaching for the door. His lifeless fingers closed over Darius's wrist as Darius moved him out of the way.

Darius went upstairs and barricaded himself inside his room. His mind was racing, wild images out of synch with the narration from his own frightened voice like a film dragged through a projector without catching in the sprockets. Vodka had the opposite effect of what he sought, speeding his brain so the film ran off the reel and spilled onto the floor. And still he drank. In SAVAK he had taught himself to assume guilt for nothing he was not directly responsible for, and not much of that; otherwise it had been impossible for him to function. But there was no escaping culpability for Rahgozar's death. Not for refusing to call the embassy—history showed that the Revolutionary Guards were not squeamish about abusing the entire legation of a foreign power. What he blamed himself for was an improbably efficient job of finding Rahgozar. Better to have let him go about his business unmolested than to lead his killers to his door. On some level, instinct told him, their interests coincided.

He shut off the lights, leaned over the low railing of his balcony. Three cars were parked on the sidewalk, and men in khaki strutted in the entrance to the lobby. A noisy crowd was forming in front of the hotel despite commands from the Guardsmen to keep moving. The spectators fell silent as two of the gunmen came out with the body trussed like a slaughtered deer, and slung it in the back of one of the cars. The young Guardsman brought Rahgozar's suitcase, followed by his companion with the bloody nose, who had exchanged his buffalo sandals for the dead man's new shoes. The crowd dispersed as the caravan raced away.

Darius ran downstairs to the seventh floor. A chambermaid unhappy to have been summoned at that late hour had pushed her cart outside Rahgozar's door. Darius waved his badge in her face as he squeezed past her. "I want a few minutes here alone," he said, "and then you can come in."

Squatting beside a splotch of blood on the runner, he might have been trying to remember the incantation that would restore life to the man from whom it came. The room had been torn apart, but not by the chambermaid. Linens were heaped on the floor along with the bedspread and blankets; the stripped mattress stood on end against a wall. The closets were empty, as was the bureau. Everything Rahgozar had carried with him had been returned to the suitcase and taken away. The chambermaid came inside uninvited, and began scraping the rug with a vacuum cleaner.

He went to the lobby, and bullied the clerk for a look at the invoice from 727, and the record of Rahgozar's phone calls. The thin man had been at the Hotel Iran two nights prior to his death. He had paid cash in advance for a week's stay, charging several breakfasts and a few bottles of overpriced mineral water to his room. The home address he had registered under was a joke, a street in northeast Teheran that he'd probably pulled from an out-of-date tourist guide: Roosevelt Road had been renamed Shahid Mofatteh in the first weeks after the Revolution.

Out of loneliness, or duty, Rahgozar had made long-distance calls approximately every other waking hour. All of them were to Teheran, to three different numbers. The shadow of the clerk's prominent nose moved across the page as Darius read.

"Do you know if Mr. Rahgozar had any visitors while he was a guest here?" Darius asked him.

"You mean a woman, sir? In his room? That is strictly forbidden."

"I mean anybody."

"I never saw him, except when he was alone. He would leave in the morning about ten and was back by noon, and did not go out again until the following day."

"Did he receive any letters?"

"No sir," the clerk said, and then turned away to steal a look at the empty box for 727.

"Did you talk with him?"

"Only to pass the time of day."

"Did he mention what he was doing in Mashad?"

"Yes." The clerk smiled, but then thought better of it. "He said he came to get away from it all."

❖ 10 ❖

Of twenty-six calls billed to Zaid Rahgozar's Iran Hotel room no fewer than fourteen had been placed to the Russian embassy in Teheran. The bulk of the remainder, a telephone company service representative reported to Darius, were rerouted via central switching to Moscow and could not be traced further. Others had been dialed each morning precisely at 8:00, and again twelve hours later, to a number in an industrial area of western Teheran on the Old Karaj Road. Not one of these had lasted as long as a minute.

By 7:30 on the morning of his first full day back in Teheran, Darius was parked outside the Old Karaj Road address, a small, square house between a factory where steel pipes were bent to shape and cut, and a commercial printer. An unusually high brick wall served as the first line of defense around an overgrown garden ringed by poplars whispering in the light breeze. The kidney-shaped goldfish pond was a dead sea capped by a mat of green scum. When his knock went unanswered, Darius peered inside the living room at flat cushions on threadbare rugs. Stale air still warm from yesterday's sun seeped from the partly open window. Darius pushed up the glass and slipped in.

The bedroom, too, was unoccupied. He turned on the single bulb in the ceiling that shined down on an unmade bed as fiercely as the fluorescent strips over Baghai's slabs. There were no papers or envelopes in the drawers of a plain pine bureau on which oak grain had been hand-painted. No mail seemed ever to have been delivered to the house, or newspapers allowed inside. The closet contained several summer dresses perfumed with sweet female perspiration that aroused him in a manner that, he decided, must violate some unwritten law. He went into the kitchen kneading the bruised ribs that had begun to hurt again, and put a flame under a pot of water. Though it occurred to him that whoever lived here had panicked when they didn't hear from Rahgozar at the usual times and were en route to Mashad— if not out of the country—he waited.

At 9:00, as he was emptying the sugar bowl into his third glass of tea, the garden gate creaked open. A shadow bobbed along the walk prodded by a woman wearing a pushiyih, a facial veil that obscured her features completely below green eyes. She set down a couple of paper bags beside the pond, and broke off a piece from a loaf of naan lavashe, pit oven–baked bread, which she tossed under the poplars. Two black birds immediately swooped down from the trees and declared a cawing tug of war. She threw another crust, but only the first was satisfactory to the birds, who carried it into the air with an end locked between their beaks. Scooping up her packages, the woman went inside to the living room and plugged a cassette player into the wall. Soft rock music manipulated the heavy air, a Beatles tune that Darius had heard a million times before, but whose title eluded him. Not until she was in the kitchen did she see him, and the pushiyih fluttered against her mouth.

The woman removed the veil, and Darius was staring at Maryam Lajevardi. She looked drawn, taller than he remembered her, and prettier, the lightness of her skin and hair not of the Caspian, or Iran. Darius could not have been startled more had she taken off all her clothes. Not because she had shown herself so casually—strange women did that all the time—but because the effect it was having on him was not much different than if he had, in fact, spied her naked.

"Who are you?" he asked.

"I'm someone else, can't you see?" She laughed without smiling. "The person you want doesn't live here. I would invite you for tea, but apparently you've already helped yourself. Good-bye," she said. "Don't forget to lock the gate on your way out."

She reached for a cabinet above the refrigerator, presenting a lush silhouette that her chador only partially obscured. She had to stand on her toes to hoist a small sack of rice inside. Darius took it from her, and slung it on the top shelf.

"Who, Miss Lajevardi?" he asked again.

"I believe I answered all your questions the last time we spoke."

"With lies," he said. "No one at the Azadi currency exchange has ever heard of you."

"*They're* the liars. I can't be held to account for the things they say. I'm resented there because I was a diligent worker and the rest were laggards."

"You mean ghosts. Azadi has been out of business at least a year. There's nothing but an empty storefront." Darius paused to study her reaction. It was he who had lied, although he would have called it probing. He had meant to go to Firdowsi Street to check out her story on a hundred occasions, but hadn't. Still he felt he was on solid ground in assuming she had never worked there.

Maryam Lajevardi took off her chador. Underneath she had on a short V-necked dress like the one she had worn in Shemiran, but of a washed-out yellow. "How did you know I was here?" she asked.

"Rahgozar told me."

She looked at him, puzzled, to say she had never heard the name before. If she was still acting, she was very good. He decided that she was.

". . . Lean, unhealthy-looking fellow attached to the Russian embassy," Darius went on. "He can't stop talking about you."

Her chin dropped. "Where did you see him?"

"In Mashad," he said. "A few days ago."

Whatever it was that differentiated fake puzzlement from the real thing vanished from her expression. What remained was made imploring by her helplessness. Darius saw that she was struggling not to ask him how he had known Rahgozar had been there. She had more questions than he did, but feared him finding out what she didn't know. It was a cumbersome way of conducting an interview—bluffing, posing misleading questions to obtain nonverbal cues to determine the next tack and then plugging ahead with more misdirection. Cumbersome for the two of them. Maybe, thought Darius, it was weariness brought on by too many interrogations like this that had driven Baraheni to take up boiling samovars and the bastinado, but he didn't like to consider it. "How does a woman from the Caspian become acquainted with a Russian diplomat?" he asked.

"In a most casual way," she said coolly.

"That isn't how it appears. I ran into him once before, at your old apartment, and he seemed at home."

Maryam said nothing.

"What was he doing there?"

"What were the police?"

"Looking for you."

"I was hiding," she said. "I was afraid you'd send me away."

"Where?"

She shrugged. "You would find a place. I'm sure you're good at that."

"Why would I want to?"

"You'd find a reason, too."

"So you came here instead?"

"It was his idea," she blurted. The change in tone struck Darius as artificial, the time having come for her to inject emotional drive into her narrative. He let her go on. "We had met through friends, and began seeing a lot of each other. He was convinced he was being watched—by his people, as well as the Komiteh—and that soon our affair would become public knowledge with all the trouble that brings. He rented this house for me. It's convenient, yet out of the way. I like—" The printing presses chugged into action next door, and she raised her voice over the racket. "I like the quiet."

Darius became aware that the Caspian accent she had practiced on him in Shemiran was giving way to a Teheran patois no less stilted. Maryam Lajevardi seemed pleased with herself. He remembered grade school classmates basking in the same glow of accomplishment after they had been called upon to recite a speech.

"What was Rahgozar doing in Mashad?" he asked.

"I don't know."

"You say you're close—"

"He *is* a diplomat, a *Russian* diplomat. Needless to say there are some things we never discuss."

"Things like heroin?"

"Why would we talk about that?"

"And mycotoxins?"

The look of helplessness deepened, and then hardened—but she had nothing on him.

"Playing dumb doesn't become such an intelligent face," Darius said. "I haven't been hunting for you to return you to your family. You're rather old to be a runaway."

"I know nothing about heroin."

"What about heroin dealers?" he asked. "What do you know about Sousan Hovanian?"

"I've never heard that name."

"And Leila Darwish?"

"Nor her," Maryam said. "Or that other word you used, my-myca . . ."

"Why, then, do you suppose Leila's body was placed under your window as a warning?"

"A warning to me? To do what?"

"To tell nothing to the police when we caught up with you." It came out as a question, a wasted one. "Rahgozar didn't install you here because you two needed a love nest. No one on Saltanatabad Avenue would care what you did, so long as you were quiet doing it and didn't frighten the children. He wanted you out of harm's way while he tried to locate the heroin and mycotoxins, those things you know nothing about."

Maryam's expression conceded little. Darius would have liked the veil in front of her face again, to be able to gauge her anxiety in much the way doctors used to employ a feather to detect the spark of life on the lips of a dying patient. He hid his frustration behind his professional stone face, an expression so rigid that he might as well have been grinning at her like the idiot she seemed to take him for.

"Right until the end," he said, "the only thing Rahgozar wanted to talk about was the mycotoxins. He never mentioned them to you?"

"Till the end of what?"

Here, he suspected, a stone face could be put to some advantage, and he fashioned it into a laser stare. "Didn't I say? His life, Miss Lajevardi. The Mashad Komiteh shot him while we talked."

She laughed in his new face, leaned so close that he could taste her hungry, morning breath. "Is that right?" she said. "You're not much of a psychologist if that's the best you can come up with to frighten me into telling you these strange things you want to hear. Zaid is perfectly well."

"Aren't you taking a lot for granted, when you haven't heard from him in forty-eight hours? He phoned twice each day before."

"You were monitoring his calls," she said. "It proves you've arrested him on some fantastic charge, and he's in one of your awful jails."

"Does it?"

She had begun to cry. Powerful sobs shook her and forced out ribbons of moisture that were not so much for Rahgozar, he guessed, as for herself. When he held out a napkin to wipe her cheeks, she twisted away. The dishrag she used instead was not clean, and left yellow streaks from fruit preserves around her eyes.

She stopped to say, "I wouldn't believe anything you told me." Then she cried some more until she was drained of tears, becalmed the way a blast of frigid air sometimes leaves a drunk momentarily sober, but, with a red running nose and chattering teeth, looking worse than ever. "I knew something terrible had happened," she said, still for her own benefit. "He wouldn't have let me worry— Why did they have to kill him?"

"The Guardsmen claim he was trying to escape."

"Where could he have run? You were there. You let it happen."

He didn't know how to answer. He pulled out his notepad and searched for an empty page. In her agitation she already had forgotten her questions.

"You're mad to think he was involved in selling drugs." Maryam looked around the squalid kitchen, and he expected to hear sobs again. "What did he need big money for? To keep me in such luxury? It was his diplomatic work that brought him to Mashad. Did you talk to the Russians? Did you ask *them* what he was doing there?"

"They refused to comment," he said, although at that point it remained only his assumption that they would. "It's an option not available to you. I must ask why he made such frequent and regular calls. What was he reporting?"

"His love," she said defiantly. "Don't you phone your wife every day when you're apart?"

Darius returned the notebook to his pocket. "Do you mind if I look around the house while we talk?"

"And if I do?"

He stood on a chair and brought down plain water glasses and cheap stoneware table settings from the cabinets. As he swept the grime from the shelves, dustballs clung to his cuff and Maryam Lajevardi seized his arm and whisked them away in embarrassment, which struck him as the first honest emotion she had demonstrated.

He lifted a corner of the sofray in the living room along with the worn carpet. Underneath, the thick dust was like a feathery rug on the scuffed floor.

"You've uncovered my dirty secret," she said. "It's damning evidence."

He checked under every corner of the carpeting, patrolled the center for telltale lumps. The Beatles rattled the crockery as the power surged, and as he went to shut off the music the chorus came around again and he remembered the name of the song: "The Fool on the Hill."

He raised the bedroom blinds and looked out at the print shop through a break in the garden wall. A workman was steering a fork lift under a wooden skid piled with glossy blue booklets, the Imam's treatise on *Fighting the Carnal Self; or: Man's Major Crusade.*

Maryam opened her bureau, and he poked through colorful garments of rayon and light cotton. The drawer below contained underwear and a black tangle of pantyhose and stockings. Women caught on the streets with bare ankles were in every bit as much trouble as those wearing makeup; all females over the age of nine kept a large supply of hosiery.

"He never talked to me about his work," Maryam volunteered after Darius had given up on getting anything from her. "Too much of the time it called him out of Teheran. We spoke twice each day by phone. Does that tell you what you want to know?"

Darius peeled back the covers from a futon clad in yellow corduroy, and felt around the cushion while Maryam hovered over his shoulder, on guard for more dust. "I want to talk to the friends who introduced you," he said.

"Leave them out of this."

"Five people have been brutally murdered, among them a Russian envoy who happened to be your boyfriend. I'm not concerned with preserving your privacy, or anyone else's."

She brought a man's handkerchief to her cheek, but there were no tears to dry. "I wasn't telling the truth," she said. "I have no friends in Teheran."

"How, then, did you meet?"

"I— It was in a tea shop on Baharestan Square. I'd gone there for lunch, and didn't have . . . had left my money at home, and he very graciously offered to pay for me. He's like that, a kind and generous man. I was lonely in Teheran, almost as lonely as he. It was natural that we should have become close."

"You're being untruthful now," Darius told her. "I need to see identification."

She took out a wallet from the chador. Aside from several postage stamps, the clear plastic sleeves were empty, as was the billfold. "Is there a law requiring that I carry any?"

"Give me the names of two relatives who can verify your story about coming to Teheran," he said.

"I refuse. It's preferable to go to jail than have my family find out I'm here and be pressured to return to them."

"Is it?"

Maryam Lajevardi nodded grimly.

She had called his bluff, showed a weak hand, and was prepared to pay the price with her freedom. More than prepared, thought Darius, she demanded it. But if her strategy called for the police to guarantee her safety now that Rahgozar was gone, she was unaware that she would be taken away by Revolutionary Guards at the first opportunity and lodged in a Komiteh prison. Was Maryam so naive that she believed she could charm them, too, or was she looking for a permanent, perhaps painless way out of a hopeless situation? He recognized a reversal in their roles in which he had gone from being her prosecutor to her protector. To take her into custody would make him her prisoner.

Maryam held her wrists together, and extended them toward him. "Well, aren't you going to arrest me?"

"As of now, there is nothing to charge you with, nothing worth the paperwork. I must insist, however, that you remain here. You have groceries for several days, you'll be all right." He gave her his card. "When you feel like talking, call me."

"I'll be bored," she said. "How many times can I listen to one old tape?"

The curtains blew inside the room. Darius stuck his head out the window into a dust storm that had sailed several of the blue pamphlets from the printers into the yard. He leaned over the sill for one. "Here's something for you to read," he said. "We'll talk soon. Good-bye."

Workmen were draping a silken banner over the street. As he drove underneath, the wind tore it down and he rolled over the shiny material.

THE QUIET OF MUSLIMS IS A BETRAYAL OF THE QUR'AN

He would talk. Maryam would say nothing, lie, do what she had to to tangle the frayed skein of her life, allow the Komiteh to silence her rather than give up her precious secrets.

Up ahead traffic was funneled into a single lane. An ambulance was parked in the narrow street with the right wheels on the sidewalk, and attendants were kneeling beside two figures wrapped in blankets.

His head began to hurt. He locked his door, placed a gun in his lap as he squeezed past a white Paycon and a Volkswagen that had collided head-on and locked bumpers. The attendants didn't look up at him, too busy ministering to the motorists in the street. Relief turned to disappointment as he put the gun away. Where were Ashfar and Baraheni now that he needed to talk?

Mehta had come up from his crypt in the sub-basement with some Padkis vodka, a prerevolutionary label, which, while not up to the standard of Caviar brand, was smoother than Caviar, and had its partisans. He filled three glasses, pushed one across Darius's desk, and gave the other to Hamid. "Where's Mansur?" he asked. "He won't forgive us for not waiting."

Hamid studied the sparkle of sunlight strained through unwashed windows in his glass. "He leaves every day at one, and that's the last we see of him."

"Hasn't anyone reminded him his job comes ahead of his women?" Darius said.

Mehta tasted the vodka, then restored the missing centimeter to his drink. "Only this does."

Darius sipped, and his frown fell apart. "Where did you find this stuff? Padkis went the way of the dodo in seventy-nine."

"It was the day the Revolutionary Guards broke into the cellars of the International Hotel," Mehta said. "A couple of cases were mixed in down there with several million rials' worth of the finest French wines. The fanatics hauled all of it to a parking lot where they could make a big show of running bulldozers over everything. The heavy equipment operators were late, and I was one of the police who volunteered to guard the site till they arrived. I've been guarding the Padkis ever since." He swallowed more, and again carefully replaced the vodka to the lip of the glass. "A pity it's not breeding stock," he said, and put an unopened bottle on the desk along with a manila folder. "Here's the file you wanted."

"What file?" On his own Darius looked for the answer in his half-empty glass.

"Maryam Lajevardi's."

"Two weeks ago there was nothing on her."

"The original description," Mehta said, "was of a blonde girl possibly from the Caspian, possibly a runaway. No one like that had been reported missing or was wanted anywhere, and she seemed too young to have a record. While you were away, I ran her name through the cards in all categories, both as victim and suspect. You didn't say she'd been a juvenile delinquent."

"I didn't know. What kind of trouble?"

Mehta riffled the yellowing pages inside the folder. "In March of eighty-three, when she was thirteen years old, she was picked up for tossing acid at a woman she claimed was dressed provocatively and wearing makeup, a woman who turned out to be the wife of a visiting Romanian businessman."

"I don't remember the incident. It would have been in the newspapers if a European had been mutilated."

"As it turned out," Mehta said, "she missed. The businessman's wife became hysterical, and had to be taken to a psychiatric hospital and left for hours in a room with mirrored walls before she accepted that she had not been injured. Since no real harm was done, the Lajevardi girl was let off with a reprimand. Next month, she pulled the same stunt again."

"Who was the victim this time?"

"A forty-three-year-old resident of Hamadan, who had come to Teheran on a shopping expedition and was going along Vali-e-Asr Avenue when she was assaulted at the Pesian intersection. She snatched away the bottle while the girl was prying the cork, and held her for the arresting officer. The Komiteh took her off our hands."

"Any harm done?" asked Darius.

"To Maryam Lajevardi only. Her right leg was burned around the knee."

"And after that?"

"There are only the two entries," Mehta said. "Presumably, the Komiteh told her to cut it out before she got into real trouble, and she did."

Between the incident reports Darius discovered a photo of a girl with shaggy yellow hair he would have guessed was no more than ten or eleven, her rage projected from tight, furious features that would blossom into Maryam Lajevardi's gorgeous insolence. Nothing in her face hinted at how a teenage religious fanatic had grown up to become a cynical taghouti involved with heroin, murder, and a Russian espionage agent.

"I don't understand."

"You mean the blonde hair?"

"No, I was just thinking—"

"The girl's father was a petroleum engineer who first came to Iran in the late 1960s as a contract worker from Milan, Italy, and converted to Islam before he was allowed to marry into the Lajevardis. They're a prominent family of bazaar merchants in Tabriz. As is the case with many converts, the old man went overboard with religion. The girl grew up in Khuzestan, in the Maroun oil fields, which," Mehta went on, "would not have been pleasant under the most ideal of circumstances. And hers certainly were not, not with a father like him."

"What was she doing on her own in Teheran at thirteen?" Darius asked.

"The father abandoned the family and went back to Italy a few years after the Revolution, and she ran off to the capital to see what the excitement was about. It says here the Komiteh returned her to her mother after both arrests."

Darius finished his drink. Mehta moved the mouth of the bottle toward Darius's glass, but Darius covered it with his palm.

"Hamid," he said, "I want you to go to Maryam Lajevardi's place and keep an eye on her for us."

Hamid reached for the photo. Darius put it out of reach. "She's not a kid anymore. The easy part of the job will be recognizing her."

"And the hard?" the criminalist asked.

"Not falling in love."

Hamid's smile dissolved in vodka.

"If you don't want to, I can get someone else."

"Bijan called. He says he has to see you at once." Hamid fiddled nervously with his glass. ". . . about the future of the homicide bureau."

Darius grabbed for the phone. "Does anyone remember the number for the Bon Yad villa?"

"He's at home."

"Where?"

"Across from the Paradise of Zahra Cemetery, near the Fountain of Blood," Hamid said. "Till one."

"For the road?" Mehta offered the bottle one more time.

Darius took his hand away, and the vodka came back automatically to his glass, and then to Hamid's.

"For paradise," he said.

Darius drove south toward the train station, then south again through mud-brick slums rising from heaps of garbage over corn-colored sand. Turning onto the Qom Highway, he broke into a procession of vehicles plodding after an old Chevrolet convertible, a dinosaur with sweeping tail fins. The top was down, and a man crouched in back bracing a loudspeaker that pulverized the thin desert air with taped prayer. Trailing the convertible were a hearse and a black limousine. Mounted on the trunk, wreathed in red-and-yellow roses, was a portrait-size photograph in a gold frame. Darius pulled close for a better look at clean-shaven features locked in a dour, hopeless gaze—the sensation of staring into a gaudy mirror. Dropping back out of range of the loudspeaker, he followed the cortege along a boulevard edged in blossoming shrubs until it entered the vast Paradise of Zahra Cemetery.

Beyond rows of marble stones where the casualties of the Revolution lay buried were glass shrines under Islam's green flag, and Shi'a's black, decked with fresh fruit and plastic tulips, the flower of martyrdom. Like the wedding bowers of the dead in Dharvazeh Ghor, they had been erected in memory of young men slain in the war with Iraq, and contained personal mementos, a favorite book, or childhood toy, the simple relics of stunted lives. Outside the cemetery fence, opposite a fountain erupting in torrents of bluish red, Darius parked at a hovel distinguishable from its neighbors by the American flag in fresh enamel on the doorstep. A mullah in a smart abayah and immaculate white turban opened the door before Darius could knock. His beard, sculpted into a perfect silver U, was lightly hennaed. "Come in, please," he said. "We have been expecting you."

Darius stepped out of his shoes and entered a living room smaller even than Maryam Lajevardi's. The cheap carpeting was covered in sofrays on which black ants gorged on spilled sugar. There would be no cassette players hidden in the corners here, no Beatles. A woman whose green silk blouse was pulled above her breast was nursing a girl at least two years old while a boy at her knees ground the wheels of a plastic army truck against a bare spot on the floor. The woman carried her daughter from the room, nearly colliding with Bijan, who had come in wearing natty brown desert fatigues, but was out of uniform in stocking feet.

"It is an honor to have you as a guest in my house," he said to Darius. "Please, let me bring you tea."

Darius squatted on a flat cushion beside the mullah with the hennaed beard.

"Ahmad," Bijan said, "I am proud to introduce you to Darius Bakhtiar, the famous homicide chief for the National Police in all of the district of Teheran."

Proud perhaps, Darius thought, but not happy. Bijan looked like a peasant forced to serve up his last scrap of food to the emissary of a malignant king.

The mullah jabbed a toothpick in his mouth beside a cigarette with a gold paper filter. He nodded.

"Hojjatoleslam Sayyid Ahmad Sarmadi has been adviser to the Bon Yad Monkerat for many years," Bijan said. "Without his help and spiritual guidance we could not have taken on the littlest part of our work for the glory of God."

Sarmadi touched a lighter to the cigarette, basking in Bijan's praise and then a cloud of blue smoke.

". . . He is also my former son-in-law."

Darius noticed a yellow stain in the hennaed silver. The mullah was in his fifties, older than Bijan by two decades. The little girl ran into the living room clinging to a rag doll dripping cotton batting. "Daddy," she said, "Fatemeh want to play with Uncle."

"Not now, my precious. Ahmad and I have important things to talk about."

Pouting, the toddler started across the room. Bijan wrapped his arms around her, and turned her toward Darius.

"You must meet my children. Muhammad," he called to the little boy, "say hello to Lieutenant Colonel Bakhtiar."

The child spun the wheels faster, drowning out his father's command. "Muhammad is eight, the light of my life," Bijan said. "His sister, Fatemeh, was two years old last month. She is Ahmad's former wife."

Bijan released the little girl, who ran to her brother. The children's mother came back, tucking a wisp of hair under a burgundy chador. She placed three glasses in saucers on the sofray along with some cookies that gave off the scent of jasmine. Darius clamped a cube of sugar in his teeth and swallowed the scalding tea watching Fatemeh bring an imaginary cup to the frayed lips of her doll.

"Ahmad," Bijan said, "is a friend of many years. Long before he began to advise the Bon Yad he was welcome at my house. As you see, we live simply, without air-conditioning or any of the luxuries you have in the northern part of the city. Not even a good breeze. In this heat it is inconvenient for my wife to have to put on her chador each time Ahmad visits. So last month, when Fatemeh turned two, we made her seegah for Ahmad. After one hour the terms of the marriage contract expired, and Fatemeh and Ahmad were single again, and free to go their own ways. But Ahmad will be our former son-in-law for all time, and now my wife no longer has to veil herself in his presence. It makes life easier sometimes when we can skirt the rules. But I don't have to tell you—"

Darius brushed ants away from his feet. "What did you want to see me about?"

"Because of criticism leveled at you from many areas," Bijan turned squarely toward Darius, "it has been decided by the Revolutionary Prosecutor, Mr. Zakir, to replace you as chief of the homicide bureau. In these perilous times, when the nation is threatened as never before, we must be able to count absolutely on persons in positions of responsibility. Your former membership in the shah's secret police disqualifies you from this trust. It is unreasonable to argue that you be allowed to continue in your present role."

"What you're telling me," Darius said, "is the Komiteh is purging Homicide."

"That is not at all the case. Other changes are anticipated gradually, over a period of years, and if God wills it you will be allowed to remain a member of the police and draw a regular salary. Your Lieutenant Ghaffari will be promoted to captain and named the new homicide commander in your place. Since he is lacking in administrative experience, he will report to Hojjatoleslam Sarmadi, who will concentrate his reforms on strengthening the men's loyalty to the regime."

Translated, Darius knew, this meant that until the Revolutionary Prosecutor was ready to move forcefully, the pompous ass with the reddened beard would be Zakir's personal spy in Homicide, harassing the men who didn't conform to the changing standard of piety, relaying bureau gossip that the resident spy was letting by—who made what joke about the way which ayatollah wound his turban—fabricating the case to bring down the National Police. Now Sarmadi picked up from Bijan, going on how the first order of business would be to issue a volume of the Imam's sermons to the men and, after they had mastered its elementary lessons, to have them study *Forbidden Occupations: The Prohibition of Seeking Profit in Filthy, Unclean and Dead Things.*

"I will demand that investigators be required to take the time for daily prayers," Sarmadi continued. "Prayer instills a favorable attitude for pursuing their heavy responsibilities . . ."

Though he had been waiting for the axe to fall, the start of its descent left Darius stunned. And nauseated by the heat, reeling from the withering assault of the Padkis, he shut his ears to what Sarmadi was saying. Why had he been summoned to this inferno when the logical place to fire him was the homicide bureau? Was Bijan so proud of his family, and of the grinding poverty that was proof of his integrity? Or did Sarmadi anticipate a rebellion when he was announced to the men as religious commissar? Still another hypothesis existed, too plausible to put out of mind—Sarmadi's mind, which Darius feared would elevate it first to strategy and then to bold tactic—that it had been decided to test Darius's reaction to the transfer of power away from headquarters, where an accident easily could be arranged should he protest too vehemently. Aware, suddenly, that his eyes were starting to glaze, he focused on the mullah, who was standing over him with his hand outstretched.

"We will confer again soon," Sarmadi said, "to discuss how to facilitate the changes with the least disruption. It was an instructive experience for me to have met you."

Sarmadi kissed the children on his way to the door, and then Darius heard the roar of a car he hadn't noticed on the street. Bijan's wife came back into the living room to clear the dishes and whisk the loose sugar into the rugs.

"Was it necessary for you to have made so obvious your resentment of Ahmad?" Bijan said to Darius. "He is a brilliant marja, a genius when it comes to the application of Islamic law to day-to-day problems, but greedy for the respect due him. He is also a sitting member of the Council of Guardians, its brightest young light, with connections that reach to the seat of power in the Islamic Republican Party, even to the President of the republic. There is nothing he cannot accomplish once he puts his mind to it."

"His ideas are inane, worse than useless."

"You will be amazed at how he makes things run better in the homicide bureau." Bijan laced up black hobnail boots. ". . . if you are still around. May I ask a favor? My car is out of service. If you are going back near police headquarters I need a ride to Khayyam Avenue, intersection of Panzdah-e-Khordad. I would like to visit my other wives and son."

Bijan shouldered his Uzi and followed Darius outside. The sun floated in chemical haze over the Paycon, which threw heat like an oven when Darius opened his door. He rolled down the windows and stood with Bijan on the shadeless sidewalk, waiting for the interior to cool.

"You must excuse my wife's behavior; it was not meant to be insulting. We have not been on the best of terms lately." Bijan's tone, not friendly, suggested the casual intimacy of shared experience. "I have been married to Bilqais for nine years. Four years ago, I contracted with another woman to be my seegah, who even now Bilqais does not accept. This is a real temporary marriage, not a sham for convenience sake, like Ahmad and Fatemeh's." Bijan pressed his hand against the passenger's seat, and then slid inside the car. Darius got in after him, sucking air through his teeth as the upholstery burned his thighs. "I have decided to leave my other wife, and take a younger seegah, a widow of the imposed war. I have a year-old boy with my second wife, and would like to keep her, but Bilqais says I cannot afford three households."

Traffic moved slowly toward a roadblock in the middle of the street. Darius let up on the gas as basijis rushed the car from both sides, teenage boys carrying Kalashnikovs at the knee. It was not uncommon to be stopped five or six times on a short trip through the city and checked for drunkenness and contraband. Unmarried couples found traveling together were at the risk of being whipped on the spot. Bijan poked his head out and snapped at the young volunteers, who waved the Paycon around the line of waiting cars and through the barricade. ". . . You know how these jealous women are," he said to Darius.

At a house behind a tumbledown wall covered in revolutionary graffiti Bijan signaled to stop. "I want you to see something," he said, and lifted the lid on a small silver paper box.

Inside was a bronze figurine of a ferocious lion. Darius's hand hovered over the open box, but he did not touch the statuette.

"Do you think my new seegah will like it? It is a Lurestan miniature, from pre-Islamic Persia."

Darius nodded. "I've seen one like it at the Archaeological Museum."

"I saw this one at the museum, too," Bijan said. "In the gift shop. It is a facsimile, but, for me, exquisite just the same. If I were as wealthy as the shah I would collect the originals for a hobby. And fine Hamadan camel's hair carpets. No other country has a culture to match ours. None."

Bijan replaced the top. He was out of the car when he said, "I have been so wrapped up in my selfish concerns that I almost forgot to ask: What did you find out about the murder of the girl in Shemiran? When will you have her killer?"

"I'm the one who was had."

"I do not understand your meaning."

"Don't you? The Revolutionary Guards followed me till I ran down my best witness in Mashad. Then they killed him."

"A heroin trader, I was told." Bijan backed toward the house. "It is just as well."

"You wanted him silenced. You used me as one of his executioners."

But what was he making a fuss about? Of course he was an executioner. Hadn't he slain Bijan's uncle for crimes that also could not be proved? Where was the authority for his protest when he was no different than the gunmen who had taken advantage of him?

"Now *you* don't understand," Bijan said. "It is a miserable business, I know, being a homicide investigator, and having to witness gruesome things, but sometimes necessary. You must look at the bright side—soon you won't have to deal with this kind of unpleasantness. You will put violent death and tortured women behind you, so you can worry about more important problems." He turned and went away, holding his rifle against his leg like the basijis, but with his hand on the trigger guard. "Problems like women who are alive."

The grossly overweight girl Darius saw at the door did not seem happy to have company, not smiling until Bijan presented her with the silver box. Not so much a gift, Darius thought, as a bribe, which she accepted without looking inside, as he had taken Rahgozar without first assessing the cost.

· 11 ·

The Islamic regime must be serious in all things, the Imam had stated. There is no fun in Islam; there can be no fun in whatever is serious. Islam does not permit swimming in the sea, and is opposed to radio and television serials. Islam, however, allows marksmanship, archery, horseback riding, wrestling, and other sports that help to develop military skills.

There were no serials on the Islamic Republic of Iran Broadcasting Network, derided throughout Teheran as mullahvision, which beamed a steady diet of religious programming, wildlife documentaries, and educational shows for children. Occasionally, one of the capital's two stations interrupted its regular schedule for a major sporting event. Tonight, following *Desert Architecture*, and prior to *Shrines of Iran*, the finals of the national weightlifting championships would be broadcast from the city of Shiraz.

Darius lay on the convertible sofa in his new apartment in the north Teheran neighborhood of Africa, trying to work up enthusiasm for the competition. He was thrilled more with the bottle of Padkis that Mehta had bestowed upon him. He drank and dozed, sometimes glancing at the screen while he toyed with an empty bottle of vodka into which he had poked his big toe, raising and slowly letting it down, going for a world record in the event in his weight division.

Around midnight, the phone rang. As he lumbered groggily across the floor, he skidded in wetness, and knew without looking that he was bleeding.

"Shit," he said, and bent to knot his handkerchief around his toe. The sound of cheering turned him back toward the screen, where a deceptively slight man hoisted a barbell almost to his shoulders before toppling from the platform. The first sensation of pain cleared his head as he grabbed the receiver. "Shit," he said again. "Who is it?"

There was no answer at first. Then, uncertainly: "This is Criminalist Hamid."

Darius was sorry he had gotten up from the comfortable sofa. For Hamid to call so late a catastrophe must have occurred or was in the works. He tightened the tourniquet, plucked jagged glass from around the base of his big toe.

"She's gone," Hamid said.

"What? Who—"

"Maryam Lajevardi. You told me to watch her place."

"Gone where?" Darius reached back for the Padkis, but couldn't get a hand on it. "She doesn't have money to go anywhere, doesn't know a soul."

"An hour ago a telephone cab came to the house and brought her east into the city. I kept close as I could without alerting the driver. It was easy. Traffic wasn't bad—"

"How did she get away?"

"There was a Pasdar roadblock on Azadi Avenue, near the freeway. The cab was waved through, but the basij had to smell my breath, and then to have me walk a straight line while they inspected the car. When they found out I was police, they tore everything apart. By the time I was let through, the cab was nowhere in sight. I tried to find it, but it was no use."

Hamid spoke quickly, bunching his words. Darius had a hard time understanding him. "Were you drinking?"

"No, absolutely not," Hamid pleaded. "I went back to the house. I hoped she had gone on a simple errand and would return soon. I didn't want to bother you, I was going to wait till morning; maybe she'd show up then." He sounded close to tears. "But she won't—I know it. What do you want me to do?"

Darius swiped at the bottle again, then gave up and carried the phone to the couch, backtracking along a trail of blood and broken glass. "Go home," he said.

"You don't want me to look anymore?"

"And get drunk, like you should have in the first place."

Darius tried to lose himself in a travelogue on the troglodyte villages of the

Khandejan region that had bumped the weightlifters from the air. Blame for losing Maryam Lajevardi did not lie with Hamid, but with himself for not taking her into custody. The immediate order of business was finding something to prop up Hamid's dwindling self-esteem. When Ghaffari took charge of Homicide, the young criminalist would be indispensable to him, if his confidence hadn't already been destroyed.

He felt completely sober, as though his system had purged itself of alcohol through the gash in his foot. Hamid was right: there was nothing to do but wait until morning, when there would be nothing left to wait for. Another search of the house was pointless. Maryam's secrets lay within herself, rather than inside her closets and bureau drawers. He turned up the volume on the television, but was uninterested in the troglodyte villages, nor in *Adventures in Arabic* on the other channel. Unable to sleep, too tired to open the bed, he hobbled into the bathroom to apply iodine and a bandage and to wake himself fully by shaving with cold water. Dressed in his banker's charcoal wool suit, soon he was back in the Paycon, speeding through the black streets of Ark.

Maryam Lajevardi's file was where he had left it on his desk, the tan cover smelling strongly of vodka. He gleaned little from the few documents inside. The girl's photograph already had told its full tale. The two episodes of her criminal career, authored by arresting officers who were not natural storytellers, were spare in detail; Mehta had left out nothing of significance in his briefing. The signatures at the bottom of each page were potentially more revealing than the accounts they attested to. Possibly the officers could be induced to remember additional facts, if they were still in the department or could be located. Darius squared one of the forms under a goose-neck lamp. The name was that of a detective who had died of a heart attack while on duty six months before. Underneath was the bunched scrawl of the Komitehman to whom the girl had been released. Darius concentrated the light through a magnifying lens until the paper gave up the name Javad Salehi, Hormoz's former student who was now a leading faculty member at "The Institute."

Salehi's signature was pure gold, which was to say that he could not refine the clue. A return to Manzarieh, even if not fatal, would accomplish nothing. Under no circumstances did he envision Salehi seeing him again, or consenting to an interview. The sheik's strained friendliness had been for Hormoz's nephew, not Darius in particular, and was exhausted by the time they had said good-bye. Some of the facts he needed on Salehi's link to the Party of God, and its camps in Lebanon, might be stitched together from secondary sources, however, and he asked the long-distance operator to dial Qom for him. The phone had rung once when he broke the connection. The summons to morning prayer would be Hormoz's alarm clock, not a 3:00 A.M. call from a desperate homicide detective, formerly his niece's husband.

He drove aimlessly from headquarters, craning for the first indication of dawn as a mariner scouts the horizon for weather. The wheel was a Ouija board that pulled him to the Old Karaj Road, and then due west. When he stopped outside Maryam Lajevardi's the black of night was still intact, enveloping the hazy moon and a single bulb that the woman evidently had overlooked in her haste to flee.

He brushed aside the bedroom curtains to play the light from a five-cell flashlight on the floor. Then he climbed in through the open window. The bed had not been slept in. He heard footsteps receding into the inner rooms, and strode purposefully after them, a warning that there was no place to run. A chair fell over in the kitchen, and silverware rattled in a drawer. The darkness swallowed the beam of light, which bounced back off a carving knife held high in a tremulous hand.

"Couldn't you have knocked?" Maryam Lajevardi lowered the blade, and Darius followed it with the flash till it hung loosely at her side, "and used the door like everybody else?"

"What are you doing here?"

"You may remember I live here. And if you don't—" Maryam's sweet, mocking tone hardened into muted anger, "then why are you in my kitchen at this hour?"

"I was informed that you'd run away. I came to see for myself."

"You were *informed?*" Maryam looked outside at the quiet commercial buildings, then pulled down the shade, stifling the dry breeze. "I have nosy neighbors, but not very reliable as witnesses," she said to him. "You can't believe what they say about me. They, or anyone else."

Darius tugged at the light string above the table, switched off his flash. "Where did you go?"

"I was bored. And lonely. I found a few thousand rials I'd forgotten about in the pockets of my chador, and went to see a friend. What's wrong with that?"

"You also told me you had no friends in Teheran."

"It could be that I was looking to make one. Is that against your rules, too?"

"Possibly the rule should be written," he said.

"If I was running away, would I be talking to you now?" She relaxed when he did not come back at her with another question. "I'd been cooped up so long I couldn't stand it by myself another minute. I called a cab and went into the city, and stopped for something to eat. Are there rules against that, too?"

It was senseless to pursue it. If he did, she would tell him the name of the restaurant and what she had ordered, how much the meal had cost and what the waiter had said when he came to her table, and how he had tried to short-change her. And none of it true, and totally beside the point.

"I find that hard to accept," he said.

"Well, that's your prob—"

"Hard to accept anything you say. You've been consistently untruthful, about working at the currency exchange, your whole past. In 1983, you were arrested for trying to toss acid at two women downtown. Do you deny it?"

"I was a naive child then, a baby. I didn't know how to think for myself. I believed in all the promises of the Revolution. Every one. If the government had allowed girls to string plastic keys around their necks and dance through the minefields of Basra, I would have been first to volunteer. That was a long time ago. Two years later, I was in high heels and lipstick, and buying Rolling Stones records on the black market. That's where my history begins." She stared into his stony face to see if any of it was sinking in. "You know nothing about me. Absolutely nothing. You've taken an isolated incident that happened half a lifetime ago, and no doubt built it into a fantastic biography."

"We know also," Darius went on as if he hadn't heard her, "of your relationship with Sheik Javad Salehi."

The color drained from Maryam's cheeks. Her brows, normally two pale smudges, emerged like invisible ink in the white ridges above her eyes.

". . . And that he is living these days in Shemiran—"

"Is that so?"

"At the Manzarieh guerrilla camp less than two kilometers from Saltan-atabad Avenue. A remarkable coincidence, your settling so near your former benefactor without knowing he was there."

"Coincidence is all it is." Maryam's tone was so reasonable that he felt himself, if not believing her, starting to consider that he had overlooked an obvious explanation. "You must give him my phone number when you see him."

"This isn't funny. Don't treat it as a joke."

"Do you hear me laughing? I'm being kept prisoner in my own home because of these crazy notions that I'm involved in murder and drugs, with no way to prove I know nothing about them. Where do you get your ideas?"

"From facts, and what must be inferred from them. Sheik Salehi is a principal instructor at Manzarieh. Considering your past relationship, it's hard to believe you've never been to the Party of God camps in Lebanon."

"He wasn't teaching anybody to be a guerrilla ten years ago. He was working for the Pasdar in central Teheran, counseling troubled youngsters to channel their energy into productive activities. After I got into trouble, it was he who returned me to my family. I shudder to think where I would be today without his kind care."

"Far from here," Darius said, "and from being the subject of a police investigation."

"Ask Javad yourself," Maryam said. "I'd love to see him again, to be able to thank him for what he did for me. How soon can you arrange a meeting?"

As tempting as it was to use her to get to Salehi, he was unwilling to try it. If the Komiteh were looking for Maryam, he'd be giving them a free chance at her, and, if not, she would be in contact with a powerful protector. He found the telephone on the living room floor and dialed in the dark, counting the holes in the rotary dial with his fingertips. "It's me, Bakhtiar," he said. "I'm sorry to wake you, but I need you to—"

Maryam had wandered in after him, and now she nudged the receiver from his ear. "No, wait. I don't—"

"One second, Hamid." Darius cupped the mouthpiece. "What do you want?" he asked her.

"Nothing." Already she had begun to walk away.

Darius still felt the pressure of her hand on his, her tag in their undeclared game. "Come back to the Old Karaj Road address," he said into the phone, "and bring a good book to read. Yes, she's here now . . . minutes ago. I want you inside this time. You'll sit twelve-hour shifts, alternating with one of the other men."

When Darius returned to the kitchen, Maryam had switched off the light and was somewhere near the table, tapping the handle of the knife against the Formica top.

"An officer is being assigned to the house, so you can't run away again," he told her.

"I didn't run away before."

"Hamid will stay indefinitely. He is a criminalist, about your age. He likes the Beatles, too. You won't be bored anymore, or lonely."

"Does he have a rich fantasy life like yours?" Maryam was a disembodied voice in the dark. "I don't want him here. Why won't you leave me alone?"

"You have information I need."

"I can't tell you what I don't know. And if I could guess what it is, I suspect you'd lock me up. You've placed me in an impossible position."

"But a safe one. You realize the police aren't alone in wanting to listen to your story. Others are getting close, and they can be persuasive."

"I see now, you're here for *my* benefit. Draw up a confession, and I'll sign it. The more heinous the crime, the better—the better for me. There isn't a thing I won't admit to."

"Not for your benefit, Miss Lajevardi."

"For whose, then? The dead girls? I would have thought it's late for them."

Darius saw himself pulling at slack strings as he attempted to manipulate her loyalty, playing the same sorry game with her future that Ashfar played with his. "You're not accused of anything," he said.

"Then it must be for your benefit. What will you give me in exchange? Isn't that the way the police operate? Promise me something, Lieutenant Colonel, and you'll have the words you need to hear, whatever you say they should be. I won't drive a hard bargain."

"It's not a confession we want."

"Nothing?" She taunted him. "That's your best offer? It seems unfair that you should profit from my remarks, and I'm to have nothing in return."

"Not a confession; but the truth."

"Oh, that's different. I'll sign right now. I'll talk," she said. "But first you have to tell me what it is."

Not as prosecutor, jailer, nor interrogator did he awe her. She tugged at the light string again, and he was blind in her pale beauty. In that instant she was nearer to all his secrets than he was to learning any of hers.

"The truth," he said again. "Is it asking so much?"

"Don't you see?" Maryam shook her head, flinging tears against his dry lips. "Don't you see that's all I have?"

❖ 12 ❖

_____

A woman with a Kurdish accent was asking the price of melons in Qom. Darius spoke louder, but was unable to drown out the cross talk in the line.

"It's good to hear your voice . . ."

Darius paused, straining to make out the words. An elderly man he thought had answered the Kurdish woman seemed to be talking to him.

"I was beginning to be afraid I had lost my favorite nephew." Over the racket Hormoz's breathy rasp was becoming clear.

"Your only nephew." Darius brushed Maryam Lajevardi's folder out of the way, and sat on his desk with his heels hooked in the handle of the bottom drawer. "How have you been, uncle?"

"As well as can be expected. Which is, truth be told, not as well as I would like to feel, although not as bad as my enemies wish."

During an instant of quiet following a false start by all the parties on the crossed wires, Darius re-created Hormoz's playful smile on his own lips. "You have no enemies," he said.

"Every man, every man who has lived as long as I, has enemies," Hormoz said, "although others may have lost some good ones along the way."

Darius missed the rest of what Hormoz said, but learned that melons had been going up all summer in Sanandaj, and now was a bad time to buy.

". . . Are you surviving? Has it been hard for you, having your freedom?"

"I've been too busy to appreciate it," Darius said.

"You're putting it to its proper use. I heard from Farib just yesterday. She is in good health, but there are hints she's unhappy."

"How's that?"

"She says she will remarry soon."

"I didn't know she was seeing anyone," Darius said. "We don't have the same friends anymore. We never did, really."

"He is an older man, a goldsmith. In no way is this a love match, but he is said to be quite well off. Alas, if that is what she wants I hope he gives her all the happiness she deserves."

A pain that was lodged permanently under Darius's ribs metastasized in his heart. He had given Farib little thought since the divorce, only in part because he was wrapped up in the investigation. A compulsive side of his personality was taunting him, making her desirable now that she would be unavailable to him forever. Though he saw through the trap, it did nothing to ease his hurt.

"I've recalled several facts about my former pupil since our last conversation," Hormoz was saying, "and talked to other people who knew him from his time at Faiziyeh."

"I didn't call about Bijan—" Darius stopped, no match for the woman inquiring about melons.

". . . Did you know he is from a family whose roots go back ten centuries in the Iraqi city of Najaf? It was his father's father who moved to Iran, settling in Khuzestan in the 1920s. During the Imam's exile in Najaf Bijan was part of his entourage until he fell from favor and was ordered back to Teheran, where he has labored in deserving obscurity ever since." Hormoz coughed. His lungs made hissing sounds as he struggled for breath.

"The phones are not secure," Darius cautioned him.

"These are not secrets. Do you need more?"

"I don't know what I need. I wanted to ask about another of your old students."

"Which one?"

"Javad Salehi."

"I hadn't been told he was in Teheran." Hormoz's voice was a feathery whisper. "He isn't murdered?"

"There hasn't been a killing in weeks. I have to find out about his past, same as Bijan's."

"We are talking about two completely different men. There are professors at Faiziyeh who to this day hold up Javad as a shining light to each new class of students. He was unusually disciplined, with no interest in worldly things, and dogmatic to a fault regarding the pronouncements of the Imam. He favored qital, the purest form of holy war, a war without mercy to convert the infidel at the point of a sword, but favored it to guarantee his redemption rather than the converts'."

Darius heard a harsh click. "*Hormoz?*"

"Yes, I'm still here."

"Where did he go from Faiziyeh?"

"We lost contact for several years. Around 1984, I received a letter of apology for having broken off with me. He had accepted an appointment to the National University, which recently had been established by the Party of God."

"I remember it," Darius said. "It was located at Evin. But it was no university. The official name was the Revolutionary Research Facility. There were a thousand students, mostly PLO."

"Javad was resident lecturer in Psychology of the Jihad. He had made himself an expert on inflicting terror on civilian populations. The National University supported what were referred to euphemistically as extension campuses at Firoughkoor and Manzarieh. The graduate centers were in south Lebanon, close to the Israeli border, and in Beirut."

"Say again?"

"After two years at Evin, he wrote to tell me he had taken up directorship of the camp in Lebanon."

"Did he mention the name?"

"No, but I recall that the student body was entirely female. Three hundred foreign women who had come to Iran to be converted to Islam had embraced a martyr's fate and were brought to the camp to await a suicide mission. There were girls from Nicaragua and El Salvador, from Germany and North Korea and Northern Ireland—"

"Were Iranian girls among them?"

"A few. The majority were Lebanese Shi'ites, and Syrians. But the loyalty of the Syrians was suspect, and they were booted out of the camp."

"Why?"

"Syrians in Lebanon care more about drugs than holy war. The dictator Assad's brother is personally in charge of the drug trade in the areas of the country under his army's control. All revenues are supposed to go to furthering the fight against the infidel West, but most of it lines the pockets of the Assads. In the camps near Israel drugs were the primary curriculum."

"Salehi told you this? He could have been shot."

"He was troubled by the commonplace hypocrisy. He had faith that the camp could do important work if the dealing in drugs ceased."

"What did you advise?"

"Javad had no business there. This I could not say directly to him. I quoted from a commentary on the chapter of the holy Qur'an on the prophet Houd:

" 'Let us be under no illusion about holy war. If we are not prepared to fight for our faith with a pure heart, our lives will be forfeit, and our resources used against us by our enemies.' "

"You meant for him to quit the camp?"

"Yes, and to divorce himself from drugs. They are an abomination in the eyes of God."

"Salehi misunderstood," Darius said. "He thought you meant he should use them to further his cause."

"He knows better. He chose deliberately to interpret my remarks that way."

Someone had come into the outer office. Darius swiveled around in time to see Ghaffari slip behind his desk like a schoolboy late for class. He lowered the receiver, and snapped his fingers to get Ghaffari's attention. "Where have you been?"

Ghaffari gestured dismissively. He looked exhausted and needed a clean shirt. Darius hadn't noticed before that his hairline had begun to recede, and he was graying at the temples. Ghaffari was thirty-two.

Hormoz was trying to impress upon Darius how perplexed he was that a man as principled as Salehi would have twisted the meaning of his words. "I will write to him today, better to explain—"

"It's late."

"I accept the blame for the damage that cannot be undone. Still, there is opportunity for him to acknowledge his error and find the correct path."

Another click signaled twenty seconds of static, and then Hormoz faded beneath a younger man's complaint about constant sandstorms and the unavailability of air filters for General Motors cars. Darius stared at Ghaffari, who sat frozen with his head in his hands. He screwed the receiver against his ear, listening for Hormoz, but it was the frustrated motorist who dominated the line.

"I can't hear you," Darius shouted, "and I've got to go. Don't send your letter till we've talked again."

Ghaffari had returned to life, and was rooting in his bottom drawer for a bottle of bootleg. "I know, I know," he said contritely when Darius got off the phone. "Listen first, then give me shit." He put a paper cup on Darius's side of the desk, and looked all over for another.

"It's Sharera's fault," he said. "She informed on me like she said she would, told the Bon Yad I was screwing around with Nahid. Lucky for me, she couldn't wait to let me know I'd be going to jail. I had one chance left, to drive through the night and hide Nahid in Tabriz, where I have cousins to look after her. We had to crash through two Pasdar roadblocks just to get out of Teheran. Nahid was in a panic—and I wasn't much better. The Komiteh grilled me for six hours straight when I got back. Without male witnesses it was my word against Sharera's, though, so she was outnumbered four to one, like in a court of law." Ghaffari's strained smile came apart when Darius didn't rise to it. "They didn't believe the first thing I told them, but what could they do? They had to take my word. The law regarding adultery is *their* law, the religious law. They let me go."

"I vouched for you," Darius said, unmoved by Ghaffari's plea for sympathy. "You've made me a liar in Sharera's eyes."

"No, no, I did nothing like that." Ghaffari gave him the cup, which he crumpled in his fist. "Really, I was trying to break off with Nahid. It just took longer than I thought. I know I failed you when you needed me in Mashad, and you hate me for it. All I ask is that you let me make it up to you."

Ghaffari's rush through the perfunctory apology, taken for granted as a nuisance for both of them, annoyed Darius less than the feeling that he was holding something back, that more dismal revelation would follow.

"You can begin by helping me to put the squeeze on Maryam Lajevardi."

"You found her?" Ghaffari stared disbelievingly. He twisted the cap off the bootleg, and gulped from the bottle. "You didn't need me after all. Where was she?"

"Everything is in my report. If I don't have the time to obtain the information we want from her, then you must."

Ghaffari wiped his mouth on his hand. "What do you mean, 'If you don't have time?' Are you going somewhere?"

"I'm being made to disappear," Darius said. "The Revolutionary Prosecutor has ordered me replaced as chief of homicide."

"You can't— He can't be serious. No one else here can even find a paper clip. How does he expect a new man to keep the bureau functioning?" Ghaffari took another long swallow. "Who is the dumb bastard bringing in, which suckass?"

"He wants you, Mansur."

Ghaffari's grin was a secret betrayed, which he wrestled back into the dark with white lips. "I'm not qualified."

"I'm out, and you're in," Darius said. "It's a sentence without appeal." No need to tell him he would be responsible to Sarmadi, the Bon Yad's adviser, and see the grin dead and buried; he would find out soon enough. "In the meantime I'll bring you to meet the Lajevardi girl."

"Since when do you want my help in getting someone to talk?"

"Positive inducements have no effect on her, and neither do threats. She doesn't care whether she lives, dies, or is jailed for a long period of time. And I don't have time."

"Is heroin so important to her, is she that far gone? Or is it the money she can get for it?"

"It's sheer obstinacy—hardened by military discipline. She was in Lebanon, in the guerrilla camps with the other girls. There's some of the fanatic in her as well."

"What do you need me to do?"

"I've established myself as her antagonist. I want you to be—"

"To be her friend? That's kindergarten stuff. What criminal won't see immediately through that?"

"She's no criminal," Darius said. "You'll play super-antagonist. Anyway, I'm tired of being the bad guy."

"But you're a natural . . ." Ghaffari stretched, raising his fists overhead. "Can't it wait? I'm beat. I'd feel plenty more ferocious after a nap."

Darius looked at his watch, stifling a yawn.

"You could stand a few winks yourself," Ghaffari said.

"Go home, read my report, patch things up with Sharera as best you can, and sleep." Darius took the bottle from him. "I'll call when I'm ready for you."

Darius walked downstairs to the basement. Fluorescent strips had been installed in the supply room, lending a sheen of newness to the blank arrest forms and reams of paper stacked haphazardly on the shelves. No, he thought, he wasn't the only one who knew where to find the paper clips. Maybe it was time for Mehta, once Homicide's bright boy, to be cast in fresh light, too, and given something to do.

Or Hamid, or one of the untried men whose names he still had not learned. Ghaffari was becoming increasingly unreliable, taking on the immature traits of the young officers like garments they had outgrown. He foresaw the new chief's tenure as a brief, unhappy period that would end with

Sarmadi assuming formal control of the bureau, and Ghaffari a discarded figurehead in limbo with himself.

The new lighting did not reach to Evidence, where the single bulb above the shelves was out. Inside the records cage Mehta dozed with his head in his arms, his usual posture when his elbow wasn't bent. Darius could not say with certainty that Mehta still left headquarters at the end of his shift; none of the men had been to his home in years. Mehta's wife was dead, and he had no children. His private life revolved around thinning the cases of whiskey that he catalogued by day. Everything of importance to him was in arm's reach in these musty rooms. Darius rattled the gate. Mehta's head rose from the cradle of his arms, and his hand swept the table. Grasping at nothing, it circled around, and he was snoring again before it settled under his ear.

The air was treacly with the aftershave that Mehta used alternately to mask the evidence of his drinking and to guzzle when even the most poisonous labels of bootleg were unavailable. This morning, there were no bottles in the cage, none of the empties filled with his urine that collected regularly in the corners and were sent upstairs as a bonus with every request for evidence or a file.

"Hey," Darius shouted, "what's so valuable in there, you've got to keep yourself locked up with it?"

Mehta rose disjointedly, gathering himself together piece by piece as he swayed over the table. To Darius the records officer appeared to have deteriorated since the last time they had talked, or rather—remembering that they had conferred just hours ago—since the last time he actually had looked at him. Mehta had been buried in the basement for so many years that no one really saw him anymore. He existed inanimately, a part of the building like the paint on the walls, the sandy dust. Even Mehta failed to see himself, overlooking the impression made by his rat's nest of hair and chalky skin. He came to the gate with long skating steps, as though fearful that if he raised his feet they would lose the floor and not find it again. He squinted through the mesh, and then unlocked the cage, and went back to the table and buried his head in his arms.

"Nader, you ought to ease up on the booze," Darius said, "and give your liver a break."

Mehta snored with his eyes open. "You woke me."

"You're not supposed to be here at this hour."

". . . To protect and serve," he mumbled.

"Tell me something, and I'll let you back to sleep. Is there any mention of Bijan Farmayan in the files?"

Mehta opened one bloodshot eye, scraped at the scaly lid with a black fingernail. "You can't count the piddlyshit cases he's handed over, the poor bastards in jail on his testimony."

"Not that. Has there ever been a time when his loyalty was suspect?"

". . . being absurd. The regime's his life's blood. He'd sooner turn against his family."

Darius shook his head at Mehta's back. "His loyalty to the nation."

Mehta turned slowly into the light like a sunbather adjusting to afternoon shadow, his skin stretched thin and glossy across the bristling thrust of his jaw. He wore a tweed jacket and vest over a long-sleeve shirt with a high starched collar. Darius found it incredible that he had been entertaining company for several minutes without going to the evidence room for a bottle.

"When things are slow, I like to see what's in the files. If I'd noticed anything to make him squirm, you would have been told a long time ago. Why do you ask?"

"I heard his family was from Iraq, and he might still have ties there. It offered an interesting avenue of investigation."

"He wouldn't betray his country. He's too straitlaced. What could he be bribed with? He wouldn't know what money is for if he had it in his hands."

Darius, recalling the fat woman on Khayyam Avenue and the silver package that had gotten Bijan past her door, said, "Not as straitlaced as you'd think. But, if there's nothing on him—"

"Is this what you ruined my sleep for?"

Files that had been brought down from the shelves never to be returned were heaped on the table, the chairs, the floor with odd bits of evidence that Mehta kept as trophies from the bureau's best cases, a rare Turkish Kerikkale pistol Darius remembered from the holdup-murder of a cab driver that remained unsolved for two years before an arrest was made, the timing device recovered intact from a pipe bomb planted by fanatics in a north Teheran cinema that claimed thirty-seven lives.

"Nader," he said, "as your friend I have to tell you, you don't look well. You ought to try to eat once in a while, and get out for some fresh air. It wouldn't be hard to develop tuberculosis in this dungeon."

"I plan to die here," Mehta said with finality, "so why bother? Worry about yourself instead. You don't look that good either—and where's *your* excuse?"

For years Darius and Mehta had been locked in a contest of dissipation, making a battlefield of their bodies as they thumbed their nose at the regime. Now that Mehta had opened a lead it struck Darius as unfair to change the rules, to declare that it had not been his intention to play until one of them was more dead than alive, a near-winner. He put his arm around Mehta's shoulder. "I meant that you should take care. I . . . all of us would be lost without you."

"Good Muslim that you are, at least indulge me in my despondency."

Darius laughed because he thought he was expected to, but Mehta didn't join in. "I'm as good a Muslim as any oil sheik at the roulette tables of London. It's an accident of birth I recovered from ages ago."

"I would have given thirty years of my life to be party to the same accident."

Mehta was slurring his words, bogged down in a sibilant quagmire. Darius glanced around the cage. What was the records officer drinking these days?

"After Islam conquered Persia," Mehta said, "we Zoroastrians believed that Ahura Mazda, the god of Good and Light, had forgotten us. Our sages had prophesied that the Messiah would appear, and instead the Arabs arrived and forced our faith underground. For fourteen centuries we have clung to our beliefs while Muslims ruined this land."

"What do you intend to do about it?"

"Persia will be redeemed when over three thousand years three saviors will appear, each one a son of Zoroaster."

"You're forgetting something, aren't you? Zoroaster's been dead a long time. How can he have kids?"

Darius was waiting for Mehta to confess that he did not subscribe to the old mythology any more than Darius did to the stories in the Qur'an. But the records chief looked at him gravely and said, "His sons will be born to a virgin who has bathed in a lake that preserved Zoroaster's semen. It is written in our holy books that one day the Messiah will help God in displacing the Islamic demons."

"Is that who I am? A demon from the forces of darkness?"

"As the spawn of invaders, you've worn out your welcome." Mehta straightened his wilted lapels. "What you have before you is a casualty of the holding action until the Messiah comes to put you smug bastards in your place."

"The son of Muslim invaders? More like the invaded, you mean. You haven't an inkling about my parents, the people I come from. Never—never talk to me like that again." Darius rarely raised his voice, not to Mehta, of whom he genuinely was fond, and now he was raving, shouting himself hoarse.

"You're a fool," Mehta said. "Every Muslim is a prince in this miserable land. If I were you, I'd—"

Drink twice as much, Darius finished the thought for him, invent crazier reasons for destroying yourself. He went out of the cage, too far for his anger and embarrassment to carry back. "Yes, Nader, what would you do in my shoes?"

". . . I'd—something . . ." Mehta sputtered, and, groping for more, rested his head on the table.

Darius remained where he was until he heard snoring. Mehta's reputation at headquarters was that of a brilliant mind ruined by drink. But his genius was overrated, consecrated in vodka and improved upon and made gospel by friends invited to share in his alcoholic bounty. This morning, Darius would credit him with rare passion—unless it was simply a better brand of bootleg that had added conviction to his drunken banalities.

He began hunting for the file on Sousan Hovanian, who had not yet been closely linked to Maryam Lajevardi at the time her body was found in Dharvazeh Ghor. The folder was not on the shelves, and he returned to the cage and searched futilely around the dozing records officer. Mehta was so far gone that he had ceased functioning on the job. Something had to be done about restoring order to the files. But not by Darius. The new homicide chief could lobby for his own man.

The door to his apartment opened without his turning the dead bolt. He remained on the threshold letting adrenaline bring him to alertness, then went inside with his shoulder gun drawn. The bureau had been torn apart, and his clothes dumped on the floor. The heap was not tall, or distinguished by style or taste; it must have taken all of a minute to go through everything. His suits and jackets were in another modest pile at the bottom of his closet. Consolation was a quick inventory that determined nothing to be missing. Had he recovered the heroin, or mycotoxins, and hidden them here, they would have been lost to him for good. His ineptitude again had proved its worth. Too tired to open the convertible bed, he lay on the sofa with his feet dangling over the armrest. Immediately, he was lost in a black void of sleep.

It was late afternoon when he woke, not rested or energized. He poured a glass of juice and drank it in the living room, digging through his underwear for his last clean white shirt, which he found on the floor wrapped around an accordion envelope that wasn't his. He had seen letter bombs in envelopes thinner than this one. A disarmed bomb sent by Mujahadeen hypocrites to Islamic Republican Party headquarters had been the prize exhibit in Mehta's trophy room until it was taken for evidence in court. He walked in wide circles around it, as though it were a wild beast chained to a stake, or else he was, and then raised the blinds and turned on all the lights, when what he would have liked was to run it through an X-ray machine. Using scissors from the medicine chest he sliced through the flap without extricating the envelope from the shirt. He inserted a finger into the opening, widened it and slid in another, pinched out a sheaf of papers five centimeters thick.

His heart was still lodged against his Adam's apple as he examined a voter registration card for the fifteenth arrondissement of Paris, a driver's license, and a French passport with his photo on the first page. Had Ashfar and Baraheni expected to find anything in the apartment, or was their sole purpose to remind him of the power they had over him? As if he didn't understand. As if he had to be told that by leaving Iran on their safe passage he would incur a debt from which he never would be allowed to free himself. All of the documentation they had promised him, and more, was here. He returned it to the envelope, and dropped that inside his suit coat. He would see the ex-SAVAK men again soon, and nothing would give him more pleasure than to make them eat the packet.

He called Ghaffari at home, but the line was busy. He tossed his things inside the drawer, and dressed in a hurry. He was impatient to get back to Maryam's. When he dialed again, Sharera answered. Without asking how he was, she brought Ghaffari to the phone.

"It's time to talk to the girl."

"You haven't heard?" Ghaffari asked him.

Watching his reflection in the window, Darius constructed a fat knot in a red-and-blue striped tie. "Heard what?"

"Nader's dead."

"What are you talking about? I was with him this morning. Six hours ago he was fine."

"He's dead now. His housekeeper found him in bed, not breathing. I was trying to reach you at the bureau when she called it in. Baghai's already on the way."

Darius's mind was racing, spinning off thoughts faster than he could articulate them, jamming the filter of his subconscious. All that registered was the fact that he had just seen Mehta, really seen him for the first time, and now, impossibly, his friend was gone.

"Meet me there," he said. "The girl will have to wait."

In a traditional house off Shabbaz Avenue near the power plant in the eastern part of the city Mehta had lived for six years with his wife, and alone for fifteen years after her death. A truck from the coroner's office was contesting space at the curb with several police cars when Darius arrived. A white Paycon from the motor pool was Ghaffari's favorite. Uniformed officers saluted as they let Darius inside, and closed the door behind him with the finality of dirt being shoveled onto a grave.

Mehta's living room was as immaculate and well ordered as the records room once had been. But then, thought Darius, a housekeeper didn't come to the basement of police headquarters twice each week to tidy up. The housekeeper in question was a woman in her fifties whose unlined features, not accustomed to grief, resisted the solemn mask occasioned by her tears. She was a short woman, the top of her head barely reaching to the chest of her interrogators, who formed a semicircle around her. They were led by Ghaffari, still in the same dirty shirt. He pointed Darius into a corridor filled with uniformed officers and coroner's assistants with nothing to do but rock on their heels and trade comments on the certitude of death and bad weather.

Baghai was in the bedroom, bent over rumpled sheets on which Mehta sprawled on his side in his undershorts and argyle socks. Like his patient the coroner appeared to have shriveled in the heat of his underground workplace until only the heavy wool suit that he wore like armor retained the original shape of his body. To Darius he still did not look well; there might have been two dead men in the room, except that Baghai moved from time to time, probing Mehta with swift hands that suddenly motioned toward the bed.

Baghai straightened Mehta's left arm, and twisted it outward. Inside the crook of the elbow a hypodermic needle protruded from a greenish vein. This was not the crude eyedropper and needle combination favored by the addicts of Dharvazeh Ghor, but the finest professional equipment. Darius noticed black-and-blue marks and a few fresh ulcerations below Mehta's bicep, but none of the scarring of a habitual user.

"Did you know he was injecting himself with drugs?" Baghai asked.

"Nader was a confirmed boozer. You see his house, the old furnishings, not even a TV or radio. He was not the kind to abandon his regular vices for something new."

"But he did—and beginning not long ago. These marks on his arm aren't old. For a man of his age, with no prior history of narcotics use, to experiment with heroin was no different than taking up Russian roulette. Even a normal dose might have killed him, and I'm skeptical he had a good idea what a normal dose was. The assumption must be that he gave himself a hot shot, either injected too much dope, or dope of such purity that his system wouldn't tolerate it."

"Mehta wasn't stupid."

"I didn't say he was. Had he been depressed?"

"He was born depressed, and then things went downhill."

"This was not an accident," Baghai said. "He had access to large amounts of drugs seized as evidence in criminal cases, and knew basically what he was getting himself into. I'm ruling suicide, and you can hold a departmental funeral tomorrow."

The bedroom was hotter than the records cage, the windows shut tight to guarantee the sweltering ambience Mehta had loved. Darius unbuttoned his collar, and blew inside his shirt. His socks were soaked through, his pants legs glued to his thighs. "Why not call it liver failure, so we can bury him with some of his pride intact? It's how his friends expected him to go."

"How many friends did he have? Who will be scandalized to find out that he did himself in this way?" Baghai lifted the wounded arm, and plucked out the needle. "Have you a more plausible interpretation for this? He was sick, miserable, alone, physically an old man at forty-eight, with nothing to live for, or even to die for, but alcohol. Until he found heroin. What are drugs and liquor anyway, but intermediate stages of death? He killed himself. Don't ask me to lie for him."

"Make out the death certificate as you see fit," Darius said.

"Will you come to the morgue to sign it?"

"Ask Ghaffari. I'm needed elsewhere."

Mehta's housekeeper had been excused by her questioners, and stood by herself in the same spot in the living room, nervously picking lint off damask bolster pillows. Ghaffari leaned against the wall with his back to her, writing in his evidence pad.

"You saw how he died?" Ghaffari looked up from the page, disgusted, a bluenose forced to compose a pornographic essay. "I didn't suspect he'd sunk so far."

"I'm leaving for Maryam Lajevardi's now."

"Wait a moment and we'll ride together. I've had the white car tuned."

"Baghai wants you at the morgue. Possibly, Hamid can be encouraged to throw a fright into the girl in your place."

"If he isn't more afraid of her," Ghaffari said. "Where is she staying? I'll join you after I'm done."

"On the Old Karaj Road, next door to a small printing plant about six kilometers beyond the Azadi Monument. Unless you can make it in the next hour or two, don't bother to come."

"I'll be there," Ghaffari promised. "For her benefit, I've primed myself to be the meanest son of a bitch on two legs. If I don't let it out soon, there'll be no living with me."

"I hadn't noticed the difference," Darius said.

· 13 ·

Maryam quit pacing. She walked to a club table where Hamid sat opposite an empty chair, and scarcely looking at the board, not having to think about it, moved a black bishop four spaces, sweeping up a pawn, which she added to a captive white army. "Check," she said wearily.

Darius looked over Hamid's shoulder at an impending three-move checkmate. "I'm glad to see you two are getting along."

"I've always regarded the police as my friends." When Darius declined the gambit, she asked, "Don't you believe me?"

"I'm sure you've never been more truthful."

"The problem with you," Maryam said, "is you don't know who *your* friends are."

Hamid hunched over the board, studying the position of the pieces. Chess, while not illegal under the law, had been frowned upon by the Imam. Chessboards and chessmen were hard to come by, traded on the same black market as Hollywood videotapes and rock CDs. No one still remembered the logic that had chased the game out of the parks and public places, and relegated it to the backrooms where card playing and Monopoly, certified evils, still held root.

"Okay, then," Darius said, "we're agreed that we're all friends. Tell your friends where you went the other night."

"I forget."

"Try to recall."

"I can't."

"Why did you come back?"

"I'd be glad to tell you," Maryam said, "if I knew why I left."

"You should have kept going, and saved us all this trouble."

"What, and miss such a good time?"

Hamid wisely was sitting this out. Darius couldn't see him as a convincing bad guy if he sprouted fangs. Worse than ineffectual, he was small and cuddly, a puppy for Maryam to cling to while Darius assumed the ogre's role. Why was Ghaffari always someplace else . . . ? "Damn it, we'll be here forever."

Darius pounded his fist on the table. Hamid embraced the chessboard, steadying the wobbly pieces.

"We will," Maryam said, "won't we?"

"If not forever," Hamid said, "at least into the foreseeable future."

And while Darius considered braining the criminalist for interrupting his good guy–bad guy soliloquy, Maryam said, "I went to see Sheik Salehi."

Darius stared at Maryam, who seemed to have gone into shock, the most amazed of any of them that she had answered. "You've known all along he was at Manzarieh?" he said.

Incapable of further speech, she nodded.

"What business did you have there?" Darius attempted to channel the rage that had startled her before. But with no one to play off he had let too much dissipate. "Why do you resent us?" he said. "Can't you see we're trying to help you?"

"I have no feelings about you one way or the other. In case you haven't heard, the National Police are of little consequence to anyone but themselves. Let me go, and I promise never to think of you again."

"She didn't reach Manzarieh," Hamid said without looking up from the board.

"How do you know?"

"There's no possibility she would have been allowed to leave the camp. Therefore," Hamid said confidently, "she never arrived."

"True?" Darius asked her.

Maryam shrugged. "What's another secret among friends?"

"You weren't allowed past the guards?"

"If it's so important to you, I never came near Manzarieh." Hamid pushed another pawn ahead one space. Maryam's knight pounced on it, and added it to the casualties on her side of the table. "Check— After you told me Rahgozar had been killed I was afraid to stay here by myself. Sheik Salehi had helped me before when I was in trouble, so I phoned him to say I would be there soon, and then called for a cab. As I rode through the plaza under the Azadi Monument I saw a woman my age knocked from her motorbike by a heavy truck. The car ahead of me ran over her, and, like the truck, kept going. I told my driver to stop, but he said it was a waste of time for him to look after a girl who was going to die anyway. I offered to pay what he asked to bring her to a hospital; he didn't want her bloodying his cab. I got out and went to help her myself. She stopped breathing while I was holding her hand. Then and there I realized there was no one I could depend on if it meant getting my blood on them, not even Sheik Salehi. I used the rest of my money to come back here."

"Who would spill such precious blood?" Darius asked.

"The same people who murdered Rahgozar."

"The Komiteh?"

"Is that who you say it was? We've been over this so many times."

"And never gotten anywhere. Look, you need us. Whoever put Leila Darwish's body outside your window in Shemiran will find you sooner or later. Unless you're frank with us, your blood will also be on people who meant only to help."

"I've told you everything. If you care what happens to me, leave now, and don't come back."

"You told us nothing," Darius said. "You didn't say that before coming to Manzarieh Salehi headed a guerrilla camp in Lebanon where drug smuggling evidently was a major activity, and that when Leila and Sousan Hovanian were at the camp they were involved in transporting heroin. Nor have you explained your relationship with the other girls, and your involvement in drugs—"

Maryam started to walk away. Darius stepped close to the table, blocking her.

"And mycotoxins."

"I've never heard that term, except from you. What are they for?"

"To be used in chemical warfare shells that may kill millions of innocent people. Do you still deny that Rahgozar was attempting to obtain them for himself?"

"I don't know what I deny anymore." Maryam slid her queen into a cluster of white pieces and confiscated a rook. "It's your move."

Hamid's remaining bishop snapped up the queen. Only then did he examine the board for a trap.

"Even the notion of drugs was repellent to Salehi," Darius said. "He would have destroyed his end of the smuggling network, but he saw in it something more, a method for bringing mycotoxins into Iran over the same route the drugs traveled. You know the details." He paused to allow her to take over the narrative.

"Don't let me interrupt," she said.

". . . know them because you were one of the couriers sent to bring heroin from the Bekaa Valley and Afghanistan into Iran, and, on your last trip, to carry back the mycotoxins. This much you didn't tell us."

Maryam tipped over her king, which rolled off the table. "I resign," she said.

". . . or what the intended destination of the mycotoxins was, whether they ever reached it, and where they are now." With the side of his hand he wiped all the pieces off the board.

In law school Darius had been taught to win a conviction from a jury by staking out a clear line of questioning and not deviating from it over the course of a trial. But that was the United States, where a preponderance of evidence was a prosecutor's strongest tool. In Iran, where confession was the goal of most legal actions, the standard prod for a recalcitrant witness, or suspect, was torture—and this he would not use. As an interrogator, psychopaths were his specialty, maniacs oblivious to pain, or else eager for it, and so to be deprived of their pleasure and tricked and cajoled out of their secrets. When these were in short supply, he withdrew from the questioning, and made himself useful by ferreting information from physical evidence and with the deductive work that guided most investigations. Against someone like Maryam Lajevardi, who was at least sane enough to recognize his games, his advantage was lost, and all that was left to him were empty threats of suffering.

Maryam was on her knees, picking chessmen off the floor. When her obfuscation had caught up to her, it seemed to Darius that she had nothing to fall back on, not the alcohol that sustained Mehta in his "holding action," or the Islam that once had fed her fires and left her spiritually vacant when they burned out. She was especially not afraid of the police, probably not even of whoever wanted her dead. She was simply afraid, so that much harder to reach.

"We're waiting for your answer," he said.

A sound like wind chimes in a sandstorm defined itself as shattering glass.

As Maryam turned toward the window, Darius felt under his arm for his gun. Yellow light sparkled in a thousand shards that were like a diamond field in the carpeting, and then fused into a fireball that devoured her couch.

A searing wind sucked a scream from Maryam's lips. Tendrils of flame backed her against the wall. The heat brought moisture to Darius's cheeks, but his body was bathed in sweat from an icy reservoir. Hamid, closest to the heart of the blaze, was agitated the most by it. He let it chase him into a corner, where he stayed too long, and with retreat cut off dashed through the flames and tore open the door.

"Get back," Darius yelled.

Hamid tottered in the doorway. His shadow danced into the yard ahead of him, flickering, struggling to break free, suddenly flying away as he fell inside. Darius saw blood erupt from the criminalist's forehead and neck before he heard shots, and afterward from his upper lip and nose. Leaping into the line of gunfire, he bowled over Maryam, who continued in Hamid's footsteps.

He lunged for her and missed, scrambled after her on hands and knees and tripped her up clutching at an ankle, climbed on her back and covered her with his body as a second fusillade stitched a circle low in the wall. "Keep your head down," he shouted into her ear. "Got that?"

She nodded, her muscles so tight that he felt the motion like a wave running down her spine. He eased his weight off her, and she slithered away on her belly. He caught up to her in the kitchen crouched between the refrigerator and stove.

"He's dead," she said. "His brain—" She choked, and flicked red matter from the back of her hand.

Darius expected tears again; but her features were set in a scowl directed not at whoever had killed Hamid, but at him for making her a part of it. "How could this happen?" she asked him.

"Do I have to tell you? Or have they dropped Molotov cocktails from the curriculum at the camps in Lebanon where you and your friends did such fine work for the glory of God?"

It was something to say to keep her anger focused on him instead of turning inward and making her want to give up right there. He peered across the yard at the crenellated roof of the printing plant rising like a washboard over the brick wall. He lifted the window and swung his legs over the sill. When he looked for her, Maryam still hadn't moved, and might have been making up her mind whether to become catatonic.

He came back in, and brought her to the window. She didn't resist as he helped her outside. He dropped down next to her, and they ran for the shadows in the furthest corner of the yard.

"Wait here," he said.

"Where are you going?" Maryam clutched at his sleeve, but didn't try to hold him there.

His answer was a finger across her lips. He walked away from her hugging the side of the house, poked his head around the corner as two men dragged Hamid onto the doorstep and knelt beside the body to wipe the blood from the criminalist's face. One of them stood up shaking his head. His heel left its imprint on Hamid's chest as both men went inside.

Darius glanced back into the yard. Maryam was plainly visible between the house and the wall, and took two quick steps toward him when he waved her further away. He ran up to the door, and slammed it, and then dashed back around the corner. The man who had cleaned Hamid's face came out on the doorstep shooting blindly in the dark. Darius squeezed off a bullet that caught him in the shoulder and spun him around, offering an easy shot at the white triangle of his shirtfront that Darius wasted. The man fired twice more before Darius's third bullet struck above the belt buckle and put him on his back beside Hamid.

Backlit by flames, the second gunman was looking out the kitchen window. Disdaining a headshot, Darius waited as a leg, then an arm, and a shoulder emerged. His bullet missed anyway, splintering the jamb. The gunman's body stiffened as he tried to pull back inside. In that instant Darius placed his next shot where he wanted to, in the rib cage under the arm. Angry at himself, the gunman said, "No—" He let go of his weapon, pitched forward, and hung head down over the sill.

Darius pulled him outside. The man's cuff was smoldering, a ribbon of fire around his ankle. Crimson froth bubbled from a hawk nose that anchored the craggy features of a thirty-year-old Darius had never seen before. Darius looked into the shadows again, but couldn't find Maryam. When he backed away, she was behind him. He took her hand, and they ran to the front of the house where the other gunman lay still but for the heaving of his broad, bloodied chest. The sound he made was like a nursing baby. Exhausted by the effort that went into one large breath, he didn't take another.

"Who are they?" Maryam asked.

"You don't know them either?"

"No," she said, and as Darius looked intently from the body back to her she added, "It's the truth. Do you think I'd be less than honest with you now?"

He bent over the dead man to search for identification. Maryam stepped in his way and pressed her hand against his chest. "You have to believe me."

"Why?" he asked.

"Why?" she repeated, fighting tears. "Why? Because I'll go out of my mind if you don't."

In late evening the industrial neighborhood was devoid of pedestrians and auto traffic. On the next block a streetlamp covered the nearest house in an umbrella of gray light. Somewhere a siren resounded, and its shrill call was answered by a pack of dogs that worshiped it. Darius put Maryam in the Paycon, and they raced eight blocks—until he pulled over for an oncoming fire company—without her taking her eyes from the gun he was holding in his lap.

"Where are you bringing me?" she asked him.

"As far away from here as we can get."

"But where?"

It was a question he was counting on to answer itself. Headquarters was as secure as his apartment. He had no close friends left, no one he trusted with a life. His only relatives were his mother and three half-sisters from whom he had been estranged forever. Someplace would come up, because it had to. In the meantime it was enough to keep moving.

"That boy," Maryam said, "Hamid. He died to save my life. He didn't even know me."

"Don't flatter yourself. He lost his head, and paid the price. There's a lesson in it for you."

"Just because you killed those two doesn't mean others like them aren't looking for me. They'll never stop."

"You have an exalted opinion of yourself," he said. "What makes you so sure it's you they were after?"

"Who else was there? You mean you? You're the police. Your methods may be smoother, but basically you're on the same side as them."

"How do you—" He hadn't meant to sound like that. But when he repeated the question, it came out with the same derision for everything she'd said. "How do you know whose side I'm on?" Except he'd almost added, *When I don't know, myself.*

He turned off the main road to avoid the Komiteh roadblocks. They wove through loud streets where whole families sought a rare night breeze on rooftop mattresses, and parked at a house behind an ivy-covered wall.

Maryam was shivering despite the heat returned by the pavement, which lingered in late summer almost till dawn. He hustled her from the curb past neighbors who looked away from her bad hejab as though bare arms and legs had the power to strike them blind. He punched the bell, pounded on the door before the ringing faded.

Light footsteps inside tapered off well back of the door. "Did you forget your key again?" an angry voice shouted. "Good. Stay out all night for all I care."

"It's Darius. Open up."

There was no more from inside. He shook the knob, rattled it till the door quivered in the frame.

"You'll tear the house down," the voice said, and then Sharera stood in the doorway with her hands on her hips. Her jet black hair was in curlers. A scowl directed at Maryam held special hatred for Darius.

"Mansur is not at home?" he asked.

"He's at the morgue. Where he belongs."

"Sharera, meet Maryam Lajevardi," he said, and pushed inside before Sharera could lock them out. "If it's all right with you, she'll be your houseguest for several days."

"Nothing is all right."

Darius would not have been surprised if Sharera went for Ghaffari's off-duty gun and came back shooting.

"She's one of Mansur's sluts, isn't she?" Sharera spat. "Or is she yours? You're no better than he. Why did you bring her here?"

"Maryam is in hiding for her life," he said.

"Hiding from who? From another woman like me, who she betrayed? Let her hide somewhere else."

"Stop, Sharera—we've been friends too long. I know you'd never turn away anyone in danger. You and Mansur are the only ones I can depend on."

"I depended on you once, too, Darius. You promised to keep Mansur in line. Where were you then?"

"You have to take her in," he said stubbornly. "It's another debt to add to my account."

"I have a nine-year-old daughter. I can't subject Shahla to this. Put her wherever Mansur keeps his girls."

"Anyplace else, and they'll find her and kill her for sure."

"That's not my problem." Sharera held her ground as she groped for the right combination of words that would banish her enemies from her house.

Maryam shivered and rubbed her hands against her arms. She moaned softly, and lifted her hem to inspect a running wound above the knee.

"This girl is hurt," Sharera said. "What's wrong with you, Darius? Why didn't you say something?"

Stepping aside, she allowed them into the living room, where Shahla was scribbling in a coloring book on the floor. "Bring mother the first-aid kit," she told the child as she tore away a fringe of charred cloth over Maryam's thigh. "How did this happen?"

"Maryam has been burned out of her house," Darius said. "She needs a place to stay until arrangements can be made for her."

"What kind of arrangements?" Sharera's tone was sharp, rebuking him for not taking better care of Maryam. Having saved her life, who better than he should understand that preserving it had become his responsibility?

"I'm working on it." Darius decided that he was jealous of Maryam for having someone, even someone like him, to look after her. Why was there no one to relieve him of the nuisance of keeping himself alive? Hamid had tried, it could be argued, but when he had gotten himself killed for his effort the weight of two lives had shifted to Darius's overburdened shoulders. "May I use your phone?"

"You know where it is."

He went into the kitchen, and dialed Homicide. "This is Bakhtiar. Criminalist Hamid has been fatally wounded at a house six kilometers west of the Azadi Monument on the Old Karaj Road. Send men right away. They'll know the address. The fire department has already responded to the scene.

"I'm going to Maryam's now," he told the women. "When Mansur gets home, tell him everything."

"When will you be back?" Maryam asked.

"Not until we're ready to move you. I can't risk leading anyone here. You're in good hands with Sharera and Ghaffari."

He could have been returning to a place he hadn't seen in years. The house was a black shell a third of its former size; the rear section alone had been left standing. The roof had caved in, and one wall was down, leaving the kitchen exposed, more like a stage set than a structure where someone had made her home until an hour ago. Firemen dragged hoses through the rubble, pouncing on hot spots that flared up at them with the crackle of sniper fire. Three bodies covered in green blankets were arranged in the yard in an orderly row that reminded Darius of the captured pieces beside Maryam's chessboard. But now the players were a uniformed sergeant and Ghaffari.

"I came as soon as I heard." In his hurry to reach Darius's side Ghaffari had left the sergeant talking to himself. "What happened here?"

Darius turned back the blanket. The men he had shot lay on either side of Hamid, the criminalist's escort into the next world. Though they were strangers to him, he was familiar with their rough type—uneducated, underemployed, deeply religious men from the southern slums who embraced the Revolution unquestioningly and achieved status commensurate with the blindness of their devotion.

"These two tossed a firebomb in the living room and then started shooting. Hamid acquitted himself with more courage than I gave him credit for, but wasn't as lucky as I."

"You're unhurt?"

Darius nodded.

"Praise Allah," Ghaffari said. "What about the girl? Where is she?"

Darius walked him out of earshot of the sergeant. "At your house, Mansur. For safekeeping."

Ghaffari yanked his arm from Darius's grasp. "What right do you have to jeopardize my family?"

He had no right—nor anything to say to Ghaffari, who knew as well as anyone that the better part of being a policeman was going along with unreasonable demands. Darius went back to the bodies alone. Murder's ruddy patina lent tragic dignity to Hamid's immature face; but embarrassment was crusted on his lips. In the moment of his death the criminalist had realized his mistake. The men who had killed him wore the slight smiles of martyrs they had not planned to be that day, still straining for a glimpse of the gates of paradise—a dumber mistake.

Darius sorted through the pockets of both corpses, finding identification for a Pihzman Bahunar, thirty-five years old, and Mahdi Attarha, twenty-eight, both of Dharvazeh Ghor. Attarha was also carrying stone worry beads and the keys to a Peugeot automobile. Darius looked across the street toward a jaunty blue sedan mixed improbably among the police cars. Neither man had as much as ten thousand rials with him. He lifted a corner of the blanket under which two .38-caliber revolvers, newer models of his own American weapon, had been collected with a pencil jammed into the muzzles.

"You can't keep the girl at my house forever." Ghaffari played his one-note song over Darius's shoulder. "What now?"

"Will your cousins in Tabriz put her up?"

"They have their hands full with Nahid. She's not easy to live with."

"Another one like her won't be noticed," Darius said.

The morgue wagons that he had left behind at Mehta's pulled up to the house ahead of a Paycon junker. Baghai limped out of the lead truck leaning heavily on an attendant's arm. "Don't you ever quit?" he asked Darius. "You're wearing me out."

"We'll try to arrange the next slaughter for a convenient hour."

"A good piece of shooting," Baghai said. "Unambiguous death is in short supply these days."

The driver of the Paycon approached the men standing over the bodies. After taking a few steps, he stopped and looked back, and the sergeant pointed at Darius.

"Sir," the young man said, "I have an important message."

"Yes?"

"I am instructed it is for your ears only." He backed off four long strides, and looked disappointed when Darius didn't follow.

"I am Probationary Patrolman Banani," he confided. "Be advised that the Revolutionary Prosecutor, Mr. Zakir, wishes to speak to you tonight, and is in his office now."

Bijan's warning that the invitation was coming had never been far from Darius's consciousness. A great weight lifting from his shoulders was not the pleasant release he had anticipated, though, and immediately was reasserted over his heart.

"If this man has brought news of another bloodbath . . ." Baghai was saying.

A basij brought Darius into the outer office to wait until the Revolutionary Prosecutor finished with a matter of national concern. The draft from the adjacent toilet pumped currents of lemon-flavored air around his head. After a long while, a bald man in a tailored suit came out of Zakir's office with an uncommonly attractive red-haired woman. Darius had seen the woman before, on more than one occasion, but couldn't say where. As the couple went past him, he heard her whisper, "Does that bastard think for one minute I would subject myself to something like that? I would die sooner than—"

"Yes, you would," her companion agreed, silencing her.

Zakir sat at his large desk jabbing a pencil without a point into a gunmetal gray box that looked to Darius like an oversize electric sharpener. On the blotter were about two dozen other new pencils sawed cleanly in half.

"Did you happen to notice the woman who just left?"

"She was quite handsome," Darius said.

"She is stunning. She is Niloofar Bihruzi, the film actress, one of the most famous faces in Iran. She finds herself embroiled in a serious conflict with the Komiteh, and has come to me for advice."

Zakir's pause was not a hint for Darius to interrupt. It was a statement that he would not proceed to such mundane business as the police until he had finished with his adventures with the movie star.

"It is an unusual case. In every one of Niloofar's films she is called upon to make love with her leading man. She is an accomplished performer; by any standard the scenes are steamy. You might say they are her bread and butter. The Komiteh have taken offense. As Niloofar is not married to the men she is kissing, they want to bring charges of prostitution against her."

"Don't they understand she's acting?"

"Ah, but you are missing the important issue they have raised. What are the faithful to conclude when they see such a beautiful woman making love with legions of men? Forget that these are movies. Are her kisses not real? Are they less than a kiss because they are captured on film? Are they anything else? Pressure is being brought to bear against Niloofar to do something about allegations of immoral behavior. Her manager advised her to see me. We have been working together on her problem for some time."

It dawned on Darius that, like Zakir, he found the movie queen's dilemma more interesting than his own, or at least was in no hurry for word that he had been relieved of his duties.

"In consultation with Ayatollah Mahallati I have decided that, starting with her next picture, Niloofar must seegah for her leading man, whoever he may be. She will become a temporary wife for the duration of each movie she makes, and her kisses will be blessed by holy law. Even better, Niloofar and her leading man can spend their nights in real lovemaking, which will lend authenticity to their performances. It is a brilliant solution, if I say so myself. No?"

"I wouldn't have thought of it," Darius said.

"Unfortunately, not all cases lend themselves to such happy resolution. I did not summon you here so you could catch a glimpse of Niloofar Bihruzi, but to let you know that after much hard debate it has been decided to reopen the investigation into the killing of Colonel Farmayan, your former boss in SAVAK. It will be necessary for you to resign from the National Police, and to surrender your weapons."

So Bijan and Sarmadi had spared him the best part, letting the news break gradually, so that he wouldn't go to pieces—or run.

"I executed the shah's torturer. For this the government wants to bring me to trial a second time?"

"Shooting Farmayan was a praiseworthy act. Even the so-called victim's nephew has come to applaud it. Does Bijan seem hostile to you? Do you have strained relations? No, the real offense is that for too long you were an obedient agent of SAVAK, an organization that perverted its charter to crack down on the activities of the communists, and instead repressed the Muslim faithful. But you will be tried for murder because it is necessary to make an example of you, and murder is the strongest charge we can prove."

"An example of what? There's not another country that would attempt to reinstitute a death sentence after so long."

"Do you dare to criticize the legal system that is the most merciful in the annals of man?" Zakir nudged the blunt tip of a pencil into the gray box. "You know what this device is," he said. "It is evidence of the compassion of Islamic justice. For centuries, when hadd was proved, and the thief sentenced to have his fingers or a hand removed, the amputation was done in an awful manner with a sword or an axe. Under the Imam's guidance the best minds of our nation, experts from the Ministry of Health, the medical faculties of Beheshti and Teheran universities, and the Islamic Scientific Institute were taken from urgent tasks to find a more humane means of performing this necessary job." Darius heard the hum of an electric motor as Zakir pressed the pencil into the box, which returned a stub to him. The other piece was expelled from the bottom, and rolled across the desk. "So spare me your complaints about the harshness of the law, because here is my rebuttal."

Zakir tore the flap from a box of pencils and lined them up beside the machine. "You were an exemplary policeman who performed his job with dedication. But that is irrelevant. Your past is bad, and the past leaves indelible stains on the present. Good deeds do not outweigh the bad, which cast a shadow over them."

Darius's outrage had been spent before Zakir's tirade was over. His fate was a foregone conclusion. The mysteries that remained he would as soon leave unanswered: how much pain could he stand, and how long would he endure beyond that; the degree of suffering before he was rewarded with the ultimate expression of Islamic justice, and then an unmarked plot in a distant corner of Behesht-e-Zahra out of sight of the Imam's mausoleum. The door opened behind him, and his hands were pinned to his sides while his gunbelts were taken away by the basij from the outer office. Five men armed with Uzis formed a circle around his chair.

"Have you anything to say?" the Revolutionary Prosecutor asked.

Darius stared straight ahead. The only crime he would admit to was not fleeing while he had the chance.

"If you will," Zakir said to the basij, "please transport Mr. Bakhtiar to Evin Prison. Show him every courtesy a former homicide chief of the National Police commands."

· 14 ·

A light rain, the season's first, turned the dust to gray-brown paste that the wipers painted across the windshield. In utter blackness they climbed the heights of the city into cool air fragrant with oleander. On the fringes of the Evin district the driver pulled over to scrub the glass with his handkerchief. As Darius strained for a glimpse of the prison wall, the basij tied a blindfold around his head.

What did they think they were hiding from him? What secrets so great that a look in that direction was a breach of security? Didn't they know that Evin had been SAVAK's prison, *his* prison, that its best secrets had been devised by him? Had it been torn down and rebuilt brick for brick on some undisclosed site? Or did they believe that, knowing as much as he did about what went on there, he would go crazy at a view of its bland facade?

They rolled into an area just inside the walls where there was no movement of air and the oleander was overpowering. Darius remembered the garden he had given permission for some prisoners to plant and where later he had worked himself, a green tangle of waxy shrubs and native desert bushes, and in one corner where the shadow of the high wall did not reach, a jungle patch that hadn't done well in the sandy earth, treeless, but for four malevolent trunks without leaves, bark, or limbs, sprouting leather straps at the height of a man's shoulders and ankles. On the side looking back to the cells bullets had eaten into the wood.

Steel doors creaked open, and the miasma of despair leaked out. The hands on his shoulders passed him on to others, hard, bony hands that felt him everywhere as they shunted him into the building. He stumbled over something like a rotted log, and would have fallen had the bony hands not seized the shackles between his wrists and jerked him upright.

A concrete maze unfolded under his feet as the plan of Block 209 winding toward the administration offices. On his right would be interrogation rooms, and opposite them the holding pens where mobs of prisoners were kept close to the engines of justice that ran round the clock. An alcoholic vapor intoxicated him; momentarily he had no idea where he was. In the map in his mind's eye he filled in the understaffed hospital where prisoners were restored between sessions under torture. By tilting his head back, he was able to see under his blindfold. Inmates lay on the floor handcuffed to the radiators, or else leaned against the wall on bloated legs while waiting their brief turn with a doctor.

To maintain an atmosphere of terror the bloodstains on the floor were never washed away. Yet no one looked anywhere else; for if they did, they would see in every doorway a man suspended by the handcuffs behind his back from a bar hammered into the lintel so that his toes barely touched the floor. Darius was ordered to halt, and his blindfold was removed. After he had blinked the improbable tableau into focus, he was brought to the end of the corridor and shoved inside one of the few doorways without a hanging sentry.

He sat in a straight-backed chair shivering in his cold sweat. Here the blood on the floor had not been left for show; it collected too fast and was crusted too thick to mop up. A picture of the Imam looked down at the blood with approval, and at Darius with regret that none was his. In half an hour a young man assumed the interrogator's place behind a plain desk. He offered Darius a cigarette, and took it for himself when it was refused. The flame from the match was reflected in his constricted pupils, which burned into Darius's eyes.

"Confession is good for the soul," he intoned in a dry voice. "Although the soul is not our concern at Evin, you will be afforded every opportunity to perfect it. You are Darius Bakhtiar, am I correct, lieutenant colonel in the National Police, Teheran district?"

"Until tonight," Darius said.

"I am Sabbagh. It is good you understand that you are no longer who you were."

"Who am I?"

"You are nobody."

"If I'm nobody, then how can I be—" Darius stopped, wary of cheap victories. The logic that was his best weapon was no match for the irrationality that was theirs. He would not fight back until he found a battlefield to his liking. "What, specifically, have I been charged with?" he asked. "Under the administrative regulations governing the revolutionary courts and public prosecutor's office I have the right to know."

"You have no rights." Sabbagh removed a ballpoint pen from his shirt pocket, and clicked the point in and out. "The charges will depend on the quality of your confession."

By this, Darius was made to understand that his crimes would be extrapolated from the information he gave up to them. It was axiomatic that the greater the pain inflicted the more encompassing the guilt acknowledged. The agonies of interrogation were but a consequence of the vile deeds they elicited, and thus the prisoner's fault. Liberation in the form of death was the hard-won gift of his torturers. And so nothing had changed since the former landlords turned over the prison to their former tenants, and took up residence in the cells.

"Have you anything to say for yourself?" Sabbagh asked. "Anything you would like me to know before we start?"

"No."

"You have a long history of anti-Iranian activity. From the time you went abroad to study you were hostile to the nation's interests. This was proven by your subsequent employment in SAVAK. When you killed the enemy of God, Ibrahim Farmayan, you were viewed as a man who had come belatedly to his senses, and so were set free by the Revolution and your past not held against you." Sabbagh studied the bare top of the desk. "This was a mistake, which we see in a continuing pattern of seditious behavior. In short, you are a saboteur."

Sabbagh's interrogatory style was amateur, grand inquisitor stuff picked up from Russian novels. Darius dropped his gaze below the table, and was surprised not to see shiny cavalry boots. "The allegation is preposterous," he said. "I demand to see a lawyer."

"You are a lawyer. Why should you have two lawyers on your case when other prisoners have none?"

There were no shortcuts through Evin Prison. Darius would not be allowed to make his confession now if he begged to tell everything. By extending the questioning over a prolonged period of time, Sabbagh expected to be rewarded with something more—whether a nugget of truth with which the prisoner hoped to buy release from pain, or a lie of nearly equal value. Though words were suspect, they were the product this harsh factory was geared to produce. There was a ready market in the press and propaganda bureaus for everything that came off the assembly lines.

Sabbagh lit another cigarette. Darius filled his lungs with its lingering smoke and pretended it relaxed him.

"I want to make a call," he said. "My friends will be alarmed when they don't hear from me."

For whom was this ruse meant? To fool Sabbagh into thinking they could not do what they wanted to him because somewhere there were important people who would raise a stink? Or was he bluffing only himself, bolstering his spirits with a fiction that Sabbagh would see through easily—that there was someone on the outside to whom he mattered.

His wrists were yanked back above his shoulders, and he was dragged from the chair.

"We will resume shortly," Sabbagh said. "In the meantime, no calls. Better that you reflect on your situation and consider the advantages of being forthcoming."

He was brought to the hospital and chained to a radiator. What was this? If he needed a doctor he would have to wait days to see one, and now, still quite well, he was given a choice place in the waiting area. Ahead of him was a prisoner whose swollen arms were thicker than his waist. Aspirin was administered by a young medic Darius recognized as Kashfi, Baghai's temporary assistant with the least affection for coroner's work. The line of patients crept around the radiator, but Darius's name wasn't called; and he realized he was not here for a checkup or treatment, but to be acquainted with the stench of ruined men and women.

When the new shift of guards came on duty he was moved to a cell with two other men, a space less than three meters by two constructed to house a single prisoner. There had been a time when it was a de facto death sentence for a SAVAK renegade to be locked up among the general population. In light of the severe crowding brought upon by revolutionary vigilance the old customs no longer applied. Or maybe they still did.

A man about his age dressed in the remnant of a fine suit was snoring on the lone mattress. Stretched out on the concrete floor was an emaciated youth whose sandy hair was pomaded with dry blood. Bare-chested, he was wrapped in a blanket. Both feet were bandaged in black rags that had been a blue shirt. By moving them out of the way one at a time with his hands he made room for Darius.

"It is Anvari's turn in the bunk," he said. "You can have it next, I can't sleep." He shifted position with difficulty, and settled back against the wall. "My name is Rajab, of the People's Mujahadeen. You are—"

Darius looked away from him.

"I know it is none of my business, but there has been no one for me to talk to in a long time. This one is a fanatic, although to his eternal credit he embezzled from the government, and will not acknowledge my existence. They are counting on us to tear each other apart.

"It's not good here," he continued after giving up on a response from Darius. "Once I needed to go to the bathroom, and when I called for the guard he beat me and kicked out two of my teeth." Rajab lifted his upper lip to expose jagged nubs festering in the gum. "Then he threw a tin can at me and told me to piss in that. For two days they did not take the can away, or feed me, or give me water. Another guard came in and asked what I was saving in the can. When I told him, he said to drink it. Naturally, I refused, but then he attacked me with a club, and beat me so bad that I did what he wanted. After, they put sweet tea in the can, and I was forced to drink it, too. I tell you these horrible things so you will know what you are up against."

Whether Rajab's story was true or not, whether he had told it out of loneliness, or because he had been instructed to, the recitation had served the purpose of focusing Darius's thoughts—as Sabbagh suggested.

"That one there," Rajab spit on the sleeping man's shoulder, "is an antenna. Have no part of him."

"What's an antenna?"

"A spy. Every word you say around him is transmitted to the administration."

Darius wanted nothing to do with either of them. Both men could be spies, or neither. Rajab could be the antenna, and his goal to isolate his sleeping enemy; or he could be the frightened man he claimed to be. The possibilities in Evin were limited only by the holding capacity of the cells. Conundrums were built upon conundrums until the process of sorting everything out, of thought itself, became torture that begged for the release of confession.

"Last night," Rajab said, "returning from being questioned, I saw a man open his wrists with a piece of glass he had secreted in the cuff of his pants."

There was no window in the cell. Light came from a metal cage in which a forty-watt bulb never went out. Darius's sense of time was the first casualty of his incarceration, but his body craved sleep. He listened to Rajab, making a pillow of his arms, letting this grisly bedtime story render him unconscious.

Breakfast was lukewarm tea and a piece of bread that he wouldn't touch. Rajab and Anvari eyed the morsel, circling like buzzards. "It's yours," Darius said, and while Anvari answered, "Thank you, sir," Rajab snatched it for himself and gobbled it in a corner with his back to them.

Waiting, a trick he had not mastered, was now an end in itself, prelude to a performance he would as soon miss. He filled his head with daydreams, and populated them with women he'd had. Farib alone eluded him. Maryam Lajevardi came uninvited in her place, her image so vivid that he saw the faint character lines around her eyes. Less clearly defined was her body, which he stripped naked and supplied with Farib's form, and then tinkered with until it was more to his liking. By taking away several centimeters from the bust, adding a slight angle to the hips where Farib was graceful curves, he attached personality to the perfect shape. He imagined Maryam as a redhead, and then with raven hair, and without having to concentrate hard as his to do with as he wanted, let his inventiveness run wild until a scream from a distant cell chased her away.

He was desperate to get a message to her, but couldn't justify an attempt for hollow assurances that would terrify her when she learned where they originated. His adversaries were aware of every one of his plans. Was the new spy in Homicide that good, a high-tech antenna beaming word even of his thoughts? Or had his work habits deteriorated into inexcusable sloppiness that would have gotten him killed had not room in Evin Prison been found for him?

When a guard came for the trays Darius asked to be taken to the toilet. The guard considered a plot before unlocking the cell. The toilet was far along the corridor, past the "one-way" stairs to the basement torture rooms. Well before he was there he was met by the smell, and no longer of the opinion that Rajab had been cruelly abused when he was made to use a can as a slop bucket. As he stepped inside, a surprise punch to the back of the head sent him reeling into the wall.

"Bloody infidel," the guard said, "don't you know the Imam has stated that upon entering a toilet the believer must set down his left foot first?"

His wrists were shackled as the corridor filled with guards. He took a tentative step wondering if the Imam used a right or left foot lead after finishing with the toilet hose. A looping punch delivered to the point of the jaw buckled his knees. He put a foot back to steady himself, and was shoved forward through a gauntlet of fists. Heavy hands pummeled his midsection. When he had wearied them he was given to others for kidney punches, passed on again and kneed in the groin, beaten with a stick. The game was "Evin soccer," and he was the ball, to be batted around until the air had hissed out of him, and he was too senseless for them to hurt anymore.

Rajab said, "Welcome home," and gave up the bunk for him. He examined Darius's bruises and said, "You're not too bad off. While you were gone, I saw something you would never believe. A boy thirteen years old was locked up in a cell for three weeks by himself. They brought him out, and he went up and down the corridor like a rabid fox, pounding on the walls, yelling gibberish at the top of his lungs. The guards could not catch him, he was so wild. They let him run till he was breathless, and then they cornered him and beat him unconscious, and threw him back in the same cell." Rajab pointed through the barred door. "That one there."

Darius shut his eyes as Rajab went on as loud and excited as the boy must have been. This time sleep didn't come, nor respite from his pain. He used his saliva to wash the blood from his face. A tooth was loose in the back of his mouth. When he wiggled it, it came off on his tongue.

Sabbagh was waiting for him reading the Imam's treatise on *The Determination of the Hour of Dawn During Moonlight—The True and False Dawns.* Although he almost never smoked, Darius accepted a cigarette. His puffy lips had no feeling, and the cigarette fell onto the table when Sabbagh gave him a light.

"Have you been to our mosque yet?" Sabbagh asked.

"No."

"It is a mistake not to go. The mosque is the wellspring of life at Evin, as it is for society as a whole. The reeducation of the miscreant begins in the mosque, because more than any other aspect of human endeavor, prayer opens the mind."

"My mind is already open," Darius said.

Sabbagh regarded him disdainfully. "Your mind is as closed as any man's that ever lived. It is just your head that is open."

And still spinning, thought Darius. He had practiced answers for anything

Sabbagh might say to him. Trying to remember them made the pain that much worse, and he fell back on tired legalisms.

"I am a political prisoner," he said, "not a criminal, and must be accorded proper standards of treatment. These are not being met in Block two-oh-nine."

"You are overly impressed with your own importance. You are no different than other inmates. We will do with you as we see fit."

"I don't see any purpose in further interviews. It's too much to expect we'll find common ground."

"Perhaps, but there is no pressure on our side to revise our attitude, while you will be given incentive to reconsider your stubborn silence."

Sabbagh glanced in his book. Darius anticipated more sparring, maybe a discussion of the true and false dawns, but the session was over. He was brought to a distant wing of the block where the cell doors were solid steel, without bars, and narrower than his shoulders. He had to duck his head as he was made to enter a pitch black opening; one step inside he was as lost as if he had stumbled into a subterranean cavern. Groping about with his hands in front of his face, he determined that he was alone in a space smaller than the cell he had shared with the other men. There was no bunk on the wall. He tipped over an object that rolled around the floor distributing the stench of human waste. His feet tangled in a stiff, dusty blanket. He balled it up in a corner and used it as a pillow. When he closed his eyes, the blackness seemed to lessen. Every punch he had taken from the guards, every kick, came back to him with renewed intensity. He amused himself by counting individual sites of pain, curious if each was matched by a dormant pleasure receptor. Past sixty he gave up and fell asleep.

He was awakened by a crawling sensation on his throat. A dream, he thought, until he felt it lingering against his cheek, and his hand closed on something that bled between his fingers. A two-day stubble had sprouted on his face. In the absence of more accurate means of measuring the passage of time, his beard would be his calendar.

Despite his protest to Sabbagh, he realized that he had been treated up to now with deferential tenderness. Soccer, while not his favorite game, was nothing he could not endure. Nor did a solitary cell hold any terror for him. The fact was that he did not mind his own company, and preferred it in extended periods to the bickering of Rajab and Anvari.

The quiet was broken by wailing that he assumed to be the pathetic residue of torture. After several minutes he proclaimed himself an expert on it, and that it was made by a woman. The women's wing of Evin was far away from the men's, and he could not figure out how the sound reached all the way to Block 209. Possibly he was imagining things. Not the crying—that was real enough. But its source. He would not be the first man obsessed with the events that brought him to Evin Prison who turned his thoughts to women, seeking reason to survive.

For three days (or four, or five—his calendar had thickened till it was too fuzzy to read) he was left alone in the cell but for the brief times he was dragged into the corridor for prayer. One day, expecting a meal tray when the door was opened, another man was pushed into his arms. They disengaged awkwardly, and sought out opposite corners.

"Who are you?" the newcomer asked.

"Call me Darius. And you?"

"Habibi. Have you been here long?"

"I don't know," Darius said. "It's a question of taste."

"It is not to my taste. Do they beat you?"

"No."

"Where I came from they whipped me every day on the soles of my feet till I was unable to walk. I wore the skin from my knees crawling. I am here to recuperate, so they can start on me again."

Darius wanted to ask what offense had brought Habibi to Evin, but this was a breach of prison etiquette.

"My crime was a terrible one . . ." Evidently, Habibi was a mind reader. "I murdered the Imam."

Darius pulled back his legs, which were tangled in the other man's. "The Imam died of old age. He was eighty-nine, and had been sick with cancer for a long time."

"So people believe," Habibi said. "But I had wished him dead every day, until it came to pass."

Darius heard the slop can scrape against the floor, and Habibi relieve himself in it.

"It is enough that I can kill by thought. But I can also project my body outside the walls. Would you like me to show you?"

"It's not necessary." For imagining what he had, Habibi was treated like a murderer and had no reason to doubt his fantasies. Though delusional, he still could be an antenna. Darius had never heard of prisoners doubling up in the solitary cells.

"My trial was three months ago. I was sentenced to die, but received a postponement until they finished questioning me."

This, at least, was not as crazy as it sounded. Interrogation continued throughout the legal process. Before arrest, during trial, or after sentence was pronounced a prisoner was grilled until prosecutors were satisfied they had every last bit of information out of him.

At the end of a week (Darius guessed it was a week—his new calendar was the arrival of his meal tray; but this was sporadic, and for long stretches he received no food) he had a cold that the Imam's confessed assassin had brought into the cell, and his head lice as well. His mental illness was contagious, too. If Habibi didn't shut up soon, Darius would declare himself a plotter in his infamous crime, and demand his help in escaping by being taught to walk through walls.

In what he believed to be his eighth day there Darius was taken from the cell. The weak light at the end of the corridor blinded him. A blanket was tossed over his head and he was marched out of the block while Habibi called after him, "You can't believe anyone, anyone but me."

He was left inside an interrogation room where a prisoner who would not speak to him used electric clippers to cut off his hair. He ran his hand over his scalp feeling the small, still painful bumps where his stitches had been. He was eager for the questioning to start. Sabbagh's studied formalities would be a relief from the raving of his cellmate. But the interrogator who arrived toting a fat leather briefcase was Bijan.

"You are to be congratulated," Bijan said as he spread papers over the desktop. "Your warders say you are a model prisoner, a marja among the inmates, to be emulated if not admired."

Darius held himself still. "I would rather be set free."

Had he faltered? To his own ears he seemed to be pleading. He did not see how he could keep from showing cracks in his demeanor that Bijan would widen until he was destroyed. Since being brought to Evin, he had been led constantly to expect torture, but the limits of his fear had not allowed for Bijan to be the arbiter of his fate. Better to have been thrown alive to the wolves.

Bijan, for his part, was as ever, but for a smile that blossomed as he sensed Darius's quandary.

"Virtue's reward must be its hunger for more of the same." The Komiteh-man riffled the papers, but did not consult them. "You are charged with the murder of Ibrahim Farmayan in the year 1979, a crime for which you have already been convicted once and sentenced to death."

"You are disqualified from these proceedings," Darius said, "as you cannot pretend to be impartial. The man I'm accused of killing was your blood relative. It's too much to expect justice under these circumstances."

"Too much to expect of *me?*" Bijan glowered at him. "What kind of justice are you asking for? Western justice—which is no justice at all, but the juridical whims of a society that has turned its back on God? Who is acquainted better than I with the consequences of your crimes, and can express grievance with them?"

"I insist that you remove yourself from the case."

"Justice is what you want? Then justice is what you will receive." Bijan paused for Darius to signal consent to the rules. "Since your guilt is not at issue, we will confine the questioning to your motivation."

"The *only* issue is guilt. I was convicted unjustly. The evidence was heard by a SAVAK court-martial. Has the government revised its opinion of SAVAK's commitment to fair trial?"

"There is no record of the murdered man's illegalities having been directed at you," Bijan bore on. "He was one of the rare officers in SAVAK whose patriotism cannot be called into question. What excesses he may have been responsible for fell on the deserving heads of the Tudeh Party cadres rather than the Muslim faithful."

"He was a sadist who raped and killed prisoners of both sexes. In the week before he was slain he tortured to death a girl not yet sixteen years old, but would not be prosecuted for it. These are crimes under Islamic law, no matter who the victims may be."

"The country was not governed by Shari'a at the time. Now that it is, why has your commendable ardor to see justice done faded?"

"What do you mean?"

"When it suited your ends, you took it upon yourself to do away with your superior in SAVAK. Yet, as a leading investigator for the National Police you were not nearly so aggressive in rooting out the enemies of society."

"Are we discussing the people who stole Ayatollah Golabi's rugs?" Darius asked.

"Zaid Rahgozar."

"I found him as you asked. He was in my custody when the Komiteh executed him."

"You were engaged in a vast ongoing conspiracy with him. When our men entered his hotel room, you were assisting his flight."

"This is pure fabrication," Darius said. "Where do you get your information?"

"In the future you may be allowed to confront your accusers. Do you dispute that upon returning from Mashad you went to the home of another conspirator, a woman you advised also to flee before the Revolutionary Guards located her?"

Using the tip of his toe Darius swept his hair into a lusterless pile. He was going gray faster than Ghaffari.

"With you, there is always another innocent victim who must be saved from the legally constituted authorities. Always a young and beautiful woman."

"No one was saved."

"Not even your soul. The persistent pattern of antistate activity stretching across three decades cannot be misread. We want to know who you are working for. For what foreign power? With which subversive elements inside Iran?"

"This kind of questioning is outside the scope of your lawful mandate. It has nothing to do with the Farmayan case."

"Everything is connected," Bijan said. "The links that are not obvious will be examined in a fresh light until they are brought out clearly."

"There are no links."

"That will not be determined by you."

He was dismissed with the flick of a finger. Resigned to another confinement with Habibi, he wanted to shout that a terrible mistake was being made when he was brought to the one-way stairs. As he descended the steep flight, his legs were kicked out from under him, and he skidded to the landing on his chest. His arrival was hailed by a cry of pain from a dark basement passage, another inside his head.

An antiseptic glow beckoned to a room with walls of blood-smeared tile. It bent his gaze to the floor, away from the bank of bulbs shining down on a hospital bed. An operating theater, he would have thought, but for the thick straps dangling from the railings. A cardboard sign read: USE OF SALT FOR DECONTAMINATION IS NECESSARY.

"Take off your shoes and socks," his guard commanded.

The tiles were cool under his bare feet. Given the chance he would perch on this small, safe spot forever. He was shoved into the glare and slammed facedown on the mattress, which smelled of blood and stale urine. The straps were buckled around his wrists and his feet elevated slightly and tied over the rail at the end of the bed. His modest wish was that he had been assigned to a disinterested, impartial torturer, who would not perform as effectively as a zealot.

A man came in treading heavily over the tiles, and walked around the bed. His broad shadow eclipsed the bright light in Darius's face. Darius stared incredulously at Baraheni, who, preoccupied with other things, did not look back. He was surprised, and yet not surprised, his capacity for astonishment overwhelmed. Had they brought in a trained ape to work him over now, he would only shrug and ask if it was done all the time.

The guards did not order Baraheni about. Darius noticed that he still had on his shoes, black brogans like those he always wore. He rolled up his sleeves, and rubbed his hands over his burly forearms. From a hook on the wall he removed several long strips of electric cable. The way he gripped each piece individually as he measured the degree of flex reminded Darius of an American baseball player deciding on a favorite bat. When he found a length to his liking, he whipped it around his head. The humming sound it made accelerated into a shrill whine, and then a whistle. He examined the cable again, and, still not pleased, used a curved blade to whittle the insulation from the frayed bundles of copper wire at the ends.

What was apparent to Darius was inconceivable; so it followed that everything was a hallucination. Why trust his senses that he was strapped beneath the broiling lights of the whipping bed, when it was as easy to accept he was taking the sun on a tropical beach? Nothing was more real than that—certainly not Baraheni lending his skills to the fanatics.

"They've turned you," Darius said. "How? What tortures were *your* weakness?"

Whistling filled the air, and then the soles of his feet were on fire. The guard jumped on his back and stuffed a filthy cloth in his mouth to catch any screams. The cable lashed out again as he struggled for breath, and white-hot pain ran up his legs and settled in his hips.

"You still don't understand what I'm doing here?"

He saw Baraheni looking at him with the same measure of disgust he'd had for Rajab when his cellmate tried to teach him the things that were essential to know in Evin.

". . . Why there are no answers that will end your agony?"

The cable shrieked in his ears. His legs twitched, but the point of impact was the middle of his back.

"The trick to this," Baraheni confided, "is to leave you wanting to talk, and still able to. If I had hit you a couple of centimeters closer to your kidneys, you would piss blood for a week and be in no condition to say much of anything. Plenty of trial and error went into perfecting my stroke. You will forgive me if I am rusty. To answer the question of why I have no questions— I'm warming up."

Darius felt the presence of another person in the room. Baraheni, for all his inventiveness, was a puppet who did not act without guidance. He raised his eyes, but saw only the copper plaits glinting in the light as the cable swung in a widening arc. The skin tearing from his feet was not a hallucination, nor the fire in his legs that flared hotter and brighter until it went out suddenly, and he thought his nervous system had overloaded.

"The perfect means of inflicting pain is yet to be discovered," Baraheni said. "Even the whipping bed has its drawbacks. After one hundred, one hundred and fifty strokes, the most obstinate man's legs go numb, and it is wasted effort after that." The cable came down higher on Darius's back, and the guard slid off and stood behind Baraheni to watch. "And so secondary areas of sensitivity must be utilized. I can beat you across the shoulders all night, but the pain has nowhere to travel. You might still resist talking."

Darius's head bobbed up and down as the cable slashed the nape of his neck; but he was unconscious, and Baraheni was talking to himself.

Opening his eyes in blackness, he feared that he had gone blind. The pressure of the blanket on his back brought tears. Someone was talking to him from far away, though he could feel hot breath in his ear.

"You see, you see—" He recognized the voice as Habibi's. "I am the only one you can trust."

When they came for him again he couldn't stand, and toppled over when he was put on his feet. More guards were called to carry him to the interrogation room.

"It was Leila Darwish who stole the mycotoxins," Bijan said, "but I do not have to tell you. If she yielded to the entreaties of a foreign power, or the Mujahadeen hypocrites, or if she had reasons of her own, or just went insane, you were in the best position to find out."

"I was unable to learn," he answered mechanically.

"That will be examined fully. Leila Darwish was an obedient member of Hezbollah who had prepared for a martyr's fate. Her defection was an insult to God. I personally blame the Lajevardi woman for turning her head. She was the corrupter who spoiled everything."

"My investigation did not lead in that direction."

Bijan leaned across the desk. "There is no alternative explanation. Maryam Lajevardi's disloyalty is not at issue. Among her lovers was a Russian agent working to deprive the Islamic Republic of a powerful chemical weapon."

"If you hadn't killed him, he would have told me where the mycotoxins are."

"Do you think we are idiots? Maryam Lajevardi had tricked him as she tricked you. He knew nothing. He was eliminated because he had made an obstacle of himself in affording her the protection of his privileged status in Iran. She was playing for higher stakes than a Russian boyfriend and a communal apartment in Moscow. By providing our enemies with the mycotoxins, she hoped to make herself a millionaire many times over."

"This is the first I've heard."

"Please, spare me your denials," Bijan said. "It is out of character for the brilliant homicide chief of the National Police to be so badly informed about the subject of a major investigation. We know of the time you spent alone with the Lajevardi woman, that you became her protector after Rahgozar was gone. She drew you into her confidence with the promise of her body and of untold riches. But she would have betrayed you as she betrayed her former comrades, her lover, and her country. Although it is too late to save yourself, you can still tell us about the mycotoxins and earn the gratitude of all good Muslims. Or would you rather I returned you to the mercies of Baraheni?"

"I can't tell you what I don't know." Darius heard Maryam's words, but without her coyness, her charm.

"No?" Bijan pushed back in his chair. "Then maybe you will tell him."

Darius clenched his teeth, held himself so tight that the muscles in his shoulders went into spasms. The cable, humming softly, spun a long, lazy arc, then crashed against his soles. His body rocked with the impact, and he convulsed against the straps. Pain was an afterthought, what he guessed it must feel like to be consumed gradually by flames.

"You are beginning to show signs of neurological impairment," Baraheni said. "Nerve tissue does not regenerate once it has been destroyed. You may never be able to walk again."

"Am I going somewhere?"

The cable screamed in air. "Well, is he?" someone asked. Baraheni dropped his arm, and the cable coiled like a black snake around his ankles.

A cold hand rested on Darius's shoulders. "You are to be commended on your perseverance, if not your intelligence." Icy fingers drummed against the quivering muscles, but did not relax them. "SAVAK training has stood you in good stead. It is always gratifying to see someone who puts principle ahead of pain."

The straps were unbuckled. Darius rolled onto his back and looked up at Ashfar.

"The tragedy in this sorry affair," Ashfar said, "the tragedy that unites the three of us, is that we did not come together again under more favorable circumstances. We could have restored Iran to its former greatness, saved it from itself."

"We tried," Baraheni said.

"Yes, we did. We have nothing to be ashamed of. Do you, Darius? Are you blushing? You're all red."

"Why aren't you dead?" Darius said.

Baraheni laughed. "We owe our lives to you. Without you, we *would* be dead."

"Dead a long time," Ashfar said. "Did I once tell you we lost our democratic zeal in our first days back in Teheran? To be precise, it was at the moment of our arrest. We had been betrayed by someone in our organization. The nature of émigré groups is that they are havens for spies." He picked up the cable, and slapped it repeatedly into his palm. "When we were brought to Evin, the fanatics were in disarray. Their precious mycotoxins had just been stolen, and they were frantic to have them back. Everyone in counterintelligence was executed immediately after the Revolution. And then suddenly here we were. The deal they broached to us was extremely attractive: return the mycotoxins, and we would be allowed to live. Otherwise, you see for yourself how vindictive they can be. We're pragmatists at heart, Darius—hardly the idealist you are. How could we say no?"

"It can be done."

"But why? What is in that for us besides an early grave? It's easier to give them what they want—or to hunt for it."

"They told you where to look for Leila Darwish," Darius said.

"They couldn't find their ass in the dark. All we had to go on was that three girls were missing, and with them the mycotoxins. Through Saeed, we already had turned up Sousan Hovanian. And Sousan knew where Leila was. They thought we were geniuses, bringing such quick results."

"You mutilated her because she wouldn't talk."

"Leila knew less about mycotoxins than we did," Ashfar said, "less even than you. Her interest was strictly in the heroin. We concluded it was the third girl alone who understood the real purpose of their mission to Afghanistan. Leila was hurt so that Maryam Lajevardi would see what was in store if she didn't cooperate with us."

Baraheni had gone away from the bed to scrub his hands in water from a steel pitcher, and now he came back and said, "I was experimenting with infibulation in the old days, but regrettably never had the chance to try it in the field. You would be amazed at the anxiety it creates in women who are threatened with it, the despondency that sets in after the procedure has been performed."

"Yes, amazed," Ashfar muttered. "We never got near Maryam," he said to Darius. "Rahgozar was constantly at her side. But we knew she had received our message through Leila. When Maryam continued to shun us, we went after Leila again. She was near death from an overdose of heroin when we found her. We put a bullet in her head so that our warning could not be missed, and left her body in the courtyard on Saltanatabad, where Maryam would have a good, long look at it. Then Rahgozar took it upon himself to move Maryam out of the apartment. We didn't know where.

"Still, we were not at a dead end. Sousan, after all, had been to Afghanistan, and we went to her place to ask again about her journey. Her boyfriend was touchy about late-night callers. He misinterpreted what we were there for. Baraheni killed him before he could tell us what we wanted to know. This, you may remember, is a recurring problem with Baraheni, but never mind. Sousan became sulky after that. We had no choice with her."

Baraheni patted his hands in a fluffy towel and left the room.

"We are not policemen. Our talents are in other areas. Maryam Lajevardi had vanished, and we needed you to locate her. Obviously, we couldn't tell you why, so we said it was the dope we wanted. The Komiteh had begun pressing us, they thought we were stalling. Then you tracked down Rahgozar, and for my partners and I it could not have come at a better time. You could have taken forever looking for Maryam, as long as there was progress for us to report."

"But I found her," Darius said. "The Komiteh doesn't need you much longer."

"It infuriated us. What right do you have to put us under this kind of pressure? If we don't come up with the mycotoxins soon, we will be in the same sorry spot as you are now."

Baraheni had returned wheeling a cart on which a bulky object was hidden under a white cloth.

"What's this?" Ashfar asked him.

"Something I picked up on Firdowsi Street." Baraheni whipped away the cloth from a samovar whose brass urn was badly in need of polish. He started a flame that burned with hard, blue light.

Darius felt the boiling samovar already strapped to his back. Baraheni let some water run out of the spigot onto the back of his hand. "Soon it will be ready."

"After reasoning things calmly," Ashfar resumed, "we came to realize what an advantageous position we are in to be this close to the mycotoxins. Who can say what avenues of opportunity will open up when we have them in our possession? Like Maryam Lajevardi, we view them as a once-in-a-lifetime chance to become extremely rich. It would be a pity if Iran does not meet our price. But we have no control over that."

Darius had not stopped staring at the samovar, which began to emit gray puffs of steam and to chug like a pocket locomotive.

"It's time," Baraheni said.

Darius's chest was hammering with a violence that made torture a secondary concern. Praise Allah, he thought, for small victories. Ashfar produced two glasses from the cart, and polished them with the fluffy towel until the last water blemish had been erased.

"I apologize for not having fine china to serve you," he said as he filled them. "These will have to do."

A guard entered with a woman wearing a tattered prison chador. The hood pulled low over her forehead did not conceal masses of blonde hair, the greenish glow of moist eyes.

"I don't expect," Ashfar was saying, "that introductions are necessary . . ."

❖ 15 ❖

She remained where she was without uttering a word until the two of them had been left alone. When she came to him she was limping. Seeing how he was watching her, she hiked the chador around her ankles to show that she had lost one sandal. "They haven't hurt me," she said. "Not yet."

He relaxed a little then, a little more after snuffing the flame under the samovar.

"I was worried about you."

"I'm well enough," he told her.

"They came for me as soon as you left Sharera's. Six of them," she blurted. "They stormed inside, and brought me straight here. I've been scared out of my wits ever since."

"That's good," he said.

"Is it?"

"You haven't lost them."

His brief replies were a kind of torture. She wanted long, rambling statements to neutralize her terror, answers for questions she hadn't raised, one on top of the other, a masculine voice to swaddle herself in.

"You can't believe what it's like in the women's wing," she said. "A day, an hour doesn't go by that a girl isn't raped before my eyes."

"You're safe. The fanatics wouldn't dare touch a Bride of Blood."

219

"Why not?"

"If they were to rape a girl who was a virgin, they'd go to hell; while any girl who dies pure will spend eternity in heaven. They didn't carry you off to Evin to give you a free pass to paradise."

"They have a way around it. All female prisoners are declared corrupt on earth and automatically made wards of the court. The judges decree the girls to be the guards' temporary wives, so they can be raped legally without the fear of hell and executed immediately after. It works out neatly for everyone concerned," she said bitterly. "Don't you think?"

A slight tremor in her voice embarrassed her. She paused till she had overcome it. "There's one guard, a foul, repulsive fellow, who already calls me his Mrs."

"Are you going to tell them?"

"Tell them what? To go to hell?" Flustered, she tasted the tea, and spilled it into the pitcher.

"Where the mycotoxins are."

"I've said it a million times." Her voice broke with emotion she couldn't disguise. "I don't know where. I just don't know."

Darius squinted into the lights where the microphones in the torture rooms customarily were secreted. After so many days in Evin Maryam would know that every breath, every scream, was recorded for analysis. The most revealing questioning took place between the formal sessions with interrogators in the conversations among the prisoners that were monitored. For what audience was she performing now?

"You may save yourself from pain," he told her.

"You've surrendered." Her face tightened with anger. "Or else never stopped working for them. Nothing has changed. You're here to frighten me into talking."

"I'm trying to help you."

"That's what they say: it will help my cause to give them everything they want. I'm glad I don't know. They can torture me to death, and still they won't find out."

It was an impassioned recitation, and he allowed himself to slip into character with it. He dropped his voice to a whisper the microphones could not hear. "Keep up your courage. Your ordeal won't be long."

"Is that so? Who's going to save me? You? You mean if I tell you what you need to know you'll put in a good word for me?"

"The grave," he said.

"That's not very comforting."

"It's honest, though. Unlike you—"

"You despise me," she said.

"Evin has made you paranoid. Personal feelings don't enter into any of this."

"But you do. You look at me like the guard who wants to rape me and kill me."

"Had you been truthful, neither of us would be in danger today."

"How can you say that? I saved your life."

". . . Did what?" He spoke loudly, but didn't care how much of what he said went on tape.

"I know even less than I let on to them." Maryam kept her voice low. "If they suspected how little, they'd have no use for either of us." Turning her back, she went away from him, and Ashfar and Baraheni rushed inside as though they were foiling an escape attempt.

"I trust you enjoyed your reunion," Ashfar said.

"We have nothing to talk about," Maryam said.

Baraheni had gone to the wall for a cable. "We may be able to provide a topic for discussion."

Maryam's expression did not change as Ashfar pushed her to the whipping bed and straightened the straps. Darius had underestimated her. He had never known a woman impervious to the threat of torture. Not until three guards burst in and buckled him to the mattress instead of her did she abandon her look of inviolability.

"Have you seen anyone undergo Islamic whipping before?" Ashfar asked her. "For some, witnessing pain is more difficult than experiencing it."

Maryam shook her head. "Don't, please—"

"It is in your hands. We cannot chance the death of the one person we *know* can give us what we want. Unfortunately—unfortunately for him—as long as you are alive, he is expendable."

"I can't—"

The cable slapped against Darius's spine, and a scream caught too late rattled around the tiles. Worse than the pain was his humiliation. His sciatic nerve was the target of the next blow, and he fought the reflex to empty his bladder. Baraheni was using every gram of strength, swinging the cable in a high, overhand arc, and then snapping it down, showing off for the girl.

Maryam averted her eyes. Ashfar took her by the shoulders, held her so close to the bed that the breeze from the whip stirred her hair.

". . . Sorry," Darius thought he heard her say. "Sorry I didn't trust—"

"You might consider how you would stand up to the same treatment," Ashfar said to her. "Darius Bakhtiar, as is well known, is a man of unusual courage. Not everyone maintains a stoic posture for so long on the whipping bed."

Darius would have argued that it was the image of himself that he carried like a millstone around his neck that was all that kept him from pleading for mercy. And if Baraheni were to remember the samovar, there was nothing he wouldn't do or say. The whip crashed into his feet, and he felt himself slipping into the unconsciousness that was the lone refuge within reach.

"You have . . ." he mumbled.

Ashfar raised his palm, and Baraheni stopped the cable in mid-stroke. "Did you say something?"

Darius turned his head toward the microphone in the lights. Somewhere Bijan would be listening.

"You already have the mycotoxins," he said. "I brought them to your place myself. Why are you doing this to me?"

The whip came down again, still harder. After that, Darius didn't have to know a thing.

He was drowning. Cold water washed over his face into his nose and mouth. His body had quit hurting everywhere except his lungs, which threatened to burst inside his chest. He measured his life in the seconds that he could hold his breath.

"He's stopped breathing," a young woman scolded. "He's dying. Somebody, please do something . . ."

He listened, but no one came, and he opened his eyes to see why. A girl about twenty years old was bent over him close enough to kiss. A wet rag in her hand was dripping onto his throat. When he brushed it aside, she turned away. A torn prison chador did not completely conceal the flowery Qashqa'i blouse she had on underneath.

He raised himself onto an elbow, but as he tried to sit up he was pulled onto his back. His left hand traced a chain that tethered his right arm to a radiator. He refilled his lungs with deep draughts of air tainted with the medicinal smell of the hospital.

"You were unconscious for a long time," the girl said. "It worried me to see you like that. The doctor is very busy, there was no one to attend to you. I asked for some water, but all they could give me was a wet towel."

Darius looked at the long line of wounded prisoners behind him. How long had he been allowed to wait now that he needed prompt medical attention? He took the rag from the girl, and wrung it out over his head. The water that ran into his eyes was pink. "Who are you?" he asked.

The girl kept her face away from him, showing a pallid, aquiline profile. "Nahid."

He knew the name, had heard it mentioned recently, but his head still felt as though he were underwater, and he couldn't remember where.

"I have been accused of adultery," she said, "but am innocent. Almost every day I am beaten while they put words in my mouth to repeat to them. I don't understand what they want."

"Do you know—" Darius stopped to consider he might still be dreaming. "Do you know an officer of the National Police by the name of Ghaffari?"

"I know a Mansur Ghaffari," she answered cautiously. "He is my fiancé. But he is not a policeman, nor is he married, as they say. He is a traveling salesman." Nahid covered her other cheek with her hand, and looked at him with both eyes. "How are you acquainted with Mansur? Is he all right?"

"They are torturing you for his sins."

"You are mistaken," she said firmly. "Mansur is clean and blameless."

The young doctor, Kashfi, called the girl into the clinic.

"Your injuries are worse than mine," she said to Darius. "You can go first."

Darius shook his head. "You've already been too kind."

Nahid was inside less than a minute before she returned clutching a foil packet of aspirin. As she brushed by him, Darius saw that the right side of her face was swollen and discolored, and hung from shattered bone like a mask that had worked loose. Kashfi came out after her, and told a guard to unlock Darius's shackles. Sensation in his legs ended at the knee. He grabbed for his feet, which were ice cold, and bloody, but at least were still attached to him.

"Help me bring him in," Kashfi said.

The clinic consisted of a single bed, an examining table, and several cabinets stocked sparsely with rudimentary medical supplies. The guard sat Darius on the table, and Kashfi raised his dead legs. From a brown bottle he applied a clear liquid to Darius's soles with a worn cotton swab. Darius felt nothing at first, then coolness, then a welcome burst of pain.

"You cannot tolerate any more, Lieutenant Colonel Bakhtiar," Kashfi said. "They have cut deeply into your arch. Tell them you need more time between sessions."

"If it's all the same," Darius said, "I'd rather not prolong my stay."

Like Nahid, Kashfi avoided looking at Darius as he applied the dressing.

"What are you doing in Evin," Darius asked him, "when you could have a pleasant posting at the morgue?"

"I did not become a doctor to attend to the dead. I requested the Ministry of Health to let me come here to fulfill the requirements of my residency."

"The one difference I see," Darius said, "is that in Evin the corpses still hobble about."

Kashfi's eyes flashed, but he didn't smile. "I believed I could provide care to people who most needed it."

There was no tape left in any of the cabinets. Kashfi knotted the bandage while looking into the corridor, where the line of patients extended around the corner.

"But this is not what I envisioned," he said. "How am I helping anyone by enabling them to stand more pain? What they have me doing is in opposition to everything that attracted me to medicine. I have asked for another assignment; even the morgue is preferable. But as I have already been moved once, it is doubtful they will rule favorably upon my request. I, too, am Evin's prisoner."

"If you're serious about helping the living," Darius said, "help me."

"I could have you walking in days if they would stop whipping you." Kashfi patted Darius's toes. "I am a good doctor."

"I need help now, help in getting out."

"I have no influence here."

"Get word to Dr. Baghai that I'm in Evin and want to see him."

Kashfi ran the water in a small sink, and his eyes darted toward the ceiling. Darius did not have to be told that a microphone was secreted there.

"Were they to find out even that I had met you before, and did not report the fact, it would be very bad for me." Kashfi dropped his voice, which was cloaked by the gushing faucets. "Really, I would like to help you, if I could."

When Darius tried to stand, Kashfi did not assist him, but watched with neither pride nor satisfaction as he balanced on his bandaged feet.

"You did a fine job," Darius said.

Kashfi shrugged. When he shook Darius's hand there was an extra packet of aspirin in it.

"Oh, you who believe! Do not take the Jews and Christians for friends; they are friends of each other; and whoever amongst you takes them for a friend, then surely he is one of them; surely Allah does not guide the unjust people."

A dirge of sermons and prayer from the reigning ayatollahs blared from Evin's loudspeakers all day long. Like most other prisoners, Darius had learned to shut his ears to the bombardment. The commentary on the surah *Al Maidah* of the holy Qur'an warning against the perfidies of the infidels was a favorite of the authorities, and the volume was turned up whenever that portion of the tape was played.

Waiting alone in the interrogation room, he had to clap his hands over his ears to blot out the racket. It was two days since his last session with Bijan, and he hadn't expected to be questioned again so soon. His feet were still swollen so badly that he couldn't fit them in his shoes; sitting too long in one spot was an ordeal that kept him constantly shifting position. A guard called to him, "You have a visitor," and Ghaffari came inside and assumed Bijan's place at the desk. They sat looking at each other in silence until an anxious frown broke across Ghaffari's face, and he said, "I worry about you, Darius. I do."

"Is that why you worked so industriously to make a place for me here?"

"I also worry about Sharera and Shahla. Sometimes, even about myself. When you don't give a damn about yourself, how can I put you ahead of my family?"

"*Guard!*" Darius shouted. "I want to go back to my cell."

No one came. The door closed, muting the attack on the Jews and Christians.

"I have nothing to say to you, Mansur."

"No? Then maybe you'll listen for once. Immense pressure is being brought to bear against me, and on others as well. The Komiteh don't care who they hurt. It will go better for everyone who ever knew you if you talk."

"I don't know anything. You can tell them I told you that."

"I did. Many, many times. They said the answer was unacceptable."

"Unacceptable? How can the truth be unacceptable?"

"You're being naive. Do you believe the truth is special to them? When it is not *their* truth it loses its usefulness and becomes heresy. Their truth is the revealed truth of God, but it has been revealed only to them. There are things they have to find out. That you don't have the information is besides the point. You must provide it."

"So you've come to ask me questions I can't answer. You'll do well in your new job."

"I don't owe them any favors."

"No, I don't suppose you do. *You* were the spy in Homicide. You fed them everything."

"You still don't see," Ghaffari said. "They know everything from the start—what we think, how we respond to any situation. All the stuff that's gone inside our head for a dozen years, they put there. Detail sometimes eludes them—as it does now—but eventually they have it, too. They know who we are better than we do ourselves. It's the function of the Revolution to decide what we must be."

"I was my own man well before the Revolution," Darius said.

"Especially you. With you there's no compromise, no complexity. You oppose them on all counts. Your type is not a mystery, merely a case for the cleaver instead of the scalpel."

"Is it part of your complicated nature to let them get to you through a girl?"

Ghaffari shook his head.

"You deny it? I saw Nahid."

"Through my family," Ghaffari told him. "Nahid was a weakness they exploited to threaten what would happen to Sharera and Shahla after I'm gone. They caught me with Nahid before you went to Mashad. Those days I spent with her here." He stripped off his jacket, and then his shirt, and swiveled around for Darius to see a crosshatch of scabs on his back. "I never wanted to be homicide chief. I didn't know they would send killers after you to the house on Old Karaj Road." When Darius said nothing, he added, "I can't stand punishment like you."

"What are they offering?"

"Tell them enough so they can recover the mycotoxins themselves, and you will have a painless death."

"It's not much of a bargain. What if I don't accept?"

"Then they will continue to torture you until you are just as dead, and Maryam Lajevardi will be declared in enmity with God. You know what that means, I'm sure."

"The penalty is crucifixion," Darius said.

"She will be tied to a cross and left there three days, or till she dies. They will get the information from her that way."

"She won't talk."

"Then they will have blood," Ghaffari said. "For them it's almost the same thing."

"Has she been told?"

"Yes."

Darius tried to put himself inside Maryam's head. Her obduracy was less complicated than his—a tropism, perhaps, or a primitive response lost over millennia of human evolution, but retained in her DNA as a fossil stubbornness so absolute that the Komiteh had to focus on him as the likelier to crack.

But what if it were not Maryam's stiff neck that made him the more attractive target? What if he *did* have what they wanted? An interesting thought, except that it meant going along with Ghaffari's notion that he had assumed the role the Revolution demanded of him—a repository of information he was too blind to recognize for what it was.

Ghaffari buttoned his shirt as Bijan came in and dropped his briefcase on the desk.

"How has the prisoner received our generous terms?"

"Ask him yourself." Ghaffari drenched the words in venom, and spit them like darts, and for that instant Darius forgave him everything.

"I can't tell you what I don't—"

"Yes, yes, I seem to have heard this before." Bijan unlocked the briefcase and ran his thumb over the stacks of papers. "It is pointless to continue. Since you refuse to cooperate, your interrogation has ended. You will be executed immediately," he said without any change in tone. "There is no appeal."

Guards came to hustle him the length of the cellblock, and then they walked three or four steps behind him through the yard. The late sun had stalled above a water tower, oozing orange light into the garden. Wintry drafts rolled down from the mountains and stirred the loose soil. Darius was brought to one of the bare trunks in front of the wall, and made to stand there while four men carrying carbines over their shoulders lined up facing him not ten meters away. He found himself asking who would be sent the bill for the bullets used to kill him, where they would find someone to whom he meant enough to share that final insult.

His wrists were lashed together behind the post, and the other strap was fastened around his knees. The ground at his feet was dark and boggy, although the rest of the yard was dry sand. In some way he felt cheated by not being given the time to unravel the mystery that had brought him to this place. Here, he decided, was his epitaph: had he lived longer, he might have found something important that was lost inside his brain.

A black hood was dropped over his head and closed with a drawstring around his throat. The cellblock door squeaked open again. Assuming that witnesses were being assembled, he listened for a woman's gait.

Bijan asked, "Do you have any requests?"

"I would like the hood removed."

"That is against the regulations."

Darius heard him walk away. His footsteps hadn't stopped when he called out, "Ready."

The firing squad shouldered rifles, cocked them, and there was a moment of remarkable clarity in which the sensation of the wind moving the hood against Darius's cheek was as fulfilling as the finest meal he had eaten, the best vodka. His heart was hammering harder than it had when the samovar was fired; but the frenzy of thought he anticipated was absent with most of his fear.

His sore shoulders ached as he backed against the trunk. Filling his lungs, he forced himself to relax. Calmness would be his small triumph over them.

"Aim."

Dust from the hood was tickling his nose. He would start sneezing if they didn't get it over with soon. A sad commentary on his spiritual decline that this would be his final concern.

"Fire!"

A ringing sensation filled his head and the concussion from the reports sent tremors through his body. His knees buckled, and he felt himself blacking out. But if he were dying, why was his heart still pounding? He wanted to consider the problem at his own pace, but someone was rushing toward him faster than he could think. He smelled the oil on the gun that would fire the coup de grace, and then there was light pressure behind his ear. As he awaited the shot the hood was yanked off, and he squinted at Bijan's thin smile. Baraheni was clapping enthusiastically beside Ashfar, who was showing his terrible gaze.

"Bravo," Baraheni shouted. "You were heroic in your fortitude. You have done the old gang proud."

"Bring him back to solitary," Bijan ordered the guards.

To Darius he said, "We have not begun with you."

Following the call to evening prayers he was taken from his cell. Marched through the block he knew the serenity of being tapped dry of fear. Whatever was in store for him held no threat after the things he'd been put through; having already experienced the moment of death, even fresh pain would be a bonus. He was left outside the clinic, but not chained. One old man was waiting in the corridor, and soon Kashfi came out and sent him away with aspirins. The young doctor did not take Darius's outstretched hand. He looked at him with annoyance for presupposing upon a friendship that did not exist.

"I didn't ask to be brought here," Darius said.

Kashfi ran water in the sink. He spoke in whispers. "I sent for you."

"You got word to Baghai?"

"The coroner is a well-meaning man, loyal to those he likes, but ineffectual away from the morgue. He would try to save you, and would fail. The single comfort you would have from him would be his company in your cell. I cannot allow that." During a long pause, Kashfi appeared to be trying to catch his breath. ". . . I have devised a plan for your escape."

"Dr. Baghai is an old man prepared to accept the consequences of his failures. You're still young. Should the Komiteh find out—"

"Do you wish to be free, or not? It will not require a brilliant argument to persuade me to be the coward I normally am."

"What do you know about breaking out of prison?"

"Next time they are done whipping you, demand to be brought to the hospital. I will hold you for treatment past midnight, when most of the guards go home. Then I will sign a death certificate, and wrap you in a shroud, and put you with the corpses that are taken before dawn to Behesht-e-Zahra. From there you will be on your own."

Of the two of them, Darius decided, Kashfi was the more grateful for the opportunity to save his life. "That's not good enough," he said.

"It puts you outside the walls. What more can you ask?"

"You have two chances to establish your credentials as a jailbreaker. Someone is coming with me."

Kashfi went back inside the hospital, and began putting away his equipment. Darius noticed a tray of surgeon's instruments beside a bloodied sheet on the examining table.

"Aren't you the doctor with no stomach for cutting?"

Kashfi grunted. He washed his hands without soap, and dried them on his gown.

"Do you perform many operations here?"

"Some."

"What kind?"

"Skin grafts. I have become expert at taking flesh from prisoners' hips, and replacing it on their soles when they have been tortured too harshly."

"Do they walk again?"

"Right back to the whipping bed." Kashfi took a deep breath, and then he sighed. "Tell me, who is the other person?"

"She's an inmate of the women's wing."

"Forget I agreed to do anything for you. The plan will fall apart, and we will both be killed—if we are lucky. A woman . . . it's dangerous enough as it is."

"Yes," Darius said, "and nearly perfect."

Several chairs had been arranged close to the whipping bed. Like judges at an erotic competition Maryam sat with Ashfar and Baraheni, who was whittling the insulation from a strip of electric flex.

"We nearly started without you today," Ashfar said when Darius was brought in.

"Don't put yourself out for *me*."

"But, you understand, we must."

Baraheni coiled the cable around his shoulder and adjusted the straps on the bed. His guards threw Darius on the mattress, and held him down while his feet were bound.

"What's this?" Baraheni ran his thumbnail against Darius's arch, scraping away a salve that Kashfi had applied. He wiped both feet with a hand towel, buffed the soles as though he was putting a shine on them.

Maryam's chair was positioned so that when Darius raised his head he was staring at her. She focused on the floor, but gradually her gaze was drawn back to him. Her expression changed from second to second, but never seemed comfortable, and as the cable began humming like a bass string she shut her eyes. The first stroke broke the scabs over the deep cuts in his feet that scarcely had begun to heal. Maryam forced herself to look, to let him know it was all right to scream.

The next blow was delivered to his heels, and was followed by others against his back. Baraheni was not in top form, possibly arm weary at the end of a long day. The cable came down across Darius's thighs, and though the pain was not unbearable, he shouted. Baraheni let up noticeably after that, and Darius rewarded him with an occasional yell.

"This is getting us nowhere," Ashfar said. "Let us try it the other way."

Darius was unstrapped and dumped in Baraheni's chair. As he waited for the samovar to be wheeled in, Ashfar extended his arm to Maryam. "If you do not mind . . ."

Maryam recoiled from him. She walked alone to the bed and swept her hand against the mattress, rubbed the grime from her fingertips.

"On your stomach, please."

Maryam glanced toward the door, and her body swayed in that direction. But then she lay down and Baraheni buckled the straps and tied her ankles to the rail.

"Notice how we do this in strict accordance with Islamic precepts." Ashfar was speaking to Darius, but his words were aimed at the ceiling. "The woman is not bared on the whipping bed, but for the soles of her feet." He brushed back the hem of the chador. "And what lovely feet these are."

Baraheni had gone to a locker for a feather pillow, which he placed under Maryam's head.

"We do not want you thrashing around and injuring your pretty neck." He hovered over the bed swinging the whip high overhead, the copper plaits shooting out sparks as they whisked the ceiling.

"One last time we are asking you," Ashfar said to Darius. "Where are the mycotoxins?"

It was clear now why they had tortured him—their purpose not to encourage information they knew he didn't have, but to get him to hate Maryam for witnessing his humiliation, and her to despise him for his helplessness, to destroy the symbiosis that preserved their silence. He lunged at Baraheni, but had no strength; Ashfar caught him before he was out of the chair, and slammed him back down.

"You are going to tell us eventually," Ashfar said to Maryam, "so why lose your pride and endure needless suffering? To allow your body to be broken is a hollow gesture. Not long ago I was in a position similar to yours. The Komiteh was determined to have everything about our organization. I am no coward, but neither am I a fool. It went against all my instincts to breach solidarity with my comrades. But I must tell you I don't lose any sleep over it. I pass on this advice because I would not like to see you hurt. Take a moment to reflect on it."

Darius was gathering himself for another charge at Baraheni when Maryam said, "I don't need a moment. They're in a locker at Mehrabad Airport. They've been there all along."

"There are thousands of lockers." The whistling began, and picked up in intensity. The cable became invisible, Baraheni's arm a gray blur. "What is the number?"

"I don't know."

"Do you have the key?"

"Yes."

"Give it to us now."

"It's in my house."

"The residence was razed by fire," Ashfar said. "A convenient excuse for not being able to turn it over."

"I kept it in a cookie tin in the kitchen. You'll find it there, if the ruins haven't been picked clean."

Ashfar placed a hand on Baraheni's shoulder, and the cable materialized, flickering in the harsh light. As the whistling died, it slipped from Baraheni's grasp and flew into a corner.

Maryam strained to make eye contact with Darius. "I had to," she pleaded. ". . . they would have gotten it out of me sooner or later." She began to sob. "I didn't want to, I didn't—"

"Had I known you were a woman susceptible to reason, much of the unpleasantness that preceded your admissions could have been avoided." Ashfar glanced triumphantly at Darius, who had gotten up from the chair and was looking toward the doorway, where Bijan stood watching them.

"It is about time," Bijan said. "Men will be sent to guard the fire scene until a search can be started at dawn." He moved to the bed where Maryam was crying softly into the pillow, and untied her feet and hands. "Pray that nothing there has been touched. You see how it will go for you should you be lying."

Maryam focused again on Darius, whose cold stare offered nothing. He did not acknowledge her when she came across the room to him, and she wrapped his arms around her shoulders and buried her face in his chest.

"Such behavior in a couple not united in marriage is immoral and may lead to stiff penalties." Bijan leered at them, immensely pleased with himself. He returned to the corridor, and Darius heard him giving orders to round up a crew for the Old Karaj Road.

Ashfar's body was rocked by great peals of laughter, which Baraheni seized on and amplified. "It must be love," he said to Maryam.

"What are you talking about?"

"That is Bijan's way of showing affection. He wants you for his seegah before it is decided what to do with you. He says it is unhealthy for a woman your age not to have regular sexual relations because the natural flow of hormones will back up into your glands. The greater tragedy, the one he will not allow, is for you to go to your grave a virgin. He will do you the great favor of permitting you to become his temporary wife."

Ashfar was laughing so hard he was having difficulty getting out the words. "Darius, have you learned the best place in Evin to obtain vodka? We would like to celebrate Maryam's betrothal."

Darius waltzed her around so that his back was to them. He took her hand from his shoulder, and slipped a sharp sliver of clear glass from his pocket against the palm.

"What's this? A diamond? I'm flattered," she said, "but as you heard I'm already spoken for." She opened her hand, but Darius caught the glass and curled her fingers around it.

"More valuable than any diamond," he whispered. "A key."

How long he had been a corpse he didn't know. He lay on a gurney inside the tiny hospital with his suit folded under the linen shroud that was all he wore. His shoes made inconspicuous bulges against his hips. Several hours more went by before he heard wailing in the corridor. He raised himself on his elbows to see what the commotion was about, and then, remembering he was a dead man, lay back again.

The lights went on, and it was all he could do to keep from shading his eyes with his hand. Several women were at the door, but the cries were Nahid's.

Rubber wheels skidded on the bare floor, and his gurney was bumped by another. Kashfi was talking over the women's voices, his adolescent drone a poor instrument of condolence. The death of her cellmate, he told Nahid, was God's will. The girl would have none of it, though, and berated herself for not taking better care of her only friend in Evin. Darius brought shallow draughts of air into the top of his lungs, and tried not to break a sweat under the hot lights till the guards took Nahid back to her cell.

Kashfi's hand was on his shoulder. Opening his eyes, he saw Maryam motionless on the gurney next to his with her right arm dangling over the edge. Redness gushed from inside her wrist and branched into separate streams along her fingers. Her cheeks were pure white; even her hair seemed to have leached color onto the floor. She sat up slowly, staring at her wrist in wonder that it belonged to her.

"Who told you to open your arm like this?" Kashfi asked. "Just to show some blood would have been enough."

"I wanted to be convincing."

"You've convinced me. A few minutes more, and you could have bled to death." Kashfi began sewing her arm with a needle and black thread. "Why did you cut so deep? Why cut along the vein like you meant it, instead of across?"

"The guards are jaded by gore. They wouldn't have taken notice of anything less."

"Maryam is a true daughter of Iran, an expert at fabrication," Darius said. "She dissembles more persuasively than the worst murderers."

"How do you know when I'm lying?" She sprayed a few drops of her blood onto his gurney. "Are these lies?"

"You've lost all feeling for the truth."

"Shhh." Kashfi cut the thread and knotted it. "The dead aren't entitled to make so much noise." He flung a shroud into Maryam's lap. "Take off your chador, and get into this, quick," he said, and shut off the light.

Darius filled his eyes with the image of a ghost in a frenzied striptease. Maryam was back on the gurney when the lights came on again, smoothing the folded chador against her body beneath the shroud. Devoid of color she was the loveliest corpse he had seen, an advertisement for the grave.

"The truck leaves for Behesht-e-Zahra in the hour before sunrise." Kashfi slipped off Maryam's rubber prison sandals and gave them to her to hide. "It does not make any stops en route. Get off the first time you feel it slow down. The cemetery is crowded at all hours these days. You don't know what you may encounter there." He shook Darius's hand. "Good luck," he said, and then went back to Maryam, and removed two silver rings from her fingers. "Find a place for these, too," he said to her, "unless you want the grave diggers all over you."

Maryam's gurney was wheeled into the corridor. Darius lay with his eyes closed and his hands folded across his heart, perfecting his attitude of death. Soon Kashfi came for him, and he was placed beside Maryam. A rough bandage chafed his wrist, and her warm hand nestled into his. Had anyone asked he would have said that indeed he must have died because already he was in heaven, a place of fantastic expectation where nothing was as it seemed to be, and falsehood was legal tender.

❖ 16 ❖

Descending from the heights of Evin, Darius shook harder with every lost meter of elevation—an inversion of physical law he explained away with the theory that absolute zero emanates from the grave. His shroud was paper thin; it afforded no protection from the wind that poured under the canvas top of the Bedford truck. The mound of bodies on which he was riding shifted as the truck careened around a corner, and a clammy crevasse opened up and swallowed him.

He touched bottom holding his breath, and began clawing his way back to the top. A moan rose from the knot of corpses, and he swept the blackness for Maryam. The hand he grabbed was ice cold and scabrous. He threw it down and searched for warm flesh, pulled Maryam close and clung to her, bobbing in a putrifying sea.

The squeal of brakes announced a sudden stop. The load pressed forward, and a body tumbled between them, a woman still wet with blood that was not quite cold. Maryam gagged as Darius freed them from her embrace.

"Are you all right?" he asked.

In the dark he heard her retching. The truck banked sharply, and he braced against the weight of their traveling companions as it speeded up again on an unpaved surface.

"How far till we're there?"

"I don't know where we are," he told her. "We must have taken a detour."

Through a tear in the canvas he looked out into a starry void in orbit around a van's single taillight. The roadbed was paved in crushed rock and dirt. Other than the van disappearing in a gray smokescreen theirs was the only vehicle on it.

"Better get dressed now," he said.

Maryam slipped on her chador over the shroud. With no place to stand Darius struggled into his pants. One leg was on when his shoes slid away, and he tunneled through the bodies to retrieve them. Maryam held his jacket behind his back, and guided his hands into the sleeves.

The dry heat of the southern slums billowed under the canvas, but neither of them could stop shivering. The truck lurched over an obstacle in the road, and as it slowed they crouched behind the tailgate. Orange traffic pylons glowed in a sodium vapor haze as a young Guardsman peeked inside, laughing nervously. A voice that otherwise was indistinct clearly pronounced the word "Advance."

Darius was certain they were entering Behesht-e-Zahra via the long avenue that led past the tomb of the Imam and the sections where the martyrs of the Revolution were buried. They turned twice more into the furthest corner of the cemetery, a potter's field where Evin disposed of martyrs to private causes.

A cement mixer was parked beside a trench from which the sun seemed to have risen out of the pebbly ground. Laborers molded of the same sandy compound lining the bottom of the excavation used long-handled hoes to prepare it to be filled and sealed.

Darius was clambering over the tailgate when the truck squeezed between the pit and a hill of turned earth, and the driver left the engine running and went around to the back. With Maryam he retreated into the mass of corpses, which had reassembled as an exclusive club that now barred them admittance. The driver held his fingers over his nose as he lowered the tailgate and glanced distastefully at his cargo. He was younger than Maryam, with the desert tan and strong white teeth of a peasant who was still new to urban living. Darius took Maryam's hand and together they came forward. The driver froze, and his skin turned as glossy as anyone's in the truck. His knees moved up and down, but his feet were stuck to the ground. Delivering himself of a girlish shriek, he ran to the gang of cement workers, and Darius saw him gesticulating wildly as he led a charge to hallowed ground.

Darius lowered himself slowly from the tailgate. The light slap of the ground against his toes was as painful as a session on the whipping bed. Maryam sprinted for the cemetery wall with Darius several steps behind. He boosted her over the waterstained bricks, and pulled himself up after her, and they kept running till they lost themselves in the twisted lanes around Bijan's house.

"Where can we go?" Maryam asked.

"I don't know."

"It doesn't matter. The important thing is that we're free."

"It was too easy," Darius said. "It worries me."

"Easy? I hope I never have to go through anything so easy again. When you relax, that's when *I'll* worry."

"Worry now. Worry for Kashfi, when they find out we're gone."

Streetlights drew them to a main thoroughfare, an avenue of shuttered food stalls and small shops. A muzzein was calling the faithful to prayer at a corner mosque, and they crossed to the other side and kept to the shadows away from the men straggling to services. A cruise cab stopped for them unasked. The driver brought them north past the railroad station following Darius's instructions for avoiding the Komiteh roadblocks. The upholstery reeked of tobacco smoke and spoiled fruit. Maryam rolled down the windows, and fumigated the interior with fresh air.

"Shabbaz Avenue," Darius said, and stone worry beads dangling from the mirror clacked rhythmically as the cab swung east. Darius looked out at street sweepers maneuvering wide brooms along sidewalks buried in trash. From the old power plant he called the turns to a gray brick wall crumbling under years of neglect. In the dying garden surrounding a traditional home a birdhouse hung in the yellow canopy of a plane tree. "Stop here," he said.

"The fare is two thousand rials," the driver said.

Darius opened the door. "My money is inside the house."

"Pay me right now." The driver reached over the seat, and pulled the door shut. "Pay me, or I will call the police."

Maryam scoured her chador, and tossed a silver ring into the front.

"This is worth tens of thousands," the driver said. "How can I make change?"

"Give us what you have," Maryam said.

The driver emptied his change maker, and raced away laughing. A finch had come out of the birdhouse, and Maryam paused in the garden to hear him sing to the early morning sun.

"Whose place is this?" she asked.

"A friend's."

"Can he be trusted?"

"Completely."

Maryam peered inside a window. "It doesn't look like anyone is home."

Through the streaked glass Darius saw tracks in the carpeting made by the cart from the morgue. He went into the garden for a dead branch, and smashed the door pane closest to the knob. Stale, arid air rushed out as though an ancient tomb had been violated. Maryam hurried inside ahead of him to explore all the rooms, and soon he heard water rumbling against the bottom of a metal tub.

"You wouldn't expect to find a bathtub in an old home like this," she said to him.

"Mehta was full of surprises."

The bedroom closet contained three or four suits that might fit him, shoes to wear over several pairs of socks. In a cardboard crate brittle with age were several shapeless dresses among a dozen black chadors. He tossed a flowery chemise with puffed sleeves at Maryam. Draping it against her body she made it youthful and exotic, but as he nodded his approval she let it drop to the floor.

"I lied," she said. "To Ashfar. There's no locker, no key. It was just something to get them to leave us alone."

"Why tell me now?"

"So you understand."

"The mycotoxins are nothing to me anymore."

"I don't want you to think I'm holding out on you. That I ever did. If I'd known where they were, I'd have told him when he had you on the whipping bed."

"Since when does it matter what I think?"

"You still don't trust me."

"I trusted you to lie to Ashfar and Bijan," he said, "and wasn't disappointed."

She was in the shower a long time, and came out wearing one of the clean chadors and with a towel wrapped like a sayyid's turban around her wet hair. The hot water was used up when it was his turn in the tub. Sitting on the bottom, he played the cold against his bruised muscles.

There was no shaving cream in the medicine chest. He toweled the mirror and stared at himself in the steamy fog. His ordeal showed in hollow cheeks, and residual swelling around the eyes. His beard had come in full and thick. With short hair and his collar open he might have been any loyal, tired son of the Revolution. In Mehta's best suit he looked ten years older.

Maryam had taken up residence in the kitchen. The oven and two burners were lighted, and he stood close and enjoyed the heat against his damp skin.

"I found some canned salmon in the pantry," she said. "It's almost ready."

She brought him fried fish and rice, and tea, and though the salmon was burned on the edges and cold inside he couldn't get enough of it. Maryam watched him eat before she served herself. She sat beside him taking slow, thoughtful bites, and when he finished before she hardly had started she filled his plate again.

"I was sixteen the year I made up my mind to martyr myself in the cause of the Shi'ites," she said abruptly. "A boy I thought I was in love with had left me for my best girlfriend, and I was going to have revenge on both of them by dying for Iran."

Darius put down his fork with a piece of salmon still on it.

"Eat," she said. "Learning to cook was my singular accomplishment as a soldier for Islam. At least have the fruits of my training." She tasted what was on her plate, but had no appetite. "I ran away to Teheran again, and Sheik Salehi arranged for me to be sent to 'The Institute' at Manzarieh for religious indoctrination. There I was taught how to hide explosives under my chador, to make myself human shrapnel. That was the extent of my instruction as a guerrilla."

"You?" Darius said. "Your vanity would allow you to die like that?"

"Don't laugh. It was what I wanted. I still hated my friend and the boy, and now I hated myself for having come to that miserable place. When we were asked who wanted to go to Lebanon to fight, I was the first to give her name." Maryam looked at her plate again, and made a meal of a forkful. "Manzarieh had been a country club compared to the camp of the Sayyidah Zaynab Brigade. 'Search for the Jew behind every depravity' was the watchword of the mullahs there. The girls all were zealots. Many were terribly ugly and had known rejection their whole life. Like me, they would take out their unhappiness on an unsuspecting world."

"But first upon themselves," he said. "It's the psychology of the camps."

"Where were you when I needed someone to tell me why I was the most miserable person on earth?"

"You saw action against the Israelis and their Christian allies?" he asked.

"Our days were spent in prayer, and in waiting. I was bored every minute until I met Leila. She also had come to Lebanon for the wrong reason, and saw no way out but the martyr's end we were promised. To ease her loneliness she had stolen some of the hashish that was used to give courage to the girls who were about to blow themselves up. To ease mine she taught me to smoke it. Things were not so dismal anymore. There was hope for us yet, if we could stay high all the time or get away."

Maryam reached under the table and brought up two bottles of Russian vodka of a fine label that Darius had never seen in the evidence room.

"Where did you find Stolichnaya?"

"There's an unopened case under the sink. I'd trade it all for two grams of hashish."

She filled his tea glass with the vodka, but took none for herself. "In the spring of this year, three girls were requested for a special mission. I had learned never to volunteer for anything unless I wanted to make good my martyrdom. Leila advised me to put my name forward as it would mean a break from our tedious existence. The other girl chosen was Sousan Hovanian, who was new to the camp and to us.

"We were returned to Iran and flown to Mashad. Revolutionary Guards drove us by night to the Afghanistan border at Jannatabad, and gave us over to a party of Islamic resistance fighters who had come to Mashad for medical treatment. We traveled with them by horse caravan over the Zulfikar Pass. The best thing I can say about the men is that they were too weak to bother us. The mountain valleys all are cultivated in opium poppies, and I began to understand what we were needed for . . . began to think I did." Maryam paused, and did not resume again.

"Yes, go on."

"I'm sorry I started. What difference does any of this make? We owe it to ourselves to forget the things that motivated us when we were in service to Iran, that seemed so important we would give up our lives for them."

"And if we could," Darius said, "what cause would take their place in your heart?"

"Myself," she said without hesitation. "All that concerns me now are my plans for the future—assuming I have a future."

"Someone has to remember those things."

"Why? To remember how we were duped, and used as if we were less than human?"

"Yes," Darius answered. "That's why."

Maryam sighed. Then she said, "The wounded fighters were bringing antihelicopter missiles into Afghanistan. On our best day in the mountains the horses made fewer than fifteen kilometers. We established contact with the main body of guerrillas at their base overlooking the highway to Herat, and were greeted with news that our camp in Lebanon had been overrun by the Israelis. We cried all night. But these were tears of joy. Without discussion we decided to return to our homes, and put out of our minds that we had ever been Brides of Blood. I was in favor of throwing the parcel the Afghanis gave us into the first lake we came to. Leila said no, that if we were picked up by the Revolutionary Guards, we would need what was inside to bargain for our lives."

Maryam sniffed the vodka bottle. "How can you drink this vile stuff?" she asked.

"We divided the plastic bags of heroin among us and taped them to our bodies as we had learned to hide explosives. Leila left for Iran in the morning, and Sousan the day after that. We were to meet one week later at the Rudaki Hall opera house. A blizzard closed the Zulfikar Pass for four days, and I lost three days more en route to Teheran. You can't imagine my relief when I found Sousan waiting for me, and she brought me to Saltanatabad Avenue."

"The apartment was hers?"

"Hers and Leila's," Maryam said. "They had sold one bag of heroin to a drug dealer from south Teheran, and were negotiating to get rid of the lot. The money that was left over from household expenses went for the first nice clothes they'd had in years. They didn't understand why I wanted no part of the deal. After talking about it long enough, neither did I. What could be more fitting, they argued, than for the people who supported the camps to be polluted by drugs, while we came away with something to show for our wasted lives?"

"Where was your part of the heroin?" Darius asked. "You weren't still carrying it taped to your body?"

"Mehrabad Airport. In a locker. So, you see, I don't lie so much as you think. The dealer was a hopeless addict who called himself Najafi. The big money he promised was always coming the next day. In time I came to feel the apartment was my home. I brought back my share of the drugs, and put it in the freezer with all the rest. While we waited to become rich, Leila began acting strangely, sleeping until noon, not eating or keeping herself clean. Najafi had taught her to smoke heroin, and it was all she cared about. Sousan and I were worried the Pasdars would pick her up on the street, so Sousan moved to Najafi's to keep a close eye on her. Next time I looked in the freezer, it was empty. I had no money, nowhere to go. I didn't even know where to reach the other girls. Then Leila came home with her insides torn up. It wasn't the Pasdars who had found her, but your friends from SAVAK."

"You've seen what good friends of mine they are."

"Leila said they would do the same to me if we didn't turn over the heroin. She became hysterical when I told her I didn't have it. Sousan had fallen in love with Najafi, and taken it all."

"And the mycotoxins?"

"The first I heard about them was from Rahgozar. He had been chasing after them for months. He was several days behind when he lost track of them near the Zulfikar Pass, and by the time he caught up to me in Teheran they were gone again."

"What did he want with them?" Darius asked. "The Russians didn't need them, since they were the first to synthesize yellow rain."

"He told me the Red Army had brought stocks of yellow rain into Afghanistan, but lost them when a cargo plane was shot down by the Islamic guerrillas. They weren't missed till the Soviets got into bed with the West, and began retrieving their chemical weapons all over the world."

"Where did you tell him they were?"

Maryam didn't try to hide her exasperation, but looked at Darius as though he were impossibly thick. "You know I don't know."

"He accepted that?"

"He was like you. He thought if he never let me out of his sight, eventually he'd have them. Them and me."

"You went along with him?"

"I'd seen what had happened to Leila. Better to let him drive me crazy asking the same question over and over than try convincing Baraheni of anything. Rahgozar was a good man, who had the best interests of two countries at heart. Whenever I think about what happened to him, I want to cry."

Reaching for the bottle again he brushed her arm, and she smiled and covered his hand in hers, a gesture that left him unmoved. In her aversion to him he'd been cast as another nuisance she was willing to put up with in order to preserve her life. He leaned across the table and kissed her.

She didn't pull away, didn't encourage him either. The sensation was like ice against his mouth—a thin layer capping a dormant hot spring. A thin fantasy, as well. He laughed out loud, and when Maryam asked, "What's funny?" he shook his head and drank more, then cupped her chin in his palm and kissed her again, watching the top of her breasts inside Mrs. Mehta's frumpy chemise.

He carried the bottle into the living room, and nestled against bolster pillows covered in red damask. Maryam came in after him, and though he concentrated on the vodka soon he had her in his arms. His hand on her breast made her heart accelerate. But she remained unresponsive when he kissed her, and he wrote off her reaction as one of alarm. On the chance that he was wrong, because he wanted to be, he nudged her onto her back. Her arm came up and stiffened against his chest.

"You heard just a small part of my story," she said. "I was a Bride of Blood in more than name only."

"I heard enough."

"No—there were rules for everything. If you broke even one of them, it might mean your life. For the girls of the Sayyidah Zaynab Brigade there was one rule that couldn't be bent, although our instructors challenged us to do so every day."

"Oh . . . ?" he said, knowing what she would tell him, already looking for his glass.

"We had to remain virgins, pure in heart and in body."

"You weren't so malleable that you agreed to everything they demanded of you?"

"I thought I was being loyal."

"Loyal to who? Of what use could the Party of God make of your virginity?"

"Those are the same arguments our instructors raised," she said, "after class was over."

She remained quiet for so long that he felt obligated to change the subject. "It's getting late . . ."

"Loyal to myself," she said then.

Women worldlier than she had given him the same rationale. From childhood, every Iranian girl had it impressed upon her that her virginity was her most precious possession. Even in cosmopolitan Teheran a young woman who was sexually experienced would have a difficult time finding a good husband. Any man who would marry a nonvirgin was deemed to be more seriously flawed than the girl he desired.

"You're falling asleep," he heard her say.

"You've hypnotized me."

He reached for her again, but embraced air as she slipped through his arms. The bottle that he snatched as a consolation prize was empty. She was scolding him, telling him he drank too much and that he needed rest if he was to regain his strength. In all her clothes, like a girl from the provinces, she wallowed in the pillows making a place to sleep for one. Darius tucked the empty under his arm and stumbled into the bedroom.

The single mattress was narrow and rutted; Mehta must have had his share of nights like this. The sheets felt gritty, and hadn't been changed since the body was taken away. He had no qualms about sleeping in his dead friend's bed. Perhaps Mehta's ghost would come down from Zoroastrian heaven where seven archangels dwelled with Ahura Mazda, and he would have companionship till morning when he would feel well enough to pursue Maryam again. Whole new areas of investigation were opening up to him now that he was no longer a detective.

He hung Mehta's suit behind the door and slipped between the sandy sheets. His eyes already were shut. The kiss that he felt on his forehead must have been a product of his imagination, for he was out by then, sleeping the deep, dreamless sleep of the dead.

Her throat was on fire. She tore open the windows and sucked cool air into her lungs, held it until she could swallow without pain. She crawled back into her nest to wait for her body to wake up, but still felt sluggish forty-five minutes later when she went into the bedroom. Darius had kicked off the covers and lay with his weight supported by both shoulders and one hip, a contortionist's trick that must have provided some relief for his wounded back. Breathing through his mouth, he made strangling sounds that she didn't like to hear. She opened the bedroom windows all the way. The breeze rustled the sheets, but Darius didn't stir. She tossed the covers over his twisted body, and walked out.

A hot morning shower was mad luxury after the weeks in Evin. She cooked some eggs and put up water for tea, and after she had eaten she made a second breakfast for Darius. His body had rearranged itself into a more intricate knot. When she raised the shades to allow the sunlight to spread over his face, she noticed an oozing rash under his beard. The light moving into his eyes didn't budge him. It was unsettling for her to see someone sleep so soundly, and she pushed at his ribs until his body rocked on one hip. "Come on," she said, "it's time you were up."

She pushed harder. His muscles contracted, and he flung himself onto his side.

"Are you all right?"

He moved his arms in front of his face, but they were heavy, and he dropped them and tried to get out of bed. The rash covered the back of his hands and ran up his other cheek in broad streaks that continued under the hairline. Thick clots of blood were stuck to his lower lip. When he opened his mouth to tell her something, he vomited up more of them, and Maryam thought she was going to be sick, too.

"Burning up," he mumbled. "No strength. Can't breathe—"

"What is it?"

"Don't know."

"Is there a doctor we can trust?"

"No. You—"

"I wouldn't know the first thing to do."

He fell back against the pillow. She lifted his head to her ear, held her breath as he tried to speak.

"Call the morgue."

Fifteen minutes went by from the time she reached the coroner's office until Baghai came on the line.

"I'm calling on behalf of Darius Bakhtiar," she said.

There was another extended silence during which she thought Baghai would hang up on her. Then she heard him clear his throat, and in an old man's reedy voice he asked, "Who is this?"

"A friend of his. He needs your help."

"Lieutenant Colonel Bakhtiar has been taken to Evin Prison. Who am I talking to?"

"He doesn't believe me," she said to Darius, and put the receiver to his mouth.

"*Baghai . . .*"

"It's you? When did you get out?"

"Yesterday. I—"

"That's wonderful news. I scarcely dared hope I'd ever hear—wonderful. Now I have some news for you."

Darius tried to interrupt, but couldn't get in a word. He shook his head, and Maryam took back the phone.

"He's very sick," she said. "He isn't able to speak."

"What's wrong with him?"

"He's throwing up blood, and can't catch his breath. His muscles are weak. He was tortured a long time in prison. He may have suffered internal injuries."

"It's a possibility."

Darius pawed at the phone until Maryam put him on again.

"I've been poisoned."

"Why do you say that?" Baghai asked.

246 ❖   Joseph Koenig

"My skin . . . like the Darwish girl's."

"*Mycotoxin* poisoning? How would you have been exposed?"

". . . No idea."

"You didn't ingest any?"

"Don't see how I could have."

"You need fluids in copious amounts to flush out your kidneys before they are permanently damaged. Drink at least three dozen glasses of water each of the next several days. Also you must remove all of the poison in contact with your body and hair. Is there a bathtub where you are?"

Darius nodded, and Maryam said yes into the phone for him.

"Take a shower right away. Put on clean clothes, and apply mineral oil to the rashes. Where are you?"

". . . Better not say."

"Well, I suppose you have your reasons," Baghai said. "What I was going to tell you is that the lab work just came back on Mehta, and it was determined conclusively that he died of mycotoxin poisoning. He took it with heroin, same as Leila Darwish. His body was one big running sore. But that doesn't explain how you got sick."

"Caught it from him."

"Don't be absurd. If you can come to my office, or I can see you there . . ."

"The Komiteh is looking for me."

"I understand. Then it is essential that you follow my instructions."

Darius touched Maryam's hand, and she put back the receiver.

"What did he tell you?" she asked. "Why were you talking about poison?"

"The mycotoxins . . . they've gotten into my system."

"How?"

He pushed her away from the bed. "Bring me water. Lots of it."

When she returned from the kitchen with a glass in each hand he had taken off his underwear and was struggling to get out of bed. Naked, he appeared mad to her; she considered that his brain had been affected. Reaching for a glass, he toppled against her, and she held him on his feet while he drank. When he finished she tried to make him sit, but his legs were churning and she couldn't move him.

"Get back into bed. Where do you think you're going?"

"Shower," he said. "I need to wash it off my body."

She pulled his arm around her shoulder, and steered him out of the room. For a lightly muscled man he seemed inordinately heavy, a highly efficient machine that had run out of gas. By the time they were in the bathroom she had as little strength left as Darius, who clutched at the shower curtain rod while she lifted his feet over the side of the tub. She saw him totter on the slippery bottom, and then stepped in after him and propped him up under the hot spray.

He was staring at her with his first smile since he had come out of prison, maybe his first ever, she thought—if a smile was what it was, and not just the sloppy grin she attributed to his loss of muscular control. She followed his gaze to the sodden rag of her dress, which was transparent over her breasts, and noticed that he had become aroused; his meager strength concentrated in that one area of his body separate and apart from him and yet at his heart. She turned him around and soaped his back. His skin came away in ragged strips that spiraled down the drain.

She worked thin lather into his scalp, rubbed it thick with her fingertips. His body was sliding down against hers. She wrapped her arms around his chest and squeezed until he had his legs under him again, and all the while he never stopped grinning. Then she sat him on the side of the tub and pulled a towel from the rack.

"A clean one," he demanded. "And a fresh change of clothes."

She came back with Turkish bath towels slung over both shoulders, covering the wet dress almost to her waist. He took one to dry his body, another for his hair, and tossed the remainder on the wet tiles.

"We have to leave now," he said.

"Why?"

"The house is full of mycotoxins."

"How can that be?"

"You tell me."

"*Me?* I've never been here before."

"I didn't absorb the poison with drugs like Leila and Mehta, I was exposed when it got on my skin. Some was in the heroin that fell into Mehta's bed the last time he injected himself. You still haven't told me how the drugs were used to smuggle the mycotoxins into Iran."

Maryam gave him clean underwear, and helped him balance while he put it on. "Inside each bag of heroin was a smaller bag containing the mycotoxins in their raw state. The Revolutionary Guards at the border were under orders to overlook any heroin coming into the country, and to allow us to continue unmolested to Teheran. They knew nothing about mycotoxins. No one did."

"Except for you."

"Not until I was informed by Rahgozar."

"Had you let me know that much—"

"At Manzarieh," she said, "all students are instructed in the art of khod'eh, the telling of half truths to guard the faith. If I was less than forthcoming, it was to save Iran."

"How did you serve the nation by losing her chemical weapons?"

"I saved it from itself."

"That's garbage. Had you told me, Mehta might still be alive."

"I never suspected the mycotoxins had become mixed with the heroin. All I knew was that they were transported in the same packages that disappeared after they were stolen by Sousan. Can you explain how they came to be here?"

Darius had found baby oil in the medicine chest, and was rubbing it into his raw skin. His breath caught every time he touched a rash. Maryam poured some into her hands, and patted it on gently.

"Can you?" she asked.

"I'm beginning to think so."

"What? Well, then, after you're better, return the mycotoxins to the Komiteh. No doubt they'll forgive everything, and honor you as a national hero."

"They may let me live," Darius said. "That would be plenty."

He started into the bedroom, and she followed after him ready to catch him if he stumbled. There were other clean shirts in the closet, more old lady dresses for her to choose from. Mehta's second-best suit had never been worn, and did not fit Darius badly after Maryam basted the cuffs.

"Where can we go with little money?" she asked, "when you're so weak you can't walk?"

"Call a telephone cab. Tell them we want the Sepahsalar Mosque on Baharestan Square."

"It's late to start praying."

"Not to pray," Darius said. "To appease."

Eight stout minarets, yellow and pale blue, reached to the heavens from the wall of the Sepahsalar Mosque. Darius stood beside the djoub on Modaress Avenue looking at the long facade of stones from a Mashad mosque destroyed in an earthquake and rebuilt on the campus of the old Army Commanders'

School, which was now the Muslim Theological Seminary. A crew of Komitehmen charged with eliminating counterrevolutionary graffiti was attacking the wall with mops and chemical solvent where vandals had spray-painted GOD BLESS AMERICA in English and Farsi. The shaded courtyard was crowded with knots of men carrying rolled prayer rugs under their arm. Darius brought Maryam across to the women's side, to the corner informally reserved for worshipers seeking to contract a temporary marriage. Here none of the women wore facial veils. Each stood in the teeth of a steady breeze that blew her chador back on her head and held the black cloth tight against her body. Darius scanned the forced smiles, looking away when any lingered too long on him. He moved toward the wall where a woman with a luxuriant figure had been following him with her eyes since he came in off the street.

"Well, now I have lived to see everything," she said. "What do *you* want at a mosque? Is some terrible crime being committed here? Or have you given up police work to become an anthropologist?"

"Perhaps both."

In her sardonic smile there was no room for his moral superiority. A short staring contest between them ended with Darius the loser. He bowed his head, allowing her to kiss him, and some of the acid went out of her expression. A resemblance to Darius became obvious the longer Maryam looked at her; but she could not guess what their relationship was, nor the woman's age, which seemed to vary between the late thirties and early sixties, depending upon which aspect of her appearance was the gauge. The smooth complexion of her handsome face was belied by slack skin under tired eyes. Delicate hands unaccustomed to hard work or household chores were heavily veined on the backs, and spotted brown. The frilly bodice of a party frock was worn to be noticed underneath her stylish chador. Although she lacked the high sculpted cheekbones that were Darius's best feature, the wide-set intelligent eyes and silky black hair, the brooding gaze, were his.

"What *are* we doing here?" Maryam asked him.

"Didn't you tell her who you've come to see?" the woman asked. "Are you too ashamed to introduce me?"

". . . I would like you to meet Shahin Khanum," he said to Maryam.

"Madame Shahin?" The smile softened into a pleased exaggeration of itself. "Since when have you become so formal?"

"Shahin Khanum," he said, "is my mother."

"This is Farib?"

"I'm divorced. Maryam is a friend."

"You don't look well," Shahin Khanum said. "Your friend is not taking good care of you. Too many women these days don't know how to look after a man."

"I've been sick."

"Marriage has made you unwell. It is a stultifying institution when it goes on for so long that inertia takes the place of love. I'm happy to learn you're single again—and that you have such a lovely friend."

"How have you been?" Darius asked.

"There is little for me to complain about. For three years on and off I was married to a mullah, a learned marja from a madreseh in Tabriz. We lived together in a nice house off Jaleh Square for a year while he had a teaching appointment in Teheran. After that he would have me for his seegah in the summer, when he would return for a month on his vacation, and pay me a generous brideprice every time.

"Now things are not so good. I have been seeing several gentlemen when their wives are having their menstrual period and are impure to them. The length of each contract is just one week, and afterward, as you know, I cannot marry again for three months. It is hard like that. Sometimes I don't wait the whole ninety days. But . . ." Shahin Khanum tucked her loose hair primly under her chador as she turned to Maryam. "But what can be more satisfying than to do God's will as the Qur'an commends us? I wish I could seegah for every man in Iran.

"Darius does not regard the holy Qur'an as a divine blueprint for the elimination of suffering," she said. "He does not approve of temporary marriage as a 'brilliant law of Islam' that meets the need of men to have many lovers without corrupting themselves by engaging prostitutes. I have devoted my life to combatting the abomination of celibacy, and the suffering that it brings. Yet, to my only son, I am not a tool of God, but an old whore." Shahin Khanum began to laugh. Just as suddenly she fell quiet and glared at Darius. "How many years has it been since you came to see me?"

"I don't know."

"Six years," she answered for him. "Six years, four months, and some days. Every one of them is burned into my heart. What have you done to ease your mother's suffering, my precious son?"

Darius shifted his weight from one sore foot to the other as his mother glanced into the men's side of the courtyard, which was filling rapidly in advance of the next summons to prayer. Her body was bathed in a young woman's perfume that also had been Farib's favorite, a premium French scent that was prohibitively expensive on those few occasions that any was to be found at the bazaar.

"To look at me," she said to Maryam, "would you believe that when I was your age I was considered a fine catch? Darius's father was so taken with me that immediately after the introduction was made he proposed a one-hour chaste marriage just to have me remove my veil for him." She paused for confirmation from Darius, which never came. "That is exactly as it happened. And right on the spot he agreed to a two-year marriage."

Maryam smiled condescendingly, as she might have if an insane woman had her ear. Darius regretted not warning her that his mother was not crazy, but thoroughly without prurience or doubt, a woman, had she been born a generation later, who would have made a perfect Bride of Blood. Maryam was groping for words, rearranging the failed smile into an inquiry of shallow concern that would fool no one, least of all Shahin Khanum.

"A member of such a powerful clan as the Bakhtiars . . ." Maryam said. "You must have been proud—"

"Bakhtiar? Bakhtiar was a man I lived with when Darius was a teenager. He is the father of Darius's sister, but was better to Darius than to his own daughter, one of those louts who measures his manhood in the number of his sons."

Maryam looked at Darius, but he had turned away from her, and she could not see his face.

". . . Were it not for the daughter we had I don't know that I would remember him. Darius's father was a religious pilgrim from a village in the Great Salt Desert, a handsome man, but shy and untalkative except in the company of God. Darius took the name Bakhtiar for himself. But it was I who called him Darius—a good Persian name. The day he was born he was already too independent to be given a name handed down from Arab slavers." Memory slipped away as Shahin Khanum paused to build a querulous frown. "Why have you come?" she asked Darius. "Is it Oil Day, or Fatemeh's Birthday, and you wish to honor your poor old mother?"

"I need a place to stay."

"You were living comfortably on Baharestan Square."

"A place to hide," he said. "The Komiteh want me."

"Wait here. I will make a good marriage before noon, and you will be my little boy again and live with me and my new husband." Shahin Khanum laughed so hard that she had to pat herself on the back to catch her breath.

She wiped tears from her eyes as she took out a leather change purse from her chador.

"I don't want money."

"No, you never did, you would not let me have the pleasure even of that." Shahin Khanum held out a tarnished key. "Take this," she said. "The house is at Mowlavi, intersection of Khayyam. You will recognize it by twin pomegranate trees in the garden. Stay as long as you need to."

"Whose is it?"

"It's mine. It was the gift of an admirer. I do not have to seegah all the time if I don't want to. It's just in my nature, like hunting murderers is in yours. To every life God assigns a purpose . . ." Still eyeing the men's side of the courtyard, she stepped out of the shadow of the wall fanning herself coyly with a loose fold of her chador. "We've been through all this before," she said. "I don't expect I will be coming home tonight. Maybe after the weekend—if you're not there."

Maryam took his arm, and they went out to Modaress Avenue. A cab brought them south past a housing project disintegrating under the sun of fewer than a dozen summers. The site had been Teheran's red light district before the ayatollahs sent earth-grading equipment against it, and Komiteh-men to round up the streetwalkers. The older women who refused to change their ways were executed, but many of the younger ones were brought to north Teheran for rehabilitation. Housed in a grand mansion abandoned by a family that had fled to the West, they spent their days cleaning, cooking, and sewing, acquiring the domestic skills needed in making a new life. To achieve the condition of grace known as "absolution through penance," they agreed to temporary marriages with their guards, short-term affairs after which they were encouraged to engage in similar relationships with the waves of soldiers returning from the Iraqi front.

Shahin Khanum's was at the end of a row of houses on the north side of Mowlavi Avenue. Like Mehta, she lived in a comfortable mix of the traditional and modern, with a kitchen equipped with new appliances, and pillows for sleeping on the richly carpeted floor. There was no vodka anywhere. Darius found a bottle of wine, which he left untouched after prizing the cork, and then stretched out in the living room on a sturdy Bakhtiari rug. Maryam came in with his water, and sat beside him drinking tea through a sugar cube in her teeth. When he put his arm around her, she didn't stiffen, or lecture him about his health. Why bother, he thought, when he was still so weak he couldn't keep his eyes open?

"Get some sleep," she said. "The refrigerator is full, and I'll have lunch ready when you wake up. It was kind of your mother to let us have her house. We'll be safe until the weekend, won't we?"

"We won't stay that long. In a day or two I should be stronger, and we'll go."

"Go where? They're hunting for us all over. We have no place to go. A couple of days is nothing."

"It's two lifetimes," Darius said.

· 17 ·

On a breezeless morning in the minute after midnight when the evening shift had gone home and the caretaker overnight crew was settling into routine, Darius slipped inside police headquarters and went down to the sub-basement by a staircase used only by janitors and the brass. The bulbs in the passageway had burned out, or been stolen, and he kept his hands in front of his face pushing back at the dense blackness. He walked on his toes, easing the weight off his sore heels and arches, making little noise. The footsteps that clattered suddenly all around caused him to flatten against the wall, to become small and quiet, but invisible only to himself.

Over the hammering of his pulse he located the sound one story above. The footsteps inscribed a misshapen circle in the ceiling, and then shuffled away. After some of the adrenaline had drained from his blood, he continued into Evidence. Two stories below street level the atmosphere of dry, dusty heat would remain constant on the dampest day of winter. Had headquarters been struck by a missile, Mehta would have been the last to find out.

The shelves had been cleared by someone attempting to externalize the order that Mehta was satisfied to keep in his brain. A huge pile had been left on the floor, to be restacked, discarded, looted. The elephant tusks were gone—probably, it would be his guess, back into the hands of the trader who had brought them into the country. Overlooked was a dagger with a rhinoceros horn handle of greater value, which had been used to kill three women in a case that was famous years before Darius was attached to Homicide. The Kerikkale pistol from Mehta's trophy collection he found in a box with counterfeit plates for ten-thousand rial notes made obsolete by new methods of printing. Out-of-date fingerprint cards had been sprinkled over a canvas knapsack that he emptied of hundreds of Uncle Sam party favors. He put the gun inside with a box of shells, and slung it over his back.

Hours of work had gone into building the evidence pile. Assuming he found a place to begin, it would take as long to tear apart. Solace was to be had inside Mehta's cage, in the double drawer of the desk where a brown bag held two more bottles of the superior Russian vodka that had been the records chief's second-best-kept secret. Underneath was a ceramic pipe with an elongated stem, and surgical tweezers for holding a crumb of flaming charcoal over the black, pasty bowl until the opium inside released its heady smoke. Below that, also in brown paper, a large bundle filled the bottom of the drawer. Without looking at the evidence tag still attached he knew it contained the packages Hamid had recovered from the toilet in Dharvazeh Ghor. He brought them out at arm's length, and tore away the wrapper in the weak light of the desk lamp.

One package was nearly twice the size of the other, and it was this one that he dissected first. The white powder exploding onto the desktop tasted of quinine, and hid six flat plastic bags. He wet his thumb and rubbed a clear spot in the plastic, a window looking in on more powder. This powder, which was the same color as the quinine, but coarser, and somewhat crystalline, he recognized as Afghani heroin processed in a crude mountain laboratory. He shook out the bag onto the floor until a smaller, tubular bag, a condom filled with a yellow sandy substance, was all that remained inside. Having the mycotoxins at last in his hands he felt no pleasure—the sole change in his emotional tenor a heightened appreciation of dread that made him interrupt what he was doing to guzzle Mehta's Russian vodka from the bottle.

Darius placed the five bags of heroin in the bottom of the knapsack and fit the condom carefully among them. Then he went through his suit for a handkerchief Maryam had made sure to put there, and tied it over his mouth and nose. Much of the milk sugar with which the other package had been stuffed had leaked out, exposing four more plastic bags. As if he were delivering frail quadruplets, he brought them out one by one and laid them on their brothers already in the knapsack. The bag he removed last was not full, and appeared to have been opened and retied. The muscular tension his body manufactured as a by-product of intense concentration did not translate into a trembling hand. With the dull edge of the blade he scraped away the milk sugar coating the plastic. The crystalline powder inside was contaminated by an off-white vein that he knew would darken to rich yellow if traced to its source. In the usual accident involving the failure of a condom, he could not help but think, the result was new life that was rarely the tragedy it seemed to be, rather a blessing in comparison to what had happened when the mycotoxins became mixed with the heroin. He exhaled through his mouth, and then held his breath until he had wrapped this last bag in the paper sack from the vodka, and placed it with everything else in the knapsack.

He heard footsteps again, and though he knew they were being made upstairs, he froze. He turned off the lights and groped for the steps. Edging open the stairwell door, he looked across the lobby toward the empty streets of Ark. Not ten meters away a night shift officer whose name was Adibi was sharing a smoke with Ghaffari in the entrance to the building.

He continued up another flight. Homicide had been left untended, not even a recruit on hand to keep the samovar fired. His old wood desk had been pushed into the outer office to make room for an executive model with Ghaffari's name on a plaque with movable letters. His top drawer had been cleaned out, his off-duty gun gone with his black book of informants' phone numbers. Among a stack of cold case files in which he had kept hidden his confidential papers the French passport was still where he'd stashed it.

The straps from the knapsack were cutting into his shoulders as he returned to the first floor. After several minutes Adibi went out and Ghaffari squashed the butt under his heel and disappeared inside headquarters. Darius hurried from the stairs, but hadn't cleared the lobby when Adibi came back with an unlit cigarette between his lips, shaking his head as he patted his pockets. He stared at Darius, obviously confused, and then looked around as if to confirm that he was in the right building. Darius scowled, and then saluted. Adibi returned the salute crisply and let out a puff of air from behind the cigarette when Darius said nothing to him, but continued to the sidewalk.

A faienced arch topped by copper cupolas marked the boundary of the administrative district. Beyond was the broad avenue renamed after the Imam where Darius would be able to hail a cruising cab. He dipped into his pockets to count the few coins that represented his fortune, and which were scarcely enough to bring him back to Maryam. Sudden, sharp pressure against his back revived the pain of his wounds, and stopped him on the spot.

"Keep walking!"

The voice was not Ghaffari's, or Adibi's, or anyone's from headquarters. His former colleagues would not be marching him out of Ark, when his maximum value was behind the bars of his old jail. The tingle of cold metal against his ear steered him into the shadows under the arch, and then turned him around so that he was looking into Djalilian's gray eyes.

"You thought you were smart." Djalilian held the gun high, pointed at Darius's face. It was an old Browning 9mm Parabellum with an intricately worked barrel, and would not be hard to swipe away, Darius thought, if his arms weren't constrained by the heavy pack. "It is a recurring problem with you—God only knows why, when you were the last to know you would lead us to the mycotoxins. That is why we let you out of Evin."

The queasy feeling that had eluded Darius for days bubbled up in the hollow of his stomach. His dry lips clung to his tongue as he licked them.

"Kashfi told us everything of your plans." Djalilian leered at him. "Or, rather, we told him. It was a clever idea for you to break out with the corpses. But it was ours. He must have forgotten to tell you that you are a corpse, too."

A Range Rover driven by a man in olive green fatigues pulled up alongside them. Darius was ordered into the backseat, where he hunched forward with the knapsack wedged against his shoulders.

"Your hopes for escape were doomed from the start." Djalilian sat next to him as they rolled out of Ark under the great arch. The driver glanced back at them, and under the flat bill of his cap Darius saw bloodshot eyes, a scraggly beard. They turned east on the avenue and raced through sparse midnight traffic. "All of Iran is looking for you. You would have been better off had your mock execution been real."

Djalilian switched the gun to his right hand and dug it into Darius's ribs.

"How does it feel to know you are going to be dead in the next few minutes?" Djalilian stopped to ponder the question himself. "By now you should be an expert on that particular sensation. Give us a hint of what it is like."

Darius looked away from him. He slipped off the pack and was thrown back in his seat as the Range Rover accelerated through a red light.

"Don't make yourself too comfortable. You won't be around long."

Djalilian jabbed the gun harder, trying for a response to his threats. Darius considered wincing, to give in to him in some way to get him to stop.

Incapable of any gesture, however, he stared out the window. They had left the avenue at Baharestan Square, and were speeding past the Sepahsalar Mosque. Along the length of the facade GOD BLESS AMERICA stood out sharper than ever where the Komitehmen had scrubbed away decades of grime with the vandals' paint.

"Let me see what's in the pack," Djalilian said.

Darius slid the webbed straps out of the buckles and pulled back the flap.

"This is heroin?" Djalilian nosed the gun inside. "What is it worth?"

"Millions."

The ornate barrel scripted the figure in air. "Did you hear that, Nasair?" Djalilian said.

The visor of his cap scraped the roof as the lightly bearded man nodded his head.

"The mycotoxins. Where are they?"

"In the heroin."

Djalilian thought about it, and then he smiled, and poked his gun between the bags.

"The plastic is torn," Darius said. "Keep playing with it, and we'll all be dead in seconds."

"Seconds, or minutes, it shouldn't make much difference to you."

"I've opened one of the bags. I'll show you what the mycotoxins look like."

Djalilian withdrew the Browning gingerly. As Darius slid his hand inside and felt beneath the heroin for Mehta's gun, Djalilian wrenched the pack away and dropped it in his own lap. "I don't want any of that stuff on me, or in the air. You're not taking anybody with you."

"I have no intention . . ." Darius probed the bottom of the knapsack until the grips of the Kerikkale rasped against his palm. He rolled his wrist, maneuvering the muzzle toward Djalilian.

"Well, where is it?" Djalilian said. "What the hell are you doing in there?"

Darius squeezed the trigger. The grinding sound it produced seemed as loud as a report. But there was no report, or bullet, no change in Djalilian but the look of scorn ripening to hatred.

"Hey," Djalilian said, and raised his gun.

Darius yanked the Kerikkale out of the pack. He snicked the safety switch above the butt, furious with himself for not having checked to see whether the clip was in place and loaded, if Mehta's prize souvenir was in killing order. A few grams of pressure on the trigger, and the automatic kicked and rode upward, and Djalilian was nailed through the shoulder to the door.

"Dog's balls!" he howled. The ferocious glare melted into indignation at lost opportunity as he switched his gun to his good hand.

A two-dimensional pancake of color spread over Djalilian's chest as Darius fired again. He pulled back on the trigger one more time, and heard grinding again as the Kerikkale jammed. He slammed the weapon into Djalilian's brow. Djalilian slid aside with his head against his shoulder, his empty jugular offered too late in submission.

The Range Rover was all over the road as the driver, Nasair, unsnapped the shiny holster on his hip. A heavy military revolver came up over the top of the seat, and Darius grabbed the barrel and twisted it away. Nasair brought his other hand from the wheel, and the Range Rover veered toward the curb, throwing Darius into Djalilian's unconscious embrace.

A shot whizzing past Darius's ear put a hole in the roof that let in a pinpoint of cool air. The side mirror snapped off as the Range Rover bounced along the line of cars at the curb. He yanked the Browning from Djalilian's hand and fired through the back of the seat. Nasair exhaled blood while the Range Rover locked bumpers with a blue Volkswagen and danced it in a circle before flinging it into the djoub. Darius scrambled into the front seat and grabbed for the wheel. Nasair's legs twitched under him, and with the same motion he would have used to punch the cigarette lighter Darius squeezed off another shot and the body spasmed onto the floor.

A streetlight was out over a yard filled with restaurant garbage. Darius backed in, and let the engine run. He pried the military revolver from Nasair's fist, then stripped the body of cash. After picking Djalilian clean, he rolled out both corpses, and the rear wheels churned a green mound over them like a dog covering a turd. A roundabout route to Mowlavi added five kilometers to a two-kilometer ride, but brought peace of mind that no one was following. When he pulled up at the twin pomegranate trees, the door swung open before he had entered the garden.

"*Where were you?*" A yawn made a mockery of Maryam's anger. "When I woke up, and you weren't anywhere, I—"

"I had to pick up some things," he said.

"What things? We have food. It's too dangerous to go out, you said so yourself."

Darius glanced toward the curb.

"That's a Komiteh Range Rover." Maryam retreated involuntarily onto the doorstep. "What's it doing here?"

"It's ours now." He pulled the door shut behind her. "We have to leave."

She walked through the garden without looking back. One foot was in the passenger's side when she stepped back out into the gutter again.

"There's blood all over the seat."

Darius spread his handkerchief on the wet spot, and she got in. The Range Rover trampled a poplar sapling in his hurry to put distance from the house, and then circled the block headed northeast toward the Old Shemiran Road.

"What's in here?" Maryam patted the knapsack he had placed between them on the seat.

"Heroin."

"You found it? Where?"

"Najafi kept his drugs in the quinine and milk sugar he used to cut them with, same as the Afghanis hid the mycotoxins in the heroin. It's a neat trick, hiding one illicit substance in another. Someone might very well scrape a lead ingot to look for smuggled gold, but who would scrape gold to look for platinum? Sousan must have taught him. The stuff was under my nose at headquarters since the night they were killed."

Maryam loosened the straps, slipped her hand in.

"*Don't touch that!*"

"You don't have to shout," she said.

"The mycotoxins are still inside."

She strapped the bag tight, and put it under her feet, wiped her palm on the hem of her chador. "What do you need with them now?" Excitement was giving way to resignation that she was taking on a burden that had grown heavier since she'd thought she had put it down for the last time.

Darius turned his head toward her. He stared so hard that she reached for the wheel.

"Well, what? Unless you're planning to go to war, what good are they?"

"They provide a valuable bargaining chip."

"For Iran? I still don't understand."

"For us," he said. "For our lives."

At the Africa-Modaress crossroads several blocks from his apartment they abandoned the Range Rover with the keys in the ignition and took a taxi back downtown. They switched cabs near the old U.S. embassy, giving as their destination an intersection near the Azadi Monument. On a factory street blasted to rubble in the war and never rebuilt Darius asked suddenly to be let out, and they hiked five blocks to the western bus terminal.

"If we move fast, we may be able to reach Azerbaijan Province," he said, anticipating her questions, "and from there continue into Turkey, or wherever. The roads are heavily patrolled. We'll be less conspicuous in a bus than in a car until we're well away from the city."

"How real are our chances?"

"Better than if we stay. In Teheran we have no chance."

The 6:00 Iran Peyma Cooperative Number One to Tabriz was the first scheduled departure of the morning. Darius paid for super-luxury-class tickets that would permit them to stretch out their legs and put back their seats. Two hours late, they were called to the gate. As Darius settled beside a man wearing a peasant's baggy trousers and white cloth slippers with camel bone soles, Maryam found room by a window in the women's section across the aisle. Another half hour was lost alongside a cinder block shed at the edge of Teheran while Komitehmen came on board for a cursory inspection of the passengers.

It was past 3:00 when they stopped in the Zanjan Province highlands midway to Tabriz, and Darius and Maryam sat together again on the patio of a truckers' restaurant looking down into the Abhar River gorge.

"I've persuaded myself we're not dead," Maryam announced to him. "Is there any truth to that rumor?"

"We still have a long way to go. The Komiteh will be looking for us at my apartment and in other places in Teheran. When the Range Rover turns up, the first thing they'll do is alert all the train stations and bus companies."

Cold, tiny portions of cello kebab that was the only item on the menu had just been brought out to them when the bus driver came by to say that he would be leaving in ten minutes. Darius dropped his napkin in his plate and got up from the table.

"I'll be right back," he said.

When the other passengers began lining up for the bus and he had not returned, Maryam walked through the restaurant to a gravel parking area where an outhouse stood away from three or four cars. She called his name, and then knocked on the door, and a little boy jumped out hitching his pants. Everyone else had boarded by the time she came back to the women's section to wait for him. Soon the driver fixed an unforgiving stare at her, and she tugged her veil across her face and stalked off to the empty table. Were it not for the knapsack that he never would have abandoned, she would have let memory claim him for its own. She dragged the heavy bag to the roadside to

watch the bus lumber over the steep grade, and then to survey the bare
highway in both directions.

A black Paycon swinging out of the lot stopped beside her with two wheels
on the pavement. The passenger door opened, and the knapsack was hauled
inside.

"Where were you? How—why did you—"

"Get in."

The engine sputtered as he came down too heavily on the gas. The light
car bucked, and then fishtailed off the gravel.

"I was starting to think you'd left without me," she said.

"Did you?"

She watched him pat the knapsack, feel it all over. "No, not really."

"We were trapped on the bus. There are roadblocks everywhere to catch
illegals bound for the Zagros Mountains. We'll attract less attention in a car
with Azerbaijan plates. We can stop in Tabriz for food and gas, and go on
from there."

The mountains steepened, the fawn-colored earth ripening to burnt ochre
in the high, rocky passes. Altitude wounded the underpowered Paycon. It
limped over each summit gasping the thin air, and then roller-coastered into
shaded valleys while Darius rode the brakes until his nostrils filled with acrid
smoke. The road leveled after Mianeh, bypassing tiny villages nearly invisible in mud-brick camouflage. Maryam fell asleep with her head against her
arm, and didn't stir when they stopped for a checkpoint. The volunteers who
rose from afternoon prayers carrying their G-3 rifles at port arms looked to
Darius to be sixteen or seventeen years old. He kicked the knapsack under the
seat, but could not hide it completely.

"Who are you?" the youngest of the Guardsmen demanded in a strong
Azerbaijan accent.

"Let us by." Darius put his hand inside his jacket where his papers
should have been, and fit his finger through the trigger guard of Djalilian's
Browning.

"Not just yet. What is your name?"

"Bakhtiar."

"And who is this woman?"

Maryam squinted at him, shielding her eyes behind her palm while her
mind cleared.

"*What is your name?*"

"Maryam Lajevardi."

The boy snorted, and stuck his head inside Darius's window. "What are you doing together on this road?"

Darius eased the gun out of his pocket. The boy was in poor position to defend himself; but with nowhere to run before Tabriz—or after—it would hardly be worth the effort to shoot him.

"We are married," Maryam said.

"I do not think so. I think you are together for immoral purposes. Let me see your marriage certificate."

"We don't take it everywhere we go," Maryam said. "We know that we are married. It is good enough for us."

"But not for me. Give me proof of who you are—your marriage license and birth certificate."

"We have nothing."

The boy was staring at her, searching for a trace of makeup or speck of color on her nails, loose wisps of hair that were the unquestionable evidence of wantonness. Every time Maryam locked on to his gaze, he averted his eyes.

"If you cannot prove that you are married," he said, "you will have to come with me."

"Not that it is any of your business," Maryam said, "but I am his seegah. He took me as a pleasure bride just last night. There is no marriage certificate, because none is required. We signed a two-week contract, but left it at home. We didn't know that we would be bothered by impudent children on our honeymoon."

"I do not believe you." He had turned away from Maryam, and was speaking to Darius. "Get out of the car."

"Do you question the holy law of God?" Maryam said.

The boy glared at her, but quickly looked at the ground, avoiding the temptation that resided in every woman's face.

"How dare you accuse us of immoral behavior when we have submitted ourselves to God's will? Did the Imam not say that a woman should surrender herself to any pleasure her husband demands, even if she is riding a camel—which is to say when they are on a great journey? If you knew more about God's law, and less about big guns, you would not have the kind of filthy mind that invents evil where none exists."

The boy backed around the Paycon, and inspected the license plate officiously. "Let me see your car registration."

Darius riffled through the papers inside the glove box. There was no registration or title, just a few torn maps and old repair bills. He heard the squeal of air brakes, and looked back at the Tabriz bus pulling up to the shed.

The door opened for a boy who might have been this one's twin. He boarded ahead of the other Guardsmen, and stepped off first in custody of a couple trying not to look at each other, the man silver-haired and wearing a crisp blue suit, and a woman close to thirty in a long Shahsavan skirt. He brought their identification to an older Guardsman, who examined the papers and then went inside the shed. The couple, making inadvertent eye contact, began to weep.

"Your papers?" Darius was asked.

He again riffled inside the glove compartment, and came out with a receipt for recapped tires and two gallons of antifreeze. A blue stamp over a column of numbers read, PAID. Darius handed it to the boy, who started toward the shed, but then returned to the Paycon as the older Guardsman came back outside with a whip coiled around his shoulder.

"What is the problem now?" Darius said angrily. "This pass was issued in Teheran by Ayatollah Golabi authorizing our travel through Azerbaijan Province without having to be bothered."

"I have never heard of such a document."

"Don't take my word for it," Darius said. "See for yourself."

The boy stared at the page as though it were a religious manuscript. He pinched a corner between his fingers, then gave it back to Darius, who refolded it carefully before returning it to the glove compartment.

"Okay, you can pass."

Darius let go of the Browning. As he steered through the roadblock, he looked back once. The man in the blue suit had taken off his jacket, and lay on his stomach across a low table. When the older Guardsman raised the whip high overhead, the Shahsavan woman fainted.

"How did you know he'd let us go?" Maryam asked.

"He's illiterate," Darius said, "at least in Farsi, and probably in his own language, but would have lost too much face in admitting that to us. You handled him well."

"There were plenty of little prigs like him in Lebanon," she said. "For him a woman is strictly an instrument of pleasure, otherwise best to be avoided. The only thing he fears worse than a woman is that he'll miss out on paradise, and the women who will be his slaves there."

"Why did you say you were my seegah?" His tone had chilled, assuming a policeman's formal inquisitiveness.

"Have you been defamed? Is it inconceivable for such a thing to happen?"

"You should have told him we were married. It's more believable."

"Any dumb kid can see I'm not your permanent wife. Your attitude toward . . . toward things in general, I doubt it's much different from his."

Darius rejected the notion with a burst of speed. "I know there's no paradise," he said.

❖ 18 ❖

P assing through the Gate of the Builders, the last sight of Tabriz was a train station of white stone and a Chaldean church crowned with a blunted cross. A blue blaze parallel to the highway came into focus as the landing strip of a regional airport. Widening circles of light scrubbed the night from the tarmac, and Darius slowed to watch three helicopters, old American Hueys, drop out of the void discharging men in khaki into the sandstorm they had brought with them.

Maryam, who had curled up on the seat with her legs under her, turned her back against the flying dust. "What is it?"

"So many refugees are trying the mountains," he said, "the Revolutionary Guards must be moving reinforcements to the border regions."

Her eyes were shutting again as she stretched to the ceiling. "Oh . . . ?"

Darius opened his window, and Maryam's loose hair whipped his cheek, the current from that sporadic contact all that was keeping him alert. Then her head lolled against his shoulder, and he tried to imagine what it would be like if she *were* his seegah, and this the first night of a two-week pleasure marriage. A preposterous idea—except that already he was lost in it. Feelings of embarrassment were complicated by a curious detachment, as though peeping through a window he had caught himself in an unsavory act and didn't know which one of him should feel the greater shame. Had Maryam never been a Bride of Blood, and not transferred her zealotry to causes still to

267

be invented, there might have been more between them than his medieval fantasy. The reality of the situation was that he was delivering goods to an unknown destination, and she had gone along for the ride.

He reached for a sack of fruit Maryam had bought in Tabriz, and gorged on dried figs to stay awake. Low-flying aircraft were somewhere overhead. With his face close to the windshield he craned toward the Hueys he had seen on the ground as they swarmed in the direction of the border. The next major town was Marand, a place he knew nothing about other than that it would be heavily patrolled by troops from a nearby military installation. More inviting was a dot on the map called Sufian, from which secondary roads wandered around Lake Urmiya to Turkey, two hundred kilometers to the west.

Hunting for the Sufian turnoff, he saw red lights strung across the highway on a wood semaphore. Men in Guardsmen's khaki came out of a floodlit shack to wait for the Paycon alongside the barricade. As he moved his hand toward Maryam's shoulder, her eyes opened and settled on the lights.

"Better get up."

"Huh? I wasn't—" She yawned, and would have smiled had the significance of the lights not begun to register. Turning her face to the breeze, she drank in cool air, then pulled the chador over her forehead and felt for stray wisps of hair. "Leave everything to me."

The red lights suddenly swept upward. Darius fed more gas, but slammed the brakes when the semaphore came down again after releasing a Bedford truck into the lane. The Paycon swerved around the truck, and continued to the barricade, where the Guardsmen shined electric lanterns into the front seat. Shielding his eyes from the glare, Darius did not see the man who asked him, "What are you doing on this road at such an hour of the night?"

"We are going to Maku."

"The border area is restricted to commercial traffic. What is your business there?"

"I am employed by a customs brokerage in Teheran. I have been sent to pick up a consignment of precious gemstones that are locked up in the customs warehouse."

"Have you proof of who you work for?"

"They know my name in Maku."

"Let me see your passport."

Darius's hand brushed the pocket where he kept his French ID. "We didn't bring passports," he said.

"Why not?"

"Of what use would they be when we are going only as far as the border?"

The light moved away from his face, and he squinted at a handsome man of about thirty whose green eyes had the Mongol cast of a native Azerbaijani, and whose lips formed an unkind smile. Why was he being given a hard time about passports? Why didn't they ask about Maryam, a grilling for which he had come well rehearsed? He looked into the sky as one of the giant Hueys floated over the checkpoint and then descended into an oat field behind the shed. The Guardsman shut his eyes, and turned his back on the whirlwind while Darius sized up his chances of crashing through the checkpoint. Since leaving Teheran he had anticipated having to make a decision like this, but wanted more than a dust cloud to cover his escape.

"Show some identification," the Guardsman said.

Maryam said, "Let us through. It's late, and we need to find a hotel. We can't waste all night here."

"Neither can we. After we have examined your papers, we will be glad to let you on your way."

Darius's hand settled on the Browning. The men with the G-3s were no more an impediment than the flimsy wood of the semaphore. As the gun slid from his pocket, a voice declared, "I know them," and Darius strained to see into the oat field, where the helicopter was cooling its engine, the rotor pinwheeling in the wind.

Three men had emerged from the Huey. One of them, clad in fatigues and black military boots, walked up to the barricade with the stiff, forceful gait of an athlete gone to seed but still to be reckoned with. Darius didn't recognize him as Baraheni until he strode into the light.

In his hurry to get at the car Baraheni pushed the Guardsman out of the way. "Did you really, in your fondest dream, believe we would let you near the border?" he said to Darius. "We have been following you in the air since before you entered Azerbaijan."

"We came this far," Darius answered. "Who is to say how far our luck would take us?"

"Luck was all you had, and already you have used up every bit of it. We are better prepared." Baraheni snatched the light from the Guardsman, and shined it into the Paycon. "Where are the mycotoxins?"

"What makes you think we found them?"

"Don't insult my intelligence. You would not leave Iran without them. We know how tenacious you are. In your way, you are also a fanatic. That is why we put obstacles in your path, so you would look that much harder."

More Guardsmen came out of the shed to surround the car on three sides, and then Ashfar broke through the circle and bore into Darius with his gaze. "We know you have them," he said. "Where are they?"

Darius eyed the knapsack between his heels.

Ashfar could not help but smile. "Personally, I would have kept them in the trunk. What if, God forbid, you had an accident?"

"Hand them over." Baraheni tugged at the driver's door. "Open it, and then step out. You, too," he said to Maryam.

As Darius hoisted the bag onto the seat, Baraheni reached inside the car. Reflexively—his hand two steps ahead of his brain, which subsequently would be asked permission for what he was about to do—Darius grabbed him by the hair, and rolled the window under the big man's chin.

Baraheni shouted, "Fuck your—"

Darius whipped out the Browning, and stuffed the barrel into Baraheni's mouth. The Guardsmen leveled their weapons and looked toward Ashfar, who said nothing as Darius tromped on the gas. The Paycon lurched ahead with the suddenness of a desert animal, but none of the grace, dragging Baraheni along with it.

Maryam covered her head in her arms as the semaphore splintered against the windshield. "You can't believe we'll outrun them."

She glanced back at the barricade. The Guardsmen were still waiting for instructions; some had pointed their guns toward the ground. Bijan stepped into the light with a finger aimed at the highway, and a ragged fusillade spurred the car faster. Maryam pressed her chin against her knees as another volley rang out, and then slowly she raised her head. "Look at *him*."

Baraheni's snub features had gone waxen, and were melting into his face. The back of his head flapped like a loose door in the wind before flying off as the Paycon picked up speed. Darius withdrew the gun, and the big man's mouth snapped shut, and then it sagged. Blood exploded into the car from both nostrils, as though an artery had been sectioned through them. Darius grabbed the window crank, but couldn't budge it.

"Steer," he said.

"I can't drive."

He wrapped her fingers around the wheel. He pushed the glass down into the door with his left hand, while trying to work Baraheni's head out through the enlarged opening. The crank still did not move, then twirled uselessly as he forced it with both hands.

A flatbed truck rounded a curve riding the center stripe, and the rear end swung into their lane. Darius took back the wheel and angled the Paycon to the right. A long load of scrap metal flying a red rag flag clipped the body dragging from his door. The Paycon caromed onto the weedy shoulder, a dry breeze sweeping the front seat over the jagged glass where Baraheni had been.

The lights in his mirror brightened while the car plodded through the tall brush. Two vehicles—possibly more—had left the checkpoint after them. Their pursuers slowed as they came alongside the truck, and a short distance beyond it they stopped. Darius saw men on the pavement. They walked six abreast, then crouched in a circle as the lights became pinpoints and then went out.

The Paycon's high beams flushed mulberry trees from the night in tidy groves behind mud-brick walls. A hairpin turn coming up without warning threw Maryam against him. She said, "Oooh," as the breath was jarred out of her, but made no comment, her silence questioning his hurry when there was no place to go. He held the Paycon at high speed for ten minutes, and just as his nerves had started to lose their edge, and Maryam was saying, "They've stopped following us," the highway was bathed in bright light.

"What's that?" Maryam lowered her window, and poked her head outside.

The eggbeater sound of the helicopter was everywhere. Darius pulled her in as gunfire raked the blacktop. He kicked harder at the gas, but his foot was already on the floor. The Huey dropped to treetop level, daring them to enter the splash of light it claimed for its own. Darius veered onto the distant shoulder as more rifle fire rained down. The helicopter floated away to position itself three hundred meters ahead. A bus was approaching in the left lane, and Darius came back onto the pavement and timed their entry into the light so that the Paycon was side by side with it. The Huey held fire, then bounded off to set up another ambush.

The farmland confined them to an asphalt corridor. Beyond the distant shoulder the mulberry trees stretched on indefinitely; but outside Maryam's window they gave way to an almond orchard surrounded by a tumbledown wall. Darius cut his lights, and the Paycon left the pavement through a gap in the brick, which it widened with its fenders. The helicopter hovered over the grove like a gargantuan dragonfly rustling the leaves with the beat of its wings, inscribing circles in the green-black canopy that encompassed a smaller area around the car with each pass. Then it banked sharply, and settled on the highway, and Guardsmen in full battle dress jumped out.

Edging through the trees, Darius did not let the speedometer needle much above five. The powdery earth afforded little traction to the light car, which spun its wheels in frustration. The grove was larger than he had anticipated, the almond trees yielding to walnuts and then a stand of immature chestnuts before the Paycon crashed through the ruins of another wall into neat grain fields pampered like garden plots. Darius estimated they had traveled two kilometers when he felt a hard surface again, and they came out onto a rutted lane of crushed rock.

"Which way?" Maryam asked.

Darius flashed his lights. In a pasture across the lane a donkey was tethered to a wagon without wheels. Darius got out of the car murmuring softly to the animal, which ignored him as it browsed on brown grass.

"What are you doing there?" Maryam said.

Darius stroked the animal's coat, and scratched behind the ears. "We'd blend into the countryside lots easier with a donkey."

"I don't want to blend in." Maryam said. "I want to get out."

He untied the animal, and tugged at the rope. The donkey did not move. He slapped its rump and the donkey stepped back without raising its head from the grass.

"Apparently, he thinks he'll be safer without us," Maryam said.

The donkey was nibbling between Darius's feet as a farm truck jolted to a halt not five meters away. One headlamp was not aimed properly. Like a wandering eye it probed the man in the patchy field. Someone called out to him in Azerbaijani, and Maryam responded in the same language.

"What did he say?" Darius asked her.

"We don't belong here. I told him to mind his own business, but he's not going to leave till he has a better answer." She cocked her head while the man said several more words. "He wants to know what we want in this field."

"Tell him privacy. Tell him we had some, and we'd like it back."

Maryam spoke slowly, her accent apparent to Darius though he had a few words of the language at best. During a prolonged silence, as she squinted at the truck unsure that anything she had said had gotten across, the men began laughing, a lunatic howl that went on so long Darius began to search the blank sky for a full moon. Gradually the hysterics subsided, one of the men coming to his senses ahead of his companions. When the old man talked to them again the humor was gone from his voice.

"Now what does he want?" Darius asked.

"He says he knows what we're doing here," Maryam said, "what we're really doing."

The farm truck clattered up to the Paycon, and Darius saw that it was a Ford, at least forty years old, with running boards eaten through with rust and a spare tire in the fender well. The old man at the wheel was wearing a karakul hat and a double-breasted suit with wide stripes that had been in fashion when the truck was new. Beside him were two men, considerably younger, although not so young that they were not showing some gray. The shallow lines in their forehead and cheeks were a blueprint for the old man's scowl; well before they were forty, Darius thought, they would weather into exact copies of him. One of them addressed Darius in a mixture of Farsi and Arabic that was as good as Maryam's Azerbaijani.

"There is a Komiteh roadblock on the highway not seventy kilometers ahead. If you would like, my father will be glad to take you around it. It is on the way to where we live."

"I wouldn't go anywhere with them," Maryam whispered to Darius.

"We don't have a choice," he said. "Thank the old man, and tell him we'll be glad to give him some money."

". . . He won't take anything." Maryam translated the reply. "He says it's his privilege to help anyone who wants to leave Iran."

"Ask him if there have been many."

Maryam spoke haltingly to the old man, who laughed again in his lunatic way.

"Not nearly enough," his son answered, and lit a cigarette from a wood match.

Under the dust Maryam saw that the truck once had been blue, but was now a colorless amalgam of primer and body putty. The passenger door opened for her. The old man's sons carried their weight in their hips and thighs, and were broad across the shoulders, a full load by themselves. She looked at Darius, who went back to the Paycon for the knapsack, and then led her around to the rear of the truck. Two dusty dogs lunged at them, spraying hot slobber as they were brought up short at the end of a heavy chain.

"There is no need for you to ride outside," one of the younger men said. "We will make room."

He hopped into the back with the dogs, and Maryam slithered onto the seat beside his brother. Darius squeezed in after her as the truck lurched forward on sagging springs. The old man ground through the gears, sending oily fumes inside the cabin, but the truck did not seem to gather speed. Maryam began to cough. With every bump her head grazed the ceiling. A hand brushed her leg, slid deliberately along her thigh, and settled close to her lap. The fingers, which did not stop moving, felt like worms.

The old man started up a rapid patter from which she could extract only an occasional phrase. The son closest to him said in Farsi, "We have a farm

not far from Khvoy. We went into Tabriz to have work done on our truck, and
to visit friends. We see refugees in this part of the mountains all the time, and
help them however we can. We are Iranian Azerbaijanis. One day, if God
wills it, we will unite with our brothers in Azerbaijan, and our nation will be
restored. In the meantime, this is what we do."

Maryam nodded at the man, but he had not been speaking to her.

"This road doesn't bypass any checkpoints," Darius said to him. "Komiteh checkpoints are positioned on main highways to catch the traffic from
feeder roads like this one."

"You are correct," the gray-haired man answered curtly. "Still, there is no
need to be concerned. The checkpoint is two hours away. When we get there,
it should be almost light. We will time our arrival for the moment of morning
prayer, and while the guards are otherwise occupied, that is when we will
pass through."

"This is the way you always do it?"

The gray-haired man mumbled a few words to his father, and both men
shrugged. "It will be the first time," he said, "but it is a good idea just the
same, don't you think?"

The truck was moving so slowly that Darius was of the opinion they would
make better time on foot. He glanced toward the speedometer, but the
dashboard gauges all had been torn out. After an hour they passed a
Shahsavan encampment in a pasture backed up against the mountains,
several dozen round tents of black goat hair arranged in no particular order,
and everywhere the great, bleating flocks the Shahsavans followed to the
summer grazing lands in the high valleys.

A washout sent them far into a meadow, which returned to a section of the
road that was axle-deep in water. The lane declined as it swung around a
shrine with a green tile dome toward a cemetery in which the graves were
designated by low lines of mud bricks that did not violate the religious edict
that burial markers must not throw a shadow. Then they were on pavement
again, and Darius saw the lights of the checkpoint. The old man laughed,
and said something to his sons, who also laughed, and Darius began to
wonder how great a bounty the government was paying in Azerbaijan for
illegal refugees.

Darius counted more than twenty Guardsmen inspecting the traffic in
both directions. A bus stopped ahead of them at the barricade, and when the
door opened for the Guardsmen a sheep scampered off followed by a boy in
baggy trousers. As the truck proceeded toward the adjacent bay, Darius
noticed the first streaks of pink in the eastern sky. The Guardsmen spotted

them, too, and turned their backs on the highway to kneel in the direction of the rising sun.

The old man did not ease up on the accelerator, but waved to the Guardsman who looked up at him in anger for disturbing his prayer. The truck shuddered as it roared away from the checkpoint, the wheel vibrating in the old man's hand. He laughed some more, and said something to his son in the middle, who told Darius:

"This is how we will do it all the time from now on."

Twenty kilometers between exits, at a place that seemed to have been chosen on a whim, the truck turned off into the hills and climbed a stone track to a poplar oasis, a muddy village hard by a stream that nurtured a few slender, silver trees. No one was about, except for a man coming down the main street on the back of a dispirited mule, and on foot alongside him a woman in a vest of red brocade and an ankle-length skirt worn over bright, pajamalike pants. The old man hailed the couple, and the woman gave him a long strip of the dimpled bread called naan sangak. He broke off a piece for himself, then passed the warm loaf to his sons. Darius pulled out several pebbles that had attached to the dough while it was being baked on a bed of stones, and shared what was left with Maryam.

The street branched off into a welter of twisting paths lined with puddled clay structures. An old woman came out of a two-story building, and looked Maryam up and down before saying something that made all the men laugh. When his sons had gone inside with her, their father brought Darius and Maryam to a shanty with a green door that crashed against the frame with every breath of wind.

"Stay here," he said. "Stay till night."

The single room behind the green door was black with the smoke from a crumbling fireplace. Disconnected patches of sunlight were projected through gaps in the wattle roof. Maryam lifted a dented teapot to her ear, and then spilled out a liter of rusty water. Ragged quilts of Kurdish design were balled up on the floor near a mound of goat droppings. Darius found matches, and ignited some khar bushes left over from an earlier blaze, and soon sooty flames threw warmth into the area immediately in front of the fireplace.

"What do we do now?" Maryam said.

"We sleep. The Zagros are full of bandits, and the army patrols for illegals along with the Revolutionary Guards. It's safer traveling after dark. We can start for the border then."

"How will we get there without a car?"

The door creaked open, and the old woman came in with a tray that she set down on the quilt. There was more of the dimpled bread, glasses of tea, yogurt, and pungent goat cheese, fresh yellow cherries, and red-and-green peaches. The woman stood looking at them for a very long time, and was laughing again as she backed outside. Moments later, she returned with a bottle containing an amber fluid. Darius lifted the cork, and sniffing sweet date wine, smiled at the woman in appreciation.

"How—there aren't any roads."

"On foot," he said. "There's no other way."

Through a chink in the clay Maryam looked out at the featureless mountains. Her teeth were chattering, and she stamped her feet on the floor. Darius spread the quilt close to the fireplace, offered her the first taste of the wine.

"You're not opposed to alcohol?"

She took a long drink, and kept her hand on his wrist when he snatched away the bottle. "I'm freezing," she announced. "Would you mind very much holding me in your arms?"

She sat between his knees, leaning toward the fire. He rubbed her shoulders, then clasped his hands together in her lap. The shaking of her body reminded him of a bird trying unsuccessfully to achieve flight. When he reached for the wine again, she wrapped his arms tightly around her. "Like this, please," she said.

He held her near, and her trembling eased. The heat of the blaze was searing his legs, but Maryam edged closer to the fireplace. Calmness came over him as she settled back against his chest. He had been craving sleep—forever, it seemed—and now, scarcely able to keep open his eyes, he fought it. Turning Maryam's face toward his, he kissed her.

Her body tensed, and she wrenched away. Maryam had lied to him about many things, but never had she pretended to be anything other than what she was, a Bride of Blood, a virgin pure in heart, vigilant against the corruption that was the essence of her female flesh. He gave her a guilty smile. "Temporary insanity," he said before he kissed her again, and pressed her down on the floor beside the fire.

Her arms came together in a hammerlock around his neck. Straining against him, she tightened the grip. Her sealed lips rubbed against his in a childish way, and then opened, instinct taking over, instinct or passion, but nothing he cared to analyze too deeply now. His hand slipped under the rough cloth of the chador. Her breasts were bathed in sweat that smelled to him like spices. A bird's heart palpitated beneath her ribs.

She pushed him away. She squirmed out from under him and turned over onto her hands and knees, looked back expectantly and a little afraid, willing to forget they had started, if he would. Here, he thought, was a *real* Iranian woman—intelligent, beautiful, politically aware, utterly compliant, approaching sex as just another suicide mission. The national fantasy—but not his.

"In a few days you'll be in the West. No sense in picking up bad habits now."

He put her on her back again, and she held herself stiffly as he tugged at the chador. Underneath she still had on her shroud. He shivered at the sight of it, then tore it from her body and balled it into the fire.

The flames saturated her skin in firelight, making something different of her beauty every second. It was impossible for him to have enough of her. She did not like to be looked at, and fluttered her hands in front of his face. "You're the first man to see me like this," she whispered.

He wanted to tell her that she was exquisite. But the superlatives in which his thoughts were arranged sounded like so much hollow flattery. He tasted the spiced moisture between her breasts, lay beside her pretending not to notice as she stole furtive glances at his body.

"You're going to be angry—"

"You aren't forcing me to do anything," she said. "How could I be angry with you? In time I think I may come to love you."

"Not with me."

"Who else is there that I'm not already furious at?"

"With yourself," he said. "For waiting so long." He smiled to let her know he was joking, and again when she saw that he meant it.

"I'm glad I did. That I waited for you."

Tears seeped through her lashes when he entered her. Her hand came up sharply against his chest.

"Am I hurting you?"

She wrapped her arms around the broadest part of his back, thrust herself at him so ardently that he was lifted off his knees. A sob answered every movement of his hips. He felt her heart beat inside his chest, an instant of perfection in which he lost himself lost in her.

"So glad," Maryam said.

She woke him with kisses to ask, "Will people be able to tell that I'm not a virgin?"

"Why would you think they would?"

"I'll be different—everything about me. People will see it, won't they?"

"I can't speak for women," Darius said. "But, yes, I suppose men can tell—those who pay that kind of attention. Most men."

She pressed her cheek against his shoulder. Her fingertips drew whorls in the hair on his thigh. "Good."

The sun roused her as it warmed her body. Not yet awake, she reached out to him; but she was alone on the quilt. She spotted him at the fireplace emptying the heroin into the embers, and would have called out to tell him how pleased she was if she hadn't seen him return the yellow bags to the knapsack. He washed his hands fastidiously in the rusty water left in the teapot, then lay down again. Her body shrunk away from his, but he pressed himself against her and didn't notice.

He couldn't stop staring. Dressed in a red waistcoat over a riotous blouse and brocade vest, a long skirt and felt boots, Maryam might have been a native of the high country, but for the blonde hair hidden under a fringed shawl that was held around her forehead with a satin sash.

"How do you like me as an Azerbaijani?"

"I like you any way," he said. "Where did you get those clothes?"

"The old woman was here while you were sleeping." A bundle of black cloth dropped onto his chest. "She brought these for you, and more bread and cheese to take on the road."

The bundle came apart into baggy trousers with a wide belt and a shirt that hung below his thighs, a felt cap and boots like hers. "That was very kind of her," he said.

"Not so kind. She wanted our old things in trade. Also some money."

She sat beside him. When she linked her arms around his neck, he nudged her onto her back. "It's getting dark," she said.

"It's not unheard of for some people to make love in the dark."

"Didn't you want to leave now? You said that by tomorrow we can be in Turkey."

He quieted her with kisses. "Today we may see heaven."

· 19 ·

The neon streaks that had opened the morning sky were holding back the dusk when he carried the knapsack outside.

"It would be nice if we could tell the old man and his wife how grateful we are for everything they've done for us," Maryam said.

"The nicest thing we can do is just to go."

They followed the color into the highest reaches of the village, continued along a cart track into barren hills.

"How far are we from Turkey?" Maryam asked.

"Too far to walk in one night. Twenty kilometers, maybe more."

"Is the border marked? How will we know we're there?"

"No one will be trying to kill us," he said.

Two riders in the blue homespun and thick felt vests of Kurdish tribesmen galloped out of the dusk on shaggy pack ponies, their faces obscured by turbans fringed in horsehair to protect against flies. They paraded their mounts in a circle they drew so tight that Maryam was all over Darius's toes, then cut between them and herded her away from him. One of the riders pinched Maryam's cheek, and when she swatted his hand away he slapped back at her face and tore the head scarf from her hair. He was pawing at her breasts when Darius got his attention with the Browning, and he traced the thrust of the barrel to his belt buckle. He backed his pony away, circled one more time in a sullen victory lap, and both men rode off with their trophy.

The trail divided around a pool of black water that trickled from a fissure in the mountainside. As Maryam cupped her hands under the seep, the whinnying of more than one horse rebounded off the cliffs. Darius turned in a full circle with the pistol in his fist, kept it out in front while a hay wagon approached from the direction of the village. The man gripping the reins was clad in filthy tatters that preceded the stink of his horses. In Azerbaijani, and again in Kurdish, he commanded Darius and Maryam out of his way. When they did not move fast enough to suit him, he stood up on the seat and invited them to ride.

The wagon took the high fork around the spring. The horses, which were not young, or lively, stretched out their necks and ploughed into a wet wind sweeping particles of frost ahead of a storm dropping down from the sum-mits. They moved at a man's pace, and then at a child's, and as the grade steepened the raggedy man ordered Darius to walk alongside the wagon. A few stars had come out, the dappled sky blending into a dome of light over the nearest deep valley. The raggedy man pointed down into the glow, and smiled. "Khvoy," he said.

The lights of the city vanished behind an escarpment where the wagon stopped to let Darius back on board. Leaning on the reins, the raggedy man walked the horses downhill to a grassy flat sheltered by willows. He put out some of the hay for them, and then unfolded an immaculate white cloth stowed under the seat and shared with his guests a supper of sweet cheese and doogh, a yogurt and mineral water drink. He did not say another word. When they reached a village more decrepit than the settlement in which Darius and Maryam had spent the afternoon, its sturdiest houses shabbier than any they had seen before, the wagon halted and he pointed the way through the mud.

A shabby dog ran out of a windowless hut, yipping at their heels as they walked the filthy streets.

"It will be getting light soon," Maryam said. "We should ask if there's somewhere we can stay."

"This is a Kurdish community," Darius said without slowing. "The Kurds resent the government in Teheran—any government—but are not famous for their incorruptibility. The army comes through the Zagros regularly to bribe them with money and food coupons to turn in refugees. It's not often that anyone cooperates. But if the mood strikes them, or times are hard, the Kurds won't hesitate to sell out their own kind. We'll find a better place . . ."

A cold rain began to fall. The brightest star in the heavens broke loose from Orion and swooped toward them.

"What *is* that?" Maryam asked him.

Darius looked into the sky, and wiped his eyes against his sleeve. "A light plane."

"A helicopter, you mean."

The aircraft swept the valley, came up behind the village swinging back toward Khvoy and the border.

"They're still hunting for us," Maryam said.

"For us, or whoever else they can find," Darius said. "We can't worry about it."

"We can't? What else can we do?"

While he adjusted the straps on the knapsack, Maryam took the lead on the narrow track. "Why not leave that here?" she asked. "We don't need the mycotoxins now. We can sneak into Turkey like other refugees."

She did not expect an answer, and took several steps toward him when he said, "Suppose you're right . . ."

"I know I am."

"Do we bury them, or burn them, or just walk away from them?" he asked. "How do you dispose of yellow rain when you don't need it anymore? If I cut open the bags will the mycotoxins dissipate, or will they fall on the village, or get into the water? Or will the wind blow it back in our face?"

"That's not the issue."

"It is until we've dealt with it," he said. "Then we can move on to less mundane considerations, like what will happen if they fall into the wrong hands."

They traced a flow of snowmelt to a barren promonotory almost in the clouds. Darius pointed across a valley to a cross on top of a black dome.

"Do you see that church?"

Maryam nodded. "That's Turkey?"

"A Turkish village," he said, "but it's inside Iran. The big mountain beyond it to the north is Mount Ararat. It's well inside Turkey. We'll go that way."

"Have you been here before? How do you know the border region?"

"This is Bakhtiari country. It was all I read about as a boy. I wanted to believe it was mine."

In Darius's steps she hiked through old snow stained by summer runoff, studying the animal tracks fossilized in the crust. The sleet came down

282 ❖ Joseph Koenig

harder, and changed all to snow, and white patches merged into fields in which the odd tree pushed its stubby crown into the storm. Fat flakes swirling around her head made her dizzy and stung her eyes. Her boots were soaked through, her feet rubbed raw. An icy stretch cost her balance, and both of them would have fallen had Darius not jerked her arm so hard that she felt something pop inside her shoulder.

They descended into a ravine clogged with boulders the size of Paycons. Chest-deep drifts forced them onto the crumbling wall. An ancient river had carved a tunnel in the soft rock, and they hiked the dry bed above the timberline and continued into a pass where two lithe poplars taunted the wind. Darius paused to stare into the teeth of what was now a blizzard. When he began walking again, Maryam pulled at his arm.

"I'm exhausted," she said.

"We'll rest soon." He brushed the snow from her eyelashes, snapping the tiny icicles that grew from her brows like glass stalactites. "But first we have to get out of the weather."

". . . Just a few minutes here, or I'll never find the strength to make it out of Iran."

"You must have—we're standing on the border."

The trackless slope looked disappointingly the same. She sighted along the ridgeline, which flattened as it passed between her feet. She took a long step over a demarcation visible only on maps, and some of the numbness went out of her legs. She kissed him, but then quickly pulled away.

"My face," she laughed, "it's so cold, I thought your lips would freeze against mine."

"I'd like that."

He pointed down the mountainside. In the whiteout she imagined a Turkish village like the one they had seen on the Iranian side, smoke rising from huts in lush, purple fields.

"Another few hours," he said.

"I can't take another step."

"We've gone far enough for one night. There are Turkish army patrols all along the border, and some of them have cozy relationships with the Revolutionary Guards. If they don't approve of a particular refugee they find inside their country, they have no compunction about sending him back. We'll look for shelter, and go down into the valley tomorrow after it's dark."

Hand in hand they plodded downhill. Their frozen boots afforded little traction in the dry powder. Darius fell, and then Maryam did, grabbing at the mountain as she slid headfirst, sweeping masses of snow in her wide-open arms to slow her descent. Darius dug her out of a modest avalanche of her own making, and brought her toward a rock wall shielded in greenish ice.

She did not see the cave until they were behind the ice and under a ledge that protruded from the mountainside like a mossy canopy. Darius struck a match and went all the way inside. The cave was ten meters deep. The low roof angling abruptly to the floor made it necessary to squat to move about. Beneath a black smudge on the ceiling was some half-burned wood and trash in a fire ring of flat stones. It took their last match to get a smoky blaze going. Then they peeled off their boots, and set them close to the flames, and babied their feet in the warmth.

"We should be close to the city of Van," Darius said. "We'll take a bus to Ankara. We can go anywhere we like from there."

"My father is Italian," Maryam said. "He lives in Milan. After he left my mother, I promised never to think of him again, to turn my back on all things European. You're not the only one to call himself by a last name less disagreeable than your own . . . now Italy is constantly on my mind. Have you ever wanted to see Italy? To spend time there?"

"I've got a French passport. Possibly, I have friends in the U.S. I might want to take up residence in either of those countries. But, yes, I'd like to visit Italy."

"We'll go to Paris also. And New York. And California. We'll travel all over the world."

"Right now, I'd be satisfied to see Van," he said.

The dry sticks quit giving heat, and Darius searched under the ash for more wood. By the time he came up with two willow branches, Maryam's eyes were half shut. He took her in his arms, and soon her head was against his chest, and his face buried in wet, fragrant hair.

He didn't know how long they had been sleeping when she slipped away and started into the back of the cave. "I have to go to the bathroom," she said.

"It's not there." He caught her by the wrist. "Till the storm lets up, this is our living room. You have to go outside."

Maryam shivered. In the first gray light of dawn the snow had relented. She squeezed water from her boots, and then climbed out through the drifts that the wind had hurled under the mossy ledge. Darius was luxuriating in the willow's dying glow when he thought he heard her call his name.

"Are you all right?" he shouted, coming alert to the realization that she had been gone for five minutes.

The wind garbled her answer. He heard other voices on top of hers, and went to stand beside the green ice at the mouth of the cave as four horses high-stepped through the snow, two men in Guardsmen's fatigues behind Ashfar and Bijan, and Maryam on foot between them like the spoils of a small war.

"It's good to see you again," Ashfar said. "Perhaps you would be so kind as to invite us all inside."

He pushed Maryam ahead. Darius noticed a gun in the lap of one of the men in the second row.

"We lost you for a while," Ashfar said, "but now it would appear that it is you who have lost someone. Consider our surprise when we found Maryam alone on the mountain. We caught her with her pants down, you might say. What is she worth to you? Is she worth something else we have lost?"

Darius did not look at Maryam, afraid of what he would see in her face, of what Ashfar would see in his.

"Go back to Iran," he said with deliberate calm. "I'll deliver the mycotoxins to our ambassador in Ankara, or anyplace else in Turkey that you say. It's the only way you'll get them."

He directed the ultimatum at Bijan, who deferred to Ashfar without comment, the threat of gunplay outside his serene realm. Ashfar laughed, and because it was expected of them, so did the men behind him. Komiteh-men did not know how to laugh. These two, thought Darius, were from Ashfar's organization.

"We would like to believe you," Ashfar said, "but we have it on good authority that you will never turn them over. That it has been your intention all along to deprive Iran of the capability of making chemical warfare."

Bijan spurred his horse alongside Ashfar's. "You will be allowed to proceed unmolested once we have the mycotoxins. You have your prostitute. She is waiting now to save your life. You have the West. We have the yellow rain. It is the trade everyone agrees should be made."

The words came in short bursts punctuated by the chattering of his teeth. He sat his mount slouched to the side, clutching the collar of a wool trenchcoat caked in snow, a general who would not lead his troops into battle, and had surrendered the right to command.

"I've given you my terms," Darius said. "Let her go, and ride back over the mountains, or I'll toss the mycotoxins in the fire."

"Do you expect us to take that seriously?" Ashfar said. "One breath, and it will be all over for you."

"Fool," Bijan said. "You know how he thinks. You're forcing him—"

It struck Darius that Bijan's warning could be meant as easily for him as for Ashfar, who had motives of his own in refusing a deal. As he retreated inside the cave, the wind delivered the report of a gunshot. Maryam lurched forward. Bijan's horse reared, nearly throwing him from the saddle. No one else moved. Maryam looked toward Ashfar in confusion as a dark splotch expanded across the faded red of her waistcoat, and then she toppled over. There was a revolver in Ashfar's fist when he dismounted and knelt over her, and tore open her blouse to show Darius the ragged exit wound in her shoulder.

"This is no fake execution," he said. "She will not be allowed to die quickly. Another bullet here, another there, and you can watch her bleed to death."

Ashfar waved the gun so that Darius could not miss it. He tugged his sleeve above his wrist as he placed the muzzle flush against Maryam's thigh. Maryam's eyes fluttered, and she screwed up her face as though a hideous insect had landed on her.

". . . It is entirely up to you."

It was not the Imam, but the Prophet himself who said that women were the rope of Satan by which the evil one ensnares men in his ruthless schemes. This, too, Darius saw now was khod'eh, the lie essential for the preservation of the faith as paradise was the lie that robbed men of their will. Did anyone understand this better than he, who having long ago lost paradise was motivated solely by the force of will? "You can have the mycotoxins," he said.

Ashfar glanced toward the cave. His old man's beard was coated white, reminding Darius of a malignant Santa Claus.

"Put her on a horse. I'll give them to you after she's away from here."

"Izzat!" Ashfar said.

One of the other men walked his horse into snow dappled with blood. Ashfar tore his handkerchief in half and balled a piece against each side of Maryam's shoulder, and then buttoned her waistcoat over the wound. Izzat made a stirrup of his hands and slung her into the saddle. She sat erect, oblivious to the color moving again over her breast. Ashfar put the reins in her fingers, and turned the horse down the mountain.

"Give the animal its head. He will bring you to a stable close to the Turkish border station in the valley. There is an Iranian army helicopter also in the valley. If I were you, I would avoid it at all cost."

To Darius he said, "We are still waiting."

"Let her go."

"Not until we have the mycotoxins. What is to prevent you from tossing them in the fire once she is gone?"

Inside the cave Darius experienced the cold in the pain of his thawing limbs. He did not linger at the blaze, the craving for its comfort a weakness as debilitating as a lack of self-confidence or the need to deliberate too long before acting. He stood beside the green ice, and flung the knapsack toward the horsemen. Arcing upward, it died on the wind, and plummeted into the no-man's-land between them.

Ashfar tightened his grip on Maryam's horse, which kicked up a squall in its eagerness to be free. "We would like to satisfy ourselves that the mycotoxins are really inside."

Izzat exhumed the knapsack from a shallow crater in the snow. He brushed off the canvas, and raised the flap.

"What do you see?" Ashfar asked him.

"Bags of yellow powder."

Darius began to plan for a holding action in which Ashfar and Bijan would lose interest in trying to outlast him in the cold. From the mouth of the cave he watched Ashfar lead Maryam's horse away. As though it were an idea he was so proud of that Darius had to see it, Ashfar turned the horse back toward him, and then pulled Maryam from the saddle. Another slug from Ashfar's gun fractured the green ice and rattled around the walls of the cave like a lead ball in a bagatelle. Darius dived out into the snow. The brilliant cold cut through his body as cleanly as a bullet.

Darius could not return fire at Ashfar, who was crouched behind Maryam. A clear shot at Izzat caught him under the jaw as he was leveling his military gun. The bullet blew him back from the knapsack. He landed in a sitting position, gushing blood from a hole above his Adam's apple. He brought up both hands to plug the leak, which ran through his fingers staining the snow to the bare earth.

Bijan had removed himself as a factor in the gun battle. An easy target, he was not worth the expenditure of a precious bullet. Ashfar's heavy revolver blasted snow into Darius's ear, but went unanswered again as Maryam crawled through the line of fire. Ashfar advanced behind her. His bullets carved a tight pattern close to Darius's head.

Darius was aware of the fourth man as a shadow in the eddying snow. While Ashfar kept him pinned down, the shadow circled wide around him.

Darius swept the battlefield with his gun. The wind diminished momentarily, presenting the man in broad profile nearly behind him. Darius's first shot was such an improbable miss that it seemed the frosted air had deflected it. The second knocked the shadow from his horse. Falling, he fired over Darius's head, and did not move again.

Maryam veered away from the crossfire. Ashfar got off a quick shot from his exposed position, and she wallowed in the snow as the bullet flew past her. Izzat's horse started into a lopsided gallop. It collapsed onto its breast like a thoroughbred breaking down, and rolled onto its flank. Ashfar threw himself behind the thrashing body, and pumped another flurry at Darius.

Darius's wet clothes were no barrier to the cold. His belt buckle scooped the snow inside his pants when he edged forward. He had begun shaking so hard that he needed to brace the gun against his forearm to shoot. Ashfar's head was in plain view above the twitching belly of the horse, but when Darius tried to squeeze the trigger he was amazed to discover that he had dropped the gun. He saw the weapon in the snow beside him, but could not move his hand. More amazing, there was blood in the hand. It streamed from a hole below the bicep, overflowing his cupped palm.

Ashfar rose cautiously onto his knees. The way he looked both ways before stepping around the steaming carcass of the horse he could have been crossing a busy street. He poked Izzat with his toe, and snatched the dead man's revolver and the knapsack. His awful stare sliced through Darius like a bitter gust of wind.

"You came close this time, closer than usual," Ashfar said. "It is in the nature of some men to succeed at everything they attempt, and in others always to fail ignobly. With you, it is routine to achieve a reasonable cause for optimism, and then to let the prize slip through your hands. Murdering Farmayan—" He turned toward Bijan, to satisfy himself that the Komiteh-man was out of earshot " was a commendable idea, but hardly worth a stay in an execution cell. And now, taking the mycotoxins all the way into Turkey to end up like this . . ." He shook his head lugubriously. "Why do you try so hard when kismet obviously is arrayed against you?"

"Had I been persuaded our scientists would end up with the mycotoxins, I might have shut my eyes and gone to Paris content to let them annihilate themselves," Darius said. "But you would never let Iran have its yellow rain. Criminal regimes more adept than ours would pay you well to have it."

Ashfar shrugged. "Who is to say the Islamic Republic will not be the winner when I put them on the market? The bidding war should be long and spirited, longer than any war in which one side is armed with such weapons."

Bijan rode up with his pistol across his knee. His lips were blue, his earlobes blood-red. Yellow mucus was congealed in his mustache, which he scraped against his sleeve. He looked impatiently at Ashfar, who raised Izzat's revolver ponderously, as though it were the big gun on a battleship that he was training on the space between Darius's eyes.

No flash accompanied the roar of the gun. The center of Ashfar's chest exploded, releasing a dam burst of blood. A fragment of bone stung Darius's cheek as he rolled out of the way of the body. Bijan's gun remained pointed at his face, a gray wisp of smoke frozen to the muzzle.

"He believed the Komiteh was stupid and cowardly, as he believed all men were but him. It appeared easy to use us for his purposes, which were in opposition to God," Bijan said. "We made no secret that we did not trust him, but his arrogance blinded him to the strength born of our faith. Were he a religious man he would have recognized what we were doing as the method by which good Muslims wage war, biding our time for the opportune moment no matter the cost in martyrs. But then, had he been a good Muslim there would have been no martyrs, none of this."

Bijan dropped down beside the body, and slung the knapsack across his chest. "You think the same way he did. You knew all along that you were being used, and still you thought you were the one who was clever. You refused to accept that I kept out of your fight not because I was afraid, but because I did not care which of you won. What alone is important to me, what is important to Iran, is that when our enemies have destroyed one another, God willing, we will be there to dance on the ashes."

Darius pressed the flat of his hand over his heart. That he felt it pumping was insufficient evidence that he was alive. By the suspension of how many physical laws had the high-powered slug that had blasted through Ashfar's ribs failed to enter his body? Pain limited the range of motion in his arm. He saw Ashfar's horse toss its head and trot away as Maryam stumbled after it. When it stopped to nuzzle the snow, she snagged the bridle and stroked its neck while it allowed her to gather the reins. Her eyes sought out Darius's and beckoned to him over Bijan's shoulder.

Bijan had a foot in the stirrups when Darius grabbed the straps of the knapsack and dragged him onto his back. He sank his knees into Bijan's chest, punching furiously with his good hand. Bijan lost his gun, and covered his head in his arms, then fought back ineffectively with a sweeping right hand. A short left got in under Darius's injured arm, and he took its full impact on the chin. Bijan went back to the looping right hands, and when none landed threw the left again. Darius saw the jab coming, but was defenseless against it. A barrage of lefts opened the brittle skin over his eyes. Bijan did not hit hard, but the accumulation of blows wore Darius down. His mouth filled with blood, his punches lost their sting. Bijan shrugged them off and scooped up the revolver.

Darius drove a shoulder into Bijan's midsection, and twined his fingers in the straps of the knapsack. A stiff left that bloodied his nose was the price to twist the straps around Bijan's throat. The gun went off with the bark of a small cannon, and Darius's ears began to ring. Bijan was angling the weapon into Darius's face when he dropped it suddenly to claw at the straps. Using the knapsack as a fulcrum Darius tightened the canvas noose, increased the pressure until the cords stood out in each man's neck. Darius noticed a hole where the bullet that killed Ashfar had torn through the cloth. His grip relaxed, and Bijan scrambled away, yellow powder seeping through the opening as he wrenched frantically at the bag. The wind spun a yellow dust devil around his turban. As he sank to his knees, he might have been under attack by a swarm of bees returning to the hive.

At the end of a mass defecation flight, Darius could not help but think.

"*Darius*—"

His name on Maryam's lips for the first time had him running to her before it registered in his consciousness, a clear channel open to his heart. She had lost control of Ashfar's horse, which reared over her, flailing its hooves. He grabbed the reins, and lifted her into the saddle. The horse bolted, feeling her weight, and Darius skidded over sharp rocks in the snow before he remembered to let go.

His momentum carried him upwind from where Bijan lay on his back. The Komitehman's features had convulsed into a blue mask behind the yellow ruff of his beard. Jabbering in a low singsong, Maryam prodded the horse toward him. Darius's knee gave way when he attempted to stand. He raised himself onto his elbows, twisting away from yellow bursts in a fresh shower of snow. "Don't come near."

The horse shied, snorting at the wind. Maryam scolded the animal, and it sidestepped into the trampled snow.

"I said stay—"

"You're in no position to order anyone around," she answered. "You may as well tell me not to love you, for all you'll accomplish."

Maryam held her breath as she marched the horse forward. Darius grabbed the bridle, and was pulled to his feet, and then climbed behind her and took the reins. The horse put back its ears, and pranced skittishly in a tight circle. A current of fear charged the muscles in its breast as it broke for the yellow bursts.

Darius turned the stallion's head almost against the ribs. The horse bucked, it kicked, it dived onto its forelegs with its ears brushing the snow; it snapped at Maryam's leg, tearing a piece from her boot, but still it ran straight ahead. With his remaining strength Darius drew back on the reins, wrestled the animal away from Bijan's body.

He dug his heels into the hocks, and they galloped off the mountaintop. The snow slanted down in pellets that scrubbed the poison from the air. Darius lifted his face into the storm, exultant in its icy freshness. On gentle, gladed slopes the horse evened its gait until they lost the sense of the ground beneath its hooves. Here the snow fell with rain that rose as vapor from the lathered hide, enveloping them in fog.

On clouds they descended into the valley.